FULL
Disclosure
Kindle Alexander

A *NICE GUYS* NOVEL

Trademark Acknowledgements

The author acknowledges the trademarked status and trademark owners of the following trademarks mentioned in this work of fiction:

F-250: Ford Motor Company
AAA: American Automobile Association, Inc.
Advil: Wyeth, LLC
American Airlines: American Airlines, Inc.
American Express: American Express Marketing & Development Corp.
Apple: Apple, Inc.
Austin-Bergstrom International Airport: City of Austin
Band-Aid: Johnson & Johnson Corporation
Bisquick: General Mills Marketing, Inc.
Blake Shelton: Blake Shelton, individual
Blue Bell: Blue Bell Creameries, L.P.
Boy Scout: Boy Scouts of America Corporation
Bud Light: Anheuser-Busch, Incorporated
Buick: General Motors LLC
Captain America: Marvel Characters, Inc.
Coke: The Coca-Cola Company
Coors: MillerCoors LLC
Crown: Diageo North America, Inc.
Doc Marten: Dr. Martens International Trading GmbH
Dr. Pepper: Dr Pepper/Seven Up, Inc.
Dodge Charger: Chrysler, LLC
Dulles International: Metropolitan Washington Airports Authority
Dumpster: Toccoa Metal Technologies, Inc.
Dunkin' Donuts: Dunkin' Donuts USA, Inc.
Embassy Suites: HLT Domestic IP LLC
ESPN: ESPN, Inc.
Glock: Glock, Inc.
Grateful Dead: Grateful Dead Productions Corporation
Harvard: President and Fellows of Harvard College Charitable Corporation
Hilton: HLT Domestic IP LLC
International Police Association: International Police Association
iPad: Apple, Inc.
Lady Antebellum (Just a Kiss): Lady A Entertainment LLC
Levi's: Levi Strauss & Co. Corporation
Linkin Park (Crawling): Linkin Park, LLC

Mack Truck: Mack Trucks, Inc.
Mavericks: Dallas Basketball Limited
McDonald's: McDonald's Corporation
Mustang GT: Ford Motor Company
Omni Hotel: Omni Hotels Management Corporation
Princess Barbie: Mattel, Inc.
Prius: Toyota Jidosha Kabushiki Kaisha AKA Toyota Motor Corporation
Ranch Style (beans): Conagra Brands, Inc.
Ray-Bans: Luxottica Group S.P.A.
Red Bull: Red Bull GMBH LLC
SEALs: The Department of the Navy
Sharpie: Sanford, L.P.
Skype: Skype Corporation
SpongeBob: Viacom International Inc.
Starbucks: Starbucks Corporation
State of Decay: Microsoft Corporation
Stepford Wives: Paramount Pictures Corporation & DreamWorks, LLC
Styrofoam: The Dow Chemical Company
Superman: DC Comics General Partnership
Tahoe: General Motors LLC
Texas Department of Public Safety: Texas Department of Public Safety, state agency
Texas Rangers (baseball): Rangers Baseball, LLC
The Matrix: Warner Bros. Entertainment Inc.
The Walking Dead: AMC Film Holdings LLC
Thunder: The Professional Basketball Club, LLC
Twilight Zone: CBS Broadcasting Inc.
Wranglers: Wrangler Apparel Corp.
YouTube: Google, Inc.

Dedication

To our amazing readers,
family and all our wonderful friends,
thank you from the bottom of our hearts.
Without your continued support and encouragement we
wouldn't be here.

Perry, you are missed every day.

Kindle, you are forever in our hearts.

Valerie, this couldn't have been done without you. Denise
Milano Sprung there are no words my dear friend.

Chapter 1

The recline of Mitch Knox's oversized leather chair fit him perfectly. This exact comfort level had required years of fine-tuning and honing the balance, but he'd invested the time, proud of the results. He sat at an angle, his Doc Marten booted feet propped securely against the file folders on his desk.

Lost in thought, Mitch's brow narrowed as he bit at his thumbnail. His eyes stayed fixed on the inner workings of the Camp Beauregard, Louisiana, United States Marshals Service field office. Like normal, he wasn't truly paying attention to anything going on outside his office door. What occupied his mind was a case on which he'd managed to get little more than a passing interest from his senior advisors and definitely zero dollars to help fund an investigation. Man, that frustrated the shit out of him.

The lingering doubt that plagued his thoughts surfaced. Why hadn't he been able to move this case any further along in all these months? Clearly, he'd completely lost his touch. Maybe his age had something to do with that. He'd just turned thirty-three. Close to middle-age, or hell, he could qualify for a solid middle-age compared to the life expectancies in this country. Good thing his people lived to ripe old ages, or he'd really be down about this latest birthday.

The shrill ring from his antiquated office telephone interrupted his thoughts, drawing his attention back into the now. Since caller ID hadn't made itself to the field office yet, Mitch was forced to answer the call blindly. He recoiled at the thought, but picked up the phone nonetheless. "Deputy Marshal Knox here."

"This is Director Skinner." The voice sounded strained on the other end, which was the norm, considering how much he'd been nagging his superior about the Colton Michaels case.

"Yes, sir, hang on." Mitch reached over his desk, extending an arm as far as he could across his small office to shut the door. The move effectively drowned out all the noise coming from the large grouping of cubicles just outside. Mitch had plopped back in his seat by the time the door slammed firmly shut. "You rang?"

"You're ignoring your email again. You're being requested on a federal warrant to transport Carlos Chavez from Dallas to Washington tomorrow morning."

"All right," Mitch said absently, raising his feet back in place on his desk as he reached out to pull up his email. He searched the incoming messages, going all the way back before lunch, because, while he would never admit the words out loud, he hadn't checked his email since he'd arrived this morning. Shit, now it was close to quitting time on a Friday. He needed to get moving.

Mitch held the receiver between his ear and shoulder as he brought the keyboard to his lap. He replied to the message quickly, letting them know he was on his way and took a second to print the details before forwarding the message to his assistant.

"Mitch, are you ignoring me again? I told you in your last performance evaluation, there's a hierarchy in all this. When you ignore me, your boss, and then the senior ranking officer who's also been emailing you this afternoon, that doesn't bode well," Director Skinner lectured.

"I'm sorry, what did you say?" Mitch paused, knowing full well it wasn't time for jokes, but he loved annoying his higher-ups. He kind of lived for these moments. He waited until he finally heard the exasperated sigh on the other end of the phone.

Score! He achieved the desired result and grinned, probably for the first time that day. "Don't worry, I already responded to the message. I'll have to make a few calls, then I'll get the first flight out. I'll be there tonight, ready for the bust in the morning."

"Then why are you still on the phone?" Skinner asked in a very lame attempt at humor.

"Ha ha. I keep telling you to leave the jokes to me. Bye." He didn't waste a second before he ended one call and started another. He dialed Ellen, his assistant, and pushed the speaker button.

"Yes, Your Grace," she answered.

"What's with all you jokesters today? This is serious law enforcement business. Not playtime!" Mitch scolded, cocking his head to the side. The blinds to his office window were raised, and if he bent a little farther, he could see her at her cubicle. She was looking directly at him. "I sent you an email. I need to arrange a trip to Dallas for departure ASAP. Once you get the details, will you forward them to the email address inside the message I sent you?"

"Yes, sir," Ellen said with a bright smile. She was young, pretty, and extremely capable. And from day one, she'd always used the 'sir' on him, but as of his last birthday, the word seemed to take on a whole new meaning.

"What have I told you about that?" he asked, irritably.

"You told me you aren't old enough to be a sir yet." She made air quotes at the word sir. "But you are." They had been through this before. He knew the comeback and could never beat her at this game, but it didn't stop him from engaging.

"You don't have to say it," Mitch said drily in her pause.

"Because my parents always taught me to be respectful of my elders." He made a show of rolling his eyes. She always had that same response, clearly very proud of her attempt at humor. She laughed and Mitch tried hard to hide his smile, not wanting to spur her on.

"You need better jokes." He gave a little chuckle as he reached across the desk to end the call. That didn't stop her. He should have known it wouldn't as she opened his office door and stuck her head inside.

"Why? When that one still works so well!" The door shut quickly, and he ignored her completely as he packed his laptop and grabbed his cellphone off the charger. By the time he hit the elevators, his cell vibrated with an incoming email. Ellen was a keeper, even in her current state of becoming a pain in his ass. She'd already arranged his flight, departure in an hour and a half. Just enough time to grab his always ready kit and get to the airport.

Chapter 2

Mitch entered the airport like he always did, in almost a dead run. An hour and half after quitting time, during rush hour traffic, even in Pineville, Louisiana, clearly wasn't enough time to get from his office to his apartment and then to the airport. He should have known better.

He slung his duffel over his shoulder as he slid his credit card into the closest kiosk and then hit continue when his name appeared on the screen. He went through the on-screen steps and grabbed his boarding pass before heading directly to TSA security. Thank god he could bypass the line and go the back way into the terminal. He handed over his badge to an employee who knew him all too well and easily passed the first checkpoint before being ushered to the next.

Mitch opened his laptop case and slid the duffel onto the conveyor belt before pulling his extra clip from a special compartment inside the bag. He unholstered the standard issue Glock he always had strapped inside the waistband of his jeans and placed both inside a tray. He liked the shock value the guys in the back got when they saw the weapon through the scanner's monitor. He figured he was doing his civic duty by giving them the jolt they needed to refocus on their tedious jobs.

The whole time he unloaded, he worked the laces of his boots until they slid off his feet. From this point, he'd have to carry those as he ran for the gate.

"Hey, Mitch. Step inside, hands up please," Velma, an older, female TSA agent, said.

"Hey, Velma, gonna pat me down this time?" he asked, standing still with his hands in the air as the machine took his body image.

"Only if I'm lucky. You know I like all those big muscles on my men. Makes for a real man," she teased. A male TSA agent stood behind her and gave a grunt in her direction.

"He's clean," the guy said.

"Guess it wasn't my day," she said, cackling as he smiled and walked past her.

"I'm late or I'd go ahead and let you feel me up," Mitch teased, grabbing his gear, waiting for the agent behind the desk to run his pistol through their computer system. He gave her a wink as she fanned herself.

"Oh lordy, Mitch Knox, you're a fine-looking tease of a man. If I was ten years younger!" Velma was five foot nothing compared to his six foot four inch frame, but he bet money she could hold her own. Maybe even outdo him when things got down to it.

"Go, Mitch. Velma's supposed to be a professional," the agent said from behind the desk. That got Mitch laughing as she shot the finger in her coworker's direction. "I'll see you guys later." Mitch took off, running toward his gate. As he hit the last call from the flight desk, Mitch stood at the end of the short line and remembered he'd wanted to call Colt Michaels before he left. Over the last eight months, he'd developed a strong bond with both Colt and his husband, Jace Montgomery.

Civilian friends were new to Mitch. He'd met both of them through his father. Colt had been the quarterback for the New York Panthers, a professional football team where his pop held the position of team doctor. Colt was a special case for his dad, drawing Mitch into their world when Colt had been injured in a suspicious accident. The conclusion everyone came to after an intensive investigation was that Jace, and not Colt, had been the target of what looked like a botched hit.

The bottom line, whoever this person or persons might be who had run the car off the road, they hadn't wanted Jace to walk away from that accident. For Mitch, that had only been the beginning as he linked several other victims throughout the US to the same type of crimes—mysterious incidents that appeared to be accidents at first glance. Most of them hadn't been as lucky as Colt.

Mitch hit the ramp to the airplane and dialed Colt's cell phone number. Jace answered on the second ring and Mitch grinned. He regularly messed with Colt, flirting shamelessly with Jace since the beginning. So much so, that he purposefully called Colt first. The guy got very protective where Jace was concerned.

"Hey, bud, I'm coming to Dallas," Mitch said.

"Does that mean you have a new lead on the case? Have you found out who did it?" Jace asked with hope in his voice, which was pretty much how Jace always sounded. It had to be the inner cheerleader in the guy. Mitch hated that he couldn't give him the answer he wanted. He'd like nothing more than to tell both Jace and Colt their culprit had been apprehended.

"We're closer," Mitch said, and those words cost him for the lie they were. He had never shared with anyone that the federal government hadn't taken an interest in their case or the others linked with the same MO.

Jace's returning silence spoke volumes. He boarded the flight, nodding at the flight attendant who mouthed a giant hello. That was the great thing about working out of a small field office—he got to personally know everyone inside the airport as well as all the flight staff. He lifted a hand to her, felt the pilot pat his back, but he kept the conversation going as he negotiated himself and his bags down the small aisle.

"I promise I'm doing everything I can do. I'll get this figured out."

"Has something else happened?" Jace asked. Mitch listened as Jace spoke away from the phone, probably catching Colt up. They must be together. Hell, they were always together. They were nauseatingly in love with one another and Mitch grinned at that thought. Colt and Jace were really quite the perfect couple.

"You know I can't give you details." Mitch used his regular excuse, which was technically a lie since the government hadn't taken the case. He could tell them anything he found out on his own. There just wasn't much to tell.

"Hey, man, ignore Jace. You're coming here, right?" Colt asked, now on the phone in place of Jace.

"Yeah, just for a day. I might have time for a quick bite if things wrap up as quickly as I like. Are you two gonna be in town?" Mitch asked, anchoring the phone on his shoulder as he hoisted his duffel into an overhead compartment in the very back of the airplane.

"We'll be here. Call and let us know if you want to have dinner. We'd really like to see you," Colt added.

"Sounds like a plan. Hey, I gotta roll. I'm in the airplane." He didn't have time for pleasantries—the engines were starting, drowning everything out. Mitch ended the call and took his seat in the last row. The flight attendants were already strapping in behind him. The roar of the engines grew as the plane started down the runway.

Chapter 3

Cody Turner rolled the tight muscles in his shoulders and downed the Red Bull he'd picked up on his way in to the Texas Department of Public Safety, Travis County field office. Normally by now, he'd have completed his paperwork, turned in his patrol car, and already be heading out to enjoy his days off. While he'd completed two of those three things already, the last had been irritatingly delayed by this afternoon's mandatory meeting in the chief's office. After working the last nine nightshifts in a row, and following those up with a day shift, the time off was much needed.

He schooled his slightly bad attitude and put it off to being tired. Besides, this whole irritable thing he had going on was his own fault. He shouldn't have picked up all those extra shifts. He'd worked back-to-back doubles over the last couple of days—but then it wasn't in his nature to not lend a hand when needed. A fellow trooper's wife gave birth unexpectedly, how could he have not taken those shifts to help the guy out? Just like agreeing to the three shifts earlier in the week to relieve another ailing officer. It was just the kind of thing he did.

The kink in the plan came with this meeting today. It was Friday afternoon. He had a scheduled two nights off, before he'd work a Sunday nightshift and then the official start of his use-it-or-lose-it vacation time. That would be two full weeks off, all in a row. He ignored the fact that his brother had claimed most of that time to help out on the family farm, because in the end, he figured he'd get a break from some of the monotony of day-to-day life as a state highway trooper. He'd come back to work stronger for it in the end.

Cody walked the long halls, rounding several corners until he came to the chief's office that took up a large chunk of the rest of the building.

"Officer Turner, Chief Hicks is expecting you," said a young man dressed in full uniform at the desk out front of the office. The guy never looked up. Cody was a little impressed with how he knew who stood before him. Since Cody had plans after work to go check out a horse just north of Dallas for his brother, he had changed into his traveling clothes—jeans, work boots, and a T-shirt. Now as he stood there, he wondered if he should have stayed dressed in his uniform.

"Can I just go in?" Cody asked, hesitating before he stepped around the desk to open the door unannounced. He'd been a trooper for four years, assigned to this location the entire time, but he'd only been in the chief's office three times, ever—once when he was hired, once when interviewing for the mounted patrol, and now. This whole scene was a little intimidating, and he suddenly worried what he might have done wrong to have been called in like this.

"Sure. He's waiting for you."

"Can I throw this away?" Cody asked and finally the guy looked up, a prominent frown marring his face.

"If you must. Sure dressed up, didn't you?" he said with more attitude than was really necessary. He produced the trash can from under his desk for Cody to place the empty can inside. The assistant's words made the nerves he had been fighting surface in full force as he knocked on the partially closed door and stuck his head inside.

"Can I come in, sir?"

"Sure. Thank you for being on time," Chief Hicks greeted him. He rose and, with his long stride, stepped forward, meeting Cody in the middle of his office with a firm handshake. They were about the same size, save an inch or two on the chief's part. At a little over six-four, Cody had earned the nickname of Biggin' around the precinct. The chief had to glance up slightly to look him in the eye. "Have a seat, Turner."

The chief waved him into the chair directly in front of his desk before he shut the office door and went back around the desk to his seat. He moved some paperwork around until he found a file. Cody sat back and watched as the folder was brought to the top of the stack, his name scrawled across the front.

"Turner, I know it's been a long wait, and I apologize for that. It's just the higher up you go, the more red tape we have to get through, but if you're still interested, we'd like to offer you the position with Mounted Patrol." The chief looked straight at him. Cody digested the words and couldn't hold in the smile that spread across his lips. The flush of adrenaline at that announcement did more to alleviate his tiredness than the recently chugged Red Bull.

"I just assumed the position had been filled," Cody replied, sitting up straighter and grinning ear to ear.

"No, it's just a slow process when every hand has to sign the papers before we can act. I'm guessing the smile means you'd still like the job?" The chief eyed him closely.

"Absolutely I would!" Cody answered.

"Good. After all this paperwork, I probably would have insisted you take the job whether you wanted it or not." The chief placed the folder across the desk for Cody to see.

"The mounted patrol's considered a promotion. Your pay grade increases and your hours will change. During training, you'll be put on days, but after that initial period, your seniority in the division will start at ground zero. Just like in here, you'll work nights, weekends, and probably holidays in the beginning," the chief explained.

"That's fine. I'll do whatever. I'm supposed to be going on vacation starting Monday. I can change that too," Cody offered.

"No, HR requires you use that time for legal liability purposes. It's in this paperwork. Your official start date is the twenty-seventh. You've got solid horsemanship skills, so they've decided to train you onsite. Look this over. Check out the pay grade. If you agree with everything, sign the bottom of the form. Let me tell you, though, if you don't agree, changes will have to be made and that could take some time," the chief stated.

"Will you continue to be over that department too?" Cody asked, looking over the offer letter in front of him. Dear god, the pay increase would be several hundred dollars more a month. Holy shit! Cody lifted the offer to look over the job description and everything looked in order there too. When he glanced up again, he realized the chief had been talking and he had no idea what about.

"Your goals in the agency are clear. You've got a solid education. I think this new position will look good on your resume when you apply to become a Texas Ranger," the chief finished, smiling at him expectantly.

"Thank you, sir," Cody said, hoping that covered whatever he'd missed on the front end.

"In the back of the packet, you'll see your mount's information. He's been waiting for his officer. I thought you'd like the name. I think he fits you. Turner, you're also the youngest trooper to be hired for this position, but I think you've got the maturity and sense to take care of you and your animal," the chief continued. Cody dug through the paperwork until he saw the information on his horse. He read over the specifics and grinned even bigger. His horse, a gelding, was named Ranger.

"He's in Waco? I'm headed that way right now. Can I stop by and see him?" Cody asked, making sure the stable's address was listed on the paper.

"I can't see where that would be a problem. I'll make a phone call and let them know you're stopping by. I think there's some paperwork in there that they need filled out too," the chief said. "If you're good with everything, sign where the tabs are located on the first three pages so I can get this processed."

"Yes, sir. Thank you." Cody's face started to ache from the grin he couldn't suppress as he scribbled his name on the official offer.

"Great! Let me get a copy of this for you, and I won't take any more of your time except to say, reporting procedures will arrive in your email before your start date. Congratulations." The chief came around the desk and shook his hand again before he left the office, leaving Cody alone. He sat back down, linked his fingers together, and smiled down at his joined hands. After three months without a word, he had actually made the elite division of the mounted patrol. He sighed deeply as he pulled his badge from his back pocket, staring down at the silver metal. It was happening. All the work and time he'd put into making these things happen in his life were paying off.

When he heard the chief at the door, he slid the badge back into his jeans pocket and absently reached up to pat the phone inside his front shirt pocket as he rose. He'd most definitely be calling his big sister Sheila and making her take a break from her always hectic schedule. They needed to celebrate!

~~~

Mitch wiggled around in his airplane seat, trying to make more room. His long legs were cramped, shoved up against the seat in front of him, and no matter how he tried, his big body just didn't fit well in these compact seats. Thank god he was alone in this row. That was the only thing making this flight bearable.

They were barely in the air with the seat belt lights off before he had the small tray lowered onto his thighs and his laptop out. The conversation with Jace weighed on him, adding pressure to his already burdened heart.

For as long as Mitch could remember, being a deputy US marshal was the only job he ever wanted. He'd always loved the idea of getting the bad guys off the street. It wasn't until he made the special teams SOG division that he finally felt like he achieved his lifelong goals. And boy, had he done everything he could to represent his badge.

In the last few years, the red tape and the concern for political correctness throughout the country really started to limit his abilities to get his job done efficiently. His seniors never wanted to step on anyone's toes, creating a Justice Department that was little more than a chess board of moves and countermoves.

Mitch had grown incredibly weary of it all. He'd even considered a career change over the last couple of months after the government's lack of support in finding the person responsible for the long line of hate crimes he'd identified. Multiple civilian deaths should have been enough to fund a task force to investigate. Instead, an entire group of people were being targeted, and his supervisors tabled his efforts, playing games with these people's lives.

Mitch closed his eyes, hoping to rein in his irritation. As punishment for his wayward thoughts, Mitch booted up his computer and logged in to the department's email system to see what else he'd missed today. He stared at the inbox as hundreds of new messages loaded. Most were annoying stupid jokes forwarded from person to person in his office.

He scanned names, saw meeting requests, department pot luck lunch signups, company baby shower invitations, just about everything completely useless until he landed on an email from his mom and dad. He smiled, knowing the message was just from his mom, but the email came with both their names.

The overly long note updated him on his entire family. Mitch stopped reading partway through and scanned to the bottom. His dad sent his love, and the last line was clear: Mitch needed to make time to come home. That was always their standard goodbye. Mitch pecked at the keyboard as he replied.

Hey Mom,

Thanks for the update. I'm heading to Dallas right now. I'll let Jace and Colt know you said hi. I was thinking about maybe taking a few days off at Thanksgiving. Tell everyone I said hey.

Love,

Your favorite son.

Smiling at the last line, as he always did, he hit enter and sent the message to his mom. Hopefully that would pacify her a little bit, and he made a mental note to ask for Thanksgiving off.

"Goddamn, you spilled the drink on my slacks." The angry words echoed in the cabin, drawing Mitch's attention.

"Sir, I'm sorry. The turbulence…" The flight attendant started to explain, and Mitch could hear the stress in her voice.

"Bullshit! You're an incompetent bitch." Mitch looked around, praying an air marshal was on the flight. All eyes appeared to be on the flight attendant, while Mitch scanned the rows, looking for anyone who might intervene. No one stood. *Fucking great!*

"Sir, please calm down." Another flight attendant made her way over to the angry passenger. She tried to defuse the situation with her attempts to clean the spill. Mitch lifted farther in his seat, watching the guy. The anger radiating off him didn't dissipate. Mitch placed his laptop in the pocket of the seat in front of him before he pushed himself across the row. Maybe if he were lucky, he could calm the situation down without further incident.

Too bad the passenger didn't clue in to Mitch's plan.

The man shoved the young flight attendant's hands out of the way, sending the towel and the water bottle she held flying across the cabin, spilling the contents everywhere. *Damn.*

"If you'll come back with me, we can get you cleaned up." Mitch had to give it to her; she tried hard to gain control. The man bolted up from his seat. Anger contorted his face, and Mitch saw he was clearly under the influence, ending any hope he had that this would end well.

The passenger awkwardly shoved the flight attendant aside as he stumbled out into the aisle. He became angrier as he tried standing without swaying. The effort caused him to trip on his feet, tumbling backward.

"Sir, get back in your seat," Mitch ordered, stalking down the aisle, trying hard not to bump against the heads of the passengers watching the show.

"Fuck you. This bitch ruined my suit." The angry man swung at a bystander who'd simply tried to help keep him on his feet. *Dammit!* He'd have to make an arrest for that move. Sighing, Mitch did his thing and wasted no time subduing the passenger in the most painful hold he could think of as he straddled the guy, locking him in handcuffs while reading him his rights.

By the time he pulled the guy to his feet, cheers erupted. That enraged the drunk. He struggled to get free, threatening to sue everyone on the plane, claiming his civil rights had been violated. Mitch tightened his grip, shoved the guy around until he stood in front of him, but the venom never stopped.

With a solid yank on his wrist, the guy stumbled backward, landing against his chest and Mitch hissed in his ear. "Shut the fuck up or so help me, I'll do it for you." The threat was idle. Mitch wouldn't jeopardize the arrest or his job by forcibly closing the guy's mouth, no matter how badly he wanted to do just that.

"Thank you," the captain said. Mitch stood there, awkwardly shaking his hand, while the passenger swayed on his feet and decided groveling might be a better choice than outright aggression.

"Just doing what needed to be done." The exchange didn't take more than a second, and he pushed the guy back to his row of seats.

"Can you move my laptop case, please?" He flashed a smile toward the flight attendant who remained close by to help.

"Yes, sir," she said as she took the laptop and the case and stored them in the overhead bin.

"Man, I'm sorry. I got outta hand," his detainee whined while they were still in the aisle.

"Shut up, sit down." Mitch wasn't in the mood for excuses.

"I'm a vice principal. I can't have this on my record. You can't do this to me." The man began to sweat bullets, and his tone grew louder as he faced off with Mitch.

"Shut up and sit down," Mitch repeated. Funny how everybody always had a reason as to why they should be excused from their shitty behavior.

"I just drank too much," he tried again with the excuses. Mitch shoved him across the seats, barely catching his head before it slammed into the window. The action hadn't stopped the guy's flow of excuses as Mitch helped get him situated in the seat.

"Why are you doing this to me? I have rights, you know!" Mitch left a seat between them and sat down, staring straight forward. On a deep sigh, he realized this was going to be one long-ass flight.

Chapter 4

Cody turned off the county highway onto the long gravel road to his family's farm in Kylie's Corner, Texas. He slowed his truck, navigating the trail they'd created through the course of his entire life. A shrill scream filled the truck cab and broke his train of thought, startling him. He smiled at the ringtone he'd assigned his sister, then fumbled for his phone to answer before the second shriek could pierce his eardrums.

"I've got news," Cody said, answering the phone.

"Well, you better! I tried to ignore your earlier call, but then I got worried. I was in an important meeting. It better be good, little Cody Turner!"

"I'm taller than you by eight inches," he teased, ignoring her complaint. Sheila considered every meeting important.

"That means nothing in the life experience department. Besides, I changed your diapers and took you out on my dates. You're still a little boy to me. Now, what did you want so late in the day on a Friday—since you're clearly not hurt or anything?" While her tone could be off-putting to some, he found her endearing, and Sheila was always the first person he called for everything.

"I got the job!" he exclaimed.

"What job? What does that mean?" she asked, very confused.

"The mounted patrol job. The one I applied for months ago, remember?"

"No, you didn't! No way! Congratulations, babe! When did you find out?" she asked. He knew she'd be excited.

"A little while ago. I got called into the chief's office and he told me. It's like a huge raise, and they have a mount waiting for me in Waco. I can stop by and see him on my way up," Cody said as the main house came in view.

"Oh, Cody, I'm so proud of you. Congratulations. You've worked hard for that. You deserve it," she praised.

"Well, I don't know about that, but I do know that I'm pretty excited. I'm close to the house. Mason's gonna be fit to be tied that I'm so late. I should go," Cody said.

"Yeah, that's right. This is your weekend to go to Dallas. Be safe, and remember, guys will make you lose your focus. Fuck 'em and leave." Sheila started to laugh.

"I'm not having this conversation with you. You'd think you'd have figured that out by now," Cody said, taking a side trail to the barn.

"It's just sex, Cody. I've done it a thousand times myself," Sheila confessed, but he wasn't in the mood to hear about his sister's love life.

"Okay, too much information, I'm hanging up now." Cody lowered the phone as he heard her yell her parting line.

"Be safe up there! And I'm proud of you, Cody. Good job!" He disconnected the call a little creeped out from hearing all that sex talk from his sister, but still incredibly happy. She'd been his number one supporter in his career.

He pulled his truck up beside Mason's and got out. Mason, his oldest brother, ran the family farm. He did just about everything on his own. His dad had become a police officer back in the eighties to help support the family during the big Texas oil bust. He'd kept that job, eventually becoming the police chief in their town, letting Mason try his hand at running things when he got old enough. Mason had done a good job of building the place back up, making the farm viable and sustaining.

By the time Cody walked around the bed of the truck, Mason was heading out of the barn door, his cell phone stuck to his ear and a checkbook in his other hand. Chester, Cody's lab, came busting around the corner, racing straight for him. Cody kneeled down, braced himself, and let Chester jump on him and lick him like crazy. He gave him a good rubdown and the doggie treat he'd brought as Mason approached.

"You're late," Mason said, the smile spreading across his face. Cody rose, figuring Mason had been talking to Sheila when he'd come out. Mason stuck out his hand, which Cody shook and got enveloped in a giant bear hug. They were similar in size and Mason gave him a good brotherly whack on the back. "Congratulations, man. I know how much you wanted that job."

Chester was right there between them, jumping up to get in on the action. Man, he missed that dog.

"It was kind of a shock. I wasn't expecting it at all." Cody's grin was as big as his brother's. "I thought they'd given the job to someone else."

"Oh come on. You were raised on the back of a horse. I had you up there with me when you were just a few years old," Mason said. "Nobody rides better than you. Besides that, you're badass at your job. I'm just real excited for you, man."

"I heard my boy has some good news." Cody's mom hollered from the front porch. "You better get over here and share what's going on with you," she yelled. They both looked her way. She was a little bitty thing, but after corralling five children she had a voice that boomed across the pasture. Cody waved at her and turned back to his brother.

"I should go talk to her because otherwise she'll hike all the way out here," he commented.

"Here's the checkbook. I wrote the farm's address on the back. I called 'em last night and you can stop by tonight or tomorrow. I'll have my cell on me, let me know what you think of her," Mason said.

"All right. Are you sure you want me to just write a check without you looking at her first?" Cody asked, walking back to his truck.

"Like I just said, you know horses better than any of us. You deem her acceptable, so will I," Mason repeated, giving him a hard pat on the back. "I'm proud for you, Cody. Chester, come here, boy!"

Cody bent down and nuzzled the dog again before he loaded himself up and drove his truck to the main house where his mom stood. She was coming off the wrap-around porch, shielding her eyes against the glare of the afternoon sun as he got out of the truck. Her smile was as big as Mason's had been.

"Sheila called, she told me you had good news and I needed to get out here." His mom met him at his truck.

"Hi, Mom." Cody leaned down to kiss her cheek. "I just met with my chief. I got that mounted patrol job I applied for all those months ago."

"No kidding? I thought it passed you up," she said, beaming bigger.

"That's what I thought. The chief just said those things take longer." Cody bent again to take her offered hug.

"I'm real proud of you, Son. None of my kids are as focused as you. You get something in your head and it's just gonna work out like that. You make me proud," she said again with another kiss on the cheek.

"I gotta get going, Mom. I'll be back for lunch on Sunday. I gotta work Sunday night."

"No church on Sunday morning?" she asked.

"Probably not, but we'll see. I love you." Cody climbed back into the cab of his truck, started the engine, and rolled down the window.

"Be safe up there in Dallas. Those people aren't as easygoing as we are down here. Did I tell you your dad's up there with your brother? They decided to go to that police conference. Good thing you got your room reserved; they had a hard time finding a hotel. I think they had to go way far south, like Grand Prairie, to finally find a place to stay," she said, shielding her eyes again as she glanced up at him to speak.

"I love you. Thanks, Mom." Cody put the truck in reverse. She waved as he pulled away. Cody stopped at the main entrance of the road and dug through the file folder of information the chief had given him. He found the address of the stables in Waco currently boarding Ranger. He had wanted that to be his first stop, but he looked at the time and changed his mind.

The Texas Ranger Hall of Fame Museum was in Waco too. He definitely wanted to stop in there, and it was already rush hour traffic, with lots of miles to go to get to Waco. He'd do the museum tonight and stop by the stable in the morning. Decision made, he pulled his well-worn Texas Rangers Major League Baseball cap from the passenger seat and slid it easily on his head, grabbed his sunglasses off the visor, and hit the highway. He had some celebrating to do.

~~~

Five hours later, one drunken arrest, and all the DPD-required paperwork completed, Mitch stood in front of his sixth different hotel. All enquiries resulted in the same dreaded response, repeated with the same deep Texas twang, topped off with a sympathetic smile and shrug of the shoulders from the staff behind the front desk: No vacancy. Mitch was tired and grumpy, definitely past the polite Texas hospitality that kept leaving him without a bed. To top everything off, he hadn't eaten since lunch. That clearly meant he was close to starvation, and now bunking down for the night in his rental car appeared to be a serious prospect.

To make matters worse, the latest establishment turned him away before he even took a step inside the lobby. What the hell? This was Dallas for Christ's sake, he'd never had a problem finding a decent place to stay…ever. Who could have anticipated the International Police Association had chosen Dallas, Texas, for its annual conference, and apparently so had Geekfest—the same freaking weekend. What was there to possibly do in Dallas that could entertain all these officers and techies at the same time? Mitch stood on the front steps of the Omni hotel, waiting for his car to be brought back around. Because of that dumbass on the flight, he was hours behind schedule, his stomach had now begun to make annoying noises, and his patience had worn thin.

From out of nowhere, six beefy men stumbled across the steps where he stood. They were loud, wobbly, and clearly drunk. One lost his footing and took a nosedive, effectively taking out all the men in his group in an attempt to save himself from the fall. Mitch took one step backward, watching the whole scene play out in slow motion in front of him. Ahh…now it began to make sense why Dallas was the place for so many tourists and conventions in October—nice weather and lots of bars within walking distance from the hotels would draw them like flies to honey.

Mitch palmed his phone, then dialed the only other option he had. Colt picked up on the third ring.

"Hello?" Colt's voice was gravely and thick. He'd clearly been sleeping.

"Please tell me you haven't become such an old married man that you're already asleep at ten o'clock at night," Mitch teased.

"It's eleven forty-five, and what's wrong?" Colt asked.

"Who is it?" Mitch heard Jace's muffled voice on the other end of the call. He'd clearly woken them both up. *Damn.*

"Mitch, babe," Colt said to Jace.

"Is everything all right?" they both asked in unison.

"Listen, apparently there're some conferences downtown. I got to the hotel late, and they gave my room away. I need a place to bunk for the night." Mitch watched as his car pulled up in front of him. The human bowling ball and his pin men finally drew enough attention, and several of the hotel staff rushed out to help them up.

"We have an extra room. Need me to come get you?" Colt asked. Mitch had to take the long way around the men being carried inside to get to the valet. He grabbed his keys, handed the guy a ten dollar bill and was in the car driving toward North Dallas where Colt and Jace lived by the time Colt finished relaying the conversation to Jace.

"I got a rental. I'm headed there now. Turn the light on and for god's sake make sure you put some clothes on. I don't wanna see anything that'll make you wanna kick my ass," Mitch chuckled.

"That's right! I still owe you an ass whoopin'," Colt started, but there was some sort of commotion on the other end of the line, then he heard Jace's voice.

"Ignore him. I'll text you the new address. Call if you get lost, we'll be waiting for you," Jace replied.

"I have your address in my phone. It's already giving me the directions. I'm on my way." Mitch ended the call as he looped around Pearl Street to hit the North Dallas Tollway straight to the new Michaels-Montgomery casa.

Chapter 5

Mitch drove the quiet streets of the Preston Hollow neighborhood amazed at the sizes of the homes. This part of Dallas reeked of money, but he had no idea places like this were tucked inside the city limits. The moonlight guided his path as he started slowing down to better read the addresses on the mailboxes. When he found his destination, he pulled in, his eyebrows lifting as he drove through a security gate into a circle driveway to one of the most beautiful homes he'd ever seen.

Not really sure what to do, Mitch parked the rental in the middle of the drive and grabbed his bags from the backseat. Colt opened the front door before he'd made it halfway up the stone walkway.

"Hey, man, I'm glad you called us. You should've just planned on staying here to begin with," Colt said, opening the door wider for Mitch to come inside.

"Thanks for taking me in." Mitch stood in the foyer, admiring the high vaulted ceilings, large chandelier, and curved stairwell.

"Come in," Colt said, drawing Mitch farther into the house.

"Who'd have thought so many police officers could leave their post to come party in big D? Nice place, man. I didn't know cheerleading paid so well," Mitch teased, smirking at Colt. Jace had become the primary breadwinner for their little family since Colt's retirement from the NFL, something Colt had taken to amazingly well.

"Yeah, neither did I. You should see the wedding gift Jace bought me. It's a 1967 Shelby Mustang GT500. I have her parked in the garage in a special place of honor," Colt announced, slapping Mitch hard on the back as he bragged.

"Fuck, man, I ended up in the wrong business from the looks of it." Mitch gave Colt a grin.

"Yeah, you and me both. I spent all those years getting knocked in the head to make a buck. Who would have thought cheerleading was the ticket? Jace has done real well. My neighbor, a few houses over, just happens to be President Bush. He hasn't invited us over for dinner yet, but I feel sure it's just a matter of time." That had Mitch laughing.

"Well, you might have had a chance if you hadn't played for New York. No hard-core Dallas fan would ever rub elbows with the likes of a New York Panther," Jace added loudly as he descended the stairs. "Good to see you, Mitch."

"Great to see you, buddy." For old times' sake, Mitch waited for Jace to reach the bottom step and grabbed him before giving him a tight hug. Jace made a humming sound and Mitch couldn't resist the urge to waggle his eyebrows at Colt.

"Jace, do you really have to encourage him?" Colt asked as Jace stepped back from the embrace. Mitch couldn't help but laugh when Colt moved in and slid an arm around his husband, drawing him close to his side. Even after all this time, Colt felt the need to radiate his possessiveness. The grin Jace gave his lover made Colt's frown widen. "You're too good-looking to have Mitch stay here. I think he needs to sleep in his car tonight. It's nice out this time of year. It'll be like a campout."

"No, he's not sleeping in his car. Come on, Mitch. I just changed the sheets in the guest bedroom. Have you had anything to eat?" Jace asked, motioning for Colt to grab the duffel by the front door. Mitch let Colt carry the bag as he brought up the rear while Jace led them to the guestroom.

It never ceased to amaze Mitch how Jace and Colt fit so well together. They had an easy way about them. The way Colt looked at Jace as if he were the only thing that mattered in the whole world, and the way Jace always knew exactly how to handle his man. Like normal, when he spent time with the two of them, Mitch felt a twinge of something pulling at his heart. Something he couldn't quite put his finger on whenever he watched them together. Was he jealous? Fuck yeah, he was, and that had him doing a mental shake to his overactive brain, quickly tamping the feeling down.

"Are you still vegan?" Mitch asked, changing the subject in his head. And that got a snicker from Colt.

"Of course, are you hungry?" Jace asked as they climbed the stairs.

"I grabbed a burger on the way."

"I get bacon for breakfast," Colt added, as if that proved he was still in charge of his own eating. Uh, yeah right. Mitch had to smile at that thought because he had firsthand experience watching Jace fuss over Colt's eating habits. No way the guy ate much meat. The only meat Colt got was the big fat cut of prime beef Jace slipped him every night, lucky guy.

"Here, this is your room," Jace stopped at the first doorway upstairs. He flipped on the lights, illuminating a large, gorgeous room with a huge king-size bed and a fifty inch flat-panel television. This was so much better than any hotel in the DFW area.

"Stay as long as you need," Jace offered as Colt dumped the duffel bag on the bed. Mitch turned in a slow circle. This guest bedroom was decorated better than his entire house.

"There's a bathroom through here," Colt said, walking over to the connecting door and turning on that light switch. "Make yourself at home. Jace leaves early in the mornings. Do I need to get you up at a certain time tomorrow?" Colt asked.

"Nah, I've got it, I'm good. By the way, this place is great. Looks like I'll be sleeping like a king tonight. I'm really sorry I woke you guys up."

"The remote's in the drawer. The Wi-Fi code is on the back," Colt said as he pulled Jace from the room, not waiting for Mitch to respond.

"It's all good. Let us know if you need anything," Jace spoke up as he was dragged away.

"Or don't," Colt called out, and Mitch laughed. He grabbed his laptop and sat at the head of the bed, putting his feet up as he booted up his computer and pulled the remote from the drawer. His gut told him Dallas had just become the safest place on the planet. What bad guy in his right mind would show up here this weekend? And why hadn't anyone figured that out before now? In a few keystrokes, he logged into his computer to check the status on the case.

~~~

"He *does* leave early." Mitch leaned against the doorframe in the kitchen, watching Colt add bacon to the frying pan.

"He works hard every day, but the weekends are big gym time because the kids are out of school all day," Colt said, moving the bacon around, turning the heat down on the burner. He obviously took great care in cooking the bacon just right.

"So, you're saying teenage girls and boys get out of bed at the butt crack of dawn to go do cheerleading? I'm not buying it." Mitch shook his head, taking the coffee mug Colt handed him, and then poured himself a cup.

"That's what I thought too, but they do. He's usually there until late into the night. He gives everything to those kids. Anything they need, he's right there helping them. You should see his gym. It's unbelievable really." Colt sounded proud and checked the fryer again until he was satisfied everything was cooking just right. "I added four pieces for you."

"Really? So that means the rest is for you? There has to be at least twenty or so slices in that packet." Mitch laughed as Colt shot him a grin of excitement, then went back to expertly turning the strips.

"Jace watches my diet closely. He hasn't gotten off the mother hen meets Florence Nightingale act. I gotta get it when I can," Colt said, pulling a carton of eggs from the refrigerator, taking his time to carefully crack each one over a bowl.

"You guys look like you're doing pretty well." Mitch lifted the steaming cup to his lips and took a welcomed drink of the hot brew.

"I think we are. I'm picking up some broadcasting and public speaking gigs, but my main focus is to try hard to be everything he needs," Colt answered, throwing the last eggshell in the trash can before whisking the eggs, then pouring them into the already heated skillet.

"That's all anyone could ask for, or at least, that's the way I see it. Jace's lucky to have you, Colt. Not trying to change the subject, but

I was thinking that if the day turns out like I think it will, this whole mission's gonna be a big waste of time. So maybe I can take you two out. Maybe dinner, dancing, that kind of thing. You do go to clubs, right? If not, dinner's fine." Mitch watched as Colt placed the cooked strips of bacon on a paper towel.

"Nah, I go anywhere. I haven't had the urge to drink since Jace took me back. We go to a club close to downtown sometimes." Colt grabbed two plates out of the cabinet dividing the scrambled eggs equally, but only adding four pieces of bacon to the plate before handing it to Mitch.

"Cool. I should know something for sure in the next couple of hours, but I'm betting I'm off tonight. I have a feeling our man's gonna be a no-show, even though they haven't called it yet."

"No problem. I'll call Jace and let him know. We haven't been out dancing in a while. Jace loves to dance, and I love watching him shake his ass," Colt said and gave him a wink before shoving a few more slices of bacon in his mouth. "Oh my god. Bacon. It's from God."

Mitch laughed at the ecstasy on Colt's face, then pointed at the pile of bacon on his friend's plate. "You really aren't planning on sharing, are you?"

"Hell no! I gave you a room to sleep in, but I draw the line at my bacon treat. If you're still hungry, there's a wide assortment of yogurt products in the refrigerator. Jace goes nuts at all the flavors. Help yourself," Colt offered, never slowing his intake of bacon.

"That's okay. This'll do," Mitch added, eating a large chunk of the scrambled eggs.

"Yeah, that's the way I feel about yogurt, too."

~~~

"Fuck you. Fuck this team and fuck this state." Mitch glared at Brody Masters, head of the Dallas field office and a longtime friend. Just like he'd assumed, Carlos Chavez was a no-show even though they had been told by their most *reliable* source he would be there today. Fucking informants sucked shit, and this was turning into nothing more than a big, bad joke as everyone flexed their muscles, trying to hide from becoming the scapegoat in the deal. What Mitch couldn't understand was why in the hell they had even bothered to call him in. He'd have been happy staying tucked in that badass room, getting a little shut-eye.

"I can see why you might feel that way," Brody started, but Mitch wasn't ready to hear any more on the subject.

"No, fuck you. I've got a case needing some serious attention, and your fucking guys can't even figure out there's a cop conference in town. It took me about a minute to know they were here and about another minute to figure out that no fugitive would be dumb enough to show his face in a town full of official enforcers of the law, thereby making it impossible for me to make the arrest." Mitch paced the back of the office, letting the venom spew from his lips. As a matter of fact, most of the frustration he'd been feeling for quite some time fueled this rant, making everything that much worse.

"Mitch," Brody started again, but he cut him off.

"No, the fucking Omni Hotel has likely been flashing 'Welcome to Dallas, International Law Enforcement conference' on the side of their building for the last week. The fucking American Airlines Center has had banners posted for the last two weeks. The barista at Starbucks downstairs told me that little bit of information when I walked into the building." Mitch gestured with his hands as he spoke, completely wound up.

"And while we're on it, why haven't any of your men been able to ID Chavez for themselves? Why am I needed in your field office? There has to be two dozen deputy marshals housed right here. The FBI's been working this case for three fucking years." Mitch stalked forward and flipped the file folder open on the desk separating the two of them. He knew the answer to the question. Chavez was a sneaky son-of-a-bitch. He could become anyone and had no problem paying people to pose as him.

Mitch only knew of the guy because fifteen years ago, way before he'd ever gotten a job with the Service, he'd been partying it up in Mexico and ran into the guy's car.

"Are you through?" Brody asked, not looking at the pages and pages Mitch flipped over with no photo of Chavez.

"No! Because I just realized why you take weapons away from your staff at the front desk. Because you know I would have had to shoot someone over all this. *Now*, I'm done." Mitch plopped down hard in the seat facing his friend. "I can't believe you went admin. Doesn't that suit and tie suck your will to live?"

"No, not at all. And I can see you didn't feel the need to dress up today. Wait! I think we actually bought that T-shirt together at the Grateful Dead concert in seventy-eight." Brody leaned back in his black leather chair, a smug grin pulled at the corners of his mouth.

"Har. Har. Har. I wasn't even born in seventy-eight. You're an old man if you even remember back that far," Mitch teased, running his palms over his T-shirt. "And there's nothing wrong with my shirt."

"I am an old man. I'll be forty-five this year. You aren't so young yourself, you know. Too old to be chasing after everything that walks." Brody's smug grin returned.

"Speak for yourself, and I don't chase everything that walks." But his friend had him. Brody was right, he wasn't getting any younger and absolutely went from guy to guy. He'd never admit it to anyone, but on some level, he envied what Brody and his wife had. He saw that same connection in Colt and Jace, but it was such a foreign concept for him.

Mitch's job demanded all his attention, and most of the guys he slept with couldn't get past the hours he worked. And he certainly didn't do clingy, he had no time for that. Maybe that was why he'd accepted the fact he'd remain single. Honestly, he blamed Jace and Colt for that little nagging feeling in his heart that insisted something was missing. *Was* he lonely? Hell, he didn't know. Colt and Jace made it look easy, but he knew better. He didn't have time to deal with all the problems, questions, and baggage, not to mention the work a relationship would bring. His job came first, end of story. It wasn't a bad thing.

"Listen, Margie and I want to take you to dinner tonight. She was just asking about you not two days ago." Brody's voice pulled him from his thoughts.

"No way am I letting you off so easy. Did I tell you I couldn't even get a room last night? I'm staying with friends. So I'm taking them to dinner for taking me in at midnight last night. Hell, I should have called and woken you up last night. Would've served your sorry ass right," Mitch declared.

"Are you staying with Colt Michaels?" Brody asked, straightening the papers Mitch had shoved all over his desk. Mitch narrowed his brow at the change in Brody's tone. He sounded a little curious and as though his mood elevated.

"Yes, how did you know that?" he questioned carefully.

"My son's been hounding me to get his autograph. He wants his Uncle Mitch to hook him up." Brody glanced up at him, a big goofy grin plastered across his face.

"Oh my god. You did not just play the kid card?" Mitch shook his head and tried not to smile.

"You know you're his god-uncle," Brody chuckled, going in for the kill.

"I am not his god-uncle. I've only met the boy once. And I'll get the autograph if you just shut up." Mitch ran his hands down his worn jeans and stood. "I'm gonna use a conference room for the next few hours."

"Sure thing. For what it's worth, I'm sorry about all this," Brody said, extending a hand to Mitch.

"Yeah, funny, I don't believe you," Mitch shot back with a smile and shook the offered hand.

"Don't let that stop you from doing the right thing for your god-nephew," Brody retorted. Mitch barked out another laugh as he opened the door. Heads turned from the weekend skeleton crew. He must have been louder in the office than he realized. Mitch ignored them all, heading back to the room he'd used as an office on many occasions throughout the years.

Hours later Mitch sat kicked back in the conference chair, his entire focus trained on the computer screen in front of him. His online gaming buddy and NSA security hacker, Aaron Stuart, had discreetly put together a report of all the known hate groups in the country. Somewhere in investigating four murders and three attempted murders, linked only through the victim's sexual orientation, he'd narrowed the suspects down to United States citizens. Since gay men were the only known targets so far, they had to be driven by homophobic hate.

What Mitch hadn't been prepared for was the extensive list of documented groups that opposed homosexuality. There were thousands and thousands of names listed. On the concept of leaving no stone unturned, he took the time to review each potential suspect, whittling down the possibilities. Age, financial ability, and background were the key qualifications as to who went where on the list.

There was a better chance of finding a needle in a haystack, but he was just getting downright desperate at this point.

On a heavy sigh, Mitch pushed away from the desk and stood, stretching out his long limbs. He ran his fingers through his close-cropped hair, then across his chin, agitated as he thought over everything he'd done off the clock and on his own dime to build this case.

He'd gone to each victim's hometown and interviewed as many of their friends and family as he could find. He'd investigated the crime scenes, gotten all of the police reports, and did everything he knew to do, trying to find how these cases tied together. He called in favors from his partner, Kreed Sinacola, who had gone over every bit of information he could put his hands on. He'd also used Aaron Stuart to gather the information he couldn't obtain easily on his own. Between Kreed's gut and Aaron's amazing hacking skills, this case should have come together easier, but it hadn't, proving the person behind these acts was very well-trained and well-funded.

If he could just have found something substantial, he was certain his director would have pulled some strings to get this case noticed, but he needed help on this one. Whoever was behind this was too clever. There were too many different methods of attack, even if the underlying cases screamed similarities.

The million dollar question surfaced again. What was Mitch missing? Over and over, he asked himself this question. And every time, he mentally ticked off the facts, hoping to identify the missed element. All of the victims were regionally high profile gay men, but none of them had contact with the others. They didn't hang out in the same social circles, nor were they in any of the same areas of the country. The only other common denominator was that all of these men were out—they accepted who they were.

It was at Aaron's insistence that they added notorious hate groups into the mix. Mitch didn't see the fit. For him, this was a one-man operation. Groups would have leaked the information by now. Somebody would have been talking or bragging, no way they could have held all this in.

Now, desperation had Mitch trying anything. If he could narrow down the groups, then dig through their hierarchy, maybe he could find a lead. From what he'd read so far, none of those groups were that well-organized, and whoever did this had his shit together. Mitch learned years ago that hate breeds hate, and those groups always had too much internal fighting to have mastered these types of crimes without someone getting pissed off in the process and blabbing their secrets.

Mitch pulled his wayward thoughts back together and sat down to continue isolating the groups. Who knew how long had passed when his phone vibrated on his desk, drawing his attention. He looked over to see Colt's name on the caller ID. Reaching for the phone, he clicked the accept button, pulling up the text.

"Jace is off tonight. We're good to go if you are. Let us know."

"Cool. I'll let you know if anything changes. Your cheer-boy's treat, right?" Mitch texted back.

"What? You said something about a thank you dinner... Thank you to me for taking you in off the streets," Colt responded immediately.

"Yeah, that's before I saw where you live and what you drive. I'm a USMS public servant. I make shit."

"I'm not overly happy with your obsession about my guy. I think I need to kick your ass." Finally! He'd had to wait almost twenty-four hours for Colt to go there this time.

"Bring it, jockstrap. I'll meet you at the house later. Pick a steakhouse," Mitch responded back, grinning at their banter. He began to pack up his work. He needed to make time for a quick workout, and he could access just about any gym anywhere—part of the Marshals' perks package. He also had to do some shopping, which he hated, but he hadn't brought anything decent to wear.

Chapter 6

The sound of the newscaster's voice had Cody looking up at the big screen television. He sat in his spacious room at the Embassy Suites hotel in the uptown area of Dallas. He halfway listened as the reporter spoke on the law enforcement and Geekfest conferences being held here in town this weekend. From Cody's perspective, outside of the intense traffic, he couldn't have picked a better time to visit the city.

The conference hadn't even crossed his mind at the time he made his reservations, but on the upside, the hotel he'd chosen was overrun with good-looking men and that couldn't be a bad thing. Honestly, he'd worked out in the hotel gym for about an hour after he first checked in, and there were so many hot guys pumping iron that he'd had to concentrate in order not to stare.

Heck, Cody had even considered going down to the free cocktail hour the hotel offered, but eventually decided against it. He really wanted to see what this JR's nightclub was all about. After all, the club was the main reason he'd come all the way up to Dallas in the first place.

For a while now, he'd tossed around the idea of taking this trip and checking out the famous night spot. Any gay club in Dallas that had made its reputation all the way down to Austin had to be experienced firsthand. It had just been a lucky coincidence that he could help Mason out by going to Anna, Texas, and checking out that horse. He'd even let Mason believe that he'd made this whole trip just for him, since Mason couldn't find the time right now to get away. Cody had justified that little white lie because that was just what brothers did to each other. But truth be told, he'd had this reservation for about a month now, right after he'd gotten his schedule and noticed he had both Friday and Saturday nights off. When had that ever happened?

The horse for Mason had been a no-brainer. She was exactly what had been sent to Mason in pictures. Cody had spent a couple of hours with her around lunch time, but he'd known right away they'd be buying her. He'd even negotiated a slightly better deal to purchase her.

As for his new patrol mount, Ranger, he spent hours with him early this morning. He really couldn't have asked for anything better. He was a five-year-old chestnut Thoroughbred mix and stood around seventeen hands tall. Cody liked the bigger horses because they held his large frame a little easier.

After Cody completed the department-required paperwork, they'd saddled Ranger up, and Cody took him out for a ride. He was truly a perfect animal, one he'd enjoy helping care for. He'd gotten lucky with that horse.

Last night, he'd stayed in Waco after several hours of touring the Texas Ranger Hall of Fame Museum. He had to have looked at everything he could find, and he spent about a hundred dollars in the gift store buying up books for himself and souvenirs for his nieces and nephews. He absolutely loved that place, and the stop had given him a renewed vigor of wanting to be one of those men someday.

Cody forced himself to stop his nervous energy masked as musing over this trip. He'd spent the last hour grooming himself, shaving, plucking, and debating over which cologne to wear. When he came out of the bathroom, he'd stood in front of the closet, looking at the choices of clothing he'd brought. When he couldn't make a decision, he sat down in the chair because he was stressing the fuck out. He had a way of doing that to himself.

It took some time to justify that it didn't matter that much what he wore. He wasn't hoping for a hookup tonight. He really wasn't a one-night stand type of guy, but he had clipped and trimmed himself down there just in case something presented itself as an option. Hell, in all honesty, he didn't know exactly what he hoped for from the club tonight. He'd never really put himself out there like this before, but he wanted to have a good time, enjoy a few drinks, celebrate his new job, and let off some steam. He also wanted to look good doing it.

Okay, that sounded reasonable, and one thing Cody knew for sure, he wouldn't have any fun sitting alone in this room, worrying about his clothing. *Screw it!* He got up, walked across the room, pulled his favorite Wranglers from his duffel bag, and slid them on. Decision made. It didn't take long for him to finish getting dressed. Ready to go, he put his wallet in his jeans back pocket, grabbed his cell phone and truck keys before placing his beloved Texas Rangers baseball cap on his head. That was sure to give him some confidence that seemed to be failing him right then.

~~~

Mitch sat across from Colt and Jace at the Dish Restaurant on Cedar Springs. Apparently the place was a hop, skip and a jump from JR's, the club they had mentioned wanting to take Mitch to. The restaurant was packed up tight. The bar area led right into the restaurant, and there wasn't a lot of space differentiating the two. The noise levels were moderate, and there was absolutely no privacy. It also seemed to be filled more with regulars than the legions of officers who packed the city. To Mitch, he didn't think this restaurant's spin on froufrou fusion Southern comfort food was really that big a draw to the normal manly man who wore a uniform.

As far as he was concerned, he couldn't have been more entertained. Jace and Colt were hilarious. Just deciding on a place to eat created an hour-long debate. Both were so focused on the other that neither would give. Jace insisted on a steakhouse for Colt, while Colt insisted on go-green health food for Jace. The debate went on so long that Mitch finally had to move them out the door, and he rode separately from them to get a little peace and quiet. He wasn't sure when they decided on this place, but they wound up here where they were apparently regulars.

The possessiveness that Colt showed toward Jace didn't just extend to Mitch. He put it out for the world to see and was actually quite amusing. Colt kept Jace close to him. He stayed attentive, even correcting the waitress when she repeated Jace's order incorrectly.

These were all such new attributes for the man he'd watched lead his father's favorite football team in back-to-back championships and the same party boy that had been implicated in more scandalous behavior than he could even begin to recall.

"I spoke to your dad the other night," Colt said. His one arm draped across the back of Jace's chair, rubbing little circles into the side of Jace's arm.

"Really?" Mitch asked. He'd foregone the beer, not wanting to drink alcohol in front of Colt, no matter how much he insisted alcohol didn't bother him. Mitch understood the everyday battle Colt faced.

"Yeah. He seems real good. Told me to tell you that you should come see them more," Colt said, a grin on his lips.

"Yeah, I got that email yesterday," Mitch replied dryly. "How's your old man doing, you ever get things straight with him?"

"We still haven't spoken. It's better this way; he made his decision," Colt said, and Jace nodded.

"Excuse me, I don't want to bother you, but can I have your autograph?" A young man, no more than seventeen or eighteen, came forward, staring straight at Colt. There was clear adulation in his eyes. He held out a black Sharpie.

"Sure," Colt said, unwrapping himself from Jace. "What do you want me to sign?"

"This." The young man lifted his shirt in the middle of the restaurant, exposing tan skin and a tight midsection. "Can you sign here?" The kid smiled, gesturing toward his flat stomach.

Colt paused and looked over at Jace who seemed to be enjoying this moment. "Is that your boyfriend?" The young man nodded his head toward Jace. "I saw you on television, but everyone was saying y'all had broken up."

"Go ahead," Jace urged Colt to sign.

"He's my husband, not my boyfriend. Do you just want me to sign my name?" Colt asked, still acting uncertain.

"Yes." He bit his bottom lip and made his stomach muscles ripple which caused Mitch to laugh into his sweet tea. No doubt the kid was trying to impress. As Colt signed, the kid locked eyes on Mitch, and that was all it took for the football hero to be forgotten. He slowly eyed Mitch up and down, letting his gaze linger on Mitch's lips, before blowing him a kiss.

"I'd tear you up, kid," Mitch grumbled, seconds before the manager approached them.

"Kenneth, behave! Leave these people alone. Go back to the bar with your friends," he scolded, ushering the kid away.

"I'm sorry he bothered you." He gave the kid an exasperated look, but turned a fond smile back toward Colt and Jace. "I'm glad you came back in tonight," he said, shaking Colt's, then Jace's, hand.

"Terrick, meet our friend Mitch. Mitch, this is Terrick. He's a co-owner of the restaurant," Jace explained.

"I'm sorry about Kenneth's behavior. He's a good guy, just a bit of a flirt. Harmless, I assure you." Terrick grasped Mitch's hand in greeting.

"He's not a problem," Mitch reassured the man. Seconds later, Kenneth was back, planting himself right next to Mitch, sliding a napkin with his phone number penned in big purple markings in front of him.

"Call me tonight. I'll bottom you so hard," he said and was gone before Terrick could shoo him away.

"That boy!" Terrick looked frustrated and shook his head, before starting off after him. Within minutes, Mitch watched as Kenneth and his group of friends were escorted from the restaurant. The kid's parting words were very clear to Mitch, though.

"Call me, handsome!"

Mitch just watched as the scene unfolded in front of him, and the smirk never left his lips. He'd taken life so seriously lately that he hadn't had this good a time in a while. And he had to admit that being propositioned by the overly forward kid left him feeling good. So good in fact, it didn't even bother him when Colt gave him hell about the encounter for the rest of the meal. The only problem? Mitch didn't do the twink thing anymore. He liked his men big, thick, and muscular, and now his mind was fully occupied with sex.

Chapter 7

Mitch slowed his ride as he passed the front doors of the two-story bar Jace had recommended. It was late in the evening, and Jace and Colt chose to walk the few blocks from the restaurant to the club. Mitch drove, wanting his rental close by, just in case the night ended with him getting lucky. Hotels were clearly not an option this weekend, but the front seat of the car could do just as well, if need be.

From the looks of the place, JR's was hopping. Guys were everywhere. They littered the sidewalks, danced along the balcony, and the big floor to ceiling window illuminated just enough to show the place packed full of men. The music blared, thumping loudly, even out into the street. Just the kind of place he was looking for. Mitch drove another fifty feet before he found a parking space freeing up. Perfect.

Mitch, never one to rest on formality, lowered the rearview mirror and checked his teeth, running a hand through his close-cropped hair. He liked to keep it short when he was out on assignments. His freshly trimmed beard was a little heavier than a five o'clock shadow. He looked down to ensure the collar of his new button-down lay right. He unbuttoned a couple of buttons, letting his muscular chest show, before getting out of the car. He hoped that did the trick. The car door slammed, and he hit the key fob, setting the locks as he took in the scene around him. From what he could see, it looked like every kind of guy was there—older, younger, it didn't seem to matter, which suited him just fine.

Mitch had been told he had a strut, some called it a swagger. Whatever it was he was damn sure going to use it tonight as he bypassed the crowd waiting for entry right outside the front door. He only made brief eye contact with the bouncer as the guy stepped back, giving him a low whistle. Mitch's shoulders and biceps were bigger than the bouncer's and that said a lot. The bouncer smiled at him and gave him immediate access.

He felt eyes on him, so he took a quick glance back over his shoulder as he passed through the door. The bouncer stared at his ass. He cocked his head to the side, drawing the guy's eyes up to his, and he gave him a real smile. His dimples were an attention-grabber so he used them to his advantage. The bouncer smiled back. Mitch let his gaze linger, then winked at the guy before heading into the bar. Maybe he could wait long enough for the guy to get off work. The bouncer was exactly his type of man. Who knew what would happen, but he needed to keep his options open.

Mitch rolled his shoulders, letting loose of any pent up energy he still held onto regarding the earlier stupidly botched case. He wasn't going to let any of that ruin his night. Keeping the natural smile on his face, he looked around for Jace and Colt, but they were probably still en route.

What a great place this turned out to be. Mitch felt free here. Every person in this room accepted him for who he was as a person. That always eased his heart, especially with the job he had. He stopped by the bar, placed a twenty on the bar top, and ordered a quick double shot and a beer. He always watched his alcohol around Colt, but if Colt could handle a place like this, it sure seemed he might have kicked his habit. On those good thoughts, Mitch turned to the dance floor. He needed to make sure he told his pop how well he believed Colt was doing.

"Hey, sexy." Mitch heard over his shoulder. He turned to see the bartender pointing downward at a full double shot glass and his beer before taking the money and moving on to the next patron. Mitch downed the shot and then the beer, watching the sea of bodies on the dance floor writhing to the music.

In times like these, he loved the fact he wasn't insecure. He didn't have any inhibitions, and he damn sure wasn't the shy type or easily embarrassed. It wasn't a bad thing, and on nights like these, it really paid off as he left the bar, strutting his way out onto the dance floor.

His dark good looks and muscular body usually had men and women alike approaching him. He'd worked hard on his body, and he had to admit he loved being a bit of an exhibitionist. Not more than a couple of minutes passed before his brand new shirt was completely unbuttoned and removed, tossed somewhere unknown. The ink that decorated his body did the rest, earning him more than a few appreciative glances.

The men at JR's were eager to make his acquaintance, and he accepted them all. It was his own little game, a kind of foreplay of sorts, zeroing in and going after what he wanted. Dragging out the process of narrowing down the person he intended to have sex with was a thrill he'd always enjoyed. Mitch loved the hunt, probably why he chose his current profession.

He danced across the floor, bodies pressed against him, and he loved the hands running across his chest, down along his ass, and over his dick. Yeah, he loved that the most. It built anticipation as he grew hard with the intentional caresses and tightened grips.

The only problem? The newly enlightened civilian culture had many gay men growing a conscience. Mitch remembered a time when any of these guys would be ripe for the picking. Sex in the restrooms had been a way of life. It wasn't so much that way anymore. He'd pick one, and only one, for the night. Pity, because there were some good-looking guys rubbing all over him.

About thirty minutes later, he needed a break. The double shot and beer combo was wearing off. He needed a refresher. Mitch wiggled his way from the middle of the dance floor, flashing those dimples as he caught the attention of each man he passed by.

He was so genuinely happy to be here and not stuck in his own head like he had been since meeting Colt and Jace. It was only then he remembered they should be there by now. Mitch did a quick search and found them dancing on the outside of the crowd. They were wrapped around each other, moving slower than the beat of the music, completely lost in each other. They were sexy hot and made for one another. The slight pang of jealousy at the closeness they shared didn't go unnoticed.

Perhaps someday he could find what they had, but for right now—Mitch cut his eyes back to the dance floor—he couldn't be bothered when there were so many other options.

The bar was unfortunately stacked three deep. Mitch snaked his way around to the side, finding a hole and sliding in. He raised a hand to get the bartender's attention. He yelled out his order, got a nod, and pulled out another twenty as he waited. He scanned the room before turning back to the bartender who was being pulled in too many different directions. This was going to take a while. It wasn't until he glanced toward the bank of tables to his left that he spotted him. The guy sat in the darkened corner of the bar, with a baseball cap pulled down low on his head, and for some reason, the way he wore the hat caught Mitch's attention.

Mitch went from giving him an over-the-shoulder look, to turning right toward him. Why hadn't he noticed him before? Mr. Ball Cap was all cowboy'd up, in little better than work boots, snug fitting worn blue jeans, and a white T-shirt with some kind of design. The T-shirt was tightly stretched across a pretty impressive chest. The bulk in his arms showed, causing Mitch's jeans to tighten that much more.

Yeah, he wouldn't mind getting to know this guy.

The guy sat there at a high-top table, peering around Mitch, looking toward the dance floor, as if he was trying to remain unseen. Mitch watched as the wallflower's long fingers circled the beer bottle in front of him and brought it to his lips.

Fuck! Those lips were a temptation he needed to sample. Mitch was spellbound. He couldn't take his eyes off the guy.

When Mr. Ball Cap tilted his head back to down his beer, Mitch actually groaned out loud as he watched his Adam's apple work up and down with every swallow. Mitch's dick took too much notice of the move, and he had to reach down to adjust himself. From his actions, Mitch surmised the guy must be newly out, or completely uncomfortable with his sexuality.

How long had it been since Mitch was right there, doing that same thing? Well that answer was clear. Never! He started exploring his sexuality at a very young age, and if the truth be told, he explored it every opportunity he got. He was who he was…always. And his family had always accepted him.

The longer he sat ogling this guy, the more he wanted him. Mitch reached over, knocking his baseball cap back, not off, but up on the top of his head.

"I can't see you if you're hiding under that cap," Mitch yelled, flashing the guy his best smile. The bartender placed his drinks on the bar, and after a minute, snatched the twenty from his hand with a loud huff.

Mitch didn't give a shit what the bartender did. He was captivated by a shockingly handsome, rugged face. One he had been completely unprepared to see.

The guy was a little older than Mitch had originally thought, and motherfucking gorgeous. Shit, those full lips and strong jaw covered with a day's worth of stubble had Mitch imagining all kinds of assorted lewd behavior. Brilliant bright blue eyes framed with thick lashes shot up to his. Panic flashed in their depths. The guy lifted his cap, ran his hand over light sandy blond hair and placed the hat back on his head. When he did, Mitch noticed a tattoo on his upper chest peeking out from under the cotton material of his shirt, and he wanted to see more. Mitch had always had a thing for big blonds with blue eyes and ink. Had he just died and gone to heaven?

"I can't decide if I wanna be seen," the guy finally said and looked down. He was no longer making eye contact, and it was hard to tell in this lighting, but Mitch could have sworn he saw a blush. *A blush?* How long had it been since he had seen one of those? Mitch pulled the hat completely off and lifted the guy's face by placing his finger under his chin.

"Just as I thought. It fits you." It *was* a blush. Damn. That was seriously hot, and his cock jerked in approval.

"Huh?"

"How old are you?" Mitch asked, running his eyes up and down Mr. Ball Cap's big frame. He had thick muscular thighs that made the jeans he wore pull tight in just the right places, showing off a very nice package.

"Can I have my hat back, please?" the guy asked, but didn't move out from under the hold Mitch had on his chin. Manners and good looks…he wanted this guy, bad.

"Maybe, if you answer the question," Mitch teased, giving him a smile and a wink for encouragement. The guy swallowed, and his eyes moved to Mitch's lips. Good sign.

"I'm twenty-six," he answered. Mitch nodded and tucked the bill of blondie's hat in the back of his waistband, before lifting a couple of fingers toward the bartender. Mitch wasn't ready to give up the ball cap just yet. He figured he'd hold on to it for a while longer, insurance that the guy wouldn't take off.

Mitch watched as the bartender worked and handed his waiting shot to the hot, young country boy. How had this gorgeous guy flown under the radar? And a better question, why wasn't he out on the dance floor?

"Drink this," Mitch said, shoving the shot in the guy's hand. The bartender placed two more shots in front of him. He absently dug another twenty out of his pocket, not even paying attention to the change being offered back.

"What is it?" the guy asked.

"Does it matter?" Mitch challenged. "Drink it. And this one too."

Mitch downed his in one swallow. The guy followed suit and then drank the other one, before slamming the glass down on the polished wood. It was liquid courage. Mitch tossed the beer chaser, encouraging the kid to drink his, and he did. Mitch placed both empty bottles back on the bar before he grabbed the guy's hand and pulled him up.

"We're dancing," Mitch informed Mr. Ball Cap, ignoring the list of objections and excuses he spewed. It was a forced deal since the guy fought him every step he made, but Mitch wasn't taking no for an answer. It took a minute to make it to the edge of the dance floor. He wasn't a big drinker, so the shot had already begun to work.

When the guy finally broke free of his hold, he flipped around. He was taller than Mitch realized, maybe taller than his own six-four frame. Mitch couldn't let him get away, that just wasn't in his plan. He reached out, hooking an arm around the guy's waist before he could bolt too far off.

The move caught Ball Cap off guard with the hold turning into a full body deal as Mitch nudged him with the weight of his body out into the middle of the dance floor.

"It's easier when you just take the plunge. You know, like a Band-Aid. Always best if you just rip it free. You're here for a reason. Be okay with it." Those words weren't whispered. The music made it impossible to not yell them from behind, but it stopped the guy's struggles. Mitch didn't let him go. Instead, he turned him around so they were face-to-face on the dance floor.

Mitch kept him close, pressing the front of his body against the guy's chest. His arms held Ball Cap caged in, and damn was he hot, far more gorgeous than Mitch had first realized. He smelled fresh, clean, like the calming light rain that falls after a summer thunderstorm, mixed with a hint of fresh cut evergreens. He leaned in and inhaled. Damn, Mitch loved the smell of rain.

"You're fucking hot," Mitch yelled, and he could feel the young guy sported a pretty impressive bulge in his jeans. So did Mitch.

"Now move. We have a little ways to go before I relieve what's going on in those Levi's." Mitch grinned as he watched deep blue eyes widen at that statement. He moved his hips rubbing his erection back and forth across the younger man's. His smile grew wider, among other things.

"They're Wranglers, and I like your dimples. I haven't been dancing in a long time, thanks for not taking no for an answer." The guy still hadn't moved, but he hadn't left either.

"Good, I like for hot twenty-six-year-olds to dance with me, and just so you know, I'm used to getting what I want," Mitch purred and ran his hand down the guy's chest to the side of his hips, urging him to move. Mitch saw the moment Mr. Ball Cap gave in and laughed. Probably the alcohol had helped him too. The guy took over the movement for himself.

He had a beautiful smile and seemed to relax into the sway.

Relieved Blue Eyes wasn't going to leave, Mitch moved both hands forward, sliding his hands under the guy's shirt and lifted the T-shirt up and over his head. He wasn't disappointed. The guy was a little fairer than Mitch, but built precisely like he had imagined. Wide chest, thick well-defined pecs dusted with light blond hair, perfectly ripped abs, and a tempting blond treasure trail disappearing into tight well-worn jeans. He smiled at the impressive art work decorating the guy's hard body. He'd always been into tattoos, but the tattoos were just icing on an already enticing piece of cake. He would enjoy exploring each and every inked line with his tongue. Yeah, Mr. Ball Cap would do just fine.

~~~

What was he thinking? From the moment Cody walked into this club, he understood the magic of the place, experienced with awe the energy that drew the massive crowds and felt better for having been there. But the longer he stayed, the more he felt a little in over his head. He was just a country bumpkin' compared to these sophisticated patrons. His own insecurities had him stuck to the far reaches of the club on purpose. Guys like him weren't seen in places like these, but damn, had he wanted to have a good time tonight. And this club's legacy should have been the place to make that happen.

The minute that guy walked inside the front doors, Cody sat back and just stared. He was tall, dark, and exceedingly handsome with all that brawn and a killer smile. When he'd come to the bar and focused on Cody, training those amber eyes his way, Cody hardened to painful degrees. It had taken everything to keep himself nonchalant because that same man who currently rubbed about seventy-five percent of his body against Cody was his wet dream walking. Someone that could make him lose his mind and quite possibly his morals just to get a single taste.

Cody had ordered his second beer of the night, just to cool off, when he watched this one's shirt come off. All those well-conditioned muscles, covered in some of the finest ink he'd ever seen, began to move and flex to whatever dance motion he made.

Now, as he danced, Cody weighed the decision to ask this guy to come back to his room for a few hours because what happened in Dallas, stayed in Dallas. The problem with that plan had to do with how completely this city filled itself with officers this weekend. His own father and middle brother were somewhere in town partying it up all in the name of unity and support of the badge—whatever that meant.

Cody had never hid who he was as a person; he'd just not ever really rubbed his sexual orientation in his peers' faces. He'd learned at a young age the importance of keeping his off-duty private life to himself. Things like public displays and adding a plus one didn't really happen for him. He was laid back, easygoing, and pretty much unattached by most people's standards. His buddies were the guys he grew up with, his dating life was separate from them, and stayed in the confines of downtown Austin.

He'd gotten brave tonight, apparently a little too comfortable in his world, and ventured out. What he hadn't expected was for the hottest guy in the room to take notice of him. When had that ever happened before? Never.

"I'm Mitch. Tell me your name," the guy said against his ear. The words and warm breath danced across his skin like a tender caress. Cody closed his eyes and let the feeling take him away.

He let his inhibitions go and let the fantasy take root. His mouth actually watered at the prospect of pushing down the dark jeans and investigating every inch of that tempting flesh for himself.

This Mitch was seriously hot.

It had taken a while for Cody to pin Mitch down as law enforcement, which was odd. He was pretty good at detecting who was who. Mitch had the short hair thing going, but not the attitude. Since Cody came from a long line of officers, he knew that I'm-a-badass-just-ask-me persona well, and Mitch didn't put that out to the world, but being a badass did radiate from every pore of his body.

A slow song began, and long, beefy arms engulfed Cody, drawing him in against a solid chest and hard body. Cody swayed to the music as Mitch's thick, solid cock rubbed against his. Mitch's hand snaked up his back, pushing his head down against his shoulder. He closed his eyes, wrapped himself around Mitch, and concentrated on breathing heavily as the spicy scent of Mitch's cologne eased his nerves.

The room began to spin. He'd most definitely had too much to drink. It was just such a turn on to be wrapped in someone's arms as the song played around them. Under the weight of such a powerful attraction, he let himself go, just feeling the moment.

"Telling me your name wouldn't kill you." Mitch drew his head back so they were face-to-face. "Did you hear me tell you my name's Mitch? I'd really like to hear you use it when I'm fucking you later." Mitch didn't bat an eye as he spoke. Those perfect eyes held his, challenging him to refuse the suggestion. Cody couldn't respond, because at the moment, he really wanted to take him up on his offer. His ass clenched, his heart thundered in his chest, and his knees threatened to give out at the thought of Mitch fucking him hard and fast.

He loved how sure and direct Mitch acted, and his dick jerked in agreement. They fit well together. Cody liked the idea of having someone that could match him move for move. And he was willing to bet Mitch wouldn't hold back in bed. He could give Cody exactly what he'd come here to get tonight, even if he hadn't known what that was until just this minute.

"Are you from around here?" Mitch asked. Cody shook his head, trying to clear the image from his mind. He'd decided early on that he wasn't going to answer any questions. He stayed silent, letting Mitch's deep rich voice lull him.

"Come on, tell me something about yourself. I know you're law enforcement," Mitch spoke against his ear, and he clearly knew what he was doing. Cody's body reacted to everything he did. Mitch had to have been out for many years, because he was too comfortable and sure of himself not to have been.

This time, when Cody didn't answer, Mitch arched his hips, grinding against his aching erection, and the warmth consumed him. The pressure of Mitch's splayed hands on the small of his back forced him to return the grind. He was like a freaking dog in heat, and so out of his league. The grin spreading across Mitch's face let him know he was in trouble. It only took another shift of hips before he matched Mitch, humping him right there on the dance floor. Damn, it felt good. Too fucking good.

Something interrupted the erotic feel of Mitch's skilled hips.

"Hey, buddy, we're out," a man yelled in their direction. Mitch cocked his head to the side, and Cody followed the gaze. His eyes landed on one of the best-looking men he'd ever laid eyes on, besides of course, the one that currently had him wrapped in his arms. The guy smiled at Mitch and lifted a hand and got even better-looking than before. Damn, Mitch traveled in fine circles.

Then recognition dawned.

"You're Colt Michaels," Cody almost yelled the words. The expressions crossing his face had to be comical.

"Come on, we'll walk you out," Mitch yelled, grabbing Cody's hand tightly, tugging him toward the door. They barely cleared the front entrance before all Cody's youthful hero worship bubbled to the top. Cody let go of the tight hold Mitch had on him and extended a hand to Colt.

"I'm a huge fan. It seems like I've followed your career my whole life. I'm from the same area you grew up in." He shook Colt's hand.

"Thank you. You're from central Texas?" Colt asked.

"Yes, sir. I'm from Kylie's Corner. It's a small town outside of Buda, where you grew up. I live in Austin now."

"That area always feels like home. Meet my husband. Jace, this is…" Colt hesitated.

"I'm Cody. It's nice to meet you," he said, extending a hand to Jace, pumping him with the same amount of vigor he had Colt's.

"Hi, Cody." Jace smiled that warm, supersexy grin he'd used on Mitch just a few minutes earlier, and he found himself a little transfixed.

"Cody, it was a pleasure to meet you. We've got a couple of blocks to walk to get back to our car. Mitch, I'll leave the laundry room door open for you. Maybe leave a T-shirt down there so you don't catch a chill," Colt teased. For the first time since they were outside, everything settled into Cody. He knew why Mitch seemed so familiar to him. He remembered the details of the Colt Michaels accident and investigation. He'd tracked that case closely, especially once he learned that Colt had come out. The puzzle pieces started falling in place, and Cody's gaze shot toward Mitch. The guy that was already so far outside of his league had to be Mitch Knox, the deputy US marshal that helped Colt in Hawaii. *Damn!* This night just kept getting better and better.

Mitch winked at Cody.

"Roger that," Mitch said, staring at Cody, but talking to Colt.

"Goodnight," Jace replied. Out of the corner of his eye, he caught Jace turning Colt away from watching them.

"You're a deputy marshal, aren't you?" Cody asked, hoping Colt and Jace were out of ear shot.

"I see you know the case." Mitch gave him a half-assed, cocky tooth-filled grin before he handed Cody back his ball cap. Cody looked down at the hat in his hands, that being the whole reason he'd followed Mitch out onto the dance floor to begin with. He slid his hat back in place on his head. The move was more a symbolic gesture, designed to create space between them. If that even made any sense.

Whatever, to Cody it made perfect sense. He shifted thoughts in his head once the invisible barriers were now set firmly between them.

For Cody, that Colt Michaels incident had kind of changed his life, made him consider things differently. Colt's case had definitely reaffirmed his lifelong convictions of wanting to make a difference in the hate of this world. Although Mitch was the hottest thing Cody might have ever laid eyes on, and he had a strong, powerful attraction to the guy, this thing they were doing tonight was all wrong. At this point, Cody couldn't risk his reputation and fucking a high-profile deputy US marshal sure didn't seem like a good idea.

Damn, how had he let this night get so far out of control? Surely Texas Ranger wannabe's didn't sit up in gay bars waiting for the first guy to come along and pick them up. He'd made a bad judgment call coming here tonight.

Chapter 8

Mitch stepped back and fought the pissed off feeling. He was jealous. What? No, surely *he wasn't...* Right? Fucking A! He was jealous! He'd been dancing with this Cody for a couple of hours, bought at least fifty dollars' worth of alcohol trying to loosen him up, and Colt got more out of him in two minutes than he'd gotten so far.

Mitch made a huge effort to mentally shrug these feelings off. To his core, the fundamental parts of Mitch's personality were the opposite of jealous—whatever that meant. He didn't do that green-eyed monster thing—ever. As he watched this whole exchange play out in front of him, Mitch did something he never did. He forced himself to act reasonably.

Through his own internal dialog, he followed Cody's hand slide inside his front jean pocket, and his first thought erased all the others floating through his head. Cody was going to adjust himself. Since Mitch always found that move sexy, he lost focus as he watched the bulge become more defined as the material stretched across that impressive cock. His mouth actually watered. Mitch had already felt the evidence showing Cody wasn't a small man. He'd ground enough against him tonight to know his dick was large and in charge, but to see the proof so clearly outlined in Cody's jeans turned his shit on. It took a second, but he kicked back in gear when he saw car keys pulled out.

"Where are you going?" Mitch asked. Something told him this was a sudden goodbye, not an invitation to ride along back to his hotel.

"Thanks for the dance and the drinks," Cody started and stepped back. The move was definitely designed to put both literal and figurative distance between them. Panic seemed to show across Cody's face as he said the words out loud. Why panic? That made no sense. Mitch was certain the guy had been just as into him as he'd been into Cody.

"Why're you freezing up on me? I'm not gonna attack you." Mitch cut to the chase. There wasn't much time to do anything more than confront this head on before Cody bolted. He certainly couldn't run after the guy, right?

"I'm not." Cody bit his lip. Right then, Mitch wondered if Cody had done those subtle moves on purpose. Coy, shy blushes and inviting lip bites... Sex on a stick came to mind, and Mitch's dick begged him to make this right.

"You can't leave now. You drank too much. My car's right over there. Give yourself time to sober up," Mitch reasoned. Where had those words come from? Actually, where was all this coming from? Cody had participated tonight, but he was clearly uncomfortable, and Mitch never got involved with self-conflicted types. That just reeked of drama and who had time for that?

Okay, Mitch was seriously arguing with himself. When had that ever happened?

Actually, this all probably came from Cody's physique. He was built like a brick house. In all likelihood, that much hotness scrambled Mitch's brain. But, damn, would they fit well together tonight. Guys like Cody didn't come around every day. It would take a lot for Mitch to wear him down. But there was something different about Cody. Hell, he sensed it the moment their eyes connected. He wanted to fuck him, no question there, but now he also wanted to know his story. He needed to get to know Cody and not just physically.

Shit! No, he didn't want to know more about Cody. That was just dumb.

This whole internal battle he waged irritated him and he scowled. It would be in his best interest to let Cody walk away. He still had time to find someone else to fuck tonight. Closeted, Dudley Do-Right types took too much time and patience. He liked his sex to be mutually hard, fast, and aggressive. Multiple times, no strings attached. Hell, what were a few bite marks in the name of a good time?

Surprising even himself and mostly definitely going against his current inner thoughts, Mitch reached out and grabbed Cody's car keys, snatching them away, then started to walk toward his car. He placed the keys he'd just swiped in his front pants pocket. Cody would have to follow to get them back. No matter how badly he wanted to, Mitch never looked over his shoulder to see how Cody had reacted to that one.

"Hey, you can't just take my truck keys," Cody yelled, and the best Mitch could tell, he hadn't moved from where he'd been standing. He would though, Mitch was certain.

"Looks like I did," Mitch called back. "You'll thank me later." He clicked his own car's key fob, unlocking both the doors and guiding himself to his rental by the flash of taillights, because right this minute, he couldn't even remember what the car looked like.

He was still a few cars away when he heard Cody's rushed footsteps approaching him. He braced himself for a tackle, because hell, he would have tackled whoever took his keys, but Cody didn't.

"Give 'em back," Cody said from right behind him.

"Give yourself time to sober up, then you can bolt. You're clearly law enforcement. It wouldn't be good for you if you got yourself a DUI," Mitch explained, rounding the trunk of his rental, still not looking back at Cody. "What are you, a police officer?"

"No, I work for the Texas DPS," Cody replied, standing near the trunk, but not moving any closer. Mitch opened the driver's door, and before he sat down, he glanced back. Mitch could see the leeriness in Cody's eyes, that he wasn't sure what to do next.

"Hmm…does that mean you're a sexy state trooper?" Mitch asked, resting both arms on the roof of the car.

"I just got assigned to mounted detail, but I really want to be a ranger. I only have another year before I can test," Cody said in probably the most honest and in-depth exchange they'd shared tonight. Mitch smiled at the bowed up chest that accompanied those words.

"Army or Texas?" Mitch asked.

"Texas," Cody answered as if that were the only logical choice. It wasn't, and it was damn hard to become a Texas Ranger.

"Good, get in," Mitch said, nodding to the passenger side.

"Good, why?" Cody called out but didn't move from his spot.

"That means you weren't lying about your age, and you're older than I originally thought you were." Mitch ducked his head inside the car and closed the door. He made a show of making sure the car was unlocked and then put the key in the ignition and turned the car on. "Crawling" by Linkin Park blared on the radio, and he reached up to lower the volume. When Cody still hadn't come to the car, Mitch cut his eyes to the rearview mirror and watched and waited. Surely Cody wouldn't leave. Mitch chuckled at the thought. If Cody knew what was good for him, he'd take off and call a locksmith, because if he got inside this car, Mitch planned to do everything it took to tap that hot Texas trooper's ass good and hard tonight.

~~~

He shouldn't get inside that car. Everything screaming through his head made it clear, he should turn around, walk away, and get AAA out there to get his truck started, lesson learned. He needed to stay in his little secluded part of the world and not venture out to the big city anymore until he grew a bigger set of metaphorical balls.

Cody removed his cap, scrubbed a hand over his face, then started cracking his knuckles, a bad habit he'd never broken himself from. But the action helped settle him, and he needed to clear his head. Mitch knew exactly what he was doing, and the guy seemed to get off on pushing at him. Besides, it would take hours to get someone out here to start his truck.

Fuck my life!

On an exaggerated huff, Cody stalked to the side of the car and tugged open the door. "Give me my keys," he huffed, bending down, glaring at Mitch.

"Get in, shut the door. It's cold out there," Mitch said as his eyes remained focused on something out the front windshield. He hadn't even bothered to look his way.

"It's not cold out here. Give me my keys," he demanded, bending in farther this time, his head all the way inside the car. Mitch said nothing as he slowly turned toward Cody and gave a fake shiver. The minute their eyes met, Cody's foot slid off the curb, and he toppled a little.

"Get in the damn car. I'm not gonna molest you. Well, not unless you ask nicely," Mitch chuckled as Cody grabbed on to the door to keep himself upright. "Look, if that's seriously what's stopping you, dude, you're my size, maybe a little bigger. You know what I do for a living and every person in that bar saw you with me. You're fine. Get in the car."

"It's not that," Cody started.

"Explain it to me in the car," Mitch suggested. For a few moments, they were again in an eye-staring standoff. Finally Cody caved and crawled inside the car with a huff. They both stared out the front window until Cody finally shut the passenger side door.

"See, no scary monsters in here," Mitch teased in a mocking tone. Cody clenched his jaw and continued the vigilant stare out the front window. The silence must not have been agreeable to Mitch because he lifted the steering wheel, turned completely in his seat, and stared directly at him. Cody's heart thundered in his chest. Without question, there was a powerful attraction between them. Well, at least from Cody's side, and the longer Mitch stared at him, the more his body stirred, pushing him to end its agony.

"So a trooper that wants to be a ranger, right?" Mitch asked, and Cody just cut his eyes over, giving Mitch what he hoped was his best are-you-seriously-asking-that glare. That caused a laugh from Mitch, and he leaned in closer. Mitch's scent surrounded him, and damn, that man smelled amazing. His traitorous cock swelled against his jeans.

"A good-lookin' guy like you must be at this club for a reason," Mitch said, slowly lifting a hand and running his knuckles down the side of Cody's cheek. Cody tried to turn away, but Mitch stopped him, grasping his chin. His brain begged his mouth to speak up—demand his car keys back—but his cock seemed to control everything he'd done since he crawled inside the car. Hell, his cock had actually controlled him from the minute he'd seen Mitch enter that stupid bar. Cody Turner did not think with his dick, he thought with his brain.

Mitch leaned in even more, coming closer to Cody's face. His eyes settled on Mitch's perfectly formed lips, and the smirk that followed made it clear Mitch knew the power he had. His eyes shot up to Mitch's deep amber gaze. "Why are you here tonight, Cody?"

"I'm celebrating," he heard himself say, lost, completely transfixed by Mitch's eyes. His answer must have surprised him. Cody dropped his gaze back down to Mitch's sexy smirk. And damn if that grin didn't go all the way to his cock.

"What are you celebrating?" Mitch moved in closer. The movement seemed to suck the oxygen from the car, and all he could do was breathe Mitch in. He was losing what little control he had. He could feel the connection and sexual tension sizzling in the air around them. There wasn't six inches separating their faces, and he welcomed the warmth of Mitch's breath on his skin. Cody remained silent for a moment, trying to gather his thoughts. There were so many things running through his head.

"My new detail, getting closer to my goal." His brain was scrambled.

"As a ranger?" Mitch's husky voice dropped an octave lower as he descended, moving closer to Cody's lips.

"Yeah." Cody lifted his face. He wanted, no needed, to feel Mitch's lips on his.

"That's hot." Mitch sealed their lips together. Cody welcomed the kiss and let Mitch take the lead.

~~~

When Cody relaxed and opened for him, he needed no further invitation. There were no awkward moments, no learning how the other kissed. They just fit from the very first press of lips.

Mitch slid his tongue along the seam of Cody's lips and pushed in. Cody's tongue met and brushed against his, caressing and swirling without hesitation. Damn, the boy could kiss, and fuck if Mitch didn't want more. The kiss deepened quickly, turning fervent as primal sounds radiated from Cody. At the same time, fingers ran through Mitch's hair and across his face. The whole encounter pleased Mitch, knowing his kiss turned Cody on so much.

Cody moved instinctively, giving Mitch better access to delve deeper, and he took the offer to its full advantage. Cody's hands moved of their own accord, skimming over every inch of his bare skin. Mitch smoothed his palm eagerly over Cody's thick chest, stopping to roll his budded nipple between two fingers before sliding down to his well-defined stomach and exploring every swell and indention under his palm.

Without any hesitation, he reached lower to massage Cody's rock hard erection entrapped behind soft, well-worn jeans. He groaned when that hard bulge thickened against his palm. Damn, his boy was a big one, just like he liked them. Mitch liked to bottom just as much as he enjoyed topping. Hell, he'd take sex any way he could get it. But tonight, he wanted to be balls deep in this hot Texas cowboy.

He massaged Cody's dick to the same rhythm he created with his tongue. He swore he would keep on till Cody was begging to be fucked. Even as he told himself to take the time to draw Cody in, Mitch made a move to speed things along. He needed to be closer to Cody. He wanted to feel that hard body under his.

"Damn fucking console," Mitch hissed, breaking from the heated lip-lock as the side of a cup holder lodged into his ribs. He pushed himself up, trying harder to get into the passenger seat with Cody. Their eyes made contact, and the need reflected in Cody's gaze took his breath away.

"I have a room," Cody whispered, lowering himself back as far as the seat would go. Mitch gasped in uneven breaths, watching Cody lie back in the seat. Fuck, that sexy hooded eye thing that Cody had going turned his shit on.

"Is it nearby?" Mitch panted, partially lying across Cody, getting as close as he could. If he couldn't be kissing the guy, he certainly needed to touch him. Mitch's hand was right back, massaging Cody's hard dick. He didn't want to lose the momentum they'd started, and he placed a simple kiss on Cody's lips, waiting for his answer.

"Fuck, that feels good," Cody whispered against Mitch's mouth, as if he hadn't already had that revelation.

Mitch weighed the risk of giving Cody a blow job right there in this very spot. The thought of sliding Cody's hot length in his mouth and teasing the guy's slit with his tongue made Mitch's mouth water. Yes, if they were caught, he'd be arrested, but his job was reasonably secure. Cody's, on the other hand, might not be so safe. And why did that even matter to him?

"Is your room close?" Mitch asked again, increasing the tempo of his hand.

"It's downtown," Cody answered breathlessly, his eyes barely opening. "There's a parking garage a little farther down that way, we could go there. It's much closer." Maybe Cody did want this as much as he did. God, he hoped so. Mitch crushed his mouth to Cody's, driving deep quickly. He used his tongue to fuck Cody's mouth like he planned to fuck his ass. Cody's lips were warm and soft, moving against his. The short stubble brushed against his cheek making him groan.

This guy flipped every switch he had. The kiss was a frenzied mix of teeth and tongues, sizzling hot and completely combustible. He was going to blow his load in his jeans if he didn't slow things down. *Damn!* He hadn't lost it like this since high school. When Mitch began to pull away in order to drive them somewhere a little more private, Cody latched roughly on to Mitch's neck and covered his palm over Mitch's hand, forcing him to massage harder until he finally guided Mitch's hand inside his jeans. The minute Mitch made skin-to-skin contact, he squeezed. A deep growl came from Cody that rivaled anything Mitch had ever heard, and it was fucking sexy as hell.

He worked that hard dick with his hand. Still wanting a taste, his mind reverted right back to the idea of a blow job, then Cody's teeth sank into his shoulder. *Motherfucker, that is some hot shit!* Screw the parking garage, he needed Cody naked, sprawled out just for him, preferably on a California king. They were big guys, and he wasn't interested in a cramped quickie in a rental anymore. He wanted the entire night to explore all of Cody's fantasies, and to do that, he needed to get them somewhere with a bed…and quick.

He drew back to tell Cody they needed to go to his hotel room, that a parking garage hookup just wouldn't do. But the words froze in his throat, all thought vanishing when he saw Cody's head positioned back against the headrest, his swollen, slightly parted lips still glistened from their kisses.

Cody drove his hips up into Mitch's hand. Dammit if Cody wasn't fucking intoxicating. Mitch couldn't remember ever having anyone so completely turned on before. Watching Cody writhe under his touch might actually be the hottest thing he'd ever seen.

From out of nowhere, a foghorn interrupted the amazing moment. Cody pitched forward, hitting Mitch in the head. Stars filled his gaze as the second foghorn sounded loudly in the car.

"Fuck." Mitch fumbled for the phone, digging in his front pocket on the third horn blast. The position was awkward. The steering wheel kept him pushed sideways as he struggled to get upright in the driver's seat. When he sent an apologetic glance Cody's way, he saw that he'd lost that sexy sensual look. Confusion and panic were now the most dominate expressions on his beautiful face.

"Don't move," Mitch demanded, holding up a finger. It was a little after one o'clock in the morning. This couldn't be a good phone call, the ringtone made that clear, so he had to answer. He waited for Cody to nod in agreement before he accepted the call. "Mitch Knox."

"Please hold, sir. I'm connecting the callers. This shouldn't take more than a minute for all parties to be on the line," a woman on the other end of the line said in a professional tone, and then suddenly, she was gone. Mitch was left with nothing but silence and a lot of questions. All parties on the line? What the fuck had that meant? Evidently he wasn't the only one being interrupted tonight.

Mitch arched his brow and again lifted his finger to Cody who seriously looked ready to bolt. He pulled the phone away from his ear for a moment. "I'm stepping out of the car to take this call. Don't move. This isn't over between us. Promise me." Mitch thought he may have gotten that halfhearted promise as a red light on his smart phone lit up, drawing his attention to the breaking news report. Mitch put the phone on speaker and clicked the flashing icon as he exited the car. His heart immediately began to race. Republican Senior Majority Leader Seth Greyson's image appeared on his screen with a headline that read, "Greyson's Son Kidnapped."

"Shit!" Wasn't Greyson's oldest son openly gay? His body immediately went on alert, the tension overriding his arousal completely as his brain kicked into overdrive.

Mitch quickly scanned the article, amassing the details offered by the press. He barely got through the first couple of paragraphs before he heard the other parties connect to the line. As every member of the call was introduced, he scanned the high points through the rest of the article. This could, unfortunately, be the break he needed to move his case along.

"Deputy Marshal Knox, are you present?" the woman asked.

"Yes, I am," he said, turning off the speaker mode and bringing the phone back to his ear.

"Go ahead, Director Skinner," the female said. There was a click as she disconnected from the call.

"We've had a situation arise. One we, unfortunately, had some knowledge of the eventuality of. Senator Greyson's son was attacked two nights ago. There was a ransom note, but that appeared to be false to throw us off. Elliot Greyson was found in the last few hours, some six hundred miles from his home. We're certain he'd been left there for dead. He's currently back in DC, in critical condition, not expected to survive. The facts as we know them: The boy dodged Secret Service, we're assuming on purpose. The FBI is all over this, but the case fits the patterns of the one Deputy Marshal Knox has put together. As a result, from this minute forward, there will be reassignment. Deputy Marshal Knox, we're pairing you with Agent Tyler Connors, the current FBI lead agent investigating this crime. Do you have any questions?"

"When do I report?" Mitch asked.

He heard the car door open behind him. He tried to listen to and concentrate on the phone conversation as he watched Cody get out of the car. Mitch pinned him with his stare, willing him to stay right there.

"Knox, you'll report to Director Carpenter first thing in the morning."

"Call me when you're on the way to the airport," Director Carpenter spoke up on the call for the first time. After those directives, the call ended as quickly as it had started. Mitch used speed dial to call Ellen while trying to keep one eye on Cody.

"Hang on, I'm almost done," Mitch said. As the phone rang, Mitch's gaze slowly drifted to Cody's lips. They were thick and full, swollen and red from their kiss, and he liked that look. As if Cody knew his thoughts, the faintest blush crossed his cheeks as he looked down. When he did, those sexy long lashes brushed his cheek.

Mitch's erection was back in full force.

Cody was about the hottest thing he'd seen. He bet that blush showed up regularly in uncomfortable situations. He knew right then that Cody was a temptation he wanted to pursue.

What was wrong with him? Mitch had just gotten the break he needed on the case that he'd fought tooth and nail for, and all he could think about right now was that he hoped he couldn't get a flight out of town until the morning.

"Yes, sir," he heard Ellen's sleepy voice come on the line.

"You're supposed to be arranging me a flight, not sleeping. I've gotta get out of Dallas ASAP. I need to be in DC in the morning. Can you get your pretty little head up and make that happen?" Mitch asked.

"You think I'm pretty? Kidding, I'm up and working now." Ellen gave a deep thorough yawn into the phone. "Why can't you guys ever get your case breaks during normal operating hours?"

"Duty calls, princess," he said as he stood there watching Cody watch him with the car still between them. "Besides, it's why you make the big bucks."

"Riiighttt. We need to talk about that raise in my next evaluation, sir," Ellen said.

"What have I told you about calling me that?" he grinned and rapped his knuckles on the car hood when Cody looked away. He wanted those eyes on him, not cast down. Down meant regret, and he didn't want there to be any of that at all.

"You told me you aren't old enough to be a sir yet," she replied back instantly.

"I'm not responding."

"But my parents always taught me to be respectful of my elders," they said the end in unison.

"Again, you need better jokes," he chuckled, giving Cody, Ellen's wink.

"Mitch, how close to the airport are you? There must be something going on in Dallas. The flights are booked up tight. I can get you out at three-thirty this morning on American Airlines. Can you make it?"

Mitch looked down at his phone. Already close to two. He lifted his eyes back up, trying to figure out if he had time for a quickie. *Dammit! Fucking shit!* He hadn't had his fill of Mr. Ball Cap yet. Mitch absolutely hated to leave like this. He swore right then, he'd definitely be back to finish what he started.

When he returned, he'd have to start from the beginning. Cody wouldn't open up to him easily, but a grin spread across his lips. He'd welcome the chase Cody seemed intent on giving him.

"Put me on it." Mitch disconnected the call as he rounded the hood.

~~~

From the time that ringtone permeated his brain, everything inside Cody told him this night was coming to a crashing halt. He'd gone from teetering on the edge to falling flat on his face in a matter of seconds. The emotions playing through him gave him a serious case of whiplash. His normal, very steady, and overly reasonable approach to life had vanished, in its place was a guy who shoved hands down his pants and begged to be taken in the front seat of a car that was parked on a busy section of a main street. What the hell was he thinking?

Cody gave an inward chuckle, laughing at himself. He knew his problem, and it stood on the other side of the car, with sexy ass dimples and a massive chest with intricate artwork. He'd lost his mind, done things he's never even considered before, for sure.

The Colt Michaels/deputy US marshal deal should have sent him packing. He'd read all about Mitch Knox as he'd followed Colt's recovery. He was thirtyish, which was reasonably young for his job, and a total badass. Cody had even aspired to be like the guy when he became a ranger. Thinking back now, he had to have seen Mitch's picture back then. How could he have not recognized him tonight? He guessed the casual biker gone rogue attire and that damn cocky attitude had thrown him off.

Now he completely understood how Mitch had been so comfortable with Colt when the rest of the entire country had focused on Colt's sexuality. Why hadn't that thought ever occurred to him? He seriously needed to work on his investigation skills.

Not knowing what to do, he looked down and began kicking the rocks at his feet. He felt like an idiot standing there trying not to listen to Mitch's phone call. Maybe he should just leave.

The knuckles rapping on the car hood drew his eyes up. This Mitch Knox he heard talking on the phone wasn't the one he'd just tried to hand fuck in the car. Even as he joked to whoever he spoke with, his tone was different.

Mitch's stare pinned him, held him in place, so he watched as Mitch rested his arms on the top of the car, the phone cradled in the palm of his hand while he spoke. Mitch's eyes conveyed the message clearly—Cody wasn't to leave this spot.

Cody waited to see if his keys, along with his will, would be returned to him. If nothing more than just to prove he could still think on his own, he reached in the backseat of the car to grab his baseball ball cap where Mitch had flipped it earlier.

He casually placed the hat back on his head. It slid easily into place. When he came back up, Mitch was gone from his spot at the driver's door and rounding the hood, tracking Cody's movements as he came closer. The predatory gaze Mitch gave had his heart slamming in his chest and again pinning him where he stood. Mitch stayed on the curb, giving him height over Cody as he backed him against the car, sliding between his parted legs. How could Mitch have that much control over him already?

Chapter 9

Mitch did quick inventory of everything he knew about Cody. He didn't know much, but what he did know, he owed to Colt and that sent a jealous twinge shooting up his spine. When he'd come around the car, he'd only planned to say his goodbyes, try and shoot for a rain check, but instead, he'd been sneaky. He snapped a picture of Cody with his phone, hoping the shot turned out well enough from the angle he held the phone against his side.

Taking Cody off guard had been a real treat. The guy acted surprised when he pushed him back against the car and leaned down, fusing their mouths together again. Mitch wasn't certain where that came from either, but later, when Cody thought over this night, he wanted to be the one remembered, not Colt Michaels. And that had him grinding himself into Cody's arousal as he tilted his head to deepen the kiss. Cody didn't resist meeting him grind for grind or swipe for swipe.

"I have to go, but I need a redo," Mitch said, wrenching from the kiss and latching on to Cody's neck. He never stopped the steady rhythm of his hips or the exploration his hands were taking as they roamed Cody's chest and slid down between his thighs. Once he gripped Cody's cock, his own hips bucked forward. Mitch had no idea of Cody's reaction until the small groan escaped, forcing Mitch's head up.

Cody was extraordinarily handsome, his muscular body on display as he lay back against the car, the baseball cap dislodged from his head once again. His eyes were shut and a fringe of lashes fluttered against his cheek. His mouth partially opened as Mitch increased the massage he gave.

"How do I find you later?" Mitch asked. He could locate Cody on his own, but he wanted Cody to tell him. When no response came, he gripped harder, causing Cody's eyes to open and focus on him. "Tell me. How do I find you?"

"Guys, you need to move it along," Mitch heard someone say from the road. The beam of a flashlight traveled across them. He moved his body to cover his hand. Cody's head snapped up, and he pushed at Mitch's chest. He didn't budge, he just pressed himself closer.

"Yes, officer," Mitch answered, never taking his eyes off Cody's. They stood there together, staring at each other until Cody reached down, gripped his hand, stopping his motion, and moved away from his touch.

"I need my keys," Cody said, bending to scoop up his hat that had fallen by the curb. He could tell Cody had been surprised by the officer and now tried to hide his flushed face and shaking hands.

"They're in your pocket." Mitch gave him a wink. He'd placed them there earlier. Maybe that was a good sign that Cody had been so into what they were doing he hadn't even noticed.

Cody's hand immediately reached inside the front pocket of his jeans, which stretched the denim across his still obviously swollen cock. Mitch felt his pain.

"When did you put them there? I didn't feel you do that." Cody sounded stunned as he took a few steps backward.

"It's one of my many skills. I'm gonna see you again, you know that right?" Mitch called out and held his ground. Cody didn't say anything more. He turned and left Mitch staring after him. Damn, that cowboy had a fine ass.

Mitch rapped his knuckles on the hood of the car for a second time as the flashlight scanned his car again. It was a cruiser. He rounded the car and dropped into the front seat, adjusting his mighty pissed off hard-on before starting the car. His phone sounded again. Director Carpenter would be chomping at the bit, no doubt. Hell,

Mitch should have been too. He shook his head, trying to clear the lust-induced haze before he answered his phone.

He dropped the rental in drive, quickly scanned the side mirror as he pulled out into the street, and answered his phone, all simultaneously. No matter how hard he'd been pushing this case to get anyone to take notice, now that administration was involved, it would be full steam ahead.

"Knox? Hello, Knox, are you there?" Shit, well apparently he wasn't so good at preforming too many tasks at once. He'd forgotten to say hello.

"Yes, sir," he answered as he applied the brake, coming to a stop in front of a red light. He reached down to adjust himself again, forcing his mind back into the work at hand, not the sexy trooper's cock he'd just had *in* his hand. "So the Greyson kid made it?"

"For now. He was unconscious when they found him, and he's in surgery now. It's going to be a waiting game and a long road to recovery for the kid if he makes it. All eyes are on this one, Knox. Looks like you got the break you needed, but now's the time to get in there and wrap this baby up," Director Skinner said. Mitch heard the concern in the director's voice. The higher you went in the agency, the more they all ran in the same circles. It was very possible Director Carpenter knew the Greyson kid. "I just hung up with Director Carpenter. He's open to anything you need. He has your case files now."

"We'll need immediate access to the family," Mitch started absently. "I know I'm assigned to Agent Connors, but I'd like official access to Aaron Stuart. No more tying his hands."

"I've got you access to the family. I just can't guarantee Stuart's full access. He's a loose cannon, Knox. " Mitch punched the gas as the light switched to green, turning on to Oak Lawn.

"That's bullshit," Mitch started, but the director jumped in.

"Stuart's on probation for the last stunt he pulled, Knox. He should've been fired. There's no telling what'll happen if we let him loose in our system."

"I'm a loose cannon…" Mitch went silent. Aaron Stuart excelled in the world of technology and hackers. He probably already had full access. "Look, I'm on my way to the airport. I need to check in with Director Carpenter."

"Get there as quick as you can." The last words Director Skinner said made him smile.

"Yes, sir," Mitch ended the call as he hit the next red light. He searched Director Carpenter's number in his contact list. As he waited for the phone to connect, a single last stray thought surfaced. He pulled up his photo gallery to see if he'd gotten a decent shot of Cody. He didn't need the picture, he could find Cody easily with the information he had, but *with* the picture, he'd let the computers handle the leg-work. Plus, he now had a little something for his spank bank.

Somehow, he'd managed to get a decent shot, and after a minute more of staring at the hot picture, he slid his finger across the screen, pushing Cody away. He had to focus on the case. Guys like Cody didn't just happen along every day. He was sure their day would come, just not today. He focused his thoughts to the business at hand. He needed to fully concentrate on the case.

The Greyson kid would make number eight. The eighth victim targeted in the last nine months. Three were still alive, the others weren't so lucky. His mind ran in overdrive as the magnitude of the situation settled in.

Chapter 10

Eight hours later, Mitch dug his thumb and forefinger into his closed eyes as he listened to the dialog going on around him. His new partner was already pissing him off. Blathering on and on about procedures, regulations, and protocols. And saying this sucked like a motherfucker would be a serious understatement.

The biggest problem right now? Connors wouldn't shut the fuck up. He was standard issue FBI. Clean-cut, clean shaven, freshly-pressed suit, in love with himself, and most definitely the smartest man on the planet—just ask him. Mitch had learned long ago you just couldn't reason with brilliant people. At that thought, Mitch rolled his eyes.

Irritatingly, once you cut through the miles of babble, Connors had a keen instinct, almost a sixth sense and a remarkable success rate when it came to the cases he worked. Mitch didn't know him well, or really at all, but he had heard about his reputation. Nothing got past the man.

Mitch needed that kind of agent on this investigation, no matter how much he droned on and on about his to-date findings on the Greyson case. Just imagine how he would react once he knew the details of the other incidents linking to this one.

As Connors repeated his last sentence for the third time, just in a different way, Mitch made a very dramatic show of rolling his eyes and dropping his head back, giving a long exaggerated yawn. It didn't seem to faze Connors or Director Carpenter.

All Mitch could do was look up at the heavens and pray for patience or a nice big bottle of tequila. The prayer was a symbolic gesture more than anything else, because he was already stuck in hell. This small office slash conference room would apparently be his home base for the next however many weeks it took to resolve this case. The décor reeked of uptight government. Chrome, black, and contemporarily boring furnishings.

The office wasn't much bigger than an oversized cubicle, and the sterile smell made him want to gag. The room was stiff, tedious, and ostentatious much like Connors who now stood, drawing things out on a dry-erase board, outlining the details of the cases he knew so far.

Mitch glanced across the room and Director Carpenter looked intrigued. *Oh hell, fuck my life.* He couldn't help the second yawn that slipped free.

"Am I boring you, Deputy Marshal Knox?" Connors asked in his perfectly correct way of saying everything.

"You know, kind of you are," Mitch answered truthfully, dropping his feet to the floor, ready for his fourth or fifth cup of coffee in the last few hours. In midstep he changed his mind. "I'm gonna see if I can get in with the Greyson family a little early. Connors, you can keep rehashing this or you can put your little red marker down and get your ass in the car and get moving on this case with me."

Mitch smirked at the open-eyed stare and the silence that greeted him. Well, whaddaya know, he'd actually stunned Connors speechless. His triumph was short-lived though as Director Carpenter's brow dropped. He honestly hadn't meant any disrespect. What was the old saying? Drastic times called for drastic measures. These were drastic times, and he was in dire need of some shut-the-fuck-up.

"Okay, okay, look," Mitch started, attempting to gather some decorum as he rambled something else to appease these two. "You can keep filling me in on the way over there, but we really need to get this show on the road." Mitch considered that a half-assed apology as he angled himself toward the door. He'd already decided FBI wonder boy might be a prodigy, but he wanted Aaron on this case, even if it were an incognito unauthorized move.

Mitch was willing to take the blame just to get this case solved faster. Cell phone calls, city surveillance videos, even identifying and tracking vehicles by just providing tire tracks were definitely within the guy's wheelhouse. Mitch just had to ditch the straight-arrow FBI agent before he made contact.

"I'm not through," Connors started, but began to rush around, gathering his things.

"If you're coming with me, you are," Mitch shot back as he lowered his laptop lid and stuffed it haphazardly into his bag.

"Deputy Marshal Knox, this may be the way the Marshals run things, but here at the Federal Bureau of Investigation there's a code of ethics and standards in professional conduct..." Director Carpenter said, clearly very put out. Mitch sighed. He didn't want to piss off the higher-ups, but he didn't have time for posturing intradepartmental bullshit.

"Sir, the trail's growing cold and I want to be in Kentucky by tonight. I'm sure Connors will talk until the plane touches down, catching me up on everything he's ever known. We'll keep you apprised every step of the way." Mitch addressed Director Carpenter with his normal straight-forward attitude. He was the new guy in the mix; he could appreciate that. But he needed to set his ground rules so everyone had a fair playing field. He certainly wasn't asking for permission nor was he retreating back to the hours-long lecture Connors clearly wanted. He took the lack of response from Carpenter as authorization to head for the door. A disgusted huff sounded behind him. He wasn't sure exactly which one of them made the noise, and he couldn't find it in himself to care.

The initial crime scene report detailed a car explosion, something that was meant to kill the kid, but he'd somehow managed to get several feet from the vehicle before detonation. For Mitch, that mess-up was the first real break he'd seen in all these cases. That left the kid able to give visual identification if he could just pull through the injuries he had from the beating that had taken place before he'd been left for dead.

Mitch made his way out of the offices and to the bank of elevators. He pushed the down button and palmed his phone quickly to text Kreed Sinacola, his partner back in Louisiana. From the beginning, he and Kreed had clicked and the man had helped Mitch in the off-the-clock investigation he'd done in these cases.

Kreed, a former Navy SEAL, bomb expert, and great friend, was as badass as they came in knowing the inner workings of explosive devices. He quickly sent Kreed a message, praying he was local this weekend and could get to Kentucky before he and Connors arrived on-site. His new partner seemed to like control, and Mitch wanted Kreed to have as much time as he could to investigate that car before Connors began micromanaging.

The elevator buzzed open and Mitch never looked up as he typed. By the smell of the cheap cologne, he could tell Connors had decided to follow after all.

"I'll call and see if we can move the appointment up," Connors stated, scooting inside the elevator as Mitch held the door open with his foot.

"Nah, let's surprise them," Mitch suggested, hitting send on his phone. He kept his eyes trained on the screen, Kreed always responded immediately.

"You might want to change clothes before you meet with the senator," Connors said matter-of-factly. Mitch could feel his eyes on him.

"This is all I got. I left everything in Dallas when I got summoned," he explained, watching Connors from the corner of his eye.

"I wondered about that whole *You Don't Know Me Witness Protection* T-shirt you're wearing. I know a quick in and out men's suit store. It's close by," Connors informed him. That had Mitch ignoring the ding that indicated an incoming text and looking straight at the guy.

"You don't like my shirt? I bought it from a street vendor on my way in. Did I get burrito juice on it? " Mitch asked, looking down to see if he might have a stain or something.

"It's inappropriate to wear. Besides that, we don't do tats around here…" Connors started, clearly on a roll.

"Wait a second. First off, I'm not FBI, and I don't do *that*." Mitch gestured wildly at the suit Connors wore. "Second, this is as good as it gets. So get used to it, fancy boy." Mitch leaned back against the mirrored elevator wall, ignoring Connors once again, and opened Kreed's message. Cool, he was still at Camp Beauregard this week and could head out soon. It did come with a huge "*you owe me big,*" but whatever. He'd happily pay that price.

"You couldn't stop to get your things?" Connors asked as if the thought had just occurred to him.

"No." Mitch sighed and stared straight ahead.

"She must have been something," Connors said, stepping out of the elevator. Mitch took the words as an attempt at levity. The agent failed miserably.

"Something like that. Let's just say he was hard to leave." Mitch gave Connors a wink, smirking as he strolled past the now-unusually-quiet agent and headed out a side door of the building. He actually laughed at the stunned look on his face when he glanced back. "I'm driving."

"You don't know the way," Connors finally said as he caught up with him in the parking lot.

"Hope you're a good navigator," Mitch retorted.

"Are you always this much of a dick?" Connors asked.

"Pretty much," he answered, sliding inside the car parked in the closest spot. Mitch started the ignition and dropped the gearshift in reverse before Connors had the seat belt buckled.

Chapter 11

Cody drove the long stretch of Interstate 35 with the driver's window of his big black four-by-four F250 rolled down. He had his Texas Rangers baseball cap flipped backward and his Ray-Ban sunglasses perched on the bridge of his nose filtering the bright Texas sun. Blake Shelton sang a tune on the radio.

The trip back to Austin hadn't been bad, even though the traffic stayed heavy pretty much the whole way back home. Probably because Cody's mind remained fully focused on Mitch Knox. Now that the night was over, he was incredibly glad he'd gone. JR's turned out to be exactly what everyone said about the place. Fantastic.

On every level, Mitch was exactly what attracted Cody to a man. He was aggressive, clever, built like a Mack Truck, and he had ambition. Not to mention he was superhot, one of the best-looking men Cody had ever seen in person, but he was also down to earth, sarcastic as hell, and damn good at his job. Based on his appearance and attitude, before he'd figured out the man's identity, he'd have thought Mitch more like a biker kind of guy instead of the decorated deputy US marshal he turned out to be.

Now all these hours later, Cody knew, he likely would have had sex with Mitch last night. The decision would have come after a lengthy internal struggle to justify his actions—because he had an inner battle with just about everything that had to do with his casual sexual needs—but no question in his mind, he'd have gone through with that one-night stand if given the opportunity.

He suspected that sexual encounter would pretty much have rocked his world, but what intrigued him more was that phone call Mitch had gotten. That call had stopped everything and sounded official. For those few seconds that he'd stood outside the car, listening to the conversation, Mitch went from the persistent, excessive flirt to a formal, hard-toned deputy marshal. It made him realize Mitch was truly badass at his job, and that was everything Cody ever wanted to be.

As he veered off the highway, taking the back roads to his family's farm, he wished he'd had the balls to ask for Mitch's phone number. At the time, he'd blamed his lack of courage on not being sophisticated enough to play the one-night stand game. Giving phone numbers meant involvement, and he didn't see Mitch as relationship material. He'd watched Mitch long enough last night to know he'd come there looking for sex. Cody easily put Mitch in the category of being the type to have a guy in every port. But now, as he lamented his missed opportunity, he recognized that fear had somewhat held him back. He had a mighty strong attraction to the guy, and it was going to take a long time to get past the appeal Mitch held. He also knew he had to up his game and get back to his priorities.

He was a twenty-six-year-old gay man who had chosen his career. He needed to stop wasting time on trying to nail party boys down to monogamous partners and start looking for something more attainable. Someone who fit him better and understood his life.

He figured that was the lesson he needed to have learned from last night. Eventually, he'd meet some professional men in law enforcement. He needed to be open to them, not shy away like he tended to do. He'd closed himself up too tight, trying to balance stereotypes, protect himself and keep the career goals of his profession.

With those thoughts, he took the long dirt road to his parents' house. He wondered what Mitch would think about weekly church services and lunch with his family. More than likely someone as badass as Mitch Knox had probably extricated himself from his family a long time ago. He couldn't see Mitch sitting inside a church, even the Cowboy Church they all attended. He even laughed at that thought. No, he couldn't see Mitch sitting in his family's pew, right up front, listening to a sermon. He wondered what Mitch would think about his father and oldest brother, Mason, being deacons of that church? That thought made him laugh out loud as he pulled up to the house.

As he suspected, all his brothers and sisters were parked right out front. What he hadn't expected was the giant banner running across the front porch that said very clearly, *Congratulations, Cody!* That had him smiling. He'd given himself all night and this entire trip back home to think about Mitch, but he'd dwelled on his missed opportunity long enough. He had people here who loved him, and in the words of his oldest sister, he needed to keep moving forward, and the past was most definitely behind him.

As he put his truck in park, the smile stayed on his face as his oldest niece, Sarah, who was seven, launched herself off the porch, running toward his truck. The rest of the brood followed. His sister-in-law caught the youngest one, Talon, as the little tyke tried to run after the others off the front porch steps. That would have been a face plant for sure since the little guy barely walked yet. Cody had decided a long time ago that his siblings were a breeding bunch.

"Uncle Cody! Congratulations!" Sarah said, hugging him tight before he'd even made it all the way out of the truck. Tucker who was six was on his other side, mimicking Sarah's hold. When four-year-old Kylie finally reached him, her little arms extended, ready for him to haul her up. He did and got a big wet kiss on his lips. He loved them all, no question, but Kylie held a special place in his heart.

"Uncle Cody, you didn't go with me to church this morning," she said as he bent over, hugging Sarah, and then patting Tucker on the head. Tanner had finally made the distance. He was a little past two and a half, and Cody hauled him up, placing him on the other hip.

"Nana made your favorite cake for Sunday lunch," Tucker declared as the group of them made their way toward the front porch. By then, the rest of his family stood outside waiting for him.

"Shhh, it was supposed to be a surprise," Sarah whispered.

"Congratulations, Son," his mom praised again as he handed Tanner over to his brother, because at the moment, Kylie had a death grip on his shirt. His mom was five-two, so he had to angle himself to keep Kylie in his arms as he bent to hug her.

"Thanks for all this," he said, accepting her kiss.

"We're so proud of you, Son." His dad was up next, giving him a tight hug, but his little nephew, Talon, wanted in on the action. He maneuvered himself from his sister-in-law's arms to where he had the same death grip on Cody that Kylie had. The congratulations continued from all his brothers and sisters as he slowly made his way inside. Even his dog, Chester, was right there, ready to greet him too.

"Was he good?" Cody asked Kylie who was finally ready to let go, once he kneeled down to pet Chester.

"No, he pooped in the dining room. Mom got mad at him," she corrected.

"No, ma'am, I didn't get mad at him. I got mad at you, little lady. You were supposed to take him outside before bedtime," she scolded.

"Uncle Cody, I didn't take him outside. The coyotes are back and Mom wouldn't let me take the BB gun out with me to protect us," Tucker chimed in. Tucker was Kylie's older brother.

"But he snuck it out anyway," Kylie said, telling on her brother. That was all it took for a fight to begin, and his sister did everything in her power to stop them before things got out of hand.

"Did we get souvenirs?" Sarah asked.

"Yep, in the front seat of the truck." Cody laughed as Sarah raced out the door in a flash.

"Tell them about the mounted patrol," Mason suggested.

"He can tell us while we're eating. We've been holding lunch," his mom spoke up from the door separating the dining room and the kitchen.

"I'm sorry I'm late, Mom," Cody apologized, moving with the group toward the table.

"Mom made your favorite dessert," Justin, his brother, added, slapping him on the shoulder. "Lucky."

The big family table, the one that kept expanding with every grandbaby born, was set, and his mom began loading the table with the huge feast she'd cooked on his behalf. Another banner, much smaller than the one out front, hung in that room too. He was even shown to his spot for this week's dinner—the prime spot in the middle of the table. Kylie made it clear she was sitting next to him. Sarah burst back inside the room with his bags of treats.

"We all got Texas Rangers baseball ball caps like Uncle Cody's," Sarah declared. She handed them out and they started to put them on.

"No hats at the table," his father said.

"Let 'em wear their hats today, Daddy. We're celebrating," his mom reasoned, carrying in his favorite pot roast dinner. The kids squealed with delight when they found the small sheriff's badges that had Dallas written across the front.

"You're going to spoil them," his sister Sheila scolded.

"That's what uncles are for." And that earned him a huge grin from Kylie who then decided dinner needed to be eaten from his lap, not her chair. "I met Colt Michaels when I was in Dallas."

"No way! Where?" Mason asked.

"He was leaving a bar." Cody picked up his napkin and placed it on his free leg.

"Did you get him to sign your hat?" Travis asked eagerly.

"Nah, I wanted to, but it wasn't really the right time."

"Tell us about the job," his brother tried again.

"Not before grace," his dad stated as his mom took her seat next to him. That was the sign to bow his head. The entire room grew silent as his father began the blessing.

Chapter 12

Mitch sat quietly, staring at Senator Greyson and his wife in a private room next to Elliot's in an undisclosed hospital west of the city. He let Connors do most of the talking for them. Apparently this was Connors second meeting with the family since the incident. Mrs. Greyson appeared exactly how he would expect an exhausted, concerned mom to look. Senator Greyson just looked angry. Then again, Greyson always appeared angry, which made it difficult to read his body language.

Honestly, as close as Mitch could tell, the Greysons had pretty standard responses to the situation. The family had no idea what happened or who would want to hurt their son. Except Senator Greyson made it clear, he believed every Democrat in the nation could be considered a suspect.

With the exception of the last remark, every other family he had interviewed felt that exact same way. When a victim had survived, they were like Colt—critically injured with very little memory of the accident. There were no leads.

There were clear differences in the Greyson case compared to the others, though. Elliot Greyson was the youngest victim targeted, he had no career, and wasn't high profile. His father held that distinction. The only similarity at the moment was that two of the cases involved a bomb. County Court Judge Bennett had been killed in a bombing accident.

Mitch began to bite at his fingernail, letting Connors go on and on with the meaningless questions until he finally just tuned him completely out and looked around the room, watching the Secret Service a little closer. The president had ordered a double-up on the Secret Service security for this family. Mitch had been given some cock and bull story about the kid ducking out of a coffee shop, dodging his security detail. Apparently this story had been backed up by the staff at the shop.

Per the family, Elliot was a good young man. An honor student throughout all his high school years and carried those same ethics into college. He was smart, well-mannered, worked hard, and was easy to get along with. Definitely not someone who fit the mold of a rebel.

One Secret Service agent stayed in the room during the questioning. Two stood by the door that hadn't been allowed to be closed. Mitch assumed the move was all that departmental posturing. The 'we're better than you' bullshit that seemed prevalent between the divisions, especially here in Washington DC.

After a few minutes more of nothing, Mitch was done. They'd find no answers here. The family knew nothing. Now they needed to move on to the next task at hand. They needed to get to Kentucky before the evidence had too much time to be tampered with.

Not exactly sure how to hurry the long-winded Connors up, Mitch stood abruptly, effectively silencing everyone, causing all eyes to look his way.

"I'll be out in the hall," Mitch announced, then strolled from the room, not waiting for a reply. He heard Connors rambling off an excuse for his lack of manners, and he rolled his eyes in his retreat. Mitch targeted the two guards at the door.

"Were either of you on this case the night the kid was abducted?" When he got the look that he was clearly stupid, he amended his sentence. "I mean the night he ran off?"

"No, sir. Special Agent Hanson was with the family that evening," the less ugly one said.

"And is he around?" Mitch asked.

"He was here earlier. We relieved him," the uglier one answered.

"Of course you did." Mitch scrubbed a hand over his face as he headed for the elevator. Then thought better of it and bypassed the elevator to take the stairs down to the lobby and out the front doors, letting the sunshine soothe his frustration. Sliding his sunglasses in place, he took a seat on the closest park bench and pulled up the message he needed to send in private. This one was to Aaron.

He'd met Aaron years ago online, playing State of Decay. As it turned out, Aaron's day job was part of the intelligence nerd herd division of the NSA. He had the highest security level clearance anyone could have, but as Mitch had come to learn, his skills didn't require a clearance. He was a hacker through and through. His sole purpose in the NSA was to hack into the government's systems. Something he did easily every single day and then assisted in fixing the areas of weakness. In other words, Aaron was badass and a great ally to have on his side even if no one else thought so.

"*Hey, you busy?*" Mitch texted.

"*In Dallas at Geekfest,*" Aaron texted back.

"*Of course you'd be there. I don't know why I didn't think of that. I just got back from there. There wasn't a room to be had,*" Mitch texted back

"*It's been greatness. Wat's up?*"

"*I'm calling in a favor. I'm on assignment and I need to figure out who someone is. Have time?*" Mitch asked

"*Sure, what's there to go on?*" Aaron asked.

"*I have a picture I'm attaching—it's not the best quality. His name is Cody. He lives somewhere in central Texas and he's a Texas State Trooper. He was just assigned to the new mounted detail for the state capitol.*" Mitch attached the photo he had and felt more than heard Connors stalking up on him. He purposely ignored him as he finished the text and waited for Aaron to respond.

"Seriously, what was that about? You never just leave an interview," Connors asked as he came to stand directly in front of Mitch.

"It was bullshit and a waste of time. Besides, someone's lying," Mitch said, never looking up. Instead, he opened Aaron's return message. "*When do you need this back?*"

"*Whenever it's convenient for you, but today would be good.*" Mitch texted back quickly.

"It's wildly assumptive to consider anyone in that room to be lying. They profile exactly as they should, and this isn't a conversation to have so publically." Mitch glanced up as Connors scanned the area, looking for wondering ears. His phone vibrated again, alerting him of another text.

"It shouldn't take long. When I get back to my room, I'll message you," Aaron responded back.

Mitch rose, making a show of stretching out his long body and rolling his shoulders. He did it all just to get a little further under the skin of his goody two-shoes partner who continued talking. Lord, did the man ever shut up? He tucked his phone in his back pocket and started for the car. Thank god he'd chosen to drive.

"You have got to stop walking away from me in midsentence!" Connors stated emphatically. Mitch did look over his shoulder, cocking his head toward their rental.

"The airport's this way," he said before lifting a finger toward the half a dozen or so cameras on the light posts around the hospital parking lot. "It's more private in the car." He never said another word, but by the time he had the car in reverse, Connors was buckling his seatbelt. God must have showed mercy on him because Connors didn't start back up again until they hit the freeway. Best half mile of his life.

Chapter 13

"You guys travel in style," Mitch said as he boarded the Federal Bureau of Investigation's luxury private jet.

"You deputy marshals seem slower than the rest of the agencies I've worked with. Do you need sign language? Honestly, this is an important case. We need answers so we get preferential treatment, or did you not hear that in the conference call we all shared?" Connors replied.

"Wait, what? Was that a joke I just heard?" Mitch stopped and looked around like he'd lost something.

"Cut the shit," Connors said over his shoulder as they were greeted by a flight attendant. In all the years Mitch had worked for the government, he'd never flown in anything this nice. For the first time in his long career, he second-guessed his decision to join the USMS. He should have gone FBI. Then again, he couldn't walk around with a stick up his ass every damn day just to get perks like this.

Even cooler than the plane…they were seated and headed for takeoff in a matter of minutes. Mitch looked up as the overhead announcement started, and he realized Connors had been talking to him again. For the first time today, he considered he might be to the point of tuning the guy out, which would be great and might actually save the case, because he was pretty close to putting his hands on Connors to get him to shut up.

"Last night I read the case files that you presented last month. You've done a lot of leg-work on this. I couldn't believe no one picked this case up. It's clearly serial," Connors said quietly as the flight attendant spoke and they began their ascent.

"Budget restraints, political infighting, whatever, I heard it all." Mitch kept his voice equally quiet.

"How did you get involved in the Michaels case?" Connors asked, looking straight at Mitch. He got the impression that Connors might have thought he and Michaels were together at the time. Mitch couldn't decide if he should string him along to humor himself or just tell the truth. Honesty won in the end.

"A personal favor. I stumbled on all this by accident."

"Gentlemen, in about twenty minutes, we'll be flying into some bad weather. We should be above the storms, but the pilot's worried about turbulence. He's asking you keep your seatbelts on," the flight attendant said.

"Can I use my laptop?" Connors asked her.

"Yes, sir, but if it gets bumpy, make sure you hang on to it. I'll be in the back if you need anything. They're requiring me to stay buckled in as well," she said with smile. Connors was all business, his laptop was on his lap and opened within seconds. Since they sat side-by-side, Mitch left his bagged. If he needed information, he'd get it, but he knew these cases too well. He thought he could answer whatever question was shot his way.

"I read you've interviewed the family and friends of all the victims," Connors said, logging in.

"Yep. Every neighbor, co-worker, all the witnesses I could find." Mitch stretched out his legs and laid the seat as far back as it would go.

"All on your own time?" Connors seemed impressed. Or that could have been shock. Mitch had no way to know.

"Yep, pretty much," Mitch responded and closed his eyes.

"But I didn't see any possible connections or theories?" Ding, ding, ding, Connors was finally on his page.

"Correct."

"Hmmm," Connors mused and sat back in his seat. "I didn't find any either. There are no patterns, nothing in the profiles, and each incident is executed with precision. The Greyson kid escaping the car is the first mistake I've seen. It's such a large one that I question if his case is related," Connors said. Mitch turned his head and stared at his partner.

"You've got nothing to add?" Connors asked.

"I do. The Greyson kid fits the profile from the standpoint that he's a pretty good guy. He didn't leave that coffee shop on his own free will, no matter what the Secret Service says. And besides, at some point, there'll always be a mistake. It's why I kept digging. This is the only break we were ever going to get; these people are too good."

"I understand that, and I can even agree, but we play nice with each other in DC. You shouldn't have just walked out of the meetings," Connors lectured.

"Forget the fucking meeting, man. That was so two hours ago. There's a reason I'm not in Washington. Now, concentrate on what's important. Keep focused on what you read in the case files. The sooner you're fully on my page, the faster this will go." He gritted his teeth, stopping the rest of the words threatening to spill out. *Fuck!* What was up with these people? After a minute, he started repeating out loud what he remembered about the cases.

"We have eight individual crimes. Each different with the exception of Greyson and Justice Bennett. Those both included bombs—different styles I think, but still two bombs. One car accident. One home invasion. One pilot error. One blood poisoning. One gunshot. One hit and run. Absolutely zero witnesses, which is incredibly hard to believe." Connors lifted a finger to halt Mitch's words.

"But clearly you've pounded the pavement searching. I focused on Kreed Sinacola's report on the justice's bombing. He's thorough, but that bomb was homegrown. It was made in America so to speak. I'm supposing you have him heading to Kentucky?" Connors asked and Mitch scowled. Dammit, he was good.

"You're smarter than you look."

"We're supposed to be a team. I need to know the decisions you're making. The FBI has more than qualified…" Mitch cut Connors off.

"Then they can take a look too, and I'm absolutely certain they already have." Mitch adjusted his seat, getting more comfortable in the leather recliner. He hadn't slept more than a couple of hours on the flight from Texas to Washington, and he was determined to take advantage of their luxury ride to Kentucky to get a little shut-eye.

"You don't work well with others. It's in your file," Connors shot back. Mitch didn't respond because it really just depended who those *others* were.

"Let's talk possibilities," Connors continued.

"It's more than likely organized," Mitch responded. He closed his eyes and relaxed his head against the headrest.

"I may disagree. Organization means multiples, and no one's talking, and someone always talks when it's organized." Mitch had thought that very same thing.

"It's more than one person. No one person is that skilled to pull off all those different accidents. It's organized, even if it's a small unit."

"Okay, I can see that. It's also well-trained. Military, law enforcement…" Connors trailed off.

"Or YouTube. Seriously, you can learn anything on the internet. And it's hate-driven," Mitch added.

"Not necessarily. Could be psychosis, probably not, but I've called in a behavioral analyst, Dr. York, to review the case. Have you heard of her?" Mitch ignored that. He had learned quickly with Connors not to engage, he would go on for hours talking about nothing but theories if Mitch fed his random thoughts.

"There's a message and meaning in these deaths. It's hate-related," Mitch said, still not looking at Connors. "They don't want recognition or fame; they're doing a service to the world."

"There are bigger ways to make that statement, not one by one isolated cases," Connors shot back.

"Individual deaths hide under the radar, much like the distance between each incident helps keep it hidden. They aren't picking the highest profile gay men, but high enough that they make the local news for their deaths."

"Colt Michaels is a very high profile gay man," Connors retorted, and Mitch slowly turned his head toward the guy.

"I thought you read the cases. Colt wasn't out yet. It was his now husband, Jace Montgomery, they targeted. That was his rental car they tampered with."

"The husband doesn't make sense," Connors argued.

"Each case has had the victim recently in the local news for some reason. Jace Montgomery had appeared on ESPN before the accident occurred. Tony Johnson had just sold his software company to Apple for an ungodly amount of money reported all over the cable news networks. Justice Bennett had just been given the trial over racial profiling. And on, and on, and on. They weren't necessarily on national news, but they were each featured in the news," Mitch explained.

"I don't remember reading that in the case information," Connors said, and Mitch totally thought he was covering his mistake.

"It's there, you just didn't retain it," Mitch shot back.

"I don't miss things." Connors stared at him in defiance now. Great, boy wonder had an ego.

"You missed that," Mitch scoffed, meeting his stare and cocking a brow. The expected turbulence hit at that moment, jolting the plane. Another big bump caused the wound-up-tight Tyler Connors to barely save his laptop before the computer hit the cabin floor. Honestly, Mitch was impressed with the guy's reflexes until another strong jolt hit, bouncing Mitch out of his seat.

"Damn," Connors swore, clutching his laptop.

"We're getting a little air turbulence. Please remain seated, with your seat belts fastened," the pilot announced rather calmly.

"Shit, this sucks," Connors declared, and Mitch took a good long look at his temporary partner. He was turning green with all the rocking they were doing. Shit, he had a hurler on his hands, motion sickness at its finest. As quickly as he could, he grabbed the laptop while reaching for the vomit bag. To Connors credit, he didn't hurl until he got the bag open, but the heaving never stopped.

Unfortunately for Connors, the turbulence continued for the rest of the trip. The violent storm raged over eastern Kentucky, causing them to circle the airport, waiting for their turn to land. He stayed sick the entire time, and finally confessed under a shroud of bad vomit breath, that he never flew well. It hadn't taken long for Mitch's initial pity to turn to irritation. How could Connors be an FBI agent and not be able to ride in an airplane? Mitch spent half his life flying from one assignment to the next.

By the time they landed, the severe weather threat had ended, but the rain was falling in sheets. Traveling in a private jet had a much different landing and exiting routine than a commercial airline, and Mitch didn't even have his ball cap to keep him from getting soaked. All he could do was hunker down and let the rain pound him until he was met with an umbrella carried by a driver.

Connors moved slower, not exiting the plane until Mitch was already tucked in tight inside the passenger seat. Mitch hadn't thought to mention to the driver that there were two of them. He watched as Connors took each step in the pouring rain as the driver scurried to get his wet umbrella from the backseat. Connors was already around to Mitch's side of the car, soaking wet, motioning him to the backseat.

When Mitch figured out Connors planned to come to his door, he hurriedly locked the car door before Connors could get it open and let the rain inside. After a minute of the guy standing firm, dripping wet and staring down at him, Mitch lowered the window about an inch or so.

"I have motion sickness. I need the front seat," Connors yelled above the pounding rain. Mitch didn't ride in the backseat, but he was also sick of watching the guy throw up and whining that little moan he made every time something came up. *Shit!*

He looked over at the driver. "Who are you in this deal? Who do you work for?"

"I was hired to drive you two to the police impound yard and wherever else you needed to go," the driver answered.

"Change of plans. You're in the backseat. I'm driving."

"Nah, man. This is my personal car," the driver started to argue, but Mitch gave him no choice as he reached past the driver to open his door for him as he scooted over the center console to avoid getting back out into the heavy rainfall.

"It'll be fine. I'm a deputy US marshal." Like that meant anything to this situation, but he pushed against the guy's hip as Connors got into the passenger seat. On a frustrated string of cuss words, the driver got in the backseat, and seconds later, Mitch sat behind the wheel.

"Don't fuck up my car," the driver said irritably.

"Where am I going?" Mitch asked, looking back in the rearview mirror. His phone began a series of vibrations, finally getting enough signal to catch up on everything he'd missed while in the air. Mitch ignored them as he put the car in drive. The driver leaned forward, pointing to the center of the dashboard.

"The address is programmed in there. Hit the volume on the right. I keep it turned down." Mitch focused on driving, and Connors began working the GPS.

"No, man, your other right." The driver said as Connors started pushing the wrong buttons. "Damn, man, you recalculated the trip."

"He's FBI, they don't make enough to afford nice cars like these," Mitch tossed out, laughing as Connors grunted and leaned his head back against the headrest, holding his stomach, clearly still recuperating.

"I'll just tell you where to go. Take a right at the entrance of the airport," the driver said. Using the back of Mitch's seat, he pulled himself forward and began reworking the address into the GPS. Mitch laughed again when he caught the very clear *what the hell* look he gave Connors as he sat back.

Luckily, the rain let up the farther they got out of town. Mitch pulled into the police impound, right up to the front of the chain link fence, and parked. He got out, surveyed the yard, and recognized Kreed's booted feet sticking out from under what looked to be a severely burned shell of a small car located inside a single car garage.

Mitch never looked back at Connors as he went through the steps of showing his badge and gaining entrance into the secured facility. From what Mitch could see, it was an incredible escape by the Greyson kid. That reality hardened Mitch's resolve. He hunched down by Kreed's boots, everything else forgotten. Kreed shoved himself out from under the mangled car, dirt and soot covering his clothing. He held Mitch's same intense look and didn't waste time on greetings.

"It's a well-constructed vehicle IED. No clear trigger visible, except there had to be a trigger from underneath and it was set purposefully for one death. It's wired for a remote detonation. The size and placement are foreign styles. I saw this in Iraq and Afghanistan. We don't do it like this in the United States. We fill our shit up for anyone to see. It's a completely different style than Bennett's. Whoever did this is well-trained," Kreed said, picking up a rag and trying to wipe the dirt from his hands.

"The kid got out of the car and far enough away that just some shrapnel hit him," Mitch said, taking in everything Kreed told him. "It's designed to send pieces flying. It would be near impossible to identify who was inside once it blew." Kreed got to his feet and Mitch stood with him. They both just stared at the car.

"What went wrong? If it was designed to kill him, then the detonation didn't respond on time... Or they thought he was already dead? Sometimes I've wondered if they were allowed to live on purpose to tell the story. But he was beaten badly. There's no reason he's alive right now," Mitch spoke, thinking over the scenarios as he went.

"The guy who did this would wanna stick around, see the explosion," Kreed replied.

"But the kid was too high profile. They'd know we'd be looking," Connors spoke from behind him. Mitch hadn't even heard him walk up and had no idea how much he'd heard.

"Then maybe it's an inside job. Maybe this is agency-related," Kreed added, ignoring Connors altogether and staring at Mitch. Through all the discussion they'd had on this case, never once had Mitch truly accepted this could be a political game, let alone an agency insider gone rogue. As he let the possibility resonate, Connors jumped in.

"Not even on the radar. You better have all your ducks in a row before you start pointing your fingers at one of them." Mitch listened and knew Kreed too well. He didn't play well between the divisions, something they had in common. Instead of firing off a smart-ass remark like he knew his friend wanted to do, Kreed stuck his greasy, dirty hand out to Connors, introducing himself. Lost in thought, Connors took the bait and shook Kreed's hand, almost immediately realizing his mistake.

"Kreed Sinacola, nice to meet you," his buddy finally let go of Connors's hand. All Connors could do was stand there looking down at his oil- and soot-stained hand.

"Really?" Connors asked, still looking at his hand.

"In the justice's case, he could have lived through his if it hadn't been a direct hit. This one right here should have killed anyone who was in range. This car was placed in that field for a reason," Kreed continued, staring back at the car. Connors walked away, looking for something to clean his hand. "I can't see how it's not organized, by multiple people. They are too well-trained and diverse. They have international experience. Probably US ex-military. If not military, then some sort of special technical training. These people are pissed off at something. There's the National United Association. I know for sure ex-military joins that group."

"Yeah, but they aren't violent," Connors chimed in, holding his hand out away from his body. Mitch tried not to laugh at the rumpled, wet, and now soiled agent. This had to be killing him.

"It's only a matter of time until a splinter-group forms. You got the League of Freedom, New Resistance Party, Keywest United, every one of them draws ex-military, and they're packed with resigned law enforcement. I also can't see how you can discount an agency insider." Kreed had apparently been here awhile, his mind already going ninety to nothing.

"At this point, we can't discount anything," Mitch said before Connors could speak.

"I'm gonna write this up in an official report. I'll get Ellen to send it to you within the next few hours. What's your plan of attack?" Kreed asked, his focus back on Mitch.

"Maybe someone saw something. They had to drive through town to get out to that field," Mitch reasoned. "The car was stolen from the owner of the field it blew in. He reported the car stolen about thirty minutes before he heard the explosion on the other side of his property. That was around midnight, right?" Mitch asked Connors.

"Correct. Local police have put together a list of possible people of interest," Connors answered.

"Aaron Stuart's pulled together a more targeted organized hate groups list for me. I got it late Friday night. He's pulled all the registered members who were military-related and government-related. He stayed with groups that had memberships of under a hundred people. My gut says it's four or five people max, probably off the radar. It's planned, executed, and never mentioned again, but someone has to be leading the pack. They don't want fame from this. They're doing this for a different reason. We can interview, but they aren't here anymore. I guarantee it," Mitch said as they left the stall.

"For the first time, I agree with you, Knox, but I don't like Aaron Stuart being involved. You need to discuss these things with me. He's under investigation…" Connors started again, but Kreed cut him off.

"I bet he never played team sports as a child," Kreed hooked a thumb in Connors's direction as they headed toward the restrooms on the side of the building.

"My thoughts exactly," Mitch gave Kreed a knuckle-bump as they kept in perfect stride.

"You know, Knox? I've had enough of all the disrespect. I'm a graduate of Harvard Law. I'm in charge of this case. I'll have someone on my team narrow this down. Stuart's out. Period. End of discussion. I'm not comfortable with him," Connors called out from a couple of steps behind them. Mitch glanced back at him as he opened the door to the bathroom. Connors still held his hand awkwardly in front of his body to keep the grime from touching anything else.

"What's his problem with Stuart?" Kreed inclined his head toward the FBI agent.

"Who could really know? You know how the feds are. All I know is what Stuart's told me. He was apparently involved in some questionable activity in college. He broke into the FBI security system as a fraternity prank. Since then, they watch him, but they fucking hired his ass to find their breaches. So it's like give him a job, but never forgive him for what he's done." Mitch let the door shut as Connors approached.

"So he's that badass then?" Kreed asked, washing his hands.

"Oh yeah, but right now he's using his power for good, not evil." Mitch looked up, catching Kreed's disbelieving stare reflected in the mirror, and gave him a wink.

"How'd you meet him?"

"Online. We play State of Decay together sometimes. I kick his ass and then he manipulates the system and cheats, but I still win," Mitch said, leaning back against the sink next to Kreed while he dried his hands. Connors finally caught up and came through the door.

"I'd stick with him, Knox. These are some serious explosives. We need all the help we can get. Have you been to the site?" Kreed asked.

"No. We were headed there next." He glanced over at Connors and got a nod from the guy.

"I'd like to see it for myself, see if I can pick up anything that might have been missed. Can I hitch a ride with you?" Kreed asked.

"All right, you can ride with us. But I need to warn you, the fed gets carsick. You're in the back," Mitch advised Kreed. "Hey, did you happen to bring me a change of clothes?"

"Yeah, I just brought you some of mine. They're in my trunk," Kreed tossed him the keys and he headed out the door as Connors ran the degreasing soap over his hands for the third time.

Chapter 14

Mitch stayed back, forcing Connors to do the same in order to give Kreed time to do his thing. Every time Connors tried to speak, Mitch silenced him. This was the agent's second trip here in the last twenty-four hours. Connors had information Kreed needed, but Mitch didn't want to taint Kreed's gut instinct, because there wasn't anything more reliable than those odd feelings his partner got. So he stood in the hot Kentucky sun, keeping a metaphorical hand held over Connors's mouth even though they'd had this conversation in the car.

"Where was his body found?" Kreed called out.

"Roughly sixty meters east." Mitch looked at Connors for confirmation and got a nod.

"Show me," Kreed said. Thankfully Connors just did as he was asked without the long-winded commentary.

"Who cleaned up the site?" Kreed asked.

"Our guys," Connors answered, moving back toward Mitch.

"The locals or ATF didn't try?" Kreed asked, continuing to scan the seared earth.

"We took precedence because of Knox's work and the Greyson kid," Connors explained. Kreed shook his head and looked over at him. Mitch gave him his not-worth-it-just-shrug-it-off look.

"His legs were tied," Kreed announced, following the visible tracks.

"His hands, too. The assumption was he was in the trunk of the car, prior to the explosion," Connor supplied.

"So he got out by pulling the safety latch?" Kreed questioned. Mitch watched as his friend bent down and ran his fingers over the ground, then brought them to his nose.

"Probably, that's our best guess," Connors finally spoke up again, keeping his eyes on Kreed.

"Guaranteed he faked unconsciousness," Kreed added.

"He's a smart kid," Mitch affirmed, following along beside Kreed, examining the tracks left by Elliot Greyson.

"He hasn't been questioned?" Kreed asked, staring at the ground.

"No. He's been in a coma since he was found," Mitch supplied

"Are the same agents with him that lost him?" Kreed asked.

"Not as of tonight," Mitch said, already palming his phone. "They're real big on him ducking out."

"You better have a good reason and something solid to back it up when you make that call," Connors cautioned Mitch. He ignored him, but got the feeling Connors was finally on board with the possibility the Secret Service might be involved. At this point, they couldn't rule anything out. Could this really be an inside job? A Secret Service agent would absolutely have the ability and know the importance of keeping things quiet. They could hide.

In mid-call, Mitch changed his mind and decided to wait. For now, the kid had extra protection and Mitch needed to think. Connors had some good points about this internal department issue they now faced. He needed time to process everything they'd learned. This could quite possibly be the first real lead he had, and for some reason, the case kept getting worse with every bit of new information found.

Kreed wrapped his end up, and Mitch drove them back to the impound lot where Kreed's rental was parked and their driver had remained after much coaxing on Mitch's part. Between Mitch, Kreed, and Connors, they all agreed they wouldn't act until they could dig a little deeper. As Connors conceded, so did Mitch. He needed evidence before he could cast stones at the Secret Service.

~~~

Mitch sat on the edge of the bed in the hotel room and waited. A knock came from the adjoining room door, one Mitch hadn't opened and debated now whether to leave closed. Kreed hadn't had enough time to do his thing, and he didn't want Connors in here rambling on and on about how the FBI handled matters such as these.

With the turn of events over the last couple of hours, paranoia began to run deep. Once they were assigned a room, Mitch immediately asked for two new ones. Now he just sat in the extreme quiet of the hotel room, waiting.

On the second knock, Mitch finally decided to let Connors in, but stood in the adjoining doorway, lifting a finger to his lips. That confused Connors a little, but he finally got the point and gave a quick nod. They just stood there, staring at each other.

"We need to ask more questions, do some leg-work. Maybe someone saw something. They had to get into town someway." Connors broke the silence, saying the words very clearly and professionally. Mitch made a mental note that the agent sucked at acting casual in complicated situations.

Finally the knock he'd been waiting for came. Mitch looked through the peep hole and there stood Kreed.

"Hey, man, thanks for coming," Mitch said.

"Nice digs. The Marshals Service doesn't usually pay for the Hilton," Kreed teased and handed one of two small handheld devices over to Mitch. They both began scanning the room. Connors stood back and watched before moving aside, letting them go over his room with the same diligence they'd surveyed the first. No part of either room remained untouched. During the sweep, Mitch noticed Connors had completely unpacked. Toiletries in their right spot, each drawer had neatly folded socks, underwear, and an undershirt. His suit was hung properly in the closet.

Kreed looked behind the bed, moved the device over the picture hanging above the headboard. "The rooms are clean." Kreed turned back around to face them, clearly thinking through the situation. "Were these the original rooms?"

"Nah, I got us two new ones."

"I think we should report in to the local PD. They need to know we're here, and I need to get the reports they filed from last night," Connors said randomly while standing in the middle of the two rooms.

"I need to get with Aaron. He can scan our computers and pull together a list of the agents assigned to Greyson. He'll do it quietly. No one'll know." Mitch ignored Kreed, who was still staring at Connors. His partner hadn't learned yet that Tyler Connors didn't fit in well with people. He was single-minded and sole-purposed. General conversation wasn't his strength.

"We keep coming right back here with Stuart. You know I don't like him." Connors gave an aggravated huff. Kreed stood back, watching both of them as if this was going be a great show. Mitch ignored him as he set up his computer and immediately turned on Skype.

"Then go check in with the police, see if they have anything new to go on. Be seen out and about. If they have a diner, stop in there. We want the word out for everyone to know that we're asking lots of questions. Leave your laptop on in your room. Aaron can remotely access it and see what devices are tracking us—if there are any, but if you haven't figured it out, Stuart's involved in this case. Get used to it." Mitch stifled a yawn. The pent up energy of worry was beginning to fade, leaving in its place the fact he hadn't slept in well over twenty-four hours.

"Guarantee me that he will only do what needs to be done. Watch every move he makes. There's sensitive information on this thing. I'll be back in a couple of hours. We can grab a bite to eat at the diner together," Connors said, bringing his laptop to Mitch.

"Agreed," he set up the computers and waited for Connors to leave before he dialed Aaron. On the first ring, his face appeared on the screen. "Did you get the text I sent you?" Aaron asked.

"I haven't checked yet, but I will. Can you check out my computer, see if I'm the only one here? I can give you my access information." Mitch could hear Kreed behind him, moving. The sound of the recliner's leg rest lifting and lowering.

"No need," Aaron said, and Skype was disconnected.

"So that's the famous Aaron Stuart. Is he straight or gay?" Kreed asked. Mitch would have sworn his friend sounded a little curious.

"I don't know. I don't know him like that. There's always a female playing with him," Mitch commented, somewhat distracted as his screen momentarily went black and then came back up, business as usual.

"He's straight then," Kreed reasoned and went back to lounging in the recliner.

"Not necessarily," Mitch said absently and waited, staring at his screen. His mouse was going crazy. Aaron had easily broken in and was working the system files. He probably kept the mouse going on purpose, letting Mitch know he was there. After a second of remaining seated, he broke his daze and dug his phone out of his pocket. There were a few missed calls and texts.

He scanned the calls, both received during the turbulent plane ride—one from Director Skinner, the other from Kreed. He'd wait to call his director when he wasn't in the middle of doing something that might be frowned upon. The incoming text message was from Aaron.

He clicked the message open to be greeted with a new photo of Cody. Damn, the guy was gorgeous, just exactly like he remembered. This had to be a professional picture. He wore a Texas State Trooper uniform and had a serious look on his face. The picture's angle perfectly accented Cody's bright blue eyes. His lips were full and pouty, and Mitch knew from experience they were totally kissable. His cock went half-mast as he recalled how soft and sexy they were. He was going to have a full-blown hard-on if he didn't stop gawking. He damn sure wasn't in any mood to explain to Kreed why he had an erection with him sitting right there in the room.

He gave Cody one last look and moved on to the information he'd requested.

Cody Turner
Birthday: June 23, 1988
Age: 26
Height: 6'4"
Address: 10410 Main Street Apt 9B, Austin, TX 78722
Phone: 512.555.6001
Email: texasranger1987@mail.com

Employed by the TxDPS as a Highway Patrol Officer for four years.

No criminal record of any kind. Looks clean. I can dig deeper if you want.

A

By the time he got to the bottom of the message, Aaron's face reappeared on his laptop screen. Aaron had re-initiated Skype himself. Mitch had no idea how he did things like that, but he did it all the time. "I can't see any evidence of devices on this machine. It's picking up the Justice Department in Louisiana, but nothing else is attached."

"Can you check another machine? I have it here with me. What do I need to do?" Mitch stared at the other computer. The screen had gone blank, so he ran a finger over the mouse.

"It's there in the room with you?" Aaron asked.

"Yes, I can't see if he has Skype installed."

"I don't need it, hang on," Aaron said, and he was gone again. The laptop next to him never changed like his had.

"How tall is he?" Kreed's voice startled him.

"Who?" Mitch responded, his eyes back on the picture of Cody. Damn, the guy was hot.

"Computer guy. How come I've never seen him before?" Kreed asked.

"You resist technology. That's my thing in this dynamic duo we have going on, and I totally suck at it. This is who I met in Dallas." He lifted his smart phone to show Kreed, and to his friend's credit, he did look at Cody, but his eyes were immediately back on Mitch's computer screen.

"Introduce me," Kreed requested.

"Fuck you. This one's mine." Mitch pressed the bar on the side of the phone to bring Cody's picture back up when the screen darkened.

"No, dumb-ass, not him…the computer geek." Kreed inclined his head toward the laptop.

"You know, I can hear everything you're saying." Aaron's voice caught him off guard, causing him and Kreed to both stare at his dark screen, and then over to Connors's darkened screen.

"How does he do that?" Kreed's brow lifted.

"I don't know. I should have warned you." He kept his eyes on his laptop, waiting for Aaron to do something else.

"So like he can watch everything you do?" Kreed probed. Mitch looked at Kreed and rolled his eyes. His buddy just wasn't going to give it up.

"This would be hearing, not seeing." A voice came from behind the darkened screen right before Skype turned back on and Aaron's face appeared. "You're not my type Deputy Marshal Sinacola."

"I'm everyone's type." Kreed obviously took offense at being shot down.

"In your dreams," Aaron responded, and Mitch had to laugh because Kreed was actually pouting now as he leaned back in the chair.

"What did you find?" Mitch finally quit laughing long enough to ask.

"He looks pretty clean too. The bureau has a way to get inside there, but nothing abnormal," Aaron said, all business again.

"Okay, thanks. I need another favor," Mitch said.

"They're stacking up," Aaron replied, smiling at him.

"Whatever—" He started to speak but Kreed cut him off.

"Is that the guy who took over your character?"

"That's fuckin' right. I told you the last time you took over my Marcus and let the zombies eat him that I was kickin' your ass." Mitch spoke to Aaron, ignoring Kreed.

"So that's the guy? Very cool. He was pissed off about that for weeks," Kreed said.

"Knox doesn't play fair," Aaron replied.

"By fair, he means I was kicking his ass. I need another favor since you owe like a million of them for that bullshit. I need a list with background information of every member of the Secret Service assigned to Senator Greyson and his family. If you can find exact times and schedules, I'd appreciate that, too," Mitch said, feeling the loss of Marcus again. He'd played forever to get that far into the game.

"Sure thing, by when?" Aaron asked.

"Tomorrow?" Mitch questioned, hoping for sooner. "And this needs to stay on the DL."

"Doesn't it all?"

"Yeah, pretty much," Mitch agreed.

"All right, I'll stay on these computers, see if anyone tries to get in this week, but then I'm off for a few days." Aaron's eyes were downcast, working on something, even as he kept the conversation going.

"You're going offline, like on a vacation?" Mitch sound incredulous.

"Going to the Keys. My brother's getting married, best man and all that bullshit," Aaron answered.

"Thanks for doing this before you go. I'll mark it off the long list you still owe me."

"Not a problem." And then Aaron was gone. Skype turned off.

"He's hot. I can't believe you haven't introduced us. Why haven't you set me up with him?" Kreed asked.

"A list of reasons. First, I'm pretty sure he's straight. Second, I can't really see how you're his type, and third, he's a seriously smart computer geek. You're barking up the wrong tree, Sinacola." Mitch lowered his laptop on another yawn.

"Hmm… Those sound like excuses. I'm heading out. Call me if you need me. If not, I'll be in touch as soon as I get to Louisiana," Kreed said, rising from the chair and stretching out his long body. Size for size, Kreed matched Mitch. He certainly beat Kreed in the tattoo count, though.

"Thanks, man," Mitch stood, keeping his phone palmed in his left hand as he shook Kreed's right. "So your gut says someone from the inside's involved?"

"Possibly yes. Maybe just feeding information out. They aren't big enough to tap you yet, but it does look like you got your first break in a pretty big way. Now, go figure out who it is," Kreed said, opening the door. "Later."

Mitch closed the door behind him before placing Connors's laptop back in his room and shutting and locking that door as well. He had a phone call to make.

Chapter 15

Cody rode with the window to his patrol car rolled down, enjoying the warmth of the October evening sun. He drove the long stretch of the country road, easily navigating the sweeping turns and speed changes like a guy who had traveled these roads for most of his life, which technically was completely true. The only difference in today than any other before, after the end of this shift, he had two weeks of vacation, then he'd be trading in his Dodge Charger for a horse named Ranger.

Cody smiled with pride at being selected for the new detail. This evening, he would turn in his keys and clear out his desk, then he'd be off for his two weeks of R&R.

As the street came to an end, Cody slowed and gave a nod to a gardener watering the flowers outside the old nursery in town. He pulled off the road, somewhat hidden behind a cluster of trees. He thought he'd spend the next few hours clocking drivers who loved to speed past this intersection, before heading back to the office.

Earlier today, he'd heard the women at headquarters whispering about a small party in honor of his new assignment. He was certain the celebration would include some of Darlene's homemade chocolate cake. First his mom's cake and now Darlene's, two of his favorite desserts, all in the same day. Cody wasn't quite sure life got any better than that.

As Cody settled in, his personal cell phone caught him off guard. It was too early in the evening to be called back to the office, beside they would do that through dispatch and his family never interrupted while he was on duty. Cody pulled the phone from his front pocket. He didn't recognize the number and the ID came up as United States. Now, that was completely weird. With a slide of his finger, he answered the phone.

"State Trooper Turner," he said, just in case this was an official call.

"Even your voice is sexy as fuck," Mitch Knox said on the other end of the line. "Did I catch you at a bad time?"

There was a pause. Something about his heart drumming in his chest and his brain going numb had Cody at a loss for words. Mitch had been on his mind pretty much since he'd left him last night at JR's. He'd caught himself about two dozen times today daydreaming about the guy. That dark, deep rich voice gave a devious chuckle during his silence.

"How did you get this number?" Cody asked lamely, trying to say something to fill the silence.

"I told you I would find you," Mitch replied with a hint of arrogance in his tone.

"I don't remember you saying that." Right then, Cody banged his forehead against the steering wheel. Was that truly the best he had? There was something about Mitch that screwed up his thought processes every single time he talked to him.

"Let's see…Cody Turner. Age twenty-six. Our birthdays are close together, yours is June twenty-third, mine's the eighteenth. Your address is 10410 Main Street, Apt 9B. Want your social?" Mitch asked.

"No, that's enough," Cody replied, and then nothing else came out; they were back to silence. He couldn't think of anything to say…again. He heard Mitch's laughter and felt the heat creeping up his cheeks.

Dammit! He must've come off like a complete idiot.

"You sure have a way of being incredibly tight-lipped. That's okay. I talk enough for the both of us. Are you working right now?" Mitch asked, filling in his silence.

"Yes, sir," he answered, watching as a car flew past him on the highway at a high rate of speed. He let them go. *Did I just say sir?*

"Why is everyone calling me sir these days? When do you get off?" Mitch asked, the humor gone, leaving just the low deep voice that sent shivers up his spine. Cody closed his eyes, and his dick perked up, tightening in his pants.

"In a few hours," Cody mumbled.

"Good, me too. Can I call you tonight? Like after ten o'clock your time?" Mitch questioned.

"Mmmm, ten? Yeah I think so... I mean, no. I've got something going on later, I think," Cody stuttered, caught off guard by the question, trying to clear his head. He had no idea how long the party at headquarters would last. And since his brain stopped working, he pretty much couldn't come up with any answers. It took a minute for him to realize Mitch had gone silent. Cody tried to explain.

"I overheard something about them having some kind of party for me this evening at the station. For the new job I got," Cody rambled, trying to fill the dead space.

"Well, text me when you're done. I should be off too. Do you ever Skype?" Mitch asked.

"I haven't before, but it's on my computer," Cody answered.

"All right, this is my cell. Save it, okay?" Mitch asked.

"Okay. It was good to hear from you." The words were out of Cody's mouth before he could stop himself, and this time he banged his head hard enough to actually make it hurt. Who said stupid shit like that?

"I bet," Mitch growled and gave that chuckle again. The call disconnected. Cody was slower to lower his hand. He was panting just from the sound of Mitch's voice. His heart had accelerated, and he was sweating from that one phone call. He'd never expected to hear that voice again.

Would he text Mitch later? Absolutely not. The whole way he'd just handled this call and the blush still on his face proved what he already suspected, Mitch Knox was far out of his league. Cody was a small town country boy. Mitch was sexy and worldly. He carried that fuck you attitude. Not to mention, Cody didn't seem to have a mind of his own when Mitch was within his vicinity. Apparently that included the phone too. Damn, just thinking of that voice and remembering their time together in the car... There was no way in hell Cody would call him. He couldn't afford this distraction. Mitch messed him up too badly.

After a solid ten minutes of staring out the front window, Cody realized he was doing it again. He was getting hard and worked up just thinking about Mitch. Damn, he really had to get a hold of himself. He just couldn't afford the trouble he imagined Mitch would bring to his life. What he needed to do was concentrate on his job and his future, nothing else.

On that thought, Cody adjusted himself, lifted his radar gun, and pretended to track the speed of the cars as his mind stayed focused on the best ways he could think of to forget Mitch.

Chapter 16

Mitch sat back, his phone still resting in the palm of his hand. He stared at the picture he'd put above the number. Why was his mind constantly on Cody Turner? Especially when he'd gotten the first real break on a case he'd not only worked but lived for the last several months?

He couldn't answer those questions, except to say Cody Turner intrigued him.

The vibration of the phone had him pushing those thoughts aside. Colt Michael's face popped up on his screen. He answered with a slide of the finger. "Hey."

"Papa Montgomery's worried. He says you should have been home hours ago," Colt said in his usual mocking tone.

"I love to think Jace is thinking about me. Makes me all warm and fluttery," Mitch shot back, laughter in his voice. "Hey, let me talk to him, so I can assure him I'm fine."

"Like hell you're talking to him. Your shit's on the front porch, Knox. No need to even ring the bell," Colt bated him.

"No, it's not, Colt. Quit being so melodramatic." Jace's voice on the other end of the line had him grinning.

"He does that 'let me talk to Jace thing' on purpose, honey. He knows it drives me crazy," Colt grumbled, but Jace got on the phone, taking over the call.

"There's no rush on coming back, we just wanted to make sure everything was good on your end," Jace said in his always reasonable tone. The man was laid-back and level-headed, which was probably why Mitch liked him so much.

"I got called out last night. I left before four this morning. I didn't want to wake you. Can you hang on to my stuff for a while? I'll be back through there soon, I'm sure."

"Sure, or I can ship it to you," Jace offered.

"If it's in the way, you can ship it. If not, I'm sure it'll be a week or so before I'm back."

"Is it the case?" Jace asked hopefully.

"I can't talk about it, you know that," Mitch answered.

"I'm wearing your ball cap," Colt yelled in the background. That was the one thing that crossed every line. It was all fun and games until his beloved baseball cap that he'd had for many years and fit him perfectly was brought into play.

"Jace, make him take it off and ask him about the sixteen to twenty pieces of bacon he ate," Mitch said, feeling completely justified that he'd just pulled out the big guns.

"Sixteen pieces of bacon?" Jace asked, clearly not talking to him.

"You suck, man. I wasn't even wearing your stupid hat," Colt hollered in the background.

"Jace, protect my hat. I'll see you guys soon." All he could hear was Colt getting the negative nutritional facts about bacon, and he laughed as he hung up. That was exactly what he needed to take his mind off a certain hot young blond.

~~~

Cody felt real good. Last call just got hollered, meaning it was close to one thirty in the morning. That meant he'd been at his regular hangout for a solid couple of hours. He'd ended up here after the celebration at DPS headquarters, and since he'd arrived, he drank his way to pretty damn drunk.

His going away slash welcome to the new mounted division party had lasted longer than he'd anticipated. He hadn't made it to the local gay club he sometimes hung out at. He also hadn't called his last boyfriend who was generally always up for a good time even though they had broken up a couple of months ago. Instead he hit The Barn, a bar below his downtown Austin apartment. They knew him by name there, and he didn't have far to get home. A nine-flight elevator ride up was all the traveling he'd have to do.

The one thing he'd needed the most hadn't happened tonight and that was sex. Man, he'd needed a good fuck, but pretty much his whole concentration now centered on not calling or texting Mitch back. After a couple of drinks, he decided it would have been simpler had he just deleted Mitch's number from his phone, but for some reason, that didn't seem to be an option. After a considerable amount of time and a few more beers, he reasoned if he deleted the number, he might not know if Mitch called again and might answer unexpectedly. So at least if he kept the number, he could ignore the call.

Yeah, that was it...

"You got my tab?" Cody called out from his end of the bar.

"Yeah, close it out?" the bartender asked.

"Yeah, tip yourself appropriately. Don't make me think tonight," Cody said, laughing at his joke that no one else seemed to think was funny. That was okay; he laughed enough for the few stragglers still lingering in the place.

Chapter 17

What the fuck! Mitch felt like a schoolboy waiting to hear from his first crush. Damn, that was so unlike him, but memories of that hot cowboy in the front seat continued to make encore appearances in his mind all night.

Mitch had spent the last few hours going over every detail of the case with Connors. In his newfound ecstatic mood, he'd even refrained from the smart-ass remarks he would have normally made to his uptight partner over things like…his less than desirable wardrobe, or frou-frou eating habits, because seriously, who still cut their hamburger with a knife and fork in this day and age? But he hadn't said a word. Mitch had other more important things to occupy his thoughts.

They had gone to the local diner earlier, asking obvious and stupid questions as they polished off homemade chocolate meringue pie, and made sure the townsfolk left talking about the two government agents in town on the outside chance they were being watched.

Even though Mitch hadn't slept, he wouldn't let them call it a night. Mitch forced an online meeting between Connors and Aaron, and Connors remained skeptical until Aaron presented them the list of the agents assigned to the Greyson family. It hadn't taken him two hours to put that information together, and the list was long. They spent the next few hours going over the list, dissecting each person and the possibility of their involvement.

In what he now considered a lame move, Mitch had left his cellphone out, close at hand the entire time they had dinner, through their impromptu meeting with Aaron, through his shower, and while he changed into the SpongeBob pajama pants Kreed loaned him. Cody never called. Why hadn't he called?

He'd thought Cody was into him. At least last night he had been. Mitch had just put all those nerves off to Cody being newly out or something like that. Mitch was reasonably certain he and Cody would have ended up doing the deed if he'd stayed in town. But on that thought, last night could have just been a hook-up for Cody. Actually, it should have just been a hook-up for Mitch too, but hell, he couldn't let this go.

If Mitch was honest with himself, Cody had walked away last night with all his information. He knew exactly who he was and how to reach him, and yet, Mitch had been the one to make the first move. Actually, he'd been the one to make all the moves—that thought caused a scowl to form as he brushed his teeth and ran a comb through his short hair. Why was he so hung up on that shy country boy?

"Fuck it. I'll call him again. I'll call him until he tells me to stop. Fuck that, I might still call him even then," he said aloud, making sure the door separating his and Connors's rooms was fully closed and locked. Mitch rolled his thick shoulders, grabbed his phone, scrolled through the numbers, and hit call. He took a seat on the edge of the bed and waited. It was two fifteen in the morning. Whatever. Cody should have called like he said he would. If he woke Cody's ass up, well that was his own damn fault.

"Hello," Cody answered in a hushed gravelly voice. He must have been asleep like Mitch really should have been.

"You didn't call." Mitch let his frustration run out of his mouth with that obvious statement. Fuck, had he already messed up calling him out like that? That was such a girl move. He tried to cover the tone he just used. "Are you home? Do you know who this is?" What was with him tonight? He lowered his head to his hand. What was it about this guy that had him so strung out?

"Yes," Cody replied, he supposed that answered both questions. The yes was slightly slurred, not completely, but enough for him to ask the next question.

"Have you been drinking?" Mitch fiddled with the top sheet on his bed, rubbing the soft fabric between his fingers.

"Some," Cody answered.

"Are you at home?" Mitch asked again.

"Yeah," Cody said. The word coming out in at least three syllables.

"Are you alone?" Not that it was any of his business, and the guy had every right to tell him so, but he had to ask.

"Yes," Cody responded. But damn what was up with the one word answers? Cody was going to make him work for any kind of conversation. Hell, why should their interactions be any different now? Cody had made him work for every single thing since the minute he approached him in the bar.

"You said you would call. Why didn't you? Is everything okay?" Mitch questioned. He hoped that came out more concerned than confrontational.

"What do you want from me?" Cody asked. Where had that come from? Mitch took the phone from his ear and stared at the lit screen, confused. Did he imagine all the hot and heavy during their little rendezvous in the small rental car or what? Because that question damn sure didn't answer anything Mitch asked, and he had no idea how to respond to Cody.

Okay, maybe what he asked wasn't as dumb as he thought. What the hell did he want? He wasn't exactly sure he knew. Sex? Sure, who didn't want sex, but it wasn't only that. Last night in the car with Cody still burned in his mind. The way he smelled, the way his lips moved against Mitch's when they kissed, the way Cody's firm body fit perfectly against his. He hadn't been able to get any part of Cody Turner out of his head, and those thoughts were driving him insane. So instead of saying all that, he said, "Are you in bed?"

That got Mitch nothing but silence. So he took the lack of response for a yes and grinned to himself. He pictured Cody's big body stretched across the bed, an impressive cock barely covered by a thin sheet, his blond hair tousled from sleep. Fuck, what an image. Clearly, he had a very active imagination.

"Mmm…the strong silent type, huh? I like that." Mitch joked, trying to get a reaction. "Cody? You still with me?" He was still there. Mitch could hear the even breathing on the other end of the line.

"Yeah." One syllable word, not slurred. Mitch smiled.

"Good. Now answer my question. Are you in bed?" He scooted over to the middle of his bed and rested against the headboard.

"Yeah," was all he got back again.

"Fuck, Cody, you're not making this easy. You're gonna make me work for this, aren't you?" Mitch was starting to think he'd made a mistake in calling Cody. Maybe he was more interested, or more likely, maybe he'd turned into a teenage girl all of the sudden.

"Work for what?" Cody sounded confused.

"I'm putting myself out here. Did I get the signals crossed or something? I thought we hit it off, was I wrong? I wanna get to know you better. I can't get you out of my fucking head...I—" Mitch stopped as he ran out of steam. It sucked being rejected.

"I...I've been thinking about you too," Cody said quietly. That had Mitch perking up, a triumphant smirk curling the corners of his lips. No teenage girls here!

"Really? When you think about me what do you think about?" He slid his knees up to plant his feet firmly on the mattress eager to hear what Cody had to say and almost laughed as he caught a glimpse of a smiling SpongeBob on his pajama's staring back at him. He was trying to be sexy and here he was in the goofiest possible set of pajamas pants. Good thing Cody couldn't see him. "Honestly, I'd like to know."

"Just, you know...stuff." Cody hesitated. He could hear the caution in his words. The sound of Cody's husky voice had him thinking about *stuff* too. Yeah, thinking about really good stuff that had his dick plumping up and filling out those damn cartoon bottoms he wore.

"Stuff, huh? What kind of stuff?" He wanted to know if Cody had been thinking about him as much as he'd been thinking about Cody. Mitch pushed his hand inside the waistband of those brightly-colored pajamas and took hold of his cock.

"Do you wanna know what I think about, Cody?" He pressed on, not waiting for a response. He didn't know how Cody would react, but he had to give this a shot. His dick had grown so fucking hard, and he needed the release. If he could get the shy country boy on board with his plan, then maybe he could fall asleep without a hard-on.

Fuckin' hell! The stupid bottoms were too restrictive so he made quick work of pushing the offending sleep pants down past his hips so he could get a better hold. Mitch ran his thumb back and forth over the sensitive head of his leaking dick as he continued talking.

"I think about the way your lips tasted against mine when you kissed me with that sweet mouth. The way your teeth scraped against my skin. Damn, that was fucking hot, Cody Turner. But what I think about the most is how much I wanted to taste that rock hard cock of yours. Swallow you all the way down, over and over again, and feel you losing yourself to me. Then I'd devour everything you gave me as you emptied your hot load down my throat. And you need to know, I would have done that had we not been interrupted." Mitch's voice lowered.

"That's what I think about, Cody, and I'm so fucking hard for you right now, my dick's dripping." He swore he heard Cody's breath hitch followed by a soft moan. Yeah, his night might just turn out better than he originally thought.

"Would you have liked that, State Trooper Turner?"

~~~

Cody couldn't help but slide his hand inside his briefs and curl his fingers around his aching cock as he listened to the cadence of Mitch's deep, sexy voice. *Fuck!* Had he moaned out loud when he pulled off a slow stroke? *Shit!* He didn't know if he was more embarrassed or turned on at his actions. He'd never touched himself while he had someone on the other end of his phone. He wasn't even sure how this worked, him being a phone sex virgin and all.

His drunken mind easily rationalized that he never had to tell anyone either. But god, the visual of Mitch's lips stretched around his dick had him hanging on every word and needing to find his own release.

"Yes," he whispered as he slowly shoved his hips into his tight grip and closed his eyes.

"Are you touching yourself, Cody?" Cody's eyes flew open, his hand stilled on his cock. How had Mitch known? What was he supposed to say?

He was most definitely touching himself, but he didn't know if he could actually say those words to Mitch. Fuck, he wished he were bolder. He wasn't sure how much time had passed when he heard Mitch's husky voice again.

"I'm touching myself, and it feels amazing. I'm pretending it's your hand stroking me, Cody. Your hand making me feel *sooo* good," Mitch said, drawing out the word, making it sound naughty. Just knowing Mitch masturbated on the other end of the line had his dick jerking in his hand even more.

"Mitch, umm…I…" he stuttered, searching for words.

"I want you to touch yourself, for me, Cody. God, I wish I could see that sexy blush thing you do, right now." Mitch's words cut off his train of thought. "Let me hear you pleasuring yourself along with me."

He could hear the rustling of the covers and Mitch's breathing change. "Fuck, it feels so good, Cody. Just touch yourself," Mitch growled. Damn, Cody was so turned on right now, he couldn't ever remember being this worked up over the sound of someone's voice. His cock was as hard as fucking stone and beading at the tip.

"I…I am," Cody managed to say. The admission was both awkward and stimulating all at the same time.

"Good. Are you stroking yourself for me, Cody?"

"Yes," he breathed, his hand keeping a slow steady pace. And it felt amazing, not only his hand on his dick, but just being able to be so open.

"Close your eyes and think about sliding your cock between my lips and deep down my throat. I wanna taste you so fucking bad. I have since the minute I laid eyes on you. It's all I think about."

"Oh god yes!" He screwed his eyes shut and tightened his grip.

"I want you to play with your balls, Cody, and pretend it's me holding them in my palm as you fuck my throat." Cody stroked himself faster and harder, adding a little twist of his wrist in just the right spot. With his free hand, he did exactly as Mitch asked and slid his palm to his balls and began tugging and playing with the sensitive sac.

He imagined his hands going to the back of Mitch's head and forcing his cock deeper down Mitch's throat. The visual had him biting his lip, drawing blood, trying to keep as quiet as he could. His orgasm built so fast he didn't know how much longer he could hold off. He was absolutely going to blow.

"Cody, I can hear you breathing, does it feel good?"

"Fuck yes! Mitch, keep talking. I'm close." He quickened the pace, arching his body as he pushed up into his fist. A light sheen of sweat coated his skin as he strained to hold back his release. He reached the point of no return, but he didn't care, he was so hot for this man.

"I wanna hear you say my name when you come. Just so you know who made you feel like this." Mitch's command went straight to his balls, drawing them up tight against his body. Jesus H. Christ he was gonna come.

"I'm so fucking close," he moaned.

"Come for me, Cody," Mitch ordered.

"Mitch! Fuck, yesss…I'm coming." His dick jerked in his grip, shooting creamy ribbons of liquid heat across his chest and stomach as he tumbled over the edge.

"*Soo* good, Cody…so fucking good," Mitch gasped. He sounded out of breath, and for some reason, that made Cody smile. He stroked his sensitive cock one last time, listening to the heavy breathing on the other end of the line. They both remained silent for a little while. He didn't really know exactly what to say. What did you say to someone you'd just jerked off with over the phone? Mitch broke the silence.

"You shouted my name. I guess I don't have to ask if it was good for you, too." Mitch chuckled, his voice huskier than before and slightly lethargic.

"Yeah, it was really good. I've never done anything like that before, with anyone," Cody confessed.

"So you do it by yourself, then?" Mitch was teasing him, but his cheeks warmed up anyway.

"Yes, I ummm… No! S-shit!" he stuttered. He could really feel the heat in his face now. He'd just embarrassed himself.

"Mmm…I'd love to watch. I'll bet you're a spectacular sight when you come," Mitch purred. Damn, that voice was making Cody hard again.

"You wanna watch me come?" His stomach tightened excitedly at the thought. He'd never been an exhibitionist, but he wasn't a prude either. To be honest, he'd love to watch Mitch come too.

"I bet you're fucking hot! If you liked what we did tonight, just wait till I get you on Skype, Cody Turner," Mitch said, and the words sent a shiver across his body and took root in his sated and alcohol-clouded mind. He'd worry about what that meant in the morning.

"Until next time, Cody Turner..." Mitch whispered, and Cody smiled as he drifted off to sleep.

Chapter 18

Monday morning, the flight from Kentucky hadn't been near as eventful as the flight there. As they ate up the miles in the air, zooming back to Washington, DC, Mitch watched as Connors changed from the reasonable, almost easygoing guy he'd finally become in Kentucky, to the stressed out, overly talkative freak Mitch had met when he'd first arrived to the DC office. To say Connors was back to being annoying was an understatement.

That caused Mitch to sigh and rub his fingers against his temples, trying to rid himself of the headache he'd had for most of the morning. His goals were simple—he was determined to sit down with every Secret Service agent assigned to Greyson and have a talk with each one individually. His plan consisted of digging further into their backgrounds, but he prepared himself for the uphill battle that would become once he hit the walls of red tape and interdepartmental rivalries. He doubted, as well-trained in discretion as they were, that he'd be able to trip them into making a stupid verbal mistake.

The plane touched down, jarring Mitch from his thoughts. He jerked his eyes open to see they had landed at the same private airstrip they'd departed from. The dings of their phones started almost immediately upon touchdown. Mitch ignored his. He'd found out this morning, if he looked at his phone, he'd think about Cody and the phone call they'd shared last night. Mitch sighed....right then, with just that thought, he grew hard again. He forced his mind back to the present, unbuckled his seat belt, and rose, stretching out his body before heading to the front of the plane for his duffel bag and laptop.

Connors had kept his bag with him. He'd never bothered to take off his suit coat either. When he exited, he looked as sharp and crisp as he did when he boarded the flight. It must have killed him to be so rumpled and wet yesterday in Kentucky. Mitch grinned at the thought.

"How do you do that?" Mitch asked, grabbing for the sunglasses he had hooked into the top of his T-shirt. The brightness of the sun blinded him as he stepped outside to the stairwell.

"How do I do what?" Connors asked as he answered his ringing phone. "What happened?"

There was silence as Connors came to an abrupt stop on the bottom step. Mitch was forced to stop or plow right into Connors from behind. Just as Mitch prepared to shove the guy off the last step, he heard him say, "Are they certain it's a break?" Mitch got the impression this was more personal than professional from the depth of concern he heard in the man's tone. "What hospital are you at?"

Mitch did reach out and move Connors over, not the shove he originally intended, but a slight nudge. He headed toward the car that had apparently replaced their company-assigned vehicle. To his surprise, the driver got out and crawled in the backseat as Mitch headed over.

"Is this thing set for the bureau?" Mitch asked as he took the now free driver's seat, waving a finger at the GPS in the dashboard.

"Yeah, I know the way, but I figured it would play out like this. I heard I was saddled with two type-A personalities. Figured neither of you would be taking the backseat. Plus word spreads quickly in our circles," the guy added with a shrug.

"I'm not like him." Mitch hooked his thumb out the side window in Connors's direction.

The guy nodded slowly. "Sure, you're not."

"Caroline, I'm on my way," Connors said as he slid inside the car. He turned to Mitch, covering a hand over the phone, and said quietly, "I need to be dropped off at St. Mary's. My son's having surgery."

"Be a big boy. I'll be there soon." Connors said into the phone. The driver hoisted himself between the seats and reprogrammed the

GPS. "Yes, you'll have a scar like me. Be brave, I'll be there in a few minutes. Kiss your mom for me."

Mitch didn't do anything more than just stare at Connors. The guy had babbled more words to him in the last twenty-four hours than Kreed had in the last ten years, yet he hadn't mentioned something as important as the fact he had a kid?

"What? Get going. My son's having surgery," Connors ordered, doing a forward finger motion thing, trying to get him moving along.

"You have a family?"

"I got you programmed in," the driver said and sat back. The GPS calculated their route, but Mitch didn't bother to move even though he was certain it wasn't hard to find his way out of the airport.

"Do I need to drive?" Connors sounded impatient.

Mitch lifted his brow at the FBI agent. "That's something a partner tells another partner. You haven't shut up since I met you, and I just now find out you have a family?"

"So what? You didn't tell me about yours, and with all that 'fuck yeah' coming through the walls last night, you sure weren't talking to your director." Point for Connors. That effectively shut Mitch up. Damn, he'd thought he'd been quiet last night.

When the GPS voice began, Mitch put the car in drive and started out of the airport.

"You heard all that, did you? And how do you know I wasn't talking to my director?" Mitch said, trying for a little shock value as he turned the blinker on and merged into the traffic.

"My bed was against the same wall as yours. Besides, I did tell you about my family. You tuned me out."

"If I listened to everything you said, I'd be a raving lunatic. Do you have one of those siren things for the top of the car? GPS says twenty minutes. I bet I can make it in seven," Mitch asked the driver as their eyes met in the rearview mirror.

"Just get us there alive," Connors cautioned at the same time the driver started to buckle himself in.

"No, sir, we're a private car service. I own this car," the driver said, sounding a little unnerved. Mitch looked into the rearview mirror again and swore he saw the sweat beading on the guy's forehead.

"But the government's liable, right? Means they have to take responsibility if I crash." Mitch hit the gas and chuckled when the tires squealed as he took the ramp to the highway. He got them to the hospital in about fifteen minutes, and pulled up to the rotunda of the hospital to let him out. "I'll be up in a minute."

That stopped Connors in his tracks. He immediately swiveled on his feet and stuck his head back in the car. "No, go back to the office."

"Nah, man, your kid's going into surgery. Even temporary partners should be there for one another." Mitch looked back at the driver. "Can you wait?"

"No. Really, just no. My wife's already too distressed. Just go back to the office."

"I'll distract her. I can be charming," Mitch said cockily, more as a joke, but gave the sexy grin he used to lure the guys in. Mitch could see Connors was clearly becoming frustrated because he wanted inside that hospital.

"No. Please, she doesn't do chaos. That's complete chaos." Connors pointed to Mitch's exposed tattoos before using his finger to circle all of Mitch's exterior. That stopped Mitch in his tracks. The driver, who had gotten out to take over driving, gave an *'oh shit'* and got back inside the backseat, shutting the door.

"Look," Connors started. "She's OCD to the max. She has a PhD in accounting, and she's very upset. So now's not the time. I gotta go." Connors wheeled around, slammed the door, and headed to the information desk as Mitch sat there staring. He wasn't sure how he felt about that encounter. Was he offended that a bunch of stuffed shirts didn't find him appropriate? Okay, no, not even a little bit. That wasn't news. He'd made the decision a long time ago to not be a part of the man's institution. Instead of driving them on, Mitch got out, walked around the car, and got in the passenger seat. The driver remained seated in the back.

"I can drive, but you know the way." Mitch stared out the front window.

"I've driven Agent Connors for years. He's always like that. Don't be offended," the driver said from the backseat.

"Not a problem. It's better anyway. I need to get badged up, access to the building. All that's going to take some time. Besides, I'd last about two point five minutes in that waiting room before I went stir crazy and drove everyone around me mad. This is for the better."

"I figured you for that type. You're a doer. It's gonna be interesting to see how you fit in around there," the driver said after he got behind the wheel. Mitch just looked at him. Yeah, he'd wondered that same thing. How would he fit in with a bunch of guys with sticks up their asses? He couldn't help but laugh at the visual.

"I've been assigned to you for the length of your time here. I laughed out loud a few minutes ago when I saw you get off that plane. You got here yesterday, right?" the driver asked as he put the car in gear and navigated the hospital parking lot.

"Yeah." Mitch cocked his brow, waiting for further explanation.

"Just wait until today. They all make Agent Connors look normal." That made Mitch laugh.

"I've been with the deputy marshal program for years, I've worked with the bureau before," Mitch informed the man.

"Not like this you haven't. I'm Derrick, by the way," the driver introduced himself.

"I'm Mitch." They awkwardly shook hands while Derrick drove through the city.

"See, right there. No one uses their first name around here. Everybody uses their title. It's good to meet you. Good luck, man. Here's my card. Call me, I'm on standby for you," he said, pulling to the front entrance of the FBI building.

"Thanks, man," Mitch took the card, got out, and started to reach for Kreed's duffel.

The driver shook his head. "Nah, I can hang on to your bags until I take you to your room, you don't want to take it in there." Mitch nodded, took his laptop case, and looked up at the massive building, before he started walking toward the front doors. There was considerably more activity than there had been yesterday when he'd arrived and, then, Director Carpenter had been waiting downstairs for him. Ignoring the fact he was the only one in jeans and a T-shirt, he entered the building through the front doors, only to be stopped immediately by FBI security.

Chapter 19

Cody woke about midmorning to a pounding headache. He opened one eye, then slowly managed to open the other, his phone lay on the pillow next to him. Damn, his head hurt. The headache had nothing on the cottonmouth drying his throat and tongue. He tried to muster enough saliva to help the situation. It didn't work. He looked around his darkened bedroom. The bright Texas sun was trying to peek its way through his dark drapes. Thank goodness Sheila had insisted on black curtains when she'd decorated his apartment.

He rolled slowly to his side and pushed himself up to where he sat on the edge of the bed, finally able to place his feet on the floor. Feeling a little nauseous, he ran his hand over his stomach. His fingers brushed across something crusty. What the hell? He looked down and saw the remnants of dried come flaking off his belly. He glanced up and noticed a dried, folded up sock laying on his nightstand. That confused him for a minute until the memories of last night came crashing back. Mitch, the phone call, and stroking himself off hadn't been a dream. *Fuck!* He fell back on the bed. His head and stomach immediately rejected the abrupt movement, and he felt like he might seriously hurl.

Navigating from his bedroom to the small kitchen happened excruciatingly slowly. He dug through one of the five cabinets until he found his Advil. Next, he opened the fridge and grabbed a cold Dr.

Pepper. He chugged the fizzy drink down in a couple of gulps, using his hip to rest against the counter, waiting for the medicine to kick in.

He rarely drank that much alcohol. Usually nights like those where reserved for playoff games or bachelor parties of his friends. They were never the result of a need to avoid thinking about a man. Cody looked down his chest and again saw the evidence of last night's extracurricular activity. What had he done? He closed his eyes tight as bits and pieces of the phone call surfaced through his fuzzy memories.

He prayed he hadn't embarrassed himself too badly. He remembered being asleep, barely hearing the phone ringing, and being shocked that Mitch was on the other end. Was it a booty call? Probably. Did he care? No... Yes, he needed to care! What was wrong with him? He'd been assigned a new job because of his steadfast dedication. The new promotion was an honor and another stepping-stone in his future to becoming a Texas Ranger. He would earn that Silver Star and six-gun reputation of being someone who could think on their feet and make the right decision when needed. Acting like a hormonal teenage girl over the new hot guy in junior high school was nowhere in that job description he'd just described. Besides, Mitch scared the crap out of him. He was all Cody could think about and that would never do.

Regardless of how he'd acted over the last forty-eight hours, Cody was determined to put Mitch aside and be the man he was destined to become, or at least die trying. And under the current state of his body, that might be sooner rather than later. Reckless, immature actions had no place in his future. His age was already liability enough to the DPS, he didn't want to come off as rash and irresponsible at such an important time in his life.

Besides, the guys he usually ended up with were cute, smaller-framed, and kind of preppy. They generally had office jobs, and could be talked into relationships. They most definitely didn't have dimples, tattoos, rocking asses, or hard bodies that could overpower him.

His oldest sister, Sheila, had always been his career counselor. She kept him focused, and he knew the real reason she stayed on him, but her message was still right. She cautioned him that the wrong guys could be a dangerous distraction and cause him to lose focus on his goals. Mitch fell in both those categories. No more games. Cody needed to get that man out of his life and his head back in the game.

Forcing himself, he pushed away from the counter and stood up straight. He ignored the jackhammer pounding in his skull and willed his stomach and body to cooperate. Grabbing his phone off the bed, he padded to the bathroom and called Mason first.

"Hello," his brother answered.

"I'm running behind, but I'm on my way." Cody could hear the wind blowing. He had no idea what was going on with the weather, but they had planned to herd cattle today. Move them from one pasture to another.

"We got this, man. We're just getting saddled up." Mason sounded laid-back as usual, even with all the work he took responsibility for at the farm.

"Nah, I need the exercise and mental break. Are you heading out to the back pasture?" Cody asked, turning on the hot water in the shower.

"Yeah. Call Jorge before you get here. He'll get you saddled up. Come around the east side. We're moving them west," Mason said.

"All right." Cody hung up the phone and stepped into the shower spray, hoping it washed away his hangover as easily as it did the dried come from his first attempt at phone sex.

Chapter 20

"Are you fucking kidding me?" Mitch asked as FBI security not only stopped him, but escorted him under almost physical force to a back room. Weapons had even been drawn as the group of eight to ten agents moved him through the facility. If he wasn't so pissed off, Mitch might have sworn he was in a Twilight Zone remake mash-up of the Stepford Wives, except incredibly well-mannered and beautiful women were replaced with Mr. Smith from The Matrix.

"Sir, you're to remain calm while we verify your credentials," Mr. Smith number one ordered, which pissed Mitch off even more. To add insult to injury, why the fuck was everyone calling him *sir*?

"I'm not a *'sir'* to you, Smith. I'm Deputy US Marshal Mitch Knox, here at the request of Director Carpenter. You already took my damn weapon, why the fuck am I going in here?" He'd stopped outside the room and swore he'd been to prisons that were nicer. He gave his best self-righteous act and all he got in return for that expression of indignation was a small shove from the back.

Mitch flipped around, fighting mad, prepared to take them all on, only to have the door shut in his face. Two Smith's stood right inside the door. Both kept their eyes on him, and Mitch kicked the door in one hard burst. The smirk he got in return made him swear when he got out, he would kick that guy's ass.

"Do you treat all invited guest this way?" Mitch yelled, fighting the need to punch something. Instead, he began pacing. Fucking FBI asshats.

"Only ones that walk through the front doors packing," the cocky Smith said, arching a brow.

"I told you idiots, Agent Tyler Connors's son had an accident. I've been assigned to work a case with him," Mitch replied through gritted teeth.

"And as soon as that's verified, we will take you directly to Director Carpenter's office where he can explain the importance of credentials when you come in here armed." Now Mitch really wanted to punch the condescending bastard. He could tell they thought he was absolutely crazy. Not only had they relieved him of his weapons, but also his badge. Stupid motherfuckers. And all Mitch could do was stand directly in front of them, take on their stance, and scowl just like them. It gave him pleasure to see he was taller and had more bulk than the condescending one.

He studied the idiot in front of him as though under a microscope. The FBI projected a persona of cool, calm, and collected. He'd never seen them ever break that façade, and they always followed the rules. They weren't given the free rein to work that his agency had. They all seriously had the same Mr. Smith wardrobe, which had to be tough to deal with. How could Washington DC men's suit stores possibly carry that many dark suits, crisp white shirts, and blue ties? What happened when a shortage caused one of them to wear a red tie? He supposed mass hysteria would surely ensue.

Right then, Mitch formulated a plan. During the duration of this assignment, he'd make these men's lives crazy. First Connors wouldn't let him meet the family, and now he'd been detained, all because of how he looked. His scowl grew fiercer and his hands balled into fists as they were tucked tight in his crossed arms. He held the stare of the arrogant one who wasn't giving an inch.

Minutes ticked by. He knew the routine. They didn't believe a word he said, but he didn't budge. He was getting under their skin. He could see the tick in the egotistic one's jaw. Mitch had years of interrogation training. He was special teams in the Marshals Service. Cocky Smith's tick didn't bother Mitch one bit. It actually gave him away. Mitch was getting to him, so he took a step closer. As close as he could without touching the guy.

"Spray tan or tanning bed?" Mitch asked, keeping his stance. "Natural never gets that orange." He guessed he hit close to the mark, because in the next moment, Mitch went sailing backward. The guy was on him. Not necessarily throwing punches, but the chest bumps meant business.

"Keep your fucking mouth shut," Cocky Smith cautioned.

"Or what?" Mitch chest bumped him back. If need be, he could take this guy, no problem. The poor Smith kid at the door tried his best to separate the two. It wasn't working.

"Or I'll shut it for you."

"Like to see you try, fake-n-bake." Mitch let the pounding happen. He never put his hands on the guy, but did give as good as he got in attempts to block the blows. He was an expert at stopping a punch, and in the process, giving a swift elbow to the gut. Besides, he knew how this was going to play out, and he shouldn't have egged the guy on, but as the other agents were pulling him off, they found his third weapon. The one they missed in the pat down. Stupid fucks could have been dead if he'd been a bad guy. So much for the FBI rules and procedures bullshit they were so fast to shove in his face.

"Let him go!" A booming voice broke up the scuffle. He recognized it as Director Carpenter's. And when he realized neither Cocky Smith, nor any agent in front of him was going after his third weapon, his demeanor changed. He smirked and blew a kiss at the supercilious one that started the brawl as he shoved past the group.

"He's Deputy Marshal Knox, here on my invitation and will be treated as a guest and colleague for the length of the time he's here," Director Carpenter instructed. Mitch didn't get to see the director's facial expression because he immediately went and stood directly behind the man and proceeded to shoot both middle fingers at all the Smith's in front of him.

"Knock it off, Knox. I know exactly what you're doing," the director barked, never looking back at Mitch. "Everyone in this room, as a matter-of-fact everyone in this entire building, better get along. No bullshit." His voice echoed in the otherwise silent room. Director Carpenter took a step back before he spun on his heel and headed straight out of the prison area.

"What about my weapons and badge?" Mitch asked, following after the director.

"You'll get them later. I want a briefing on what you found. Connors called. I missed the call, so I didn't get a chance to let anyone know you were arriving alone. They were just following protocol for anyone who would walk inside this building armed," the director said, leading him through a maze of halls until they reached the back elevator he'd used yesterday. Mitch guessed they were in about the center of the building.

"I didn't take the time to show you around yesterday. Administrative offices are on the fourth floor. You'll have access to the entire building. My secretary—sorry, assistant—has your access cards and ID badge. We usually put more thought into what we wear around here than that." He pointed to Kreed's *I don't cuddle...but I'll hold you tight while I fuck you* T-shirt that he now wore. "You'll have to find a suit coat to wear. It's part of the dress code."

The director walked straight to the elevator that just opened, bypassing all the people who stood waiting for its arrival. Apparently, they knew this one wasn't for them. He stared at the group as no one else entered the elevator with the two of them and the doors slid shut.

"My boss, Director Young, is going to sit in on our briefing. Connors has about an hour before he reports in. We'll see if he makes it in time for the meeting." Mitch knew that Director Young was as high as it went in the FBI. Senator Greyson would surely be dialing him directly, wanting answers.

He just continued to follow as he left the elevator and weaved his way through the few cubicles at the front of the office. Like everywhere else in this building, the offices were sterile and cold. No matter how many people they passed, no one spoke a word or even bothered to look his way.

What the hell was everyone's problem?

"These are my offices." The director pointed to a bank of offices in the corner. An older woman, dressed in a severe, formal business suit sat out front, her only acknowledgement of their arrival was a lift of the eyes.

"Gladys, meet Deputy Marshal Knox." She nodded and did manage a look at him, but that was about all he got.

"It's nice to meet you," he said, trying for nice.

"Here's your code. It allows access to every floor in this building. If it's forgotten, please report to bureau security on the first floor.

They will assist you. Please memorize the number and return this page to me before you leave this building today," she said, handing him a sheet of paper with directions on how to work the keypad in the elevator along with the four-digit number.

"This is your badge. You'll be asked to present it every time you enter the building. Since you carry a weapon, you'll have to have it logged and go through the formal procedures every time you enter," she said crisply.

"Yes, ma'am," he tried again. Who knew if Gladys here would be his go-to assistant during the duration of his assignment.

"This is the bureau's policy on the dress code. I understand this is a delicate situation, but as long as you are in this building, you'll need to cover up the tattoos and no vulgar or obscene clothing." She glanced at his T-shirt, then lifted her perfectly arched brows as her eyes caught his. "Director Young doesn't give on that breach. And what you're wearing right now, Deputy Marshal Knox, is completely inappropriate for most situations."

She stood and went to a door behind her. Several suit jackets and ties hung in the closet. Mitch said nothing to this. He understood most agencies frowned on profanity on T-shirts and didn't allow their agents to have tattoos, but never in all his years working for the Marshals Service had he been asked to cover himself up.

"I'll guess this is about your size," she said, pulling a jacket from the closet. He didn't reach out and take the suit jacket because he could already feel the fabric sucking his will to live.

"Wear the coat, Knox. It's not an option while you're in this part of the building," Director Carpenter ordered as he walked away from the desk heading toward the back of the building. Reluctantly he took the jacket, sliding the restrictive fabric on as he followed behind, quickening his steps to catch up. Director Carpenter rapped his knuckles on a big oak door and walked straight in to what Mitch assumed was the big guy's office. Mitch looked around and, to his surprise, the office was bigger than his entire apartment in Pineville, Louisiana. It may have actually encompassed the entire side of the fourth floor of the FBI building.

Director Young, the biggest dog of the FBI, sat behind his ultra-clean desk, motioning them in while ending a phone call. There was a large desk and credenza area, but also a small conference table that sat about eight people. Directly beside that, a sitting area. Two long sofas and several matching upholstered chairs sat around a large coffee table. Again, for about the thousandth time in the last two days, the opulence of how this bureau ran itself overwhelmed him.

Mitch followed Director Carpenter's lead and took a seat in front of the desk. "Sorry about that. That was Agent Connors," Director Young said while standing and extending a hand across his desk. He was shorter than Mitch had imagined. He stood to shake the man's hand.

"Nice to meet you, Deputy Marshal Knox. Thank you for taking on this case. Director Skinner's waiting on the other line to be conferenced in." There was no pause on Young's end. He punched a couple of numbers on the phone. "Tom, you here with us?"

"Yes, I'm here," Director Skinner acknowledged.

"Director Carpenter as well as Deputy Marshal Knox are also here. Special Agent Tyler Connors has had a family emergency. He should be available later this evening. Knox and Connors just returned from Kentucky, from what I understand." Director Young quickly got everyone caught up.

"Yes, sir," Mitch responded and tugged at the uncomfortable suit jacket he'd been given.

"Senator Greyson wasn't pleased with the interview he received," Director Young started right in, his tone changed, becoming a little harder.

"Knox, we need you to play a little more diplomatically when dealing with members of Congress," Director Skinner said.

"Sir, I'm not unsympathetic to the senator's plight, but the meeting and interview were bullshit. Two and two never equal five, even if you're in Congress," Mitch said. He could hear his own director sighing, but Director Carpenter was the first to reply.

"And what is it exactly that doesn't equal up for you?"

"I'm afraid none of this is. Connors feels like we should tread lightly here, and he's probably right. He clearly understands this bureau more than I do." Mitch gestured wildly with his hand, waving it around the room and then down the suit jacket he'd been forced to wear.

"Just talk, Knox," Director Skinner pressed.

"My gut says that we didn't need to waste our time in Kentucky. Our first viable lead was right here, and no one wants to see it. Look, the Greyson kid's a straight A student. He's well-mannered and well-behaved. He's Ivy League, wants his own political career someday, and he's openly gay, but yet still very respectful of his father's political views on the matter. Now, all of a sudden, in a matter of a few minutes, he becomes this unmanageable rebel and ducks out on his security detail to find himself kidnapped? He's not sixteen years old. He's a sophomore in college with no history of defiance. That tells me someone on the inside helped this 'accident' along." Mitch raised his two fingers, making air quotes, stressing the word accident.

"That was my initial conclusion too. I've met the kid a few times, know the family," Director Skinner added, backing Mitch up. It shocked him a little, but since he'd already gone against what he, Connors, and Kreed had decided and gone off half-cocked, pointing fingers without proof, he needed Skinner on his side.

"I called in some favors and got a full list of the security detail on the Greysons for the past six months. We dug a little deeper and nothing's obvious," Mitch said, sitting forward in the seat.

"Your information's reliable?" Director Young questioned.

"Yes, sir, it is, so we're in this holding phase. The kid's gotta wake up, or we need time to find out who on the inside had motive." Mitch sat back, let the weight of that information settle and then ran his hand through his hair as he thought about what more he should say.

"My concern, and what makes me toss this out with nothing more than my gut to go on, is that if that kid wakes and the person or persons responsible for this is there with him, then we might lose our chance of getting him to talk. Fear will hold his tongue, and out of all of the victims, he's the only one that might be able to lead us in a solid direction." Mitch ran a hand over the stubble on his chin. He could feel himself growing impatient with the silence in the room.

"Then we change the detail," Director Skinner said reasonably.

"Greyson's against it." Director Carpenter stared directly at Mitch. "We thought there should be a change when the accident happened."

"He's not thinking clearly. I'll take care of it," Director Young stated.

"I'd like every Secret Service agent assigned to the Greysons to stay in town so they can be interviewed." Mitch decided to throw that out there since he was already on a roll.

"Agreed," Director Young said as he picked up the phone, dialing a number while Director Skinner stayed on speaker. After a second, the phone was answered and Young turned casual and cordial again.

"Don, it's Hank, how busy are you right now?" Director Young asked. So his first name was Hank. Who knew? And "Don" had to be Don Smethsad, the head of Homeland Security.

"Hang tight, I'm on my way over," Director Young disconnected the call. "I'm going to talk to Don. See if we can find an easy solution to all this. Carpenter, come with me. Knox, you'll be shown the facility. If everything goes well with Smethsad, we'll begin interviews with Secret Service tomorrow." Director Young stood, speaking to everyone at once.

"Keep me updated, gentlemen," Director Skinner instructed, before he disconnected the call.

"Knox, get Agent Connors caught up when you talk to him again." Young gave him a nod and headed toward the door.

"Yes, sir," he said and pushed to his feet.

"We'll call the president on the way over to Homeland Security," Director Young said to Carpenter as the men walked out the door. Mitch found himself standing alone in the office still wearing the stupid suit jacket with no clue where to go.

"Deputy Marshal Knox, come with me." He turned to greet the person with the first pleasant voice he'd heard since he got there. A young woman stood in the doorway, and he gave her a slow smile. She was pretty and dressed properly according to the dress code, although that skirt might be a little short...

"Do you have my weapons and badge?" he asked as he got to the door.

"Yes, sir, they're downstairs. I'll show you around. I made you a copy of your code information so you can return that to Gladys. She's very old school," she said, snaking back around to Director Carpenter's office. Thank god Gladys wasn't around, so he left the paper she'd given him on her desk and continued to follow his new tour guide as they headed toward the elevator again.

"You can lose the jacket now, Deputy Marshal Knox," she said as the elevator doors opened and they stepped inside. "You know, you've caused quite a stir here this afternoon," she added, her tone very friendly as they exited the elevator one floor down. She walked him to the end of a long hall. Every eye stared at them as they passed by. She didn't seem to notice, but Mitch did.

"I'm Anne, by the way. I know Ellen," she said, and that caused him to give her one of his real smiles as he slid the jacket off, draping it over an arm.

"Oh great, that's just wonderful," he teased.

"Ellen said keeping you in line's a full-time job." As she spoke, her Southern accent became a little more pronounced.

"Where are you from?" he asked, his guess would be Texas or Louisiana.

"I started off in Texas, but landed in North Carolina. My father was military," Anne replied, giving him the first genuine smile he'd received since arriving in DC.

"The guy I'm seeing's from Texas. I could hear that accent in your voice," he said casually and then mentally stopped. Why had he said that? What in the world would have made him say he was seeing Cody? He'd had a make-out session and phone sex with the guy. That certainly didn't constitute *seeing* anyone. Did it?

"Figures. All the good ones are either taken or gay. You're both," Anne said, laughing at her little joke. He was still stuck on the potential Freudian slip regarding Cody.

"Here we are. This will be your office while you're here, but I think you met in here yesterday." She flipped a switch, illuminating the small, ugly vacant room. Funny, the room hadn't magically gotten any better since he'd been here last. "Agent Connors office is right next door. His regular partner's door is to the right." She gestured to the open door. He looked where she pointed, and from his angle, he could see someone diligently working away, dressed as severely as Connors. "Come on, I'll introduce you."

"Agent Paul Brown, I want you to meet Deputy Marshal Knox, Connors temporary partner," Anne introduced him. Brown looked up at Knox, then back down to his computer only to glance back up at him again with wide eyes.

"Oh my god, that's hilarious," Brown said, laughing as he dropped back in his seat.

"I know, right?" Anne said, leaning against the doorjamb, the same big smile on her face.

"You know, I might be getting a complex here," Mitch said, watching them both.

"Nah, it's not you, man, it's my partner. Have you not noticed how OCD he is? Just wait till you meet his family," Brown snickered.

"I've already been informed I won't have that honor. I tried to go to the hospital with him, but he wouldn't let me," Mitch shrugged.

"What happened?" Brown's demeanor changed instantly, and he was already reaching for his cell.

"His son broke a bone. Needed an operation, he'll be fine. That's all I know."

"I hope he's okay." Anne sounded concerned.

"I'll go now. Knox, it was nice meeting you." Brown was up and out of his office, shaking his hand as he passed by.

"They've been partners for almost three weeks. Agent Connors is one of the top in the field, but he's a little intense. Agent Brown's the only one that works reasonably well with him," she said, flipping off the office light and closing the door. "The doors lock behind you. That code you were given earlier will allow you access. Just punch it in the keypad at the door. Now let me take you down to the cafeteria and the workout room. Then we'll get your weapons."

Mitch followed along beside her, trying to memorize his way around. They stopped at the second floor. He followed her as she hit the highlights of every office and room along the way. The cafeteria looked more like a dining area at a mall. It had everything you could possibly want. A little farther down was a workout room.

"The bureau requires every agent to log in forty-five minutes of daily activity. They swipe their badges here. Director Young's a stickler about it. Since we're open twenty-four seven, each agent must abide by the rule unless they're in the field," Anne advised him as she pushed open the door. "So the entire facility's usually packed with men and women training."

"During office hours?" He couldn't believe it.

"Absolutely," she nodded.

"Damn. We have the same physical fitness criteria, but we aren't getting paid to work out, that's for damn sure." Okay, he had to admit to just a little twinge of jealousy over the FBI's sweet setup, but all this still wouldn't make up for having to wear the damn suits.

"I understand this office runs differently than most federal agencies. You'll see Director Young runs a tight ship. I'll be available as your assistant," she said, efficiently navigating them back around, now a different way. They took stairs down to security.

"We're here to pick up Deputy Marshal Knox's weapons and badge." She smiled sweetly.

"Right." Cocky Smith, the one he'd stood up against while being detained, sat behind the desk. That smirk was still there on that smug face, and damn if the guy didn't purposefully move slowly just to irritate him. Mitch lifted his brow and smirked right back. The agent was probably still pissed about earlier. They held eye contact, and Mitch wasn't about to back down.

"Okay, boys, the cock measuring contest is officially over. Play nice," she scolded, and that caused them both to look up at her at the same time. The smirks on their faces now aimed at her, and she gave one back and didn't even bat a pretty eyelash in the process.

"Deputy Marshal Knox, I want you to meet my husband, Agent Roger Covington. And from this point forward, he's here for anything you need," she said, smiling as she nodded at her husband. Mitch laughed when the guy looked over at his pretty wife and gave in, then lifted a brow in his direction. He decided he might end up liking this guy after all.

"Policy, you know…" Agent Covington said, handing Mitch his pistol, which he took and immediately secured the safety. He slid the gun into his waistband holster in the back of his jeans. The next one he did the same thing and placed the firearm in the holster attached to his belt on the side of his jeans.

"Right," Mitch started, preparing to do a bit of trash talking about the pat down he got, but Anne spoke up before he had the chance.

"Roger's always wanted a tattoo," Anne said, watching as the final items were handed to Mitch—his wallet, computer bag, and badge. He checked his wallet and badge before shoving them both in his back pocket.

"Oh, that's right. You guys can't have ink. Too bad." He shrugged.

"You stick out like a sore thumb," Roger grumbled, but was clearly inspecting the sleeve Mitch was about seventy percent finished with.

"Better than being a Mr. Smith," Mitch shot back.

"Yeah, listen, The Matrix and nineteen ninety-nine called and they want their joke back," Roger laughed. It was lame, but Mitch laughed too.

"So do I have a place to stay tonight?" Mitch asked Anne.

"Yes, that information's back on the fourth floor, and I'm afraid you'll have to put this back on." She pointed to the suit jacket he'd placed across the desk while holstering his weapons. All he could do was look up and roll his eyes. Was he absolutely certain solving this case was worth all this?

Chapter 21

Mitch got word that Director Young had been successful in changing out the Secret Service for the Greyson family. Connors called—he wouldn't be back until the morning. To kill time, Mitch somewhat set up his new office and managed to hit the bureau's gym. While in there, he'd actually worked out harder than he had in years. He ran ten miles on the treadmill, lifted weights heavier than he'd ever lifted before, and he'd done the workout wearing shorts and a too tight wife-beater he found in Connors's locker after he'd picked the lock.

Mitch made sure he gave his standard nod greeting to anyone who came close to him. Then set to outdo them on every level. His body would hurt tonight, no question there, but he hoped he'd gained a few points in this over-the-top, self-righteous group of men.

A sweat-soaked Mitch decided to shower in the locker room of the bureau before heading to his temporary home. After his shower, he went in search of his driver, who took him to a rental car place where Mitch rented a small SUV. From there he went in search of food and clothing. As he hunted for something to wear, he decided on Spencer's and carefully chose the most annoying T-shirts he could find, but decided to grab a leather bomber jacket to help hide himself when needed. Besides, it was October in Washington, DC. The nights were cold even if the days were still relatively warm.

Mitch found his hotel and busied himself, keeping his mind occupied as completely as he could. The hotel room was a suite, and he set up an office in the living room area. On a whim he printed a picture of every victim that had been brutalized by these crimes. He taped each picture above his desk and stared at each one intently.

What he hadn't allowed himself to think about since landing this morning was Cody Turner. He didn't understand what had him acting like this. He'd never chased anyone before. Actually, he never gave anyone a second thought. A good hard fuck and he sent them on their way. But Cody, damn, he wanted that cowboy, and he knew if he had him just once, he wouldn't be sending him away. If he had sex with Cody, everything would change for him. Hell, who was he kidding? Everything had already changed for him.

Mitch ran his hands over his short hair. Cody was clearly not as into him. But there was something more there for Mitch. Something more than the intense attraction he felt for the guy. He actually got butterflies in his stomach when he thought about that hot as shit trooper. He couldn't wait to talk to him again. He needed to know how his day went, and if he had enjoyed last night as much as Mitch had. He wanted to know Cody's favorite things and hear about his life growing up on a farm.

As he stared at the pictures of these men, many who had lost their lives, Mitch's heart sank. He got a gnawing feeling in the pit of his stomach. Men were being victimized. Gay men weren't safe with this psychopath still on the loose, and that included Cody. Vehemence gripped his body on a level he'd never experienced before.

There was no more playing. No more guessing and absolutely zero pussyfooting around this stupid politically correct game. The accuracy and brutality of the acts had him certain the suspect was very well-trained. Someone who had gone through battle. Maybe someone who could pay handsomely to carry out these type jobs against their enemy. All in the name of justice or righteousness or morality.

Mitch's gut twisted. He pulled up the short list of hate groups again and studied it for several long minutes before pushing away from the desk, completely frustrated. The answers didn't lie in that report. He'd known from the beginning the answer was obvious, but he just wasn't seeing it yet.

Instead of letting the anger manifest until he threw his laptop across the room like he wanted to do, he picked up his cell and ran his finger over the screen. He thought for sure Cody would have called him today. At least responded to the text he'd sent last night, but he hadn't. He picked up his laptop, still hanging on to his phone as he made his way to his bed. He turned on the television, lowering the volume to background noise and sat there staring at the TV.

Focus, Mitch. *You can't stalk the guy. If he's interested, he'll call.* Besides this was all fucking Colt and Jace's fault anyway. Just watching them together and seeing the love they shared made him want that kind of a connection. Colt and Jace knew what it felt like to have that someone special waiting for them at home. Someone who missed them if they were gone or laughed at Colt's corny jokes. They shared secrets together and cuddled up on the couch to play video games with one another. Someone to share the bed with on long, cold nights.

Hell, he bet they even woke up wrapped around each other every morning too. He had his head all stuck around wanting a relationship and then fucking Cody Turner showed up in his line of sight. Why did any of this even matter to him? None of it had before. He anchored himself against the headboard and resolutely sat the computer on his lap. He couldn't sit around hoping and dreaming, not when he had work to do.

~~~

Cody came through the front door of his apartment and was surrounded by complete darkness. He'd left the place closed up tight, the drapes all drawn and the lights off, when he'd left this morning. He flipped the switch, then went to the kitchen and tossed his keys toward the counter. The bright light flashing on immediately blinded him, and he heard his keys tumble from the counter onto the floor. Damn, he didn't even have enough wits about him to toss his keys on a counter like he did every single time he walked through this door.

The clock on the kitchen stove read ten. He'd eaten dinner at his sister-in-law's house tonight. The guys were so dirty from the hard day's work that she'd made them eat on the back porch. He got it. His mom had always made them do those kinds of things too.

He was almost OCD about his own cleanliness. So he stripped in the tiled entryway, leaving his dirty clothes and shoes lying right where they fell as he padded to his bathroom. He didn't touch anything but the knobs to the faucet and stood patiently in one spot until the water warmed. He stepped under the hot stream and allowed the water to do its job. After a few minutes, a steady beat of warmth began to soothe and loosen the knots left from a hard day's work. He shut his eyes and relaxed against the tile.

Today had been an eye-opener. He'd figured out pretty quickly that all those daily workouts hadn't prepared him for a full day of manual labor. And whatever his problem was with guiding and leading his horse needed to be worked out quickly. He'd been raised on a horse. He was going into the horse patrol mainly due to his handling skills, so he absolutely couldn't be making stupid mistakes like he had today. He made so many that his own brothers laughed and gave him hell over his rusty saddle skills.

In the beginning of the day, he'd blamed his performance on all the alcohol he'd drunk the night before, but as the effects of the hangover wore off, he was forced to deal with the truth. And unfortunately, the evidence of that truth stuck straight out in front of him right now. Ignoring the hard-on he sported, he dunked his face into the hot water.

His problems today weren't rusty skills or the pounding hangover, his problem related to Mitch Knox. No matter how much he tried. He couldn't focus on anything but him. How had this gotten so far out of control in such a short amount of time?

He reached for the shampoo and lathered his hair before scrubbing down his body. He continued to ignore his dick. As the moments ticked by, the ache only got worse, but he was not going to give in. After he'd cleaned himself, he turned the nobs and the water ran ice cold. *Shit!* He jumped back and shut the faucet off, completely frustrated as he left the shower stall.

Why was he acting like this? And just like he'd done all day, he started thinking about Mitch again. He dried himself and then ran the towel over his fog-covered mirror. He could see the evidence of a blush creeping up his neck and cheeks as he remembered last night's phone call. Mitch had so easily gotten him off. He had been asleep and drunk when Mitch called. All things considered, it should have taken him much, much longer to orgasm. Then he must have fallen asleep afterward, because when he woke, he found his phone still lying on the pillow next to his head.

How fucking embarrassing was that? Had he really fallen asleep with Mitch still on the line?

Cody tossed the terrycloth towel over the shower rod to dry. As he brushed his teeth and ran a comb over his short hair, he noticed his flushed skin was made worse by the hints of sunburn across his cheeks and nose. His arms and neck were burned too.

Much like he was doing with his dick, he ignored the sunburn. The bedroom was still dark, and he bypassed the underwear and went for the bed, flopping his exhausted body onto the mattress. The sheets were cold against his freshly showered skin. He tucked himself in, rubbing his legs together to build some warmth. His hand hit his cellphone. That was another thing he'd done today. He'd forgotten his phone when he left this morning. He never forgot his phone.

Palming his cell, he checked the missed calls. Those were all normal. He hadn't missed anything too important. Then he went straight to his text messages. There were two. He opened them, and his eyes stopped over Mitch's phone number. Mitch had sent him a text? Instead of opening his family's first, he tapped the screen and read the few words Mitch had sent him. The time of the text was five fifty-eight this morning. Okay, close to seven Eastern time. His heart did a flip-flop as he read the words.

"I enjoyed last night. I got off a couple of times before you fell asleep. Your voice is amazing. Call me today when you get a chance."

He dropped the phone and looked up at the dark ceiling and closed his eyes. He let himself reminisce over the few details he vividly remembered from last night. His eyes snapped open when his hand moved to his rock hard cock and his hips automatically arched for the touch.

"No…No!" He picked up the phone and reread the text. It came in fifteen hours ago. Surely since he hadn't responded, Mitch would get the hint and move on, right? Cody stared back up at the ceiling and then back at the phone. It was already ten thirty at night, eleven thirty in Washington, DC. Ah hell, he needed to man up, and end this thing. He couldn't leave Mitch on the hook like that. Cody decided on a text.

"I don't think this is a good idea." It took him a second before he finally hit send. There, he'd replied. Technically he should have called, but Mitch messed with his head too much. He chose the chicken's way out by sending the text. As he continued to lie there, he reasoned everything out again reaffirming his decision to stand strong

and stop all this non-sense. He was twenty-six years old. He had a certain time frame laid out for his life. He had goals. None of those goals included having his heart trampled on by a player who enjoyed the sex 'em and leave 'em game as well as Mitch Knox probably did. Distractions like those were bad if he wanted to achieve his dreams.

"What's not a good idea?" That reply text had him narrowing his brow. He thought he'd been pretty clear.

"Us, we're not a good idea." Cody explained quickly. There, no confusion in those words. Seconds later his phone vibrated, and he opened the message.

"There's an "Us"? You elevated you and I to an us, like a couple?" Okay, now that made Cody feel like an ass. Had he misunderstood Mitch's intentions? No, he hadn't, right? Oh, man.

"No, I'm not saying we're a couple, I'm just saying, we should probably not do this." Cody typed back.

"It might be all right to say "us". I like the idea, not opposed to it in any way. Probably should spend more time getting to know each other first though. I think that's kind of the more natural way of it. But you don't like texting?" Mitch texted back to him. Cody looked at the phone, read the words, and then re-read them. What? How had Mitch come to the conclusion that he didn't like texting? And then the phone began to ring in his hand. Glancing down at the screen, his stomach twisted and his heartbeat sped up. Mitch. He so didn't need this, not right now. He let the phone ring four times before he decided to answer.

"Hello?" It came out more as an uncertainty than a greeting.

"You don't like texting?" Mitch's smooth deep voice made his body tighten and his dick pay even closer attention. Fuck, he was in serious trouble here. Why had he even texted Mitch back tonight?

"No, texting's fine," Cody managed, even though his mouth went dry and his voice was a little shaky. Mitch had a way of making him like that, all hot and flustered.

"Okay. Texting's generally easier for me too, especially when I'm working. What about this *us* thing? I'm confused about that," Mitch said.

"I didn't mean us like that," Cody said, slightly at a loss for words.

"What did you mean?" Mitch sounded confused, and Cody didn't know how to explain. This was why he'd chosen to text. Texting was so much easier than a one-on-one conversation. And how did he make Mitch understand what he meant? How did he say that Mitch was too far out of his league? He didn't play those kinds of games. Mitch was too hot and too smooth….Cody was more of a relationship kind of guy. All that sounded way too lame and he closed his eyes, running his palm over his face. Why had he even texted Mitch in the first place? Mitch's voice caught him off guard. "Are you there? Did I lose you?"

"No, I'm here," Cody finally answered.

"What are you doing right now?" Mitch asked. Cody froze. He certainly couldn't say lying in bed, right? Yeah, no that would definitely be a bad idea. "Is that a hard question too?" Mitch laughed this time, and Cody gave an inner groan.

"That sounded hot. What are you doing that you're making sounds like that, I'd really like to watch." Mitch's voice had dropped an octave or two lower. Cody sighed and pushed himself up in bed, resting against the headboard since he couldn't find it in himself to just tell Mitch to stop calling him.

"I was thinking about going to bed. You know like sleep, and I saw your text," Cody answered truthfully.

"You just got my text from this morning?" Mitch sounded surprised.

"I left my phone at home today. It's been that kind of day. I forgot it this morning when I headed out the door." He crossed his legs at the ankles and pulled the cover across his waist silently berating himself. His stupid heart was connecting during his break-up call and that was what scared him the very most, the fear of a broken heart.

"I wondered why you didn't text me back. My ego was a little hurt today because of it. But I'm good now. So, what did you do on your day off?" Mitch questioned.

"I moved cattle. My family has a farm down by Austin."

"I figured something like that. You look like a cowboy. Do you have a laptop?" Mitch asked.

"Yes," Cody answered wearily.

"Can you get it? I'll Skype you," Mitch said. "Tell me your email address again?"

Cody paused and forced himself to stop this before it started. He opened his mouth to say the words he'd tried to use in the very first text, but those didn't come out. Instead he rattled off his email address. "Give me a minute."

He left the phone on the bed, went to the living room, grabbed the laptop, and returned to his bedroom. He looked in the dresser mirror to make sure his hair wasn't sticking every which way and debated putting on some athletic shorts. Instead he opted to tuck himself back in bed, covering everything below the waist. He opened his laptop and put the phone to his ear again.

"Okay, I opened the program, what do I do now?"

After a moment, Mitch's profile picture filled the screen. Oh fucking hell, the guy was hotter than he remembered. Need instantly slammed into his body causing his dick to tent the sheet. Thank god Mitch couldn't see that.

What the hell was wrong with him? He was such a fucking contradiction. He'd just relaxed on this bed and decided to end this stupid intense infatuation, and now he was answering Mitch's call on Skype. The reasoning side of his brain finally made an appearance. He clearly wanted Mitch. That was obvious. He just didn't *want* to want him.

As the call connected and video initiated, all Cody could do was stare down at the screen—Mitch reclined against his headboard with his laptop in his lap, too, and not wearing a shirt. Damn, the man was so freaking fine, with all that bulked up, tattooed chest showing. A detailed cross decorating his left pectoral muscle and the words 'Only God Can Judge Me' inked in black scroll across his collarbone stood out like a beacon against his olive skin. The man's dimples showed, big and tempting. All Cody could think about was pressing his lips to one of them.

Fuck my life.

"You can put the phone down now," Mitch chuckled. Cody slowly lowered the cell and kept his eyes on the screen with his mouth shut tight. Like he'd thought a hundred times since meeting Mitch, he was so in over his head. Cody closed his eyes at the thought and ran a hand over his face and through his still damp hair.

"We were talking about what you did today. Your family has a farm in Texas? It's like big enough to run cattle?" Mitch questioned.

Cody nodded. He'd lost count of how much land they still owned. Over the last ten or so years, the area where they lived had started to grow. They had slowly sold part off. He guessed maybe they still had six to eight hundred acres, but who knew for sure with his brain so jumbled.

"Did you grow up there?" Mitch asked.

"I did," Cody finally said something. He was proud of himself.

"I grew up in New York. I'm a Yankee, I guess," Mitch smiled. Those damn dimples were back. "Do you live at home still?"

"I have a place in Austin," Cody answered.

"That's right. I think you told me that last night. You live alone."

"Right." Cody couldn't take his eyes off Mitch. How in the world had someone like him drawn the interest of a guy like Mitch?

"I'm gonna tell you something… You sure look good against that headboard. That's a headboard, isn't it? Are you in bed?" The smile spread further across Mitch's face.

"Yes. I'm sitting in bed. Are you in bed?" Seeing that smile on Mitch's face and admitting he was in bed made his body tighten even more.

"Your voice got lower. I get it. I feel the same way. And yes, I'm in bed too," Mitch said, and Cody watched as Mitch rested his hands behind his head. His chest muscles flexing as he settled into position. *Fuck!* His dick swelled with every movement Mitch made.

"This, between us. It isn't very good timing for me," Cody finally blurted out.

"Is that what you were trying to say in your text?" Mitch's face softened as he stared back at him.

"Yes, I…I can't…" Mitch cut him off before he could finish his sentence.

"I agree. It's terrible timing for me too, but I can't seem to get you out of my head."

Besides the fact that was exactly the problem Cody was having about Mitch, no one had ever said anything like that to him before. He had no idea how to respond to those words. All he could do was stare at the screen. His heart picked up an even faster beat, his breath slightly panted, and he focused on Mitch's chest, once again reading the words 'Only God Can Judge Me' tattooed on his chest. He could already tell that was Mitch's motto for life. The guy was perfect, and he wanted to take him all in, so he let his gaze slide lower, as far as the screen would let him.

"Ah, you're killing me, man. And it's that right there. That thing you do right there. It's that distance you carry, but when you open yourself up and let yourself feel, you're hot as hell," Mitch said, leaning his face into the webcam as he spoke.

"What?" Cody wasn't sure he understood. Mitch paused, clearly thinking before he spoke again.

"You're telling me you don't want me, but you're eye-fucking me all at the same time. That's hot as hell. You're fucking gorgeous, Cody. Last night got me off like you were right here fucking me. I closed my eyes, and damn, I could just imagine the look on your face when you came." Mitch moved so his face completely filled the screen. "Let me see you, let me watch you."

Cody sat there waging an internal battle. The problem keeping him from closing the screen was, deep down, Cody was too drawn to Mitch. He wanted him in the worst way, more than he'd ever wanted any other man before. Maybe he should give in and do what his body and instinct begged him to do.

"Push the sheet down, show me what's under there. I need to see you, Cody." Mitch's voice sent chills across his body. Damn, he couldn't speak. He couldn't tear his eyes away from Mitch's gaze. His eyes were the most perfect shade of amber he'd ever seen, compelling and provoking. His body heated under their scrutiny. Cody found himself obeying the command and slowly started to push the sheet lower. Damn it to hell, he wanted to give Mitch Knox exactly what he asked for.

~~~

Mitch had known from the minute he received Cody's text that this was a pivotal step in getting to know Cody Turner. He'd played dumb, acted like he didn't understand the point Cody tried to make. Hell, he knew exactly what the guy meant, because he was usually the one making the damn excuses. But there was something so innocent and sweet about this hot cowboy that had him breaking protocol. He'd even teased the guy about rushing them into a relationship, but there was just no way to describe how excited he was to have Cody reaching out to him. Texting him, even if it was to tell him to back off.

Guy code dictated—if you aren't interested, you never respond. Even if it was fifteen hours later, Cody responded. That meant he was in, no matter what he'd said.

"Push it lower. I want to see all of you." Mitch watched as the sheet slid down Cody's body, revealing a flat stomach and treasure trail of dark blond hair that had Mitch's mouth watering at the promise of what was to come. That promise had him reaching for his own cock.

Mitch saw hesitation in the way Cody looked at him. "That's it, don't freak out on me now, cowboy, go ahead show me. Damn, I'm so fucking hard, Cody. You make me so motherfucking hard just thinking about what your dick looks like." His eyes stayed focused on the screen as Cody's perfect cock came into view.

"So beautiful, I knew you'd be," he groaned.

"Yeah?" Cody looked like a deer caught in headlights.

"Oh, yeah. Look at what you've done to me." He pushed he laptop past his aching dick, spread his legs, and sat the computer on the bed between them. He bent his knees, adjusted the screen, propping his feet on either side of the laptop. From Cody's intake of breath, he knew exactly what view Cody had. Fuck, his cock was already leaking just knowing that Cody watched him.

"See how hard you make me, Cody Turner?" He leaned back, his fingers circled his dick, and he started to slowly stroke himself. "Fuck, this feels so good."

"Shit, that's hot…I…I've never done anything like this before." Mitch could hear the nervousness in Cody's voice, but he hadn't run away and that was a good thing.

"You mean you've never done anything this sexy before?" He gave Cody a wink and his own cock a few long, slow tugs, for Cody's benefit of course.

"No, I guess not." A shy smile lit up Cody's face.

"Good then, I'll be your first. I'm so going to pop your online cherry." He waggled his brows and shot Cody a grin. "You want that, Trooper Turner?"

"Ye…yeah, I do." Cody's sexy blue eyes locked on his.

"Then touch yourself for me and don't hold anything back." It was Mitch's turn to groan when Cody wrapped his big fist around that swollen ruddy cock and started stroking.

"Mmm…that's it. I love watching you, Cody. So beautiful. I need to taste that gorgeous dick," Mitch murmured.

"Oh, god…" Cody's hand picked up speed, and his breathing grew deeper, but his eyes stayed on Mitch, and then all of a sudden he was out of the picture. Mitch could hear his moans, and he could see part of the headboard, but Cody wasn't there.

"Umm…Cody? Hey, Cody, I can't see you, where did you go?" He spoke as loudly as he could without yelling.

He heard a rustling of the covers as the picture on the screen moved, and then Cody's beautiful smile came into focus. "Oh, shit, sorry, I kinda moved and the laptop slid. I'm not that experienced at this." Mitch could tell Cody was adjusting the laptop. He must have placed it on the nightstand because now he could see all of Cody's big perfect body as he sprawled out on the bed and Cody's hand returned to his cock.

"That's much better, I can see everything and I like it. Do you like jacking off for me?"

Cody turned his head toward the camera and nodded. "I do," he said breathlessly.

"That's it babe, fuck your fist and pretend it's my ass you're driving into." Mitch brought two fingers to his mouth and sucked them in, getting them wet. He stopped stroking his dick long enough to reach down, spread his cheeks, and work his fingers into his ass. He pumped them in and out slowly, watching as Cody fucked his fist, his hips thrusting hard up into his palm. Cody's hooded eyes taking in every movement he made.

"Oh, god, Mitch. That's so hot," Cody moaned.

Mitch kept his fingers in his ass and pulled slowly on his cock with his other hand. He looked at the screen. Fuck, the look in Cody's eyes was enough to force his orgasm from his body. He bucked up into his rough palm, his eyes drawn to Cody's hand, stroking that big dick.

"Fuck, Cody…I'm gonna come." He withdrew his fingers from his ass and fisted the sheet, spreading his legs as he stroked himself faster. He fought to keep his eyes from slamming shut from all the pleasure coursing through his body. And mostly because he damn sure didn't want to miss the sight of Cody coming. He'd held off as long as he could manage.

"Come for me, Cody," Mitch roared as the first jets of come erupted from his cock and splattered against his chest. He rode out his orgasm with gritted teeth. His eyes stayed glued to Cody, watching him strain for release as Mitch emptied the last of his seed.

"Aghh…yes!" Mitch watched in awe as Cody tripped over the edge. Cody's eyes were screwed tightly shut, his head thrown back against the pillow. His full lips parted slightly as he mumbled incoherently. Cody's big body shook as he arched off the bed, and his stomach muscles contracted in spasms as that perfect cock painted his chest and stomach with thick ribbons of come. Cody was fucking beautiful when he came.

"Motherfucker, that was good," Mitch panted. He couldn't move, so he just laid there watching Cody and catching his breath. After a few minutes, Cody turned his head toward Mitch, and bright blue eyes opened, capturing his attention.

"Beautiful, just fucking beautiful," Mitch whispered, and that earned him a genuine smile. He reached over and grabbed his shirt, swiping it across his chest, cleaning himself up before repositioning the laptop on his stomach. "Damn, Cody, I don't know what to say except that popping your online cherry was…just so fucking hot."

Cody laughed at that and rolled to his side, fully facing Mitch. "I really enjoyed it too. So you must do this a lot, huh?"

"No, I don't. I mean, I have, but only once or twice just playing around on a webcam site. Nothing ever like this. This was fucking intense." He couldn't explain to Cody. Hell, he couldn't even explain this to himself. Mitch felt something for this guy, and the emotion actually scared the shit out of him. He'd never been so mixed up in his feelings about anyone.

"I'd have to agree with you, losing your online cherry's a very intense experience," Cody chuckled. "Maybe next time I won't be so nervous."

"So you're already planning a next time? Just let me know when. Better yet, why don't you fly here to DC and spend some time with me. I know you have some vacation days coming." The look on Cody's face changed as if he were truly considering the offer.

"I really wanna see you, Cody," he added sincerely.

"I'm not sure…" There was hesitation in Cody's voice, and Mitch knew what that meant, so he stopped him mid-sentence.

"Shh…it's okay. You don't have to answer me right now. Think it over," Mitch threw in before Cody could say no.

"I will," Cody mumbled. Mitch saw his eyes slowly closing. "I should go. I'm exhausted."

"Promise me you will really think about this, Cody, and text me in the morning."

"I promise. Goodnight. Thanks for this tonight," Cody said and lifted a hand to close Skype.

"Goodnight," Mitch whispered. Cody hadn't closed the program correctly; he was still on Mitch's screen as he drifted off to sleep.

He couldn't take his eyes off him or force himself to close the program. Cody snored and all Mitch could do was stare at the peacefully sleeping, gorgeous, still nude man that lay there for him to get his visual fill. And he did, watching Cody for a long time. He let his overactive imagination run wild with visions of them falling asleep wrapped in each other's arms. Cody would be so fucking hot in person. Probably the hottest he'd ever had, but he needed to focus, put all his mental energy toward solving this case.

As he stared at Cody, a yawn finally tore free. He had to get Cody Turner out of his mind, and there was only one way to do that. He typed Cody a Skype message, and he also texted him so he wouldn't forget.

"Come to DC for a day or two. I have a lot going on, I'll be busy, but I want you like I've never wanted anything else in my life. Don't fight me on this. Just come, you have the time off. I'll buy your ticket."

Chapter 22

Mitch surveyed the T-shirts he'd bought the day before, trying to decide which one might be the least offensive of the bunch. He didn't give a shit what the director thought about his choice in clothing, but Gladys, now that was a totally different story. Her evil eye carried across the entire floor.

Even though he'd had just a few hours sleep, not more than seven in the last couple of days, he felt alive, invigorated, and ready to start this day. He was positive he could talk Cody into coming to DC for a couple of days. So sure in fact, he abandoned his wardrobe search and left the clothes hanging in the closet to go in search of his cell phone.

He sent a quick text to his assistant in Louisiana asking her to book an open-ended flight in the next few days from Austin to DC and charge his personal credit card. He had no idea how much that was going to cost him, since he hadn't had to pay for a flight in the last six years, but whatever the cost, it would be worth it, of that, he was certain.

Mitch chose the T-shirt that had a print screen across the front saying, *'I'm not gay, but twenty bucks is twenty bucks',* and smiled, looking in the mirror. He'd save the one that read, *'I'd bottom you so hard,'* for tomorrow. Hopefully he'd be picking Cody up from the airport wearing that one.

Mitch opted for the shoulder holster today. He'd bought the jacket, but for some reason adding the outside, under the arm holster to the T-shirt just seemed all the more fun to poke at his temporary partner. And honestly, he knew he shouldn't. Connors's son was hurt. Released from the hospital last night, but still down for a good long time. He should be considerate, but whatever. He was in such a flipping good mood, and he loved giving people shit when he was having a good day.

Mitch looked himself over in the mirror once more and barked out a laugh. He looked perfectly ridiculous. He grabbed his jacket and laptop as he made his way out the door. It was a little before six in the morning, and Starbucks was right downstairs. A venti coffee and blueberry muffin would be absolutely awesome.

"Hey," Mitch said, getting on the elevator. Damn, he hadn't paid attention, and now he was going up, instead of down.

"Good Morning," the woman replied. She was just coming in from what looked like a very long, but good night. Her dress rumpled, her makeup smeared, and her hair still partly up, well, he supposed that was what some would call it.

"Good time last night?" he asked, with a lift of his brow.

"You know it. Made some good money, that's for sure." She gave him a wink. "No one tips like the religious freaks."

"That was more than likely keep-your-mouth-shut money, not a tip," Mitch chuckled.

"I'm here for the rest of the week. Room eight-oh-one. Come see me" she said, as the elevator door opened. She moved forward, then leaned against the frame of the elevator, half in and half out. "You don't even have to tip me, handsome."

He was absolutely certain that was meant to be a sexy pose and certainly might have been without the mascara running down her cheek and her lipstick smeared across her face. She stifled a yawn and straightened her stance. He gave a nod and wink, not mentioning how that was never going to happen. She stepped out, still looking at him.

"I love the T-shirt. It's the motto of my life," she winked again. He wondered if she knew she closed both eyes when she winked. Thank god the elevator door closed just as she dropped her key card on the hallway floor and bent over to retrieve it. He would have gotten a full shot of what was going on under that micro mini and no one wanted to see that this early in the morning, especially before breakfast.

~~~

Questioning the Secret Service sucked. Mitch scrubbed a hand over his face and listened as the fourth agent repeated exactly the same spiel as the others. He bit at his thumbnail and ran his fingers across his chin. Good cop, bad cop interrogation tactics didn't work on this crowd. Mitch sat in a room with the senior directors of both departments, along with legal counsel from each. It was all incredibly ridiculous.

Apparently things hadn't gone so well yesterday in Director Young's meeting with Don. They were now sitting in a neutral building, not FBI headquarters. They had been given very strict guidelines as to what could happen. Needless to say, the initial fun of the *'twenty bucks is twenty bucks'* T-shirt had worn off, so Mitch now sat with his jacket zipped up, a cold cup of coffee in front of him, and just let Connors do all the talking.

Apparently the guy hadn't clued in that every question was answered the same way—they were definitely pre-versed and rehearsed. If any question was deemed inappropriate, the attorneys stepped in, stopping the flow.

Mitch shoved back in his chair and stood. When he saw all eyes were on him, he realized he'd fucked up again. Well, nothing he could do about it now, so he started to leave in mid-question. Connors gave him one serious go-to-hell look and Mitch conceded, attempting to keep the situation civil.

"I'm just taking a bathroom break, please continue," he said, waving a hand toward the conference room table where they all sat.

Mitch left and headed straight for the elevators. He needed sun, even though a cold front had blown through. He punched the down button with his thumb, then punched the button again for good measure. Just a few days ago, he'd been so relieved someone picked up this case. Mitch had known things were going to finally get done. This was the FBI for Christ's sake. No matter how much trash talking he did, Mitch absolutely had respect for this division. These agents were badasses. Well, at least in the field they were hot shit. Here in

DC, they played a political game. Corporate politics meets political correctness at its finest. All the things Mitch totally hated.

The elevator opened, granting his access to freedom. He wove his way into the overly full box and listened as a little female beside him said something about this elevator being the only one working today.

They stopped on every floor on their way down, delaying his escape, but luckily after the second stop, no one got on. As he hit the lobby of the high-rise, his phone immediately started vibrating. He must have finally gotten a signal. He dug the cell out of his front pocket as he hit the front doors, surveying the area. He came to a halt a few steps from a water fountain.

Mitch scanned through the calls and then the texts, choosing Ellen's message first. The text message started out with her trying to be funny several hours ago and then ended with her declaring she wanted pictures of the guy he was willing to spend a thousand dollars on for a couple of days together.

A thousand dollars? For a damn plane ticket?

Mitch had always thought he made decent money. Well, sort of, his salary wasn't that great, but he didn't have to pay for much. His benefits were amazing. Reduced housing, car allowance, health insurance paid for… add all that together and he did okay for himself, but a thousand dollars for a plane flight? He thought about that for a minute and decided he would pay whatever it took to be able to hold that cowboy in his arms again.

Instead of letting himself overthink this, he forwarded Ellen's message with the arrangements straight to Cody. Who he had technically not even talked to today, although Cody promised to text him when he got up.

Damn. A thousand dollars on a guy that keeps blowing you off. Mitch Knox, what the fuck is wrong with you?

No! Stop overthinking. Cody's worth it.

He sent a quick note to Cody. *"Attached are the details for the flight we talked about last night. I don't know the exact specifics, my assistant made the arrangements, but I think you can leave tomorrow or the next day, even today if you want and return whenever you want. She can set up your dates if you want her to. Don't stand me up on this. It's been a pretty sucky day to have started so good. I really want to see you. M."*

Mitch hit send before he could talk himself out of the text. He sat and leaned back on the steps, letting the sun hit his face. His phone rang and Cody's picture popped up on his screen.

"You didn't seriously pay that much money to fly me up there," Cody stated as soon as he answered the phone.

"Yes, I did. I told you I would. Have you looked at your schedule?" Mitch asked, ignoring the money part and stood to move away from people after guessing where this conversation might lead.

"You spent a thousand dollars so I could come there and fuck you and turn around and come home. You're insane."

"I'm not insane. I spent the money because I wanna spend time with you. I don't have much free time, but I'd like those hours to be spent with you," Mitch said sensitively. And he meant every word. He truly wanted to spend time with Cody and learn everything about him. But he was also kind of proud of himself for not saying that he couldn't wait to be buried balls deep in Cody's hot ass.

"Just to fuck me." Cody ignored everything he'd just said and still sounded incredulous.

"Or you could fuck me." Mitch paused. Damn, he wanted that too. Wanted Cody driving into him so fucking bad. "I'm guessing you didn't go to your brother's again today since you're talking about sex so loudly?"

"Shit, man, you're killing me," Cody said ardently, and Mitch stopped in his tracks. What had he done now? He thought over everything he'd said. Confused, he finally asked, "What did I say wrong?"

"You paid attention enough to remember my plans for today." Mitch smiled at Cody's answer.

"I did. I told you, I want to see what this is that I'm feeling, why I'm so far out of my element when it comes to you. When are you coming?" Mitch asked.

"I don't know. I didn't think you were serious. I'll have to figure it out." Mitch grinned. That definitely sounded like a yes to him.

"Okay, well, sooner's better than later for me." Mitch resumed his pacing around the front of the water fountain.

"I don't have Skype sex. I don't do things like that," Cody replied, and Mitch narrowed his eyes to follow that train of thought. His guy could be really random at times.

"I know, you said that several times last night, while we were having Skype sex. And to my disappointment, you kept moving out of view at the most critical times. We'll have to get better at keeping you angled toward the camera. I loved watching you, though. You're seriously hot. I've already jacked my dick raw just thinking about the look on your face when you came. I loved everything we did. I just wish you had actually been in my bed so I could feel your shudder and smell your release," Mitch said, pretty proud of those words. He wanted to romance Cody, and he hoped that worked a little magic for him.

Cody didn't respond.

"If you come tomorrow, I'll have someone pick you up. And please text me this time, let me know something. I have a hard time waiting to hear from you. It drives me crazy with all the wondering." Did he really just say that? The silence that ensued let him know he had. Damn, that had sounded needy, but he didn't know how to get out of it now. He could try for witty.

"It'll probably be Friday before I can get there," Cody spoke up.

"That's fine, just let me know the details. I gotta go back inside. All that investigating needs an investigator you know." Lame, not witty at all.

"You shouldn't have spent that much money on me," Cody mumbled softly.

"Let the money go. I hope to see you soon. Bye." He disconnected the call and strolled back inside, much happier than when he'd left.

Chapter 23

"Little brother, are you sure you know what you're doing?" Sheila asked. Cody realized at that moment he shouldn't have told her his plans to go out of town. He just felt like someone should know he was leaving for a few days.

"I'm almost a foot taller than you, and it's just a weekend away. No big deal," he said, smiling. He hoped that reached his voice as he tried for nonchalant. He walked through the long-term parking garage at the airport, hoofing it inside as quickly as possible.

"Hmm….you're taller, I'll give you that. But I'm not sure about this just being a weekend away, Cody. It took forever for you to make those plans to go to Dallas and that's three hours away. And getting you to talk to me is like pulling teeth. Why are guys like that?" she asked.

"I don't know, sis." He laughed at her randomness, she was always like that.

"You know the Turners are a fertile bunch, and when we fall, we fall hard. You gotta stay strong," she advised.

"I'm gay. No chance of babies," he laughed again, sidestepping a woman texting and not paying attention to where she was going.

"You know what I mean. Washington's a long way from Texas," she said a little more seriously.

"He doesn't live there. He's just working there right now. He lives like in Louisiana," Cody answered.

"Still a long commute, and Louisiana's more backwoods than even Texas. It's not safe for you there," she shot right back.

"Sis, you're gonna make me say it, aren't you? I'm just going up there…" He placed his mouth closer to his phone and slid his duffel over his shoulder as he checked the flight board in the terminal.

To fuck his brains out! He just couldn't say the words to his sister, even as close as they were. Truthfully, Cody wanted this time with Mitch, just to be with him, however that might work out. Hell, he'd probably come home and never talk to the guy again, but at least he'd given this a try.

"You could easily find that here, if it's sex you're talking about. There's a guy in my office I've been meaning to talk to you about," she said, breaking his train of thought. "He's a cutie. I think he's just your type too. He's in our accounting department. Lots of stimulating conversation," she laughed. She'd never been overly fond of the guys he'd dated. Regularly making fun of him and them.

"No, I'm good. I can't even imagine what you think I think my type of guy really is," he said, standing in line for his security check.

"I'll snap a picture of him," she said.

"No! I gotta go. I'm going through security," he said. "Love you!"

"Cody, please be watchful and safe. I know you're a big guy and can take care of yourself, but that's a new place and…yeah. Promise me you'll be safe," Sheila said in all honesty. He knew she worried.

"I will, I promise. I gotta go." He ended the call before she could say anything more. Cody held his driver's license and boarding pass in one hand and had his duffel bag still slung over his left shoulder. He'd called Mitch earlier and left a voice message letting him know about the weather delay they were experiencing.

At this point, Cody refused to let his analytical or negative side keep him from boarding this flight. He'd almost let the weather delay be a sign from God that he shouldn't go, but he fought that too. As he made his way through the security screening, he tucked his phone back in his front pocket and began walking toward his gate. The farther he got into this airport, the less chances he had to ditch this weekend.

Besides, he had to keep his perspective. All this weekend really meant was a fuck-fest with a super good-looking US Marshal, while spending most of the entire day alone. It really wasn't much different than what he did here at home. Well, except he would be in Washington, DC, and his head was really weird about Mitch.

There was just something about him that kept driving Cody to do things completely out of character, like having phone sex and smokin' hot webcam sex. When they'd had video sex, he'd come so hard his toes cramped up, and he swore they'd heard him all the way over on Sixth Street when he came.

When he boarded, Cody tucked his bag in the overhead bin, refusing the help of the flight attendant right at his side. Mitch's assistant had contacted him today on her own and let him know she'd done some wiggling and Cody had been upgraded to first class.

He had an aisle seat big enough to fit his large frame. He smiled and had just gotten comfortable when his phone vibrated. He leaned forward and pulled his phone from his pocket, then slid a finger across the screen, pulling up the text message.

Mitch had sent a selfie giving a thumbs up. His grin stretched from ear to ear, accentuating his handsomeness. The message was short and sweet.

"Good, I should be able to pick you up myself."

That got his heart thumping. He was excited and nervous about seeing Mitch again.

"He's handsome," the older woman sitting beside him said. He looked up at her, grinning.

"Thank you." He looked at the picture again, and his stomach did a flip-flop at the thought of kissing those smiling lips in a few hours. "Yeah, he is, isn't he?"

"Yes, he is." The woman took off her sweater and placed it across her lap.

"This is my first time in first class," he admitted.

"Oh, it's such a better experience. You'll never want to fly any other way," she said, patting his leg as the flight attendant's voice came through the speaker. He turned off his phone, put his seatbelt on, and actually did have the best flight of his life.

~~~

Mitch stood in baggage claim, his hands tucked into his jeans pocket, his knee bouncing erratically, and his eyes glued to the doors waiting for Cody to walk through. The update he'd been waiting for had just come over the paging system. The plane had landed. It shouldn't be long now.

Shit, if he wasn't a bundle of nerves. He checked his breath—it was fine, but he decided to pop a piece of cinnamon gum in his mouth just in case.

He'd bought himself a dress shirt, the one he had on now, a long sleeve button-down that he'd left untucked. He didn't want to look like he was trying too hard, but he still wanted to impress Cody.

The first few passengers came through the door. Mitch lifted on his tiptoes trying to see if Cody had been in the first group to enter before the door shut again. The next few came through, and he stood on his toes again, this time seeing a blond head towering over the rest of the passengers making their way into the area. His heart picked up a beat, his stomach did cartwheels. Cody was really here.

He watched as Cody held the door open for several women and then some men. He never grew impatient, just nodded his head until someone relieved him of door duty. He was such a Southern gentleman. Damn that made Mitch want him even more than he already did. Mitch watched from the corner of the room as Cody looked around until their eyes connected and his heart stopped. He actually felt it stop and pause before starting the thumping shit again. He could feel his smile growing bigger. Cody stared at him from across the room with a huge smile lighting his face as well.

Cody was bigger than he remembered, more handsome too. They wound their way through the crowd, Mitch's eyes never leaving his, until they came to a stop in the middle of the room, facing each other, the baggage carousel close by.

The machine started, and Cody was bumped a little from the back as other passengers grabbed their bags, forcing him to take a step closer to Mitch. They were a little awkward at first. Mitch wasn't necessarily sure what to do, so after just a second's pause, he reached in, gently placing his hands on Cody's muscular forearms and placed a simple kiss on his cheek.

"I'm glad you're here." Mitch held Cody's eyes with his, meaning every word he said. He was so thankful Cody hadn't changed his mind. Mitch didn't miss the instant flush of color creeping over Cody's face or how his smile seemed to brighten. "Did you bring any other luggage?"

"No, just the carry-on." Cody looked down at the duffel slung over his arm as he answered. Mitch loved they were about the same height and build. All he could do was just stare. Cody smelled incredible and looked so damn good in those tight jeans, cowboy boots, and a button-down gray and black striped shirt under a black leather jacket.

Mitch couldn't wait to peel him out of those tight Wranglers. He finally managed to get his carnal thoughts under control and extended a hand toward the door, ushering the cowboy out of the baggage claim area. He let Cody go in front of him toward an exit door. When Cody headed for the wrong door, Mitch used that as an excuse to touch him and reached out for Cody's arm, stopping him from going farther. Damn, he liked the feel of Cody's muscles flexing beneath his hand.

"No, I parked this way," Mitch said and slid his hand down to link his fingers with Cody's. Cody was a little more hesitant to wrap his fingers back around Mitch's. He wasn't certain what that meant, but after a minute, Cody complied. Mitch walked a step or two in front of him, guiding him out the door as he held it open. The move was awkward and Mitch was forced to let go of his hand.

"I parked on the first level, in the garage." Mitch pointed in the general direction as he came up behind Cody. Mitch took the duffel bag strap off Cody's arm and dropped it on his own shoulder, then entwined their fingers again.

The evening air was brisk and cool against his skin, and he loved the warmth and feel of Cody's hand in his. In this moment, everything was fucking perfect. "Come on."

He pulled Cody out on the crosswalk and made them jog the last couple of steps as he dug the keys out of his pocket. Since all white SUVs looked about the same to him, he hit the lock button on the key fob and made the vehicle honk to pinpoint his rental.

He also hit the trunk button and raised the rear door, dropping Cody's bag inside. Damn, he'd really wanted to hold the passenger door for Cody, but unfortunately, they had too tight a fit to allow that. He remembered watching Colt jump ahead to get Jace's door more times than he could count. You could see how Jace loved that move by the expression on his face. He wanted that moment for himself and Cody and looked again to see how to navigate the move a little easier. The moment of indecision had Cody taking matters into his own hands. He released the hold Mitch had on his hand and went for the passenger door.

"Are you hungry?" Mitch asked and hit the car fob again, making sure all the doors unlocked. He slid inside the driver's side, starting the keyless remote while looking at Cody. "I'm so glad you're here."

"You said that," Cody said with a big grin. "And, yeah. I'm hungry. I was too wound up to eat before I left."

"Why were you wound up?" Mitch asked, placing the Tahoe in reverse and backing out of the tight parking spot. "Oh that's right, the weather was bad."

"It wasn't that. I was trying not to chicken out," Cody confessed, and that caused Mitch to look over at him, splitting his attention between the road and Cody. There was hesitation on Cody's face and questions in those blue eyes. Mitch wasn't sure he liked that and reached over and took his hand.

"Tell me why would you back out?" Mitch asked. They'd touched on this a little last night when they talked, and he knew how hard he had to pursue Cody to get them this far in the game. Cody needed to explain this further so he'd better understand what he was up against.

"I don't really know. I worked hard to get where I am. I've got just about another year before I can apply for the Rangers. I need to keep myself focused," Cody said as he turned to look out the front window.

"You keep saying things like that, but how does coming here affect you becoming a Texas Ranger?" Mitch asked, genuinely confused. He'd thought this might be Cody's problem, but he couldn't fully wrap his head around how dating Mitch factored into the Texas Ranger's application process.

"You're a deputy US marshal." Like that answered the question. It didn't.

"Well, I am, yes, and now you've confused me even more." Mitch glanced over at Cody, who didn't respond right away. "How does my being a deputy marshal factor into your job plans? I mean, I have helped the Rangers when they call. I've done a couple of arrests internationally with one guy, but I don't think he held any power or authority. I don't get the problem."

"I don't know, it's just...never mind," Cody said after a minute more of silence, letting Mitch know there was more to this than just the job situation.

"No, tell me. I really want to know," Mitch pressed. He needed to know what was going on in that pretty blond head of Cody's.

"Not now."

"Okay, when?" Mitch persisted.

"Just not now. Where are we eating?" Cody asked, changing the subject. So Mitch let the topic go and filed it away for later discussion. But Mitch needed that answer before Cody left this weekend. If he had to reassure Cody that he was discreet, he would.

"We can go out to just about any place around here, or there's a nice grill at the hotel. Either's good with me," Mitch said, watching the signs in downtown DC, making sure he hit all the right turns.

"The grill at the hotel sounds good, if I'm dressed all right."

"Cool. We can drop your bag off in the room and then go back downstairs to eat." Mitch watched as Cody eased back in the seat and relaxed.

Chapter 24

A valet opened Cody's door when they arrived at the hotel. Another greeted Mitch and took his keys after a brief conversation that Cody couldn't hear. He watched as Mitch clicked the back hatch, handed money to the valet, and exited the driver's seat, leaving the door open for the attendant. Cody took a moment to make sure his shirt was tucked in and straightened out the crease in his jeans as he made his way to the back of the vehicle. When he was almost there, he ran his hands across his short hair, making sure nothing was sticking up or out of place.

Mitch had beat him to the back, again grabbing his duffel bag and slinging the long strap over his shoulder before he took his hand again. Now, this was something new to Cody. He was totally out, he didn't hide, but he also didn't flaunt his sexuality. He never held hands with any guy. He certainly had never been kissed in public by a guy, even on the cheek.

On so many levels, everything about this weekend was already new to him. He tried hard to just go with the flow. Not be the kink in the chain. Washington, DC, was definitely more liberal than Texas, and he prayed he didn't stick out like a sore thumb.

Interestingly enough, Mitch didn't care at all. This seemed so natural to him. Mitch kept their pace, letting Cody go through the doors first even though Mitch led the way.

"That's the grill. The elevators are this way," Mitch said, heading to the main lobby of the hotel. The restaurant slash bar didn't look overly crowded. The lobby in front of the elevators, on the other hand, was packed. Apparently a wedding party had reserved ballrooms on two floors for the reception, and the actual wedding had just ended. There was a wait as all the guests filtered to the next location, and Mitch got in line toward the back of the group before turning to face Cody. They stood almost toe to toe, and that silly little smile that showcased those two perfect dimples spread across his face.

God, that smile did it for Cody. Everything about Mitch turned him on. His cock began to plump up in his tight jeans. When he reached down to adjust himself, he hoped the move wasn't too obvious to the people around him. Cody returned the smile, focusing on Mitch's bottom lip.

"Look what I'm wearing," Mitch said excitedly. Cody lifted his eyes to see a mischievous sparkle in Mitch's gaze. It took a second for Cody to realize Mitch was unbuttoning his shirt. That confused him, and he drew his eyes away from those perfect lips and that heated gaze to watch Mitch make quick work of the shirt buttons. He executed a Superman move and flashed Cody the T-shirt underneath the button-down.

Cody burst out laughing as he read the words, *'I'm going to bottom you so hard,'* written in big white letters on Mitch's dark gray shirt. He shook his head, smiling at the grin on Mitch's face. "I wondered what you liked. You know, we could always call room service." Cody's eyes were back on Mitch's.

"Oh hell," Mitch muttered, looking around. Cody followed his gaze to see a number of faces staring at them with curiosity. Mitch didn't waste any time tugging Cody away from the crowd. Mitch stayed two steps in front of him the whole way, until they turned down a hall and ducked into an alcove. Cody only had seconds to see the swimming pool restrooms were this way before he was shoved backward and Mitch was on him. That big body pressing him roughly against the wall.

There wasn't a sweet invitation on those lips, but instead Mitch came at him with a blistering kiss, taking what he wanted. His tongue probed and brushed against Cody's, and he answered Mitch stroke for stroke. Their mouths were fused together as Mitch ground his entire body against Cody's. Fuck, this was hot! He wrapped his arms around

Mitch, drawing him in tighter, loving the feel of their cocks pushed up against each other. Mitch left no question that he was just as hard as Cody as he ground himself against Cody's now rock hard erection.

It was only the need to breathe that had either of them breaking free. When Cody came up for air, Mitch latched on to his neck, sucking hard. He was sure to leave a mark.

"Not too hard," Cody whispered as he turned his neck up for Mitch. He did that a lot with Mitch. He said one thing, but his actions told another story.

"You're going home marked up," Mitch whispered before sliding his tongue inside Cody's ear. His hips rolled forward into Mitch on their own accord. Damn, he liked that tongue in the ear move. His hands caressed Mitch's back and up his shoulders with one settling on the back of Mitch's neck, keeping him right there at his ear.

"I want you like I've never wanted anything in my life," Mitch whispered. His warm breath caressed the moist trail he'd just made with his tongue. Cody shivered under the assault.

"Let's go upstairs," Cody responded, turning to take Mitch's lips once again. The kiss deepened immediately, and several minutes passed as Mitch completely rocked his world.

Cody felt deprived when Mitch pulled away. He used the strength in his hands to draw Mitch back down. Mitch's insistent resistance prompted Cody to finally open his eyes.

"We don't have to rush this." Mitch's face was so close that the sweet cinnamon breath he'd just tasted now filled his lungs. He loved that sensation.

"That's why I'm here, isn't it?" It made perfect sense to Cody, but he watched as Mitch's lust-filled gaze turned thoughtful.

"It's not the only reason," Mitch answered and pushed against the wall, tugging free of Cody's hold.

"It's not?" That had him wanting Mitch right back in his arms. He reached to try and pull Mitch back against him, but Mitch shook his head.

"You're damn sexy, I'll give you that." Mitch took a step back. "But sex isn't the only reason you're here, so stop with that line of thinking. I want you to go back to the grill. I'll drop this off in my room. If you go up with me, we won't make it out of the room and you know it. Good intentions or not." Mitch just turned and left him standing right there. By the time Cody got his wits about him and ran his fingers over his face and through his hair to get his arousal under control, he heard Mitch's voice a distance away.

"Get moving, cowboy!" Mitch said. Cody ducked his head around the corner, and Mitch stood at the end of the hallway. "And don't go in there and jackoff. Hold on for me," Mitch whispered loudly. Cody could feel the instant heat in his cheeks and quickly glanced all around to see who might have heard. "The pool's closed this time of year. The restaurant's that way." Mitch motioned with his right hand and then he was gone in the same direction, leaving Cody red-faced with a giant hard-on.

"Fuck my life," Cody said on a long groan. He did debate jacking off for a minute, just because he was painfully hard. He could easily relieve himself, especially if the pool was closed, but in the end, he agreed with Mitch. He'd wait. Anticipating what Mitch would do next had become almost a habit to him. One, he found he didn't want to break.

~~~

Mitch did his best to wine and dine Cody. He wasn't an expert at romance or seduction by any stretch of the imagination, but he wanted both those things for Cody. So he had kept them in the restaurant for a few hours by ordering slowly, plying Cody with alcohol, and insisting on picking up the tab. A relaxed Cody was a magical thing. The longer they sat in that oversized booth, the more Cody loosened up, and the more he learned.

They actually had very similar backgrounds. Cody's parents were still alive and married. He had several brothers and sisters, and just like Mitch's siblings, they were a fertile bunch. Cody's crew was slightly bigger, and he had a sister he talked about a lot—the oldest of the bunch and more career-oriented than the others. Mitch figured she had a strong influence in his life.

They were both the youngest in their families, although Mitch was seven years older than Cody. He'd laid that bit of information out there carefully. He wasn't sure how Cody would feel about his almost old man status. There were lots of differences between mid-twenties and early thirties, but luckily, he hadn't blinked an eye or started calling him sir or grandpa like he would have done if the situation were reversed.

The biggest difference in their life story was that Cody saw and talked to his family just about every day. Mitch hadn't seen his father and mother since Jace and Colt's Dallas wedding, and he had a hard time recalling the last time he'd seen his siblings or their children. But enough of those mental wanderings, it was time to get to the fun and games part of the evening.

"You ready to go upstairs?" Mitch asked, draining the last of his Coors light. Cody's gaze intensified, that sexy-ass blush appeared, and he nodded. Mitch raised his hand for the waitress, and they both dug in their back pockets for their wallets.

"I got this, you're my guest," Mitch said, opening up his stuffed wallet and fingering through the cards until he found his American Express.

"I need to cover this. That flight—" Mitch cut Cody off.

"Enough with the flight. This is my weekend. When I come to Texas, you can pay." He laid the card on the table as they waited for the waitress to bring their check.

"When you come to Texas, you can just stay at my place," Cody said. He drained his Bud Light, and set the empty bottle back on the table.

"See? That's you paying," Mitch said casually, as though they were actually planning for the future. He hoped that held throughout the weekend. So far, they fit well. Washington, DC, was a gay-friendly location. They had been easily accepted in the restaurant. He even saw guys from the bar checking Cody out. It made him proud that Cody only seemed to have eyes for him. He hoped that held too.

"Not the same thing," Cody argued.

"You can charge this to your room. I just need your signature and room number," the waitress said.

"Nah, I got this one." He handed over his credit card wanting to buy Cody's meal, not put it on the FBI's tab. A minute later he added the tip in and signed his name across the bottom of the receipt. He scooped up his card and receipt, shoving them inside the dollar bill slot of his wallet to deal with later.

"Thank you," he nodded to the waitress, before sliding out of the booth.

"What were you saying?" he asked, waiting for Cody to stand.

"Who knows? Nothing worth the argument, I guess," Cody answered, giving him a smile that set his dick on fire. Damn, Cody turned his shit on.

"Come on, this way." Mitch extended an arm. For the first time, he got why Colt did all those seemingly romantic gestures for Jace. Colt didn't do it to make Jace feel good. He doubted Colt even realized that part. It rocked Mitch's world to place his hand on the small of Cody's back and guide him out of the restaurant. This was a two-part deal. He got one hell of a rewarding view of Cody's ass as he walked in front of him and everyone in this place knew Cody had come here with him.

"Those elevators?" he asked. Cody suddenly turned around while Mitch stared down at his perfect bubble butt.

"I'm sorry what?" Mitch looked up.

"Were you just staring at my ass?" Cody asked, coming to a complete stop.

"I think you'll probably catch me staring a lot this weekend. Front or back, doesn't matter to me." Mitch laughed at his small joke, dropping his eyes to Cody's package that he swore expanded under his gaze.

"Shit, you're killing me. Come on, Casanova," Cody said, pulling him along across the foyer.

Chapter 25

Mitch held the hotel room door open for Cody. Only then did it occur to him that Mitch purposely opened his doors, letting him go first. Cody's eyes collided with Mitch's as he braced the door with his foot and extended an arm. The gesture was incredibly endearing, and he couldn't remember ever being on the receiving end like this until tonight.

The uncertainty Cody had been holding on to broke free as he stepped fully inside the room. The emotions that flooded were strong and created their own kind of panic. More than just physical need, this deep attraction for Mitch had him off balance. He needed a moment to deal, just to get some breathing room. Cody could so easily fall for Mitch. Hell, truthfully he was already tumbling and that freaked him out completely.

The intensity of those thoughts had him taking several steps in front of Mitch. He found the bedroom with his bag sitting on the end of bed, and he headed there. The duffel could be enough distraction to give him the minute he needed to regroup and set his head straight.

He stood over his things and closed his eyes. His hands absently worked the zipper open with his back to the door. Allowing himself to finally admit his feelings about Mitch had been almost a spiritual awakening. His sister had been absolutely right about what a distraction love could be, but in return for his single-minded focus on his career, he'd become an incredibly lonely guy.

Stop being a girl, Cody chastised himself and began to tug his shirt over his head.

"Let's take this slow," Mitch said, and Cody looked over his shoulder, seeing Mitch propped up against the door frame. "Unpack, I left a drawer for you. And there are hangers in the closet. Or you don't have to do any of that, whatever you want. I'll be in the bathroom," he said, disappearing through a side door Cody had missed when he'd walked in. How the hell had he missed that door? He was trained to observe his surroundings. A soft groan escaped him as he sat on the end of the bed. What had he gotten himself into?

~~~

Mitch closed his eyes as he inserted two lubed fingers slowly into his ass, conjuring a mental image of Cody while he worked himself from behind. He should have asked Cody how he liked sex. He shouldn't just assume, but he thought he'd made his position clear when he'd Superman'd the T-shirt for Cody at the elevators. He didn't usually bottom, but all he could think of since their Skype sex was having Cody top him. If Cody wanted first crack bottoming, he'd still be ready for later because he was completely certain there would be a round two.

Working himself open, massaging himself, so he would be ready for Cody wasn't turning out like he'd planned. He kept thinking about Cody's big body pumping into his, and that image had his knees going weak and him already teetering on the brink. He couldn't ever remember being this close to climax just from stretching himself, but instead of stroking off like he normally would, he clamped his free hand around his cock and opened his eyes, pushing Cody's image from his mind. He damn sure didn't want to shoot his load on the bathroom floor before he'd even touched his cowboy.

Minutes later, Mitch stopped. He washed his hands and brushed his teeth. In a round of nervous energy waiting for Cody to arrive, he'd gotten as clean as he could get and all nice and groomed too. After a second more, he ran a brush over the top of his head where his hair was the longest and then brushed his teeth again.

He left his underwear off, put the jeans back on, leaving the button open and, at the last minute, added the T-shirt back on with a smirk, just in case Cody needed a reminder.

He checked his appearance one last time and left the room, hoping he hadn't taken too long.

~~~

Cody sat on the sofa in the living room, unsure what to do while Mitch was in the restroom. He had his arm over the back of the sofa with his booted foot crossed over his knee. He'd turned on the television, keeping the volume low but his attention trained on the door separating the two rooms. Mitch was right through that door.

When the door opened, Mitch came out looking hot as hell. He wore that T-shirt, his jeans unbuttoned and his feet bare. The long-sleeve button-down shirt had hidden Mitch's sheer bulk. His massive arms, one with an intricate tribal sleeve and the other decorated with an inked serpent that coiled around his bicep and ran down his forearm, attracted Cody's attention. He'd caught glimpses of his body in the darkened club, and he'd seen him on Skype, but to have this in front of him now, had his hands itching to pull that T-shirt off and explore every inch of the broad, marked flesh.

"Do you need the restroom?" Mitch asked. Cody'd left his toiletries on the dresser. He should at least brush his teeth. Besides, if Mitch could play things cool, so could he.

"Yeah, I do," Cody said, rising, stretching his body as he stood. He flipped off the TV with the remote control and headed toward Mitch who didn't move out of his way.

"Don't take as long as I did," Mitch said, drawing Cody up against him. Mitch didn't try to kiss him which might have been a testament to his breath, but he did place both hands on his hips and grind forward. He matched the move. Only then did Mitch press a soft kiss to his lips.

Cody simply pulled away and stepped into the bedroom. If Mitch could control himself, then he could too. "I'll be back." He grabbed his stuff and headed inside the bathroom.

~~~

Mitch undressed completely, tossing his clothes over the back of a chair. He flipped on the bedside lamp and turned off all the other lights throughout the suite. He'd stashed a new box of condoms and a bottle of lubricant in the bedside table, so he laid those out in easy reach and climbed on the big bed.

He stretched out on top of the cool blankets, then decided to crawl under the folded down bedspread. He wanted to look hot and sexy for Cody. He rested back against the headboard, laid there a second before he got up, folded all the blankets down, and grabbed only the sheet, draping it across his waist. He anchored himself back against the headboard again, this time placing one arm casually behind his head.

Right when he was about to reposition again, the door opened up. Now he was committed to the pose. Mitch looked up as Cody came toward the light. He was still dressed, and when his eyes landed on Mitch, Cody mouthed the word *fuck* and automatically began tugging the T-shirt over his head as he toed off his boots at the same time.

Mitch stroked himself as he watched Cody hurriedly toss the garment over the chair and kick his boots out of the way toward the end of the bed. Just as the sexy trooper went to unbutton his jeans, Mitch was up off the bed. "Hang on, let me do that."

Mitch dropped to his knees in front of Cody. The urgency of Cody's loud groan filled the room as Mitch reached for the button on the jeans. Working quickly, he unfastened the Wranglers and tugged the zipper down. He glanced up, taking in all the ridges and depressions in Cody's chest and stomach. His gaze lingered, before sliding down Cody's six-pack, following the dark blond treasure trail that disappeared into the jeans he worked to rid Cody of.

"I need to taste you, Cody." After pushing the jeans down those thick, muscular thighs, he pressed a kiss against the pistol tattooed on Cody's hip, then buried his face in Cody's brief-covered groin, inhaling the clean, musky scent that was all Cody Turner. Mitch rubbed his face against the material preventing him from tasting Cody's naked flesh. The movement had Cody's cock lengthening against his cheek.

"Fuck, cowboy," he gasped, and his own cock reacted with a jerk as he slid his fingers in the waistband of Cody's briefs and tugged them, along with the denim down his legs. Cody placed his hands on

Mitch's shoulders to keep his balance as he stepped out of the jeans and kicked them to the side.

Fingers slid across his scalp and fisted in his short hair as he took in the sight of Cody's perfectly cut and blushing with color cock. He wrapped his fingers around Cody and slowly stroked him from base to tip. Mitch had seen his share of dicks, but Cody's had to be the most perfect he'd ever laid eyes on. He lifted his gaze to find Cody staring down at him, his blue eyes hooded with lust.

"Your cock's so fucking beautiful, Cody. So thick and perfect, and I'll bet you taste as delicious as you look." Mitch lowered his head, whispering against Cody's skin while he placed soft kisses along his thighs. He tongued the tattoo covering Cody's hip bone. Mitch's hand worked Cody all the while, stroking him, as he nibbled his way lower and sucked one of Cody's balls in his mouth.

Cody widened his stance as Mitch licked and mouthed the soft sac between the hot trooper's legs. Cody's thighs quivered in response to Mitch's lips as he moved in to sample his cock. He took his time tasting Cody, exploring every vein on that thick shaft before tonguing the cowboy's perfect slit. Cody's essence burst across his palate. He loved the sweet and salty bitterness of Cody's arousal filling his senses. He sucked on the flared crown of Cody's dick, lapping at the pre-come beading at the tip.

"Damn, baby, you do taste fucking delicious." Mitch dropped his head and devoured Cody in one swift motion, loosening his jaw as he swallowed Cody to the back of his throat. Cody gasped, and the fingers in his hair tightened, stinging his scalp. Cody's hips thrust forward driving that long dick farther down his throat, cutting off his air. *Fuck yes!* His throat constricted around the decadent invasion. Cody quickened his rhythm, thrusting deep, and he let the hot cowboy plunder his mouth.

Only a few minutes passed before Cody's cock swelled against his tongue. He was close. Mitch felt Cody's balls draw tight against his body. But since he had other plans in mind, he used his hand and squeezed the base tightly then reluctantly pulled off of Cody's cock.

"You can't come, not yet...I want you in me." He didn't care about the desperation in his voice. Mitch needed Cody in him, the sooner the better.

"Mitch?" Cody's ragged breath hitched on what sounded like both a question and a plea.

He stood and took Cody's mouth with his, breathing heavily as he spoke. "Fuck me, Cody, I want you inside me."

"I thought you…" Cody started, but Mitch cut him off.

"Didn't you pay attention to my shirt, Turner? For a trooper, you aren't very observant, are you?" Mitch grinned and watched the corners of Cody's mouth tip up as the man thought over what he'd just said.

"I did but…but you don't wanna fuck me?" Cody's head tilted to one side. Mitch caught his bottom lip with his teeth as those bright blue eyes questioned him.

"Later. Right now, I want this in me." He gripped Cody's dick, squeezing tightly, making his intentions known. Cody groaned, and in less than a heartbeat, the cowboy's mouth was fused to his. The kiss was anything but gentle. Their tongues tangled, twisting, as Cody's hands slid around his back and down his ass, forcing them together. Mitch rocked into Cody's hips, his erection brushing roughly against Cody's. They both moaned at the contact.

Cody pushed him against the wall, pinning him, easily holding Mitch in place as he ravished his mouth. Cody tore his lips away and buried them against the side of his neck. Mitch heard a deep inhale right before his cowboy latched on to his neck. Cody sucked hard at the tender skin and ground sensually against his cock. The sweet pain of Cody marking him traveled straight to Mitch's balls. He hissed at the sting of Cody's teeth sinking into his skin and the feel of the rock hard arousal nudging his.

"Yes, god, yes." He wanted Cody in him right now. He lifted his head offering his neck as he thrust his hips forward. Cody's movements were as heated and frenzied as his.

"I do want your ass, Mitch," Cody growled against his ear. "So fucking bad."

Cody's warm palm tightened around his aching dick, and those full, eager lips took his again. He almost came from the rough friction Cody unleashed on his cock. Mitch's head spun from the fevered kiss, all teeth and tongues, lips, heat and need. His stomach flip-flopped, and he couldn't ever recall a kiss as passionate as this. Mitch felt as if Cody were kissing him with his entire body.

Minutes passed as Mitch surfaced enough to find Cody guiding him toward the bed. He stopped when the edge of the mattress hit the back of his knee. Mitch wrapped his arms around Cody and fell back, pulling the cowboy down with him.

Mitch scooted toward the middle of the bed, and Cody crawled up his body, kissing him, as he settled that big body between his open legs. Cody sat back on his heels, stroking his own dick, regarding him curiously. And damn, Mitch enjoyed the show.

"You make me so damn crazy, Cody."

"Do I?" Cody smiled, let go of his dick, and lowered to his stomach. Cody kept his eyes on Mitch as he wrapped his hand around Mitch's cock and dropped his head, licking up him like a lollipop before circling his leaking tip with his warm tongue.

"Uh-huh." Mitch couldn't take his eyes off the beautiful blond lapping playfully at his dick.

Cody's warm wet mouth engulfed him to the root. *Holy mother of god!* The cowboy evidently didn't have any sort of gag reflex to speak of. Mitch thrust his hips up, and Cody took every inch of him. He fucked into Cody's warm mouth, loving the wet heat surrounding him.

"Shit, babe, that's one sweet mouth you've got on you. Damn, I think I'm falling in love, Cody Turner." Cody pulled off his dick and grinned up at him.

"Well, if you like that, Deputy Marshal Knox, then this is gonna have you asking for my hand in marriage. Now roll over." Cody swatted at his thigh. Mitch complied and rolled to his stomach.

"Lift up your ass for me," Cody demanded and moved to the edge of the bed, sitting up on his shins. Cody held onto Mitch's hip as he lifted and went to all fours. Widening his knees, he offered his ass to Cody. The hot trooper smoothed his hands down Mitch's back and over the curve of his ass, before kneading the globes and spreading him wide.

"You're so damn hot," Cody rumbled and buried his face between Mitch's ass cheeks. His warm tongue probing and licking with vigor at his most sensitive area. Cody reached forward, his fingers circling Mitch's shaft and began to stroke. Mitch couldn't help but shudder as Cody stiffened his tongue and began probing him with purpose.

The stroking on his dick never stopped. Mitch was in fucking heaven, and he never wanted this to end. Cody gave him a few long licks before thick fingers circled then tapped at his entrance. The tip of one of those torturous fingers barely slipped inside, stealing his breath.

"Mmm…you're already relaxed for me," Cody purred. Mitch nodded and rocked his hips back, needing badly for the cowboy to breach him, to give him more.

"I opened myself for you. I'm ready… I need you now," he groaned as Cody's fingers pressed inside and began working him further open.

"Without me?" Cody leaned over and pressed wet kisses down his spine.

"Uh-huh." All he could think about were the big fingers buried in him, spreading him, and Cody's groin rubbing his butt cheek and the back of his thighs. The light fuzz that covered Cody's leg brushed against his and drove him absolutely mad.

"Damn, Mitch, that's hot and all, but why?" Cody questioned, still leaning over him. His breath caressed his sensitive skin as he spoke the words, sending a shiver racing down to his ass. The attention and sensations of the scene made it incredibly hard to think.

"When?" Cody asked as he curled his fingers. Damn, that cowboy knew exactly what he was doing.

"In the bathroom. I didn't wanna wait," Mitch replied honestly. Cody picked up the pace, and he rode those fingers, pressing his ass back as Cody pushed in and out, twisting his fingers, scraping that delicious knot. He just about lost his load right then.

"I'm fucking almost there, but I need to come with your dick in my ass, not your fingers, cowboy," Mitch panted breathlessly with desire.

"Demanding, aren't you?" Cody chuckled and withdrew his fingers. Mitch turned his head and looked over his shoulder, watching as Cody rolled the condom down his impressive dick. Mitch's ass clenched in anticipation, and his dick wept with need. He had waited far too long for this moment.

If he had to admit it, he was a little nervous about Cody's girth, but he really wanted to bottom for his cowboy. He'd stretched himself in the bathroom earlier for that very reason. Out of the corner of his eye, he watched Cody reach for the lube lying next to him and drizzle the liquid onto his cock. Mitch bit his lip as Cody took himself in hand, dragging the blunt head of his dick up and down his crevice.

"Is this what you want?" Cody's cock pressed against his hole, barely breaching him. He tried to push back and impale himself with the heat of that hard prick.

"Not so quick, Deputy Marshal," Cody teased, then slapped his ass. *Fuck!* That made his dick twitch.

"God, Cody, stop teasing and fuck me. Hard," he groaned. He couldn't wait another second, he needed to be fucked good and proper, and Cody was big enough to give him exactly what he craved.

Cody gripped on to his hips, and in one solid move, he slammed into him, burying his cock to the hilt in a single smooth thrust. Mitch's ass burned. He reared up as he adjusted to the sudden, but welcomed, invasion. The pain morphed into sweet pleasure as Cody began to move in and out. He threw his head back at the breathtakingly full sensation in his ass.

"So tight. Mitch…" Cody uttered on a sigh. He drew back and thrust into him again.

Cody's hands gripped his hips, driving Mitch forward then tugging him backward straight onto his cock, rocking into him with purpose. He was sure to have finger-shaped bruises with as deep as they sank into his skin. Cody rode his ass, hard and fast, causing unintelligible sounds to fall from his lips as the warmth spread up his spine.

Cody wrapped his arms around Mitch and pulled his upper body up, drawing him tightly against his chest so he was no longer balancing on his hands. Mitch's knees and the big cowboy held all his weight now.

"So fucking good." Cody's uneven breaths caressed his ear. He sat back on his calves, pulling Mitch with him, bucking hard and fast up into him. All Mitch could do was hang on for the mind-numbing ride. Cody was the first guy that had ever fucked him like this, and he loved the feel of all that power and muscle holding him in place. Mitch pressed back, losing himself in the sensations.

"Fuck, yes…" Mitch hissed.

Cody slid his hand around his neck, drawing his head back as his hips pistoned wildly in and out of his body. Their grunts and moans filled the room.

"Kiss me," Cody panted.

"Yes." Mitch angled his head. Cody nipped, then licked at the seam of his lips, drawing him in. That hot mouth moved over his, and he parted his lips as Cody's tongue plunged inside and tangled with his. Their teeth knocked together, and Mitch lost his mind.

A hard thrust sent Cody's cock sliding over his prostate, and he just about came off the bed in ecstasy. His balls tightened and churned as the pleasure spread from his ass and bloomed in his groin. He rocked himself back against Cody, chasing his orgasm with focus. And it wouldn't take long with the way Cody kept hitting against his spot with every roll of his hips.

Cody wrapped his free hand around Mitch's cock and pulled, jerking him off with fast unsteady movements.

"Come for me, Mitch," Cody whispered huskily against his ear. He licked a wet trail down his neck, then sank his teeth into Mitch's shoulder. His body tensed at Cody's command, his ass clenched around Cody's cock, and his dick jerked in obedience. Intense pleasure shot through him as he emptied his balls into Cody's fist in multiple mind-numbing surges. Thick ribbons of come escaped Cody's grip and splattered in warm globs against his stomach while his heart pounded wildly in his chest and his body quivered from release.

"Oh god, yes...Mitch!" Cody moaned and thrust into him. Mitch could feel the heat of Cody's orgasm filling the condom as his lover's cock twitched eagerly in his contracting ass. One last stroke to his cock drew a final shudder from both of them.

They fell forward with Cody's full weight collapsing across his back. Neither moved, only Cody's loud pants filled his ear, and Mitch could feel Cody's heart beating in perfect rhythm with his.

"Damn," Cody finally said and slowly started to pull out of him. Mitch's ass constricted, gripping him. "Fuck, that feels amazing," Cody moaned and slid the rest of the way out. Mitch couldn't move. He was a boneless heap, drifting in pure bliss. Out of the corner of his eye, he watched as Cody slid the condom off his semi-erect cock and tied the end in a knot before tossing it into the trash can by the bed. Cody crawled back to the center of the mattress, kissing Mitch's back and shoulders as he cuddled in close to him.

"Ready for round two when you are, Deputy Marshal," Cody yawned.

When Mitch finally gathered enough strength, he turned to Cody and gave a cheeky grin as he teased his cowboy with the words his heart wanted him to take seriously. "Yep, those words just sealed the deal. I believe I've fallen for you, cowboy Cody."

Chapter 26

Cody woke to the sound of the heater rumbling on. Mitch's chest was pressed close to his back, a heavy leg thrown across his thigh, and the guy's morning erection poked against his ass cheeks. They'd only been asleep for a couple of hours.

Last night had been a frenzied fuck-fest, both taking and giving pleasure. They'd screwed on the bed, and then couch. They ordered food, talked, and made love again before soaking in a hot bath. Cody fell asleep in Mitch's arms, sated, exhausted, and happy.

After last night, Cody's concern about his feelings for Mitch only increased. He'd figured coming here would have helped get Mitch out of his system. But from the need coursing through his body, he doubted the possibility existed. Now, all he could think was how he didn't want to leave him.

Mitch had jokingly said he had fallen for him. Cody knew he shouldn't hope too much for those words to be true. He wasn't dumb; he would only get hurt if he expected more than just this one weekend. Besides, they couldn't work even if they tried. They both had jobs they loved, and Mitch lived a whole state away from him. Sheila was right about all that. So, Cody would enjoy these few days and then go back to Texas and throw himself into his career. Wasn't that what he kept saying to Mitch? That he wanted his career above all else?

"Stop overthinking it, cowboy." Mitch's warm breath ghosted across his skin, giving him instant chills.

"Morning, Deputy Marshal, hope I didn't wake you." Cody smiled and pushed his ass back against Mitch's morning wood. Mitch groaned and canted his hips forward, pulling him closer. Cody's cock plumped up immediately.

How did Mitch always read his moods so well? More importantly, he needed to heed Mitch's words. What Mitch really meant by "don't overthink it" was he put too much emotion into what they had done.

Cody rose up, looked over at the alarm clock, and gave a slight yawn he tried to hide.

"You didn't. What time is it?" Mitch asked, his voice still in the after-sex husky mode.

"It's close to four," Cody whispered, snuggling back down against Mitch. "What time do you have to go in?"

"I think ten is like the official start time on the weekends," Mitch said, keeping steady work at stroking his fingertips up and down Cody's back.

"Did you sleep well?" Cody asked. Mitch lifted his head, and Cody turned, arching his neck to give Mitch a soft kiss.

"I did. I believe I slept better in the past couple of hours than I have my whole life. Thanks to you," Mitch answered, rubbing against him. The wet tip of his cock pressed against his ass, slipping close to his hole.

"That feels good." Cody loved the way Mitch's body fit perfectly against his. And he also loved the feel of Mitch's arousal sliding up and down his crevice, slicking him with pre-come.

"Are you sore?" Mitch asked as he rubbed a thumb across his nipple, then slid his palm down his stomach, bypassing Cody's dick to cup his balls.

"Yes, but only in the best way." Cody wiggled back against him, seeking more of his touch. He was a fool for Mitch's touch. "Make love to me, Mitch."

"Not if you're sore. I don't wanna hurt you." Mitch sucked on the tender skin below his ear and continued fondling his sac.

"I'll be fine, just go slow." He reached an arm behind him and pulled Mitch's mouth to his, giving him a deep, passionate kiss.

"You sure, cowboy?" Mitch playfully licked at the corner of his lips.

"I'm positive, Knox…I just need to feel you." Cody was already halfway there and completely unwilling to take no for an answer. He rose up on his elbow and reached for the lube. Cody popped open the cap, pouring a generous amount onto Mitch's fingers and palm. He lay down again and scooted his butt back into Mitch, moaning when Mitch's fingers found his hole.

Mitch gently massaged him. He drew a knee to his chest, allowing his lover better access. Mitch carefully eased one long digit into him, followed by another, kissing and sucking on his neck as he slowly worked him open. Cody couldn't think of a better way to start the morning.

"Mmm…so warm and tight in there. You sure you're not too sore?" Mitch's fingers twisted and curled, and damn, it felt good.

"Positive. You're not gonna hurt me." The fingers in his ass were suddenly gone. The bed shifted, and he heard Mitch rip open the condom packet. And it wasn't three seconds later he felt the delicious burn of Mitch pushing into his body. Mitch froze as soon as that blunt head breached his entrance.

"You okay?" Mitch asked and pressed his mouth against Cody's neck, lightly sucking. The man was so tender and loving that Mitch filled his body and heart with desire. In the last few hours, he had seen both sides of Mitch Knox—the wild, rough one who sought pleasure with abandon, and then this sweet caring side. Cody had fallen for both.

"Mmm-huh. I love the way you feel in me," Cody confessed, and he meant every word. Mitch licked and nipped at his neck, drawing back and pushing into him a little farther with each roll of his hips. Mitch was being so slow and tender. And with each movement, he was stealing Cody's heart like he stole his breath.

"Mmm…me too, cowboy," Mitch moaned, his thrusts now more determined. "Feels so damn good."

Cody melted against Mitch and those big arms wrapped around him, enveloping him in all that masculine warmth, something he doubted he would ever get enough of. His heart stuttered. How was he supposed to leave and go back to his life after having this? How was he supposed to just walk away from Mitch Knox?

This wasn't just the sex, although that was fucking amazing too, but it was the deep connection they shared. Cody couldn't sense where he ended and Mitch began. Even when they weren't together, he could feel the powerful bond between them. That bond connected them from the first night they met, but he'd been too scared and overwhelmed to act on his feelings.

"I wanna make you feel good." Mitch stroked him harder and faster, keeping in time with his powerful thrusts. He fucked Mitch's palm while his cock pushed in and out of his body. Mitch's free hand found his, and they linked their fingers, entwining them tightly. Mitch bucked into him. His movements became erratic, every thrust rubbed relentlessly against Cody's gland.

Each snap of Mitch's hips seared his insides like liquid fire. He rested his head back against Mitch's shoulder as he fell over the edge, quickly heading for spontaneous combustion. Cody didn't fight it or try to hold back, he let Mitch consume him. And that delicious heat gathering at the base of his spine spread through his body and boiled in his veins until it erupted from him in long hard spurts, coating Mitch's hand and the sheets with his seed.

"Cody." Mitch's breath hitched in his ear, his body stiffened behind him, and he felt every spasm of Mitch's trembling body deep in his ass.

"Fuck, that was…" Mitch panted into the back of his neck and kissed his shoulder.

"I know," Cody agreed.

After a few seconds, the light on the nightstand flipped on. Mitch rolled from the bed and disappeared into the bathroom, coming back with a warm wet towel, which he used to carefully clean Cody, then crawled back in the bed after tossing the towel to the floor.

"We should try to get some more sleep. I can't see where you've slept much since you've been here," Cody whispered and pushed the sheet to the end of the bed, while pulling the covers across their bodies.

"I haven't, but every waking moment has been so worth these last few hours with you," Mitch said sleepily and kissed the top of his head.

"I was afraid that thousand dollar plane ticket would give me performance anxiety," Cody teased. Mitch reached under his arms and turned them quickly so Cody rested in the crook of his arm.

"Stop saying it like that." Mitch stared down at him now. "I consider that money well spent. Maybe the best money I've ever spent. Plus you're paying when I come to Texas, cowboy." Mitch chuckled and leaned to kiss him. "Besides, I'm hoping that after tonight I can look at the case with a clear head. You've been on my mind too much lately. I can't think straight."

"The case. You haven't talked much about it, except to say it was Colt's case," Cody said, running a palm over Mitch's cheek until his fingers ran across the fine hairs at the back of his neck.

"I've actually started referring to it as the Impossible Case From Fucking Hell. I might have to pass it off." Mitch almost sounded defeated.

"What does that mean?" Cody asked.

"It means the FBI's mother ship sucks. It's not about solving the case as much as not stepping on anyone's well-manicured toenails. I'm not cut out for here. There's so much red tape involved. I should give it up. I just know I'm missing something, but I can't fucking figure it out."

"Are those the men taped to the wall? The men that have been injured or killed in this case? I noticed earlier, but didn't say anything," Cody said.

"Yeah," Mitch responded after a minute and leaned in to place a simple kiss on his lips.

"Were they all gay or just Colt?" Cody asked and watched as Mitch warred with himself about how much to say.

"They're all gay," he said after a long minute. The defeat returned, and Cody definitely picked up the empathy Mitch had for those eight men.

"Don't give it up. Keep going. They need you pushing for them, Mitch. If you leave the case, they won't have anyone as devoted as you." Cody switched their position, rolling Mitch over as he lifted and looked down directly into Mitch's eyes.

"It's not that. I just think the case needs fresh eyes," Mitch said, tenderly palming Cody's cheek.

"It doesn't always work like that, and you have to know, lots of officials are still put off by people like you and me. We don't matter because of our lifestyle. Most people don't get the injustice of being discriminated against because of who they choose to love. This case is too important, not just for those men on the wall, but for the men who loved them, for their families, for our entire community. They need you and your team to be tenacious. To push and push until they get answers and justice is served."

After a few seconds of watching Cody, Mitch narrowed his eyes and rolled him back over. "That sounds more like personal experience talking, not just an observation. What happened?"

Several more moments passed and Cody knew his face had to be a cloud of emotion. Should he say anything to Mitch? Every part of him said absolutely not. Outside of his family, he'd never spoken the words aloud. "This can't be good, Cody. Tell me. Is it why you've been so reluctant to be with me? Did something happen to you?"

Cody shook his head. "Not to me personally. Shit, Mitch, I don't know. Maybe it's part of the reason I hold myself back. I hadn't thought about it like that," Cody finally answered.

"Tell me," Mitch encouraged.

"It happened a long time ago. I was like six or seven. My oldest sister Sheila was babysitting me. I was her shadow back then; I went everywhere with her. We were driving through town to go see my dad at work. I always liked to hang out at the police station. We were close to the station, and we drove past this guy getting the shit beat out of him. I mean they were killing him. Even at six years old, I remember them kicking him in the head and one used a tire iron on him. My sister jumped out of the car, screaming for my dad. He came running outside, realized what was going on and took off across the street. He stopped that fight and took those three guys down by himself."

"That had to be hard for a boy your age." Mitch's eyes were full of compassion.

"No, wait, the thing is, the guy getting the shit beat out of him, his name was Mr. Spencer, and he was *the gay* in town. Everybody knew him, but no one really ever talked to him. No matter how hard my dad tried, he couldn't get the county judge to take the case seriously. Mr. Spencer spent months in the hospital recuperating, but he never was quite right after he got out. They beat him so bad he ended up in the mental institution, and the guys that attacked him just got probation. Where was the justice? Mitch, no one's gonna have the compassion or conviction you have for those guys hanging on your wall. If you give up, it might be years before anyone really takes this seriously again. The victims and families deserve closure."

Mitch stared at Cody for a long while. Slowly Cody saw the spark coming back in Mitch's eyes.

"Is that the way you go about your job?" Mitch asked, maybe smiling, but probably more smirking up at him.

"Don't make fun of me," Cody said seriously.

"I'm not at all. You take it seriously; I do too. I just hide that side of me," Mitch replied. "I like that about you. I like that you worry about your future, and if I could complicate your goals. It means you're driven…I like my men driven with purpose in their lives," Mitch said and smiled a real smile at him. Cody returned the grin and rested his head back on Mitch's chest.

"I'll stay on the case. You're right, and I lost sight of the facts. Thank you for opening up like that. I needed to hear those words."

"It's the true reason I got into law enforcement. I remember thinking if a Texas Ranger would have seen that fight, he'd have gotten justice. I don't know if that's true or not, but since then I wanted to be that man." Cody confessed it all to Mitch who kissed the top of his head.

"When I first started with the Marshals I had some guys look down on me because I was gay. They're the reason I got this tattoo across my collarbone and wear all those silly shirts. No one has the right to judge anyone." He ran his hand over Cody's back in a tender caress. "Can you go back to sleep like this?" Mitch asked.

"I think so," he answered. Actually, he was quite certain he could spend his life sleeping like this.

"Good, I think I can too," Mitch said and reached for the lamp, plunging the room into darkness.

Chapter 27

Mitch came rolling through the front doors of the main FBI building with his hands filled with perfectly folded white, orange, and pink boxes of donuts, coffee, and whatever he'd found on the shelf at the Dunkin' Donuts down the street.

He showed his ID badge with a little help from the security guard and treated the guy with a bag of donut holes. "What's gotten into you, man?"

"Just feelin' good this morning." Mitch laughed at the security guard's lifted brows.

"Uh huh," he said as he let Mitch through the gate. He kept that strut in his step and caught the eye of several employees he'd seen before, all were looking at him like he'd lost his mind, which wasn't really abnormal.

He got to the elevator as the doors opened. This whole day was turning out better and better. He whistled a tune as he stepped into a completely deserted elevator and got a full shot of himself in the mirror in the back.

He caught the big grin on his face. It was probably bigger than the arms full of food he carried. Now he understood things around here a little better. He'd been in a pretty foul mood just about every day he'd walked into this building. Whatever. All those guys out there could just suck it. Maybe if one of those guys would have blown him as well as Cody had last night, he would have already lightened up some. And besides, all that deliciously sexy, hot as hell man was currently back in his hotel room, sleeping in his bed, waiting for him to return.

Mitch had a lot to be happy about.

The automated voice announced the third floor, and the elevator doors opened to a much quieter, yet still every bit as sterile, FBI work floor. Mitch skirted the cubicles and headed to the back. It was a little past ten, actually more like ten thirty, and he knew Connors would already be there working. Not necessarily waiting on him, most definitely moving full steam ahead, and he was certain Connors would be pissed off. Not necessarily because he was late, but because he hadn't had anyone to talk to for the last half hour.

Except, as he got closer to their bank of offices, he could hear the guy's voice. Mitch never considered that Connors might talk out loud just to hear himself speak. Was the guy in his office just talking? Brown said something at the same time as well as their assistant, Anne. Ah, the whole team had arrived. As he rounded the corner and entered the conference room, everything stopped and all eyes were on him.

"What?" Mitch asked, dropping all his goodies on the table. "I didn't know you guys would be here. We can share these," Mitch said, looking up.

"What?" he probed again when no one spoke.

"I think he got laid last night." Mitch turned at the sound of Aaron Stuart's voice. "For the record, I already guessed that when you were late." Aaron beamed at him from the monitor as if he'd won a huge prize.

"You have insider information," Mitch said and took a seat, grabbing for the first bag of donuts he could put his hands on. He wasn't sure what happened to have this group here or how Connors magically accepted Aaron's involvement with the case enough to allow him into the meeting without Mitch forcing the issue, but he didn't question them. He didn't want to do anything to slow their progress.

"You're really a very handsome man," Anne said, reaching for the coffee. She didn't waste any time topping off her cup.

"It's the food." Mitch nudged the bag he opened toward her. He'd gotten a little bit of everything, but he was certain they had given him some sort of blueberry cake donut, and he wanted that thing bad.

"Nah, it's those dimples. Who would have known how effective they could be?" Anne said and dug through the bag before pushing that one toward Brown.

"For me, I wouldn't have ever guessed your face would smooth out. I thought the scowl was permanent," Brown tossed out as he reached over and grabbed a bag, inspecting the contents before taking out a pastry.

"The blueberry donut's mine." Mitch just thought he'd throw that out there if anyone found the thing before him. Giving in to his curiosity, he finally looked at the screen and asked, "Why's Aaron involved? I thought he gave Connors the heebie-jeebies."

"I asked for the report he sent you earlier this week about the Secret Service members," Connors said, ignoring the whole previous conversation with his head still stuck in the report.

"How did you know about that?" Mitch asked, looking at Aaron for the answer.

"I'm your partner, Knox. You need to run things past me; I run them past you. When you're gathering this kind of information, I need to know."

"Sorry, dude." Stuart looked directly at Mitch, sporting an extreme case of bedhead. "He messaged me and asked for the same report. I got the wires crossed."

"By the way, thank you for the gift. My son's a huge Captain America fan," Connors said, glancing up for the first time, looking genuinely thankful. The problem was that Mitch had no idea what the guy was talking about. Mitch slowly lost the smile as Brown began to laugh. That was when he clued in—Anne must have had his back and sent something to the boy.

"You don't read your text messages, do you?" she asked. Mitch looked over at her. Even though it was late, he quickly turned back to Connors.

"You're more than welcome. I was glad to do it," Mitch said, finally taking credit for the gift he hadn't sent.

"Oh fuck you," Connors mumbled, burying his head back in the report.

"Did he just say a cuss word? Did the proper Agent Tyler Connors tell me to, let's see, *fuck off*?"

Brown laughed, but Connors pushed away from the table and the donuts and started pacing the small room. Brown used the opportunity to grab the coffee cup left sitting between Mitch and Connors. He gave a salute as the agent sat back down.

"It's too fucking clean! This whole fucking case is too clean. I've read every report you've done, Knox. I thought you had to be missing something. I reviewed all the investigators' reports on each accident. I called the friends and family myself. It's too clean. There are no mistakes. None! Now, I've reverted to calling in this guy," Connors said, whipping his hand toward Aaron.

"No offense," Mitch called toward the webcam.

"None taken," Aaron called back. Connors never stopped his rant.

"I reviewed your files on the smaller, unknown homosexual hate crimes in the country over the last two years. I'm supposing that information came from Stuart too." Mitch didn't respond. "It would take years to investigate all those crimes and find the cases so clean that they fit these patterns."

A duplicate of Mitch's wall of pictures had also made its way to the wall of the conference room. Connors stood in front of them, staring. "Not one survivor knows anything about who attacked them, including the Greyson kid."

"What? He's awake?" Mitch asked.

"You seriously don't look at your messages. I went over there last night when I couldn't get you. He's blacked out on everything," Connors explained.

"Shit. I honestly didn't expect anything different." Mitch leaned back in his chair, staring at Connors. He ignored the phone reference. He hadn't even heard his phone going off last night, and he certainly hadn't checked the thing this morning.

"I'd say we need to expand our tactical team. We're missing something," Connors said, still staring at the pictures as though the answers were hidden within them. He stood, coming to stand beside Connors, looking over the photos.

"Do you know how many millions of case files in the FBI are worked and never solved?" Connors asked now in a much lower voice. It was a voice of defeat. Mitch knew it well. He'd had his moment last night with Cody. Mitch did the calm-down-man pat on Connors, then gripped his shoulder in a gesture of understanding.

"I get it. I swear I do, but you're the best we've got. No one's better than you. I hear that shit all the time," Mitch said quietly, trying to add compassion to his tone. "Now come back to the table and let's start this over."

"I've got nothing," Connors shook his head, looking straight at Mitch. "Not one single lead after a solid week's worth of work."

"Imagine then how I feel about working this case for the last eight months? Come on. Are you guys here for the day?" Mitch asked Brown and Anne.

"Yes," Anne responded with a firm nod.

"Stuart, you staying or going?" Mitch asked, sitting Connors back down on his seat.

"I'm going. I'm already in enough hot water for not being at my brother's wedding breakfast. I mean, seriously, who has a breakfast on the day of their wedding? Ring if you need me," Stuart offered and clicked off the screen.

"I'll get Kreed to come back and join this team, too. I'll request him officially on Monday. We can do this, guys. There's enough intelligence and tenacity right here to get this job done. We need to think outside the box. Think like competent, well-trained serial killers. These guys need us." Mitch used Cody's words from earlier as he pointed to the photo wall. He took his seat, draining the last of his coffee before taking a big bite of the donut. They had this. "All right, guys, let's start from the beginning."

Chapter 28

"No, I can hangout and pick you up," Mitch said into the phone as he ran buck-naked across the hotel bedroom to grab their beer bottles left in the living room. He and Cody had gone out, but made an early night, opting for a twelve-pack and the privacy of Mitch's hotel room for Cody's second and final night in DC.

"I can grab a rental," Kreed started, but Mitch cut him off, diving under the covers Cody held open. They had turned the heat off and the AC down low, needing human contact to stay warm.

"No, it's not a problem. I'll be there anyway," Mitch tried to explain again.

"Why will you be at the airport?" Kreed sounded confused.

"I'll tell you later. Text me your arrival info. Bye," Mitch hung up the phone, tossing the cell somewhere on the bedside table. When he heard the thump, he realized he must have missed the table all together and the phone fell to the floor. He immediately descended on Cody's perfect, smiling lips. When he decided he needed more of that instead of the beer break they'd decided on, a loud shrill scream had him looking around the room to see what had happened.

"My sister's ringtone. Hand me my phone or she'll just keep sending me texts." Cody scowled, looking in the direction of the phone, and as if on command, the scream sounded again.

"She thinks she's funny," Cody explained, extending a hand for the phone he couldn't quite reach.

Mitch rose, gave Cody the phone, and turned around on the bed. Screaming sisters sounded drama-filled, but he smiled and kissed the top of Cody's head as he rested his back against Mitch. It was funny how comfortable they'd gotten. That stiff, uptight Cody he'd first met was long gone, except for sometimes in public Mitch could feel him pulling away. When Cody did turn shy, Mitch refused to let him. He was quickly learning how to handle his man.

They had about fifteen more hours together, and he sure as hell didn't want Cody to close up on him now. He'd been intrigued with Cody Turner since the night they'd met, and now he was just plain taken with the man.

"The room gets seriously cold," Cody said and Mitch wrapped him tighter in his arms, drawing the covers up around them as Cody worked his phone. Another scream filled the cold hotel room. That one had Mitch smiling, and he made the mistake of looking down at the cell phone as a guy's picture filled the screen. The smile fled and Mitch's brow narrowed.

"Who's that?" he asked. He shouldn't have. He shouldn't have even looked at the phone, but, too late, he had.

"I'm not sure," Cody answered vaguely and the phone screamed again. "Damn she can be a pain in the ass."

Cody worked his phone until he brought up a box. Mitch's eyes stayed glued to the screen—he shouldn't be snooping, but he couldn't keep himself from reading the series of messages that Cody and his sister sent back and forth. Cody shot off a quick *'that's enough. I'm busy and I'll call you tomorrow'* text message.

Once he hit send, he started to put the phone away, but Mitch stopped him. "Who's Jonathan Klive Barlett, age twenty-seven, five-eight with okay looking blue eyes?" The text screamed again before he got his answer.

"She's such a pain in the ass," Cody repeated, ignoring the incoming text. He silenced his phone.

"Answer the question," Mitch pushed. He really needed to know the answer. He didn't think Cody had a boyfriend, but had he ever asked that question? Maybe he didn't want to know the answer after all. Cody turned in his arms, lying on his chest, then he tossed the phone on the nightstand and sighed. Mitch pulled the blankets up around them.

"Someone my sister suggested I meet," Cody answered, his piercing blue eyes were back on Mitch, right where they should be. He liked that.

"Are you going to meet him?" Mitch asked. *Please say no...please say no!* He didn't want Cody hooking up with this Klive guy or any other dude for that matter.

"I don't know. Probably not. She has terrible taste in men," Cody said and shrugged.

"Are those the kinds of guys you usually date?" Mitch nodded toward the phone.

"Yeah, I mean, sure, sometimes. Yes. And I usually prefer to date guys more than just having a quick fuck. I mean it's not like serious dating, but someone to hang out with until the next one comes along. I honestly haven't dated all that much since I've been focused on my career," Cody said, reaching for the Bud Light bottle on the nightstand. "I bet you're a fuck 'em and leave 'em kind of guy, aren't you?"

"Quit changing the subject." Mitch's gaze stayed trained on Cody.

"I didn't know we were on a subject," Cody replied after a long swallow. "Is this like an interrogation thing?" Cody asked and reached up to kiss Mitch. Cody sucked his lip in his mouth and kissed him a little longer than a standard kiss. Cody tasted like beer and pure hot sexed-up male, and that stirred Mitch's body. Who was he kidding? His body came to life the minute Cody walked into baggage claim and hadn't stopped since.

"No, but I'm pretty sure I'd like to be the next guy you date," Mitch growled, rolling them over to where he ended up on top of Cody. He settled between his legs, adjusted his cock so it nestled beside Cody's as he stared down at the cowboy. "I mean, I'm absolutely sure I want that spot."

Cody just looked up at him with the most beautiful expression on his face, one that made Mitch shiver. He rose again, tenting the covers over them and anchored up on his elbows, holding Cody's head in place. "What do you think?"

"I think I wasn't expecting that. And Louisiana's a long way away from Austin, Texas."

"I can be anywhere, just about any time. I catch flights like most people catch cabs," Mitch said and arched his hips, pushing himself against Cody's belly, angling himself so his and Cody's dicks got a sensual rub.

"All right," Cody finally said, and a throaty moan escaped his lips as his eyes fluttered closed. "Damn, I already need to come again. Shit, the things you do to me."

"So I've got the spot?" Mitch reached out of the blankets to grab the lube and condoms, but changed his mind. He hadn't finished giving Cody one of his mind-altering, down his throat blow-jobs. He'd been saving that for in the morning. A parting gift, but now seemed a better time. "Say it, Cody, and I'll suck your dick."

Why was he pressing this? He'd already gotten a basic yes, because really 'all right' could be a solid yes. Mitch leaned down and licked then gently bit at the pebble of Cody's nipple. He swirled his tongue around the erect nub and slid his hand lower, grabbing both their cocks in his fist. Cody moaned and Mitch kind of lost his mind right there along with Cody. Cody writhed beneath him, all those thick muscles flexing against his. Mitch gave a few good pumps then released his own cock and concentrated only on Cody. "Say it, cowboy…tell me we're dating."

"We're dating." Cody gasped.

Mitch kissed a trail down Cody's flat stomach, stroking him with purpose. He took Cody deep down his throat in the first try, and a string of curse words tore free from Cody's lips. Mitch could feel Cody lift his head and adjust the blankets to watch him. The look in Cody's eyes gripped his heart. He was so lost to the moment, so lost to this man.

Chapter 29

"I'm glad I came." Cody looked over at Mitch. The weather was mild today. He'd been told at breakfast this was an unusual occurrence for this time of year. The sun was out, the temperature warm, and he strolled hand in hand with Mitch through the parking garage toward the airport. The sun was so bright he still squinted behind his Ray Bans.

"I haven't ever been here before. It's nice. Everybody's very open here," Cody said. He wished he could feel as supported in Texas.

"Yeah, I think this area was one of the first to legalize gay marriage," Mitch said. He easily kept pace with Cody, stride for stride. Cody found he liked those types of things about Mitch; they were perfectly matched in so many ways.

"In my part of the world, they're gonna have to be forced to treat us equal. They won't do it on their own," Cody said, stepping through the door Mitch held for him and smiling as he passed him by. Mitch had kept that routine for the entire weekend. Now that Cody knew how much Mitch tried to please him, those little acts made him feel special.

"Check-in's over here." Mitch pointed toward a row of ticket counters. It took a second for Cody's eyes to adjust to the interior lighting. He followed along behind Mitch as they approached the desk. As Cody went through the procedures of getting his boarding pass, Mitch stayed close by, kind of anchored against the counter, just watching everything that happened, but not saying much.

When he finished, Mitch guided him down to TSA security, the line was long and Mitch waited with him. "I wish you would stay," Mitch said, the familiar refrain that started earlier today. Mitch wanted him to stay the week. Finish his vacation out with him in DC.

"I want to too, but I can't. Thank you for flying me out." Cody hoped to change the subject. He'd considered staying. Truth was that he didn't have anything really going on, but in his mind, staying only showed that he was needy somehow. He'd declined Mitch's offer even though Mitch was hell bent on trying to keep him there.

"You're changing the subject," Mitch said.

"And you don't take no for an answer very well," he replied.

"True, but if I had, you wouldn't be standing here," Mitch shot back. "We're getting to the front of the line. If you get on the other side and decide you can't live without me this week, I'll be here, waiting."

"I'll be fine. I'm a big boy."

"Yes, you are." Mitch grinned broadly and winked at him.

"You know what I mean. I'll be okay." Cody laughed him off, trying to mentally distance himself. He wanted so badly to tell Mitch he'd changed his mind, that he wanted to spend the rest of his vacation right here with him. But the few extra days would only make saying goodbye so much harder. Mitch was right, the line went quickly, and they were at the front as he moved to the security desk.

"But I might not be," Mitch said quietly. Cody looked over his shoulder, surprised at the words. The man was so open with his feelings. He didn't hide anything. He was just completely comfortable with who he was and what he wanted. After a second of Cody just staring, Mitch pushed his sunglasses up on his head and smiled that dimpled smile. God, he had it bad for this guy.

"Sir, we're waiting. If you aren't ready, please step aside," the security guard said to Cody.

"I'm ready," Cody said and showed his identification along with his boarding pass. A second later, he was nodded through.

"Hey, Mitch," the TSA agent said. Cody watched as Mitch handed over his badge. He'd taken a couple of steps away, but he could still hear Mitch talking quietly with the guy, and they both looked in his direction at the same time. Mitch made his way over to Cody, he'd apparently gotten access to pass through the security checkpoint and began pulling the bins and placing his stuff on the conveyors.

"I thought this was goodbye," Cody said, watching Mitch work.

"Shhhh, he's doing me a favor. I'm going with you through security," Mitch whispered, urging Cody to get moving. They were backing up the line. Cody complied, sliding off his boots as Mitch placed his carry-on on the belt.

"Step through the box, place your hands above you head." Cody went through the motions of airport security. Mitch did too, and they came out the other side. Mitch hadn't lied; he was a pro at the whole thing, never faltering where Cody, with his lack of travel skills, had to be guided through the processes.

"Over here." Mitch motioned, Cody's duffel hanging over his shoulder.

"Your gate's all the way down there." Mitch pointed to the right, again taking his hand, walking him in a different direction than he'd indicated. "I have to go out this way."

Just to the right of security was a small hall with a door at the end. It wasn't a crowded area like the rest of the airport, but they weren't alone either. Mitch took several steps toward the door before stopping and turning, drawing Cody against him by a tug of the hips.

"Thank you for coming," Mitch said, dropping Cody's bag to the floor.

"You've already said that, and I had a good time. Thank you," Cody replied.

"I'm gonna kiss you, cowboy." Mitch's amber eyes bore into his soul.

"But we did that in the car. There're so many people." Cody couldn't look away.

"I can't help it. I'm not sure when I'll see you again." Mitch moved in so close their chests touched.

"It'll make people uncomfortable." Cody pretended to protest, but Mitch was already moving forward.

"Just a small kiss," Mitch whispered and leaned in, pressing his lips against Cody's with a teasing swipe of his tongue. Cody couldn't resist and opened slightly. When the tip of his tongue met the tip of Mitch's, something happened. The entire busy airport faded away, and Cody opened fully for Mitch's kiss. The kiss was intensely passionate and filled with promise. It took his breath away and reached out to capture Cody's heart, right there in the airport terminal. This might have been the best goodbye kiss ever on the planet.

Desperation, more than the need to breathe, had Cody pulling away. He bit his bottom lip and just stared at Mitch.

"Hold my spot for me," Mitch said, and again those dang eyes pinned Cody where he stood.

"I will," he promised. Mitch leaned in again and kissed him with a soft brush of lips before he stepped away from the wall.

"You're probably gonna have to jog to your gate. It's a little bit of a hike. Remember, if you change your mind and wanna stay, I'm just a phone call away." Mitch kissed his lips again.

"All right," Cody nodded and scrubbed a hand over his face before picking up his duffel bag at Mitch's feet. "All right." He turned on his heel and took off to the left.

"Wrong way," Mitch called out. *Dammit!* He *had* gone the wrong way. He turned around to see Mitch standing there, a huge smile on his handsome face. Cody waved and headed in the other direction. He had fifteen minutes to figure out where he was and get on that plane.

~~~

Mitch sat directly outside the airport arrival doors where he'd dropped Cody off. He found a park bench and kicked back, letting the heat of the sun warm his skin. He stayed like that for about thirty minutes. He kept his phone in his hand and waited just in case Cody changed his mind. Damn, he really hoped Cody changed his mind.

He'd be working long hours from now until they solved this case, and he got that Cody would be completely alone while he worked, but he had grown fond of the idea of coming home and having Cody waiting for him. And yes, he also got how silly that sounded, but he couldn't care less.

When he figured enough time had passed and Cody hadn't bailed on the flight, he let the disappointment settle in as hope faded away. He looked at his phone to assess the time. It was noon, and Kreed arrived at one fifteen. The two of them were to meet at the office with the rest of the team by two thirty. Mitch thought over his options. It was time for lunch. He loved food, but eating with all the stupid feelings of loss he had flipping through his stomach didn't seem like a good idea.

Instead he picked up his phone and sent Cody a text he'd get once he landed. *"You should have stayed. I miss you already. Text me and let me know you got home okay. This weekend was the best weekend that I've had in a very long time, thank you."*

Then he did something he never did, he voluntarily called his mom just to chat. On the third ring, he got a winded, "Is everything okay, Son?"

He winced. He supposed he deserved that kind of greeting, but he hated that when his mom saw his name, she worried.

"Of course everything's fine. Can't I just call and talk to the best mom ever?" There was a pause on his mother's part, a long one, and Mitch laughed. "Mom, I'm fine. I realized that I haven't talked to you since Jace and Colt's wedding. How are you doing?" Mitch asked. He closed his eyes and leaned his head back, facing the sun.

"You've met someone special, haven't you, Son?" That had him sitting forward, looking around. How did she know that?

"Nah, not really… I mean, maybe. I don't know. How do you know? Am I that transparent?" Mitch stumbled on his words as he danced around the subject.

"I know my children. You all are all the same. Flying the nest, being free, and then settling right back here when it's family time," she said. "Besides, I always said you got your investigative skills from my side of the family."

His mom laughed as he absorbed her words. He weighed how much he should say. He loved his family, his mom was the best, but regardless of how he'd acted with Cody, he was an incredibly private person.

"Mitch, did you hang up on me?" she asked.

"No, I'm here," he answered.

"Well, then, stop overthinking this. I've warmed my tea from a little bit ago, and I'm sitting down. I'm alone until your sister comes over in about an hour. Tell me about him."

"Mom. I don't know what you're..." Mitch stopped himself and rested his elbows on his knees. Was he going to tell her? He sighed and hung his head a moment. Apparently so. "His name's Cody Turner. He's younger than me. Not that much younger, but enough to say he's younger—he's twenty-six. He lives in Texas. He works for Texas DPS, he's a State Trooper."

"Oh good, is he friends with Jace and Colt?" she asked.

"No, but I met him the last time I was in Dallas. He lives in Austin, but he was in town for some business," Mitch said, staring a hole in the small patch of grass at his feet.

"And you've spent time with him?" she asked. These were all questions designed to keep him talking. He knew the tactic, had perfected the skill, but it worked like a charm on him nevertheless.

"This weekend, he flew up here. I'm in DC, and we spent the weekend together," Mitch confessed.

"Was it a nice weekend?" she asked.

"Very nice," he said, smiling at the grass. "He's good-looking and funny," Mitch added and then he trailed off. "He gets my job. That's a big one right there."

"Have you told him how you feel?" she asked.

"Not really. I don't really know how I feel. You kind of took me off guard with all this. I was really just calling to say hi. He's got a big family like ours. His parents are still married. He's got pain-in-the-butt brothers and sisters and lots of nephews and nieces. We have a lot of similarities like that in common."

"That's important, I think, to have similar backgrounds," she said. "What does he look like?"

"He's tall, a little taller than me. He works out pretty heavily, I think. He's got blond hair..."

"When are you going to bring him home to meet the family?" she asked.

"Not for a long time, Mom. I'm trying to keep him, not send him away screaming," he laughed. "Now, tell me how you're doing?"

"Honey, we're all just fine. All the grandkids are growing so big. You won't recognize any of them. Your dad's working too much. He's always gone, but he loves it. The team's bouncing back from Colton being gone. It's an exciting time. We watched Colt broadcast a game this weekend. He did very well. Your father called him afterward. He got a kick out of that," his mom said, efficiently catching him up.

"That's good, Mom. I'm glad to hear it. Listen, I love you. Tell Dad too."

"I will, Mitch, and you need to tell that man how you feel. You certainly aren't getting any younger, Son."

"Was that a joke? Did Ellen tell you to say that if I called?" Mitch asked.

"You know, I've told you that you get your sense of humor from my side of the family," she said, laughing.

"I love you, Mom. Bye."

"Bye, baby," she said, and he could hear the smile in her voice. Conversation about flying the nest and coming back home…Wait! Did she just tell him he was like his brothers and sister? Surely not, right?

Mitch cringed as he realized the truth. He did want Cody to meet his family.

Chapter 30

"Thanks, man, for picking me up," Kreed said as they drove down the highway toward FBI headquarters.

"Not a problem. I planned to let you walk in the FBI building armed, but I decided to spare you this time. You owe me," Mitch teased, keeping his eyes on the road.

"What's that mean?" Kreed sounded completely confused.

"They let me walk in the front doors of the FBI building unannounced. Connors wasn't there; his kid was in the hospital. I got detained for a little while. Had all the FBI attitude in my face trying to figure out what the hell was wrong with me." Mitch gave an exaggerated eye roll. They'd worked enough with the FBI for Kreed to know exactly what he was talking about.

"Oh hell, I bet that was epic. Sorry I missed that," Kreed said, laughing out loud.

"I was gonna let you experience the same welcome, but I've decided to keep my fun to myself since you came all this way to help out," Mitch chuckled.

"That's mighty nice of you, Knox." He couldn't help but catch the moment of realization on Kreed's face. "What's wrong with you? Are you dying or something?"

"What? No, nothing's wrong."

"Tell me why you were already at the airport today," Kreed prodded, looking at him speculatively.

"No, and stop looking at me like that." Mitch focused his eyes fully back on the road and angled his body so his right arm rested on the wheel. He didn't want to explain anything to Kreed right now.

"What's with you, man? Picking me up at the airport, choosing not to set me up for your own enjoyment? What the hell?" Mitch refused to speak, so Kreed narrowed the questions. "Why were you at the airport? Who were you seeing off?"

Mitch sighed. Kreed would eventually get it out of him, so Mitch broke and spoke.

"I met someone. I showed you his picture," Mitch said casually.

"And he flew out here to be with you while you're in the middle of a big break for the case you've had a hard-on about for the last nine months?" Yep, he knew that was exactly where Kreed would go.

"Fuck you, man. It's none of your fucking business. See if I tell you anything else," Mitch countered.

"Ahh, that's right, you've been mentioning that nonsense about a relationship since you met the football guy and the cheerleader. Are you just settling for anyone?" Kreed asked.

"Aren't you just Mary fucking Sunshine? And I'm not settling for shit. You're pissing me off," Mitch replied, refusing to look at Kreed.

"Good, then my job is done. I'm hungry. Stop by Mickey D's up there," Kreed said and pointed to the McDonald's sign up ahead.

"Fuck you. You can wave as we go by."

~~~

Four hours later, Mitch, Connors, Brown, and Kreed sat in the conference room, scouring over all the case information they'd accumulated. The wall of photos had become a maze of information, a puzzle of sorts. They had been thorough with each individual incident. Mitch had done a good job gathering and fact-finding. Even putting in all the hours and having all these eyes and minds working the information, nothing changed except a growing victim tally.

"So we have the Greyson kid. He's the odd man out," Kreed stated as he led this round of discussion while they all sat back studying the wall.

"Correct," Brown agreed.

"He's different from the rest," Kreed repeated. Mitch answered with a nod, and Connors shook his head no.

"Let him finish," Mitch said, holding up a hand as Connors started to speak.

"He's different, Connors, because he's not in the public eye." Kreed kept talking as he rounded the table.

"That's Mitch's theory, but I disagree," Connors argued.

"Hold up, man, and let him finish. You can have the floor next, but listen for once," Mitch said, aggravated. Kreed continued without ever taking his eyes off the board.

"Yes, Greyson's in the public eye for negative reasons. His father's a hard-core republican with a gay son. I get that. But these others are established men who appeared in the news for some recent success they had. The Greyson kid hadn't. My theory is when they left their original plan of going after middle-aged, publicized gay men that that's when they started making mistakes. If they continue going outside their target base, that means something in all this. These mistakes could continue to happen with everyone they target. Besides, we know they have to have a huge ego by now. They've gotten away with murder. Or the kid might not actually be a part of the big plan. He might be a message."

"I don't know," Brown started.

"Let's play the what-if game for a minute." Kreed jumped back in to take the floor. "They got cocky and went off their original plan of attack. The kid wasn't intended to get out of the exploding car. That's the first mistake these guys ever made, because it wasn't a well-executed or organized plan."

"We all agree with you on that," Connors said drily, clearly still not completely on board, but participating.

"He was abducted from a coffee shop. His Secret Service agent was out front. The kid's background check and record are coming back clean, plus surveillance shows his agent sitting out front, waiting for the kid to leave. Security cameras in the front and the back of the shop never showed him exiting the building. We have two mistakes right there. You can't vanish into thin air, and he was able to work himself out of the car before it detonated."

"Correct, but we've interviewed every person we could find who patronized the coffee shop at the time of the alleged kidnapping. We followed the receipt trail. We also interviewed the entire staff of the place," Connors said.

"And what did you find from all that talking?" Kreed asked.

"Elliot Greyson was in the coffee shop for about an hour, studying. He went to the restroom and never came out," Connors answered.

"And there're no windows?" Kreed asked. Mitch kicked back in his chair, concentrating on the conversation. He'd gotten this far on his own, but had also read the investigation reports on the customers and helped interview the employees himself.

"Not a one," Brown said, looking down at the report in front of him. "Connors did you look for yourself?"

"Of course I looked for myself," Connors retorted.

"You still can't vanish into thin air," Kreed said. "This is where I think we concentrate. Someone had to see something. They had to get him out of the building. Whether they dressed him up or what." Kreed looked over at Mitch.

"I believe that was the conclusion we made. There are no cameras in that part of the shop," Mitch said as he bit at his fingernail.

"And the perps would have to know that," Mitch added. He was on board with this. They'd been down this road already, actually a couple of times, but it was all they had after the debacle of interviewing the Secret Service.

"The video from the camera on the street's too grainy to make out every person who entered or exited the building. About thirty percent of the nightly receipts are unaccounted for," Mitch stated, thinking through everything they'd found.

Mitch's phone vibrated at his hip, and he automatically took the cell from the holder, smiling when he saw the text from Cody. He didn't want to lose the momentum the team had going right now, so he forced himself to slide the phone back in its holder. He'd call Cody when they took a break.

"Did you get your computer guy on it?" Kreed turned to Mitch and asked.

"Yeah, he couldn't do much without enhancing the video beyond recognition. It lost too much integrity or something like that. The camera equipment at the coffee shop isn't great."

"And the garbage?" Kreed questioned.

"We took it all. It came back clean, or relatively clean." Connors jumped in. "I still think it's impossible to gather more from the shop. We were thorough in our investigation. We know where you're at on this, Sinacola. That was the strategy we had," Connors said.

"Then it won't hurt to take a second look." Kreed rounded the table as he began to gather his laptop and paperwork. "Let's go by there now," Kreed said to Mitch.

"Or we could do this the courteous way since we've disrupted their business quite a bit over the last week." Both Mitch and Kreed stared at Connors. Out of the corner of his eye, he could see Brown was surprised too.

"Let's just go give it a walk-through. If it's slow, we'll interview whoever's there before we make a formal request to bring the employees in," Mitch offered.

Brown seemed on board, but Connors shook his head no. Honestly, Connors was always slower to agree. Mitch dropped his feet to the floor.

"What's it hurt, man?" Mitch threw out the question as he stood.

"It doesn't hurt anything, but if we put these people on the suspect list, it will change how they respond to us," Connors began.

"Exactly. That's exactly it. We need to change things up. That's why we have Brown and Kreed here full time now," Mitch said.

"He hasn't even been officially assigned to the case," Connors pointed out about Kreed.

"That's why we're just getting a cup of coffee." Mitch grinned. Kreed was first out the door; Mitch following along after him.

"I'm driving if you want a ride," he called over his shoulder.

"We'll meet you over there," Brown yelled. He and Connors were still in the conference room.

"He's a fucking douche, man. Are you sure he isn't involved?" Kreed asked in the relative privacy of the elevators.

"I'm gonna say yes, but who knows," Mitch said, thinking over the possibility. Connors had fought him every step of the way through this case.

Chapter 31

The four of them stood outside the coffee shop, staring at the note on the locked door. They were closed tonight. One of their busiest nights of the week, and they were closed. That seemed off to Mitch.

"Closed for the day, praying justice is served," Brown read the note out loud.

"Huh, what the hell does that mean?" Kreed asked, eyeing the note like the answer would pop off the paper. "Did they tell you they were closing?"

"They aren't suspects. They don't have to keep us informed. It would do you good to read up on the policies and procedures handbook," Connors replied in his usual asshole manner.

"Man, what's your fucking problem?" Kreed turned to confront Connors on his attitude, and Mitch got between them.

"We'll come back in the morning. No big deal," Mitch soothed. "It's late anyway."

"That's what I've been trying to say this whole time. This way we can make sure the owner's available to sit in on the interviews," Connors said, making sure his suit was still laying correctly.

"For real?" Kreed looked at Mitch with a huge *What The Fuck* expression on his face. "This is what you've been dealing with? How do you maintain?"

"The rules and procedures are here to make our jobs easier," Connors began. He sounded very much like the bullshit film they watched in training, certainly not a seasoned professional. Mitch flipped around and looked at Connors.

"Are you fucking kidding me? I should let him kick your ass because you won't read people's body language and learn you're seriously annoying," Mitch started in on him.

"Guys, not here. The cameras are on. United front and all that shit," Brown said, smiling big and motioning them back to their cars.

Kreed slammed the passenger door, rolled his window down, and yelled at Connors from the safety of Mitch's rental which was far away from the cameras on the building. "He's a douche bag."

"That's what I thought too, but since I've been here, I've changed my mind. He's just navigating the political waters to do his job," Brown replied, walking past them toward Connors's car.

"I can't believe he ever gets anything done," Kreed said.

"He does. He gets his cases closed so tight they never stand a chance in court. I've heard all about it, he just follows all the rules in getting them there. We're lucky to have him," Brown yelled out several feet from them. Mitch regrettably tended to agree.

~~~

With a slide of his finger, Cody went through his entire collection of photos from the past weekend. He'd visited museums and monuments, even visited George Washington's plantation in Mt. Vernon on Saturday. He'd taken so many pictures, even some selfies of them together on Saturday night after Mitch got off work. They took one in the cab together, another with Mitch turning quickly to kiss him on the cheek. Mitch had even taken a picture of his breakfast this morning with Cody's phone, just so he'd remember what he was missing by not choosing to stay longer.

Cody flipped through a few more pictures, but went back to the ones where they were together. Had he made a mistake by not staying? Probably, but there was a game to this dating thing. If he'd have stayed, he would have risked looking desperate, and as he sat alone in his apartment right now, he did feel pretty miserable. Why hadn't Mitch returned his text this evening when he got home?

The entire week, Mitch had answered him within minutes of his sent text. Now that he was back home, there was nothing. Maybe Mitch had been at work the whole night... And Mitch did have bad reception in the FBI building. But it was close to nine at night, ten in DC. Surely he'd be back at the hotel by now.

Maybe Mitch was out with his partner? Maybe this whole thing had just been a fuck-fest like Cody had originally assumed. Maybe he was being blown off right now. Actually, he was about ninety-nine percent certain the lack of communication meant he'd been solidly played. But if that was true, why had Mitch referenced holding his spot over and over again? Perhaps Mitch liked to string guys along, wear down their defenses. Or maybe he liked having the connection while they were there and when they were gone...out of sight, out of mind.

Cody thumbed back to the pictures of them together. Mitch was a really good-looking guy. Cody wasn't terrible to look at, but Mitch took everything to the next level. His hair, eyes, and skin tone were all dark, making him the perfect description of tall, dark, and handsome. His lips were full and grew fuller the longer they kissed, and damn, he could kiss. Those dimples though. Cody loved those dimples. He loved the sex with Mitch even more than he loved those sexy dimples. Mitch was the total package of smart, accomplished and sexy as hell. He'd known that going in and knew Mitch was out of his league. Cody should have never gone to DC in the first place.

Guys like Mitch didn't just fall in your lap and stay there. Disillusionment and disappointment filled his thoughts. Cody understood how guys like Mitch worked. They liked the chase, but didn't like to stick.

How would this affect his future? US Marshals worked with the Texas Rangers on occasion. Would Mitch be strolling in and out of the picture for the rest of his life? Shit. He probably would. The way Cody had so easily agreed to hold the spot... The way he'd gone the opposite direction in the airport after that last mind-blowing kiss... Thank god he hadn't stayed around for the week.

Trying to gain some anger to help remove the pain slicing through his heart, Cody slid the pictures away, shut down the screen, and put the phone on the charger.

He grabbed a beer from the refrigerator and pulled a steak from the freezer, dropping it in the microwave on auto defrost before he headed to the patio to light the grill. He twisted the cap off the beer bottle and took a long swig. Steak and beer, the perfect you're-such-a-freaking-fool meal. He supposed women would turn to ice cream and chocolate right about now. He did have a brand new container of Blue Bell chocolate ice cream in the freezer. He'd probably open that up when he was done and catch up on a few episodes of The Walking Dead.

Flipping the knobs to the grill, he looked out over his balcony. He lived in a ninth-floor apartment. Not too high up, but still a perfect view of the parking lot and garage below. If he cocked his head and bent far to the right, he could see Sixth Street. He had a great view of the Austin skyline, one of the things that had drawn him to this apartment. Well, that and the bar downstairs.

He could definitely hear activity going on in the streets below. Maybe he should venture down there tonight. The weather was absolutely perfect for a night out. The smells and sounds of the city were carried on the light breeze. The town was just coming to life at this hour. He could get out, have a drink, and push this sour feeling away before morning.

He decided against that and went back to the microwave as it dinged. He passed his radio, flipped the button on, and Lady Antebellum's "Just A Kiss" filled the space.

"Just perfect," Cody sighed out loud. Why did everything have to remind him of Mitch? It wasn't until he had the steak on a plate, perfectly seasoned and ready to grill, that he heard the shrill ring of his cell. His heart slammed in his chest. It was most likely one of his brothers or sisters, but he took off running, struggling to switch everything into one hand in order to grab the phone. He'd got there as the phone went to voice mail.

"Dammit!" The beer bottle he braced up against his chest with his forearm slipped forward, spilling on to the plate as he pushed the button to see who'd called. A text came through with a whistle. One of those exaggerated construction worker catcall kind of whistles that had him narrowing his brow. That was new. He picked up his phone and opened the text. It was Mitch.

"Call me when you get this. It doesn't matter the time." Plain, simple, and to the point. Those few words lifted his spirits like nothing else ever had before.

There was no hesitation; he immediately dialed Mitch while placing the beer bottle on the nightstand.

"I just tried to call you," Mitch answered. No hello, nothing like that.

"I was trying to get to the phone," Cody said, rounding the corner back into the living room to turn off the radio.

"Are you out?" Mitch asked, he sounded a little defensive.

"No, I just turned on the radio in my apartment. I'm cooking a steak," Cody replied, coming to stand in the middle of the living room.

"It sucked coming back to the hotel and you not being here. Sucks even more now. My partner's bunking in with me tonight. The place's packed, something's going on in town, and his room isn't ready until tomorrow," Mitch said, and there was a definite whine in his husky voice.

"Well, see, it's better that I left then," Cody said, finally moving forward when he remembered the steak he held. He took the phone outside with him as he lifted the grill lid and dropped the steak on the grate.

"No, I don't think so at all," Mitch answered.

"Did you put the whistle on my phone?" Cody asked, walking back into his room to grab the beer off the nightstand and heading back out to the balcony where he had a couple of lawn chairs set up. He'd kept his tone light and easygoing in order to gauge Mitch's. Did players call like this when they were blowing people off?

"Yeah," Mitch laughed. "You liked that, eh?"

"Yeah, it surprised me. I looked around the room wondering what the hell?" Cody sat back in the lounge chair and looked out over the city. That intense happiness he had in Washington slowly crept back in.

"I wanted you to know that's what I think about you," Mitch said.

Okay, well, that sure didn't sound like a guy who was trying to get rid of him. Cody ran a hand over his face and through his hair. When he was talking to Mitch, it was like the universe aligned itself in proper position.

"You get weird when I say things like that." Mitch's voice sounded thoughtful.

"Not weird, just quiet. Where's your partner now?" He had to change subject. He got up from his lounge chair and made his way over to check his steak, trying to get out from under all this emotion coursing through him.

"In the bedroom," Mitch answered, his voice dropped lower. "I can't...you know. He can hear me."

"Does he know I was there?" Cody asked.

"Yeah, he figured it out pretty quick. I was happy, which is apparently uncommon for me. Who knew?" Mitch said. Cody laughed at that. "I was in a meeting when you texted earlier. Watching Connors and Kreed face off was pretty funny."

"Yeah?"

"Yeah. It's like oil and water with those two," Mitch chuckled.

"I thought you might be blowing me off," Cody uttered randomly. He'd finally mustered the nerve and just said the words. Seconds felt like hours as he waited for Mitch to respond.

"What? No. Not even a little bit. I wanted some privacy to talk to you. We worked all afternoon into tonight and then I had to get Kreed situated. I actually miss you like crazy," Mitch replied. He sounded sincere. The words made perfect sense, and Cody's relief level soared through the roof.

"You're quiet again. Tell me, what're you doing?" Mitch asked after a full minute of his silence. He took his seat back on the patio and kicked his legs up on the rail.

"I just put a steak on the grill," Cody answered.

"You could add that you're missing me," Mitch suggested, and Cody got quiet again. "There's the silence. I liked it better when you were here, and I could gauge your reaction. Damn, I miss you, Cody. I don't want that to freak you out, but I do. It was only two days, but when I came in tonight, the hotel seemed lonely. Fuck, Cody, look what you're doing to me. You have me assessing the feelings of a fucking hotel room."

"I miss you, too," Cody confessed.

"You sound like it pained you to say that" Mitch laughed.

"What about the case? Do you think it's moving in a different direction?" Cody questioned, moving the conversation away from the sentimental stuff. He wasn't good at expressing his feelings, so they needed to talk about something different.

"We're going backward again. I told you, we're missing something. Kreed'll help us. He's a pain in the ass sometimes, but good at his job." Mitch let out a giant yawn in the middle of his sentence. "I'm beat, cowboy. It's late here, and I'm sleeping on the sofa bed. Besides, somebody kept me up all weekend. Hell, when I think about it, you kept me up all week, Cody Turner." Mitch chuckled again.

"I'm glad you called," Cody replied.

"What're you doing tomorrow?" Mitch asked.

"Hanging shingles on the barn at my parents place," Cody answered.

"Cool. I'll call you tomorrow night. Text me if you want, but remember, I have shoddy signal. It might take me a little while to reply."

"All right," Cody said, and there was a pause.

"Damn, I don't want to hang up this phone," Mitch whispered.

"Go to sleep, I'll talk to you tomorrow," Cody offered.

"All right, goodnight," Mitch responded.

"Bye." Cody ended the call and stared out into the night. Mitch had called and made everything right in his world with just the sound of his voice. What the hell was that about? Cody let the smell of sizzling meat pull him from his thoughts. He jumped up, letting the chair slam back as he lifted the lid to his grill and tried to salvage the steak he'd let overcook on one side.

Chapter 32

"What the hell are you doing in here?" Mitch asked. He'd left his office for no less than five minutes and returned to Kreed kicked back in his office chair. Mitch's computer was pushed to the side, and Kreed had his laptop placed right in the center of the desk.

"We're bunking together here too. Apparently the bureau's short of space right now," Kreed said, typing away on his computer.

"That shit doesn't mean you take over my spot," Mitch said, placing his coffee on the edge of the desk. On a second thought, he picked the hot paper cup back up and downed several gulps. He needed the liquid energy because he'd only gotten about twenty minutes of sleep last night on that damn uncomfortable fucking sofa.

"Sure, I can. You can sit over there." Kreed pointed to the other side of the desk.

"The hell I am!" Mitch grabbed the laptop out from under Kreed's hands and laid it on the decorative office chair facing the desk.

"Hey, man!"

"You have five seconds before I physically move you out of my chair," Mitch warned.

"Try it," Kreed taunted, gripping on the sides of the chair. "This chair's badass. The Marshals Service needs to invest. I refuse to go willingly."

"Four." Mitch started rounding the desk toward the back of the chair.

"Three," Mitch growled, and Kreed anchored his feet to the ground.

"Two." Mitch continued the countdown and gripped the back of the chair.

"No fair! You gave me your lumpy bed, and I bet it was covered in undesirable shit, too," Kreed protested.

"One." Mitch used his brute force, dumping Kreed out of the chair. He didn't hesitate jumping in the vacant seat as Kreed landed on his knees and hands, breaking the fall.

"You suck, man. Can't say you've never had me on my hands and knees, Knox," Kreed chuckled.

"Whatever. The promise of personal favors won't help either, Sinacola," he said smugly, reaching for his coffee.

"And I thought you cared. Hell, you didn't even bring me a cup of coffee," Kreed replied, getting to his feet. "Speaking of coffee, shouldn't we be heading over to the coffee shop?"

"Connors will be here soon. He's running behind," Mitch supplied, pulling his laptop back in front him.

"Of course he is. And why do we have to wait?" Kreed questioned.

"Because he happens to be my partner on this fucking case. The coffee's right around the corner. No, to the left not the right," Mitch called out when Kreed went the wrong way. Seconds later, he was back with Brown on his heels.

"Brown agrees, let's get moving. Connors can meet us there," Kreed announced.

"All right, but you guys are explaining this when Connors gets his panties in a wad. Did you get your official reassignment?" Mitch asked, reaching for the jacket he'd tossed on the coat rack by the door.

"The email was waiting for me when I came in this morning," Kreed offered, heading for the elevator.

The three of them made it as far as the elevator before the doors opened to Director Young. Mitch could feel the collective sigh from both Brown and Kreed.

"I was coming down to see you," Director Young said.

"We're headed down," Mitch offered up quickly.

"I'll ride down with," he said, holding the door open. Kreed entered first, Mitch followed, and Brown was working at a much slower pace.

"I'm Kreed Sinacola." He held out his hand to the director who reluctantly offered his. He didn't introduce himself.

"Since the team has doubled, we're expecting quicker results," Director Young said.

"Sir—" Brown started, but the director cut him off.

"I need daily reports from this point forward. It's been well over a week and you've got nothing. Now we're having to double your team. No one's pleased," the director's tone was sharp and clear. Mitch stayed quiet, because no one wanted to hear what he had to say after three days of pussyfooting around the legal department with the Secret Service interviews.

The elevator opened on the first floor parking garage. The director never said another word or looked back in their direction.

"Well, isn't he just a breath of fresh air," Kreed mumbled, as they walked off at a slower pace.

"You have no idea," Brown replied.

"I vote Connors to be the one to give the daily updates," Mitch recommended, finally stepping off the elevator as the doors started to close.

"I second it," Brown said.

"It unanimous then. Serves him right for being late," Kreed added, heading for Mitch's rental.

~~~

Eight o'clock in the morning and the coffee shop bustled with business. Long lines streamed from each order station and every so often names were called with coffee handed over the end of the counter. The place worked like a well-oiled machine, and no one had to wait too long for an order.

Their whole game plan for the visit came to three men there just having coffee. It was a brilliant plan, didn't take long to formulate, and might have holes. They'd have to wait and see. Mitch and Kreed followed along behind Brown, but Kreed's attention stayed focused elsewhere.

Mitch led Kreed down the hall where Elliot Greyson was last seen. They entered the men's bathroom, running everyone off inside. Kreed pulled out his tools to sweep the room to see if any taps had been left behind. They both did a thorough search for hidden exit routes. Even the ceiling was concrete. Just like the original reports, there was nothing amiss with the room. Elliot couldn't have exited this room without going through the door.

"Gentlemen, we need to move it along." A voice came from the hall outside the locked bathroom door. Mitch recognized the voice, and he used his hand codes to try to let Kreed know who was at the door.

"Deputy Marshal Knox," the owner said. Damn, he remembered Mitch's name. For a one-time chance meeting that seemed odd to him, but some people were just like that. He hadn't pegged that guy as one of them.

"Mr. DeGeorge, I want you to meet my partner, Kreed Sinacola." Mitch turned to Kreed as he opened the door. Kreed stood right there in the doorway, blocking customers who waited to use the facilities while Mitch made the introductions.

"Has anything else happened?" Mr. DeGeorge asked, concerned.

"No, sir, Deputy Marshal Sinacola's new to the case. He mentioned he wanted to have a look at the scene, so I brought him over." Mitch took another glance around the restroom.

"I do have a few questions. Are you busy?" Kreed asked as he stepped into the hallway.

"It's rush hour for us," Mr. DeGeorge said, somewhat defensively.

"It won't take long," Kreed announced and straightened to his full height, towering over the guy.

"All right, I guess I'm willing to spare a few minutes to help. I hope you're getting closer to identifying the scum who did this. Business is suffering with all this police presence all the time," Mr. DeGeorge replied. He was a small man with a graying beard and had always seemed nice enough until right this minute. He motioned for them to follow him, and he lead them down the same hall, but in the opposite direction and a little deeper in to the building, until they were almost at the back door. Mr. DeGeorge turned right and ushered them toward the small office.

"Is this the only back door to the building?" Kreed questioned the owner as he looked over the door.

"Yes, it leads to the Dumpster and alley," DeGeorge said.

"Can I take a look?" Kreed asked

"Of course, but your men scoured the area…"

"Humor me," Kreed replied, not stepping inside the office, but staying close to the door. Mr. DeGeorge skirted around Mitch toward the back door. He entered a security code.

"Who has this code?" Kreed inquired. Mitch listened to see if an answer might change, but so far everything was on the up and up.

"Every employee here. The Dumpster's out back." DeGeorge opened the back door, and Kreed walked out first, spotting the security camera by the door.

"Who controls the security camera?" Kreed asked, keeping an eye on the owner.

"We do. It's set up in the computer you guys confiscated. Any word when we can get it back?" Mitch and Kreed ignored the owner's question. Kreed climbed the side of the Dumpster and pushed on the protective security gate. Mitch watched him closely. The only way Elliot could have gotten over the top of the fence would have been with help. The spiral barbwire had no DNA. And the only other way out was down the alley, which would have passed by the assigned Secret Service agent out front.

"The Dumpster contents?" Kreed looked over at Mitch and asked.

"It's still in FBI custody," Mitch answered.

Kreed jumped down and turned to Mr. DeGeorge. "This is the only way out?"

"Correct. And the agent sitting on the road never saw anyone else," Mr. DeGeorge offered.

"No disturbance, nothing abnormal that night?" Kreed kept probing. He was relentless, which was exactly why Mitch wanted his friend on this case.

"No one noticed anything until we locked up and the Secret Service agents were banging on the doors." The man looked down at the ground and wiped his hands on his apron.

"Someone's lying," Kreed said to Mitch.

"Now wait a minute," Mr. DeGeorge spoke up.

"We aren't talking to you," Kreed blurted, flashing an intimidating gaze toward the man as he started to walk the alley toward the street. Mitch followed. He'd been through these things with Kreed for years. Kreed had an innate ability to flesh out a situation. His expertise was unprecedented, and Mitch had called him more times than he could count to run things past him, see what he was missing.

Kreed walked slowly, undoubtedly checking for any holes, any way the roof might have been used. Once he got to the street and retraced his steps to where they'd started, they'd lost the owner. He'd vanished. Kreed started to push the Dumpster toward the wall.

"Help me, I want to get up there," Kreed said. Mitch grabbed an end and helped roll the Dumpster to the back wall. First Kreed, then Mitch, hoisted himself up onto the roof. The surface was flat, with an awning stuck out from the front making it appear angled. Kreed walked the entire length as Mitch went for the canopy. He'd seen this area before. They'd actually wiped it down for fingerprints and DNA, but he checked again, trying to find anything that might help them with this case.

"He's lying," Kreed whispered and scared the shit out of Mitch. Kreed had that way of just being quiet all the fucking time. Mitch supposed that was from all those years as a Navy SEAL.

"How do you know?" Mitch asked.

"Gut," Kreed turned to him and shrugged. "Did we background check him?"

"You read the report." Mitch sat down on the roof and looked out over the building. What were they missing?

"No, I mean your online guy. Did you send this through him?" Kreed's brows knitted together, and he let out a long sigh as he sat down beside Mitch.

"I don't know, maybe. I put so much in front of him," Mitch answered honestly.

"Get him to dig. That man's hiding something, I'm sure of it." Kreed nodded his head toward the coffee shop.

"We could bring him in, but, man, there's absolutely no good-cop, bad-cop types here. Can you see Connors playing bad cop?"

Mitch laughed at the thought. "We wouldn't get much more out of him."

"No, and we don't need to bring him in just yet." Kreed lowered his voice. "You need to bug his office tonight. His house today." Mitch rolled his eyes. Of course, he'd be the one that had to do it. "And don't get caught," Kreed added.

"I don't ever get caught, ass," Mitch hissed quietly.

"Stop looking like that. I know he's hiding something. We'll get a direction out of this, I guarantee it," Kreed said before getting up and strolling across the roof. Mitch was slower. He'd never hesitated on doing things like this. Hell, he and Aaron did some shit that would have earned them both jail time if they'd been caught, but in those cases, he'd been pretty damn sure of what he was dealing with. Not this time, though, but Kreed had never let him down before. So invasion of privacy, here they came.

Chapter 33

Mitch had three objectives. He needed access to the coffee shop's incoming and outgoing calls on his cell phone. He needed DeGeorge's phone tapped, and he needed the information from the man's computer at work, as well as at his home. Thank god they lived in a time where most of those objectives could be achieved without setting foot outside the FBI building.

His only problem? He didn't want to involve the director to achieve any of those goals. Nor did he have anything other than Kreed's gut to go on. Definitely not enough to convince anyone in this building to possibly take someone's civil liberties away.

He had two choices. Mitch had developed some pretty decent relationships with a federal judge who now sat on the FISA court. Not allowing himself to overthink this, he palmed his phone and sent a message to the judge, praying for an expedited approval on wiretap for DeGeorge's office, shop, and home. He quickly and efficiently bullet-pointed the information the judge might need to pull this together as soon as possible. To his surprise, the judge responded back immediately that he'd have approval back to him in the next hour. Mitch gave himself a mental high-five. One obstacle down, another to go.

Second, Mitch had to call Anne into their secret plan. She had bureau clout. Being the administrative assistant to the top guy gave her a certain authority around the building. Anne was smart, sharp as a tack, and beautiful. On a very firm second decision to not overthink things, Mitch grabbed his suit coat and tossed it over his arm, ready to slide it on if needed. He entered the elevator, pushed the fourth floor button, and swiped his tag to gain entrance to the elite floor.

Every eye in the room stopped what they were doing in order to look his way as he walked past. The disapproving looks were still right there on their faces. After all this time, he actually got used to the stares and even laughed now because envy had to crawl up their asses that he got away with things and they couldn't.

He rounded the corner and saw the director's door closed. Thank god for small favors. He stopped in front of Anne's desk.

"Hi, Mitch," Anne said, never looking up from the computer screen as she typed.

"How'd you know it was me?" Mitch was impressed.

"If I said cologne, would you believe me?" she questioned, finally turning her smiling face up to his.

"What's the real reason?" he asked skeptically.

"The room always becomes quiet when you walk through. I've thought it's because you're such a good-looking guy, but today I suspect it's the shirt without the required jacket on, not just close by." Anne pointed at his shirt and suit coat hanging over his arm.

"It's a cool shirt," he defended in a mock tone of shock, ignoring the jacket comment. He was past tired of that stupid rule.

"Ass Bandit. Really, Mitch? You know you do it on purpose," she said, all attention on him now as she held laughter in her eyes, and a growing smile.

"I might do that, but it's funny, and it got you smiling, so it works," he said and realized he might have turned the sweetness on a little too much.

"What do you want?" Anne sighed.

"I need you for a minute," he answered.

"Okay, what's up?"

"Not here," he leaned in and whispered, pointing toward the elevator. "Can you come with me?"

She nodded and stood. He led the way, not speaking until they hit the lobby. Mitch didn't stop until he reached the water fountain where he took a seat. Anne did the same, sitting on the seat right next to his.

"I need extreme confidentiality. Can you give that to me?" he asked as she sat down beside him.

"Of course," she replied.

"No, I mean no one knows." He couldn't stress this point enough.

"All right, you have my word. I told you Saturday I was in to help get this resolved."

"I contemplated calling my office in Louisiana, but it's bigger than that. We need people closer," Mitch confided.

"And you feel like the director wouldn't go along with this plan?" She looked up at him, and he gave her a smile. No, he *knew* the director wouldn't go along with this plan.

"I'd rather say it like this to you. Director Young gave me carte blanche and I've gotten judicial approval." Mitch changed the words around to fit his need. It was a skill he'd perfected over the years.

"And that's to protect me for doing what you want?" Anne asked.

Mitch nodded and looked down at his Doc Martens. "Yeah, maybe."

"Okay, I'm in. I haven't told you, but this case holds special interest to me. My brother's gay. His life hasn't been easy. People like you, help. I want to help, Mitch. What do you need?" She'd surprised him with that one.

"I need complete surveillance on Mr. DeGeorge, the owner of the coffee shop Elliot Greyson was abducted from," Mitch said honestly.

"Director Young would have to commission our Information Technologies' agents…" Mitch cut her off.

"I'm working on a court order now. You have to know some of those guys in the IT department. You know everyone. Go down there with me. Don't lie to them, just sort of insinuate the approval I've gotten. Get me the equipment, I'll get it set, but I need it monitored," Mitch said.

"The way I understand it, they can tap into his phone easy," Anne offered.

"Right, and I can do that myself, but I need people monitoring the activity, listening twenty-four seven, not just recording for me to go through later. I want his conversations, text messages, and all the conversations going on around him. I want everything," Mitch said.

"All right, and you want web-tapping too, I'm guessing?" Anne asked.

"Yes, absolutely." Mitch nodded.

"And you will never tell my husband what you witness, correct?" she asked randomly.

"Absolutely not. Scout's honor." He suspected what she might be about to do and held up his three fingers, flashing her a big grin.

"Then come on." Anne was up, walking back into the building and in a new direction. She took him to the back freight elevator, forgoing the standard employee elevators up front. She spent the two minute ride unbuttoning one of her top buttons of her blouse, rolling the waistband of her skirt over one time to shorten the length, and she reached inside of her bra, then paused when she caught him watching, and motioned for him to turn around. Mitch did, not pointing out that he had absolutely no interest in what she had going on. As the doors opened, she tousled her hair, and all Mitch could do was stare at her because she had managed to transform herself from the proper administrative assistant to a hot little number in a hundred and twenty seconds.

"Get that look off your face. You're making it obvious," she whispered as she gave an exaggerated walk in front of him, much like she was taking a stroll down an imaginary catwalk.

Damn, if he hadn't picked the right person for this job.

Mitch smiled as he followed along behind her. For the first time since he started working here, he wasn't the focus of attention when he entered a room. Anne rounded a corner, Mitch followed and stopped dead in his tracks. She was anchored on the side of a cubical ledge, her arms crossed, effectively shoving her breasts up even farther, and she kept a wide stance, showing a nice view of her mile long legs.

"Jordie, I need help with something. Can you come with me to the conference room?" she asked, her voice a little low. She had the guy's complete attention.

Mitch had gotten close enough to see this Jordie was typical FBI meets extreme computer nerd, and he fumbled with his words and finally croaked, "Sure."

Jordie never saw Mitch as he rounded the corner to his cubicle and followed Anne to a small room. Mitch trailed along behind them, shutting the door as they entered. It was the first time Jordie looked his way. The lust-filled gaze turned somewhat panicked until Anne took over again.

"Jordie, this is the new deputy marshal working for Director Young, remember me telling you about him?" she asked and crossed her legs in front of him. *Damn, she's good.*

"Nice to meet you," Jordie replied, sticking out a hand, but his eyes remained focused on Anne.

"They're looking for someone to help in the investigation. Someone who won't say a word, keep things on the down low. I told them I know just the person. You're smart, trustworthy, and I know you'll put your all into this. I've watched you work for years, what do you say? Will you help them?" she asked and batted her eyelashes a little bit.

"What do I need to do?" he asked, and for the first time since they entered the room, Mitch felt like the guy had a brain in his head.

"Well, Deputy Marshal Knox knows the ins and outs more than I do. You know he's the one Director Young personally assigned to handle this case," Mitch just looked at her. She was clever as shit. She never one time said the director approved this, but used his name two times and implied it all over the place.

"I need to monitor someone's activity through their cell and online. I need equipment. I'll get the wiretaps set in his office myself. I just need the cell phone monitored and some web-tapping," Mitch said quickly.

"Who's gonna monitor once it's set," Jordie asked. He looked excited at the prospect. Finally, something that took Jordie's eyes off Anne's breasts.

"We could use your help," Mitch offered.

"That's all you need?" Jordie asked, acting like that was the easiest thing in the world. Aaron would have probably said about the same thing.

"That's it, man. I see Anne brought me to the right person." That caused Jordie to sit up straighter in his chair.

"How do you want this to work?" Jordie asked.

"You can go through me. Mitch's going to give me all the details as he knows them. As soon as I have them, I'll forward them to you and so we begin," she explained.

"Okay, I'll get started as soon as you give me the green light. I'll also stay in touch with you, Anne. Does your husband know?" There was disdain in his voice. Jordie must have had the hots for Anne for a while now.

"Absolutely not," Anne replied, flashing the computer guy a big smile.

"So we'll talk in code," Jordie instructed.

"That would be great, Jordie," Anne rose, all legs and boobs in Jordie's face. "Thank you so much!" She kissed him on the cheek. Good thing she was on his side.

Chapter 34

Once the warrant had come through, Mitch laid out his plan to Connors and Brown in a very private, closed-door meeting. Mitch came prepared to fight to the death to make sure Connors didn't leave that office and tell one single person their strategy to tackle the case.

Connors caught him completely off guard when he declared his complete acceptance of the wiretapping, and even thanked him for taking the steps to have a federal judge review the case.

Connors stepped up and began calling in favors to the short list of his trusted support staff. As a senior agent, no one questioned him when he asked for onsite, around the clock surveillance on both the coffee shop and monitoring the taps they planned to place.

"They're moving. They should be in front of the coffee shop within the hour," Connors said as he hung up the phone.

Mitch actually reached across the table and high-fived the guy. "I thought you'd fight me."

"We were told to use whatever means necessary to bring this case to a close. You covered our asses, and since we don't know who to trust anymore, it's not like we can ask for permission," Connors reasoned, and Mitch wondered right then if aliens had taken over his temporary partner's body.

"Better to beg for forgiveness, than to ask for permission anyway," Kreed added. Mitch leaned over and gave him a fist bump. That had totally been their motto over the years they had worked together.

"So you're going to break into the office tonight?" Brown asked.

"We'll go. He'll be the distraction." Mitch hooked his thumb toward Kreed.

"I can cause some chaos," Kreed affirmed confidently. "I'll set the tap under the bar while Knox works the office. Connors, you and Brown will be with surveillance to verify everything works."

"I'll have a surveillance van about a block over. They can pick up both signals as needed."

"Jordie's also hacking into DeGeorge's computer and setting up the web-tapping at his home and the office," Mitch added.

"Anne must be involved. He falls all over himself to impress her." Brown laughed.

"No shit. He was putty in her hands," Mitch added, laughing when he thought about how effectively she'd worked him.

"So how long do we give this to work?" Brown asked.

"Our warrant gives us three weeks, but with our presence back in there, it shouldn't be more than a couple of days—no more than a week. DeGeorge'll get spooked, we'll know it. Besides, eight hits in nine months dictates it's time for another strike. They have to be getting cocky as hell by now," Mitch said.

"We'll need to take shifts. Someone should be with surveillance at all times," Kreed detailed.

"That's not the way it works here," Connors began.

"We're deputy US marshals apprehending a fugitive. It's definitely how it works with us," Mitch said.

"But we don't have a fugitive yet. Let them do their job. They'll keep us updated," Connors suggested.

"You take the first shift," Mitch said to Kreed, ignoring Connors altogether.

"I'll take the next shift," Brown offered.

"Then that leaves me overnight, because Connors has a family— he gets the morning shift. Great, thanks!" Mitch feigned a smile at drawing the graveyard shift.

"Whatever, man! That'll give you plenty of time to sex up your boyfriend and still get a couple of hours sleep." Kreed aimed his smirk right at him. Mitch shot him the finger and picked up the closest thing to him, his stapler, and threw it at Kreed who caught it before it could make contact with his head.

"Shut the fuck up, man." Mitch couldn't help the grin that broke out across his face.

Kreed gave him a kissing sound and mocked him with a pretend phone in his hand. "I'll call you as soon as I can... I miss you already... Ohh! Yes, that's it..." Kreed ducked out of the room, but his laughter could be heard down the hall.

"For the record, I don't sound like that," Mitch said good-naturedly to Connors and Brown. He didn't care what anyone thought. Cody was a keeper he planned to have around awhile. They all needed to get used to him.

Chapter 35

Mitch and Kreed entered the coffee shop a little before closing. The time of day where the staff was at the end of their shift, ready to lock the doors, clean the place, and get the hell out of Dodge. He learned early on this was always the perfect time to get information or have free access to just about anything in the building. No one ever seemed to care.

Kreed took on the job as distractor. If possible, he would plant a bug under the main counter. Mitch would take care of the rest of the place, including DeGeorge's personal office. Brown, along with the surveillance crew, sat parked in an unmarked van down the street.

As luck would have it, a young woman manned the counter. The stars and moon must have aligned because Kreed could be very charming in certain situations. Girls usually lost their minds where he was concerned.

"Hey there, pretty eyes, they have you working here all alone tonight?" Kreed asked in a deep Southern drawl. Mitch watched as her smile grew bigger and her eyes glazed over.

"Nah, Denise's in the back, getting ready to close. But you guys came in yesterday, didn't you? You were with the investigators, right?" she asked, all perky and eager to talk.

"You have a really good memory, Jazzy. I'm impressed," Kreed said, staring straight into her eyes, anchoring an arm on the counter.

"Have they figured out what happened to Elliot Greyson?" she asked.

"I just consult. I'm a deputy US marshal, but this looks like a cool place. What's the best drink you have here?" Kreed had her hook, line, and sinker.

"I'm heading to the john," Mitch mumbled, neither Kreed nor Jazzy, at least that was what her name badge read, looked his way.

"It depends on what you're looking for. Do you want a hot or cold drink?" she asked, her voice turning coy, and just like clockwork, Mitch even mouthed the words as Kreed spoke them.

"I always like it hot." Mitch even gave that wink he knew Kreed bestowed on the girl as he turned the corner to the bathroom. Instead of going left to the men's room, he went right. He reached for the doorknob and found it locked. No problem there, he just had to hurry.

Mitch reached inside his jacket pocket, pulled out a small black leather case, and within seconds, jimmied the lock free. He quickly stepped in, shutting the door behind him. The office was filled with boxes, probably overflow storage, and the desk was stacked high with paperwork. Actually, clutter filled the entire space. Better for him. Mitch worked fast at inserting the listening device into the phone. Once complete, he dialed Brown's cell to make sure they were picking up the signal.

"Kreed works faster than you," Brown said as he answered the phone.

"Fuck you, can you get a signal?" Mitch said.

"Hang on, they're working it."

"I don't have all day," Mitch added.

"They got it," Brown responded. Mitch's triumph was short-lived when heard a key being inserted in the doorknob.

"Shit," he barely whispered and quietly placed the phone back on the hook before ducking to the only place he could find to hide in the overcrowded office. He slid under the desk. So not the best place, but maybe this would buy him a little more time before being spotted.

"The Styrofoam cups are in here," he heard Jazzy say as she opened the door. *Shit! Where the fuck are you, Sinacola?*

"Isn't this the office?" Mitch rolled his eyes up, thanking god for the good karma being tossed his way when he heard his friend's voice.

"Yeah, it's a mess right now," she said as she stepped inside the dark office. The lights flashed on, blinding Mitch, and he pulled his body even farther under the desk.

"Here, let me carry that for you." Kreed's smooth voice almost made him laugh. He could just imagine Kreed batting his eyelashes.

"I can get it," she said, but her tone was clear—*I'd love for you to carry that for me.*

"Anything else?' Kreed drawled.

"I need to enter the sales for the night, but I can do that after you leave. Your friend has been in the bathroom a long time. I hope he's okay," she said. Mitch could tell she was retreating toward the door, thank god.

"He's got that irritable bowel syndrome. Keeps him in there awhile," Kreed said in a low voice, as though he was telling her a secret, and right then, Mitch decided to kick Kreed's ass when they got out of there. Besides, how the fuck had he let her come to this office?

"Oh poor guy, my granddad has that. He can't always make it to the restroom in time." Mitch scowled as the light turned off and the door shut behind them.

"Motherfucker," Mitch hissed, untucking himself from under the desk. His big body wasn't made for such tight places, and he rolled his shoulders and then his neck.

He needed to call Brown back. Apparently he hadn't hung up the office phone in his scurry to get under the desk. It was sitting slightly askew in its cradle.

"You still there?" he asked, picking up the phone.

"Irritable bowel syndrome?" Brown asked. Mitch could hear them all laughing in the background.

"Fuck you, fuck him. What the hell else am I doing in here?" Mitch hissed, running his fingers across his jaw.

"Turn the computer on," Brown said, still laughing. Mitch didn't say a word as he reached down to the CPU and pushed the button on. The screen slowly lit up, and he waited for Brown's next instruction.

"All right, we're in," he said.

"Everything's good?" Mitch wanted confirmation before he left. This might be the only chance they had.

"Yep, get the hell out of there," Brown said, and Mitch disconnected the call. He doubled checked the phone, making sure it looked untouched, and went to the door. With his ear stuck close to the door, he listened for any sounds in the hallway. When he heard nothing, he cracked open the door and slid out, making sure the lock re-engaged when he closed the door. Kreed now had captured both women's attention and was talking at the front of the store.

"Hey, buddy, everything come out all right?" Kreed asked, acting concerned. Mitch cocked a brow, but stayed silent.

"I guess that means no then." Kreed pretended to wince.

"I'm sorry about that. I know it's a hard thing to deal with," Jazzy said, sympathy written all over her face. He gave her a nod and a small smile.

"Are you ready?" Mitch turned to Kreed and asked.

"What, you don't want a drink now?" Kreed asked, holding his cup in his hand. He lifted it, taking a long drink to hide his smile.

"No, I don't." Mitch turned around and hurried out of the building. Every word they spoke was being recorded and he wasn't giving that bunch anymore ammunition to harass him. Kreed took a little longer to exit. When he did, he held out a piece of paper.

"Fuck you, I ought to kick your ass," Mitch rumbled, stalking toward his rental.

"But you won't." Kreed chuckled.

"I might. Irritable bowel syndrome? Are you fucking kidding me, that's all you could come up with?" Mitch opened the door, sliding in the driver's seat.

"I had to think fast," Kreed said, shutting the passenger door and putting on his seat belt.

"Your job was to keep her out of the fucking office," Mitch hissed, starting the SUV.

"How was I supposed to know that's where they kept the fucking Styrofoam cups? I was louder than a herd of elephants coming down the hall. You had time to hide." Mitch's phone began to ring as he pulled out of his parking spot.

"You're the worst fucking partner on the planet. Hello," he barked into the phone.

"Is this a bad time?" Cody asked, and Mitch's ruffled feathers were immediately soothed. This was the first time Cody had spontaneously and voluntarily called him. He could feel the smile spreading on his face.

"No, of course not. Not for you. What're you doing?" His voice became softer and his heart raced.

"Oh god, here we go again," Kreed spouted as he rolled his eyes and slumped down in the seat, being completely overdramatic.

"Fuck you," he snarled at Kreed, but he was in too good a mood right now to be serious. He gave Kreed his I-mean-it stare before he continued. "Ignore him, Cody. We just left an assignment that he fucked up, but I don't want to talk about that. I'd rather talk about you. What are you up to tonight?"

~~~

Cody stretched out on his bed completely nude, his hardened cock already in his hand. It was eleven o'clock his time, so midnight in DC, and he was more than ready for some of that hot as hell phone sex Mitch was so good at giving him. He'd even put his laptop on the bed in case Mitch could Skype. He'd grown to love their video chat sessions.

But dammit if his night hadn't just came to a screeching halt. Mitch was with people—well, his buddy Kreed. How in the hell did he even begin to answer the question Mitch asked now? What was he up to? He couldn't just say what he really wanted. Which was to jack off with Mitch.

"Is this a bad time?" he asked again, trying to keep his voice even. Mitch was silent for a minute, maybe even catching on, maybe not, but Cody waited for him to answer.

"It's not a good time for me, but you sound like you might be ready." Mitch's voice lowered to little more than a whisper.

"I can still hear you, ass. I'm sitting right next to you," Kreed said loud enough for Cody to hear.

"I can call you later." Cody suddenly wished he'd never made this call. He should have texted first, but Mitch stopped him.

"No, hang on." Mitch replied, and Cody could hear the screech of the car tires in the background.

"What the hell? Are you trying to kill us?" Kreed shouted.

"Shut up," Mitch grumbled and Cody heard the car door slam. "Okay, we're alone now."

"What did you do?" Cody asked, completely confused.

"I pulled over and got out. So what are you really doing?" Mitch questioned. It took a second for Cody's mind to switch in so many different directions.

"I was thinking about you," he confessed, feeling a little vulnerable and still worried he shouldn't have made this call.

"You're always on my mind. Are you alone?" Mitch asked, making everything right again in Cody's world.

"Yeah."

"Are you naked?" Mitch purred. Cody could hear the smile in Mitch's tone. It made him smile too, and he reached for his cock again.

"Yeah." The heat of his blush warmed his cheeks. He'd gone from turned on, to losing the erection, back to so turned on in a matter of two or three minutes, and it all happened with the sound of Mitch's voice. He gripped himself, moving his fist up and down his swollen shaft.

"Are you touching yourself? I bet you are. I wish I was there to do that for you."

Cody said nothing because he wanted that exact thing so badly right now.

"I want it to be me touching you, stroking you, Cody. Me tasting you, sucking you till you give up your load. Mmm…damn. Just thinking about you fucking my mouth…" The horn to Mitch's rental sounded off in the background. Cody heard Mitch curse under his breath. He had been so close, and he was horny as hell. His dick wept with need. Kreed must have rolled down the window because he could hear him shouting at Mitch.

"Get in the car. I know what you're doing. You have to be on duty tonight. Phone fuck him later, Mitch. Job before hos." And Kreed honked the horn again.

"You need to go." Cody couldn't help the disappointment, but he completely understood. He had plenty of images of Mitch in his spank bank, so he'd be just fine.

"He's such a pain in the ass," Mitch growled into the phone. Cody loved that sexy growl Mitch had, and so did his dick.

"He's your partner. You're on a big case. I shouldn't have called."

"No, you always call. Don't stop calling. I love when you call me. It's just, I've got surveillance tonight, and I'll be off around six in the morning. Can I call you then?" Mitch sounded hopeful.

"We're on the last leg of repairing the fence line. I'm meeting my brothers at five. We need to get it done before I start back to work," Cody answered. He still gripped himself tightly. He'd finish this when he hung up.

"Dammit! Then call me when you take a break," Mitch instructed.

"You need to sleep sometime, Mitch."

"Just call me," Mitch repeated, and the horn blared again in the background. "Cowboy, I want you to send me a picture of yourself right now. Get that angle from the webcam when you put it on the nightstand or whatever's by your head. And promise me you'll keep doing what you're doing, just make sure it's me you're thinking about. It's my lips on you, my fingers inside you, pleasuring you till you explode. And I expect you to say my name when you come."

"I don't think that'll be a problem, but I'm not sure about that picture." Cody continued stroking himself to the sound of Mitch's voice.

"I promise to protect it with my life and cut your head out. No one will know," Mitch whispered softly. "I need to see you like this. I miss us together."

Cody rode his fist harder and faster with each word Mitch spoke. The image of Mitch's mouth on his cock had his balls tingling and drawing up tight against his body.

"You're all I can think about anymore..." Cody uttered the words he held so secretly inside his heart as he pumped up into his fist one last time, his body arched as hot thick come splashed on his stomach and chest. "Mitch," he breathed out on a long moan.

"God, you're killing me, Turner, I'm so fucking hard right now. I'm coming there as soon as I can. And you better be ready for me."

Cody didn't say anything, nor did he immediately clean himself up. He just laid there, his eyes closed, thinking about Mitch's full lips and those perfect dimples.

"Fuck it! I really like you a lot. More than a lot," Mitch whispered his confession.

"Me too," Cody sighed. He loved hearing those words from Mitch, especially after what he let out. His body was completely relaxed now, enveloped in a state of bliss.

"Save it for me, no one else. You're holding my spot, right?" The horn beeped again.

"Yeah," Cody answered quietly.

"I'm trying, Cody. I don't know when I'll see you again, but I'm trying," Mitch said. His voice sounded a little desperate. Cody had no idea what he was trying for, what Mitch wanted to say.

"I wanna see you too," he finally answered.

"Good, I gotta go kick Kreed's ass. I'll talk to you tomorrow. Sweet dreams, cowboy." Mitch ended the call.

Cody still refused to move and laid there silently contemplating everything they'd just said. He'd planned for a little phone sex, not confessions of the heart. He did like Mitch. He liked him a lot. Maybe a little too much. Tomorrow he'd worry about the repercussions of admitting his interest in someone as extraordinary as Mitch Knox.

Chapter 36

Days turned into a week as Mitch and the team listened to endless hours of conversation from the coffee shop and the private discussions of the owner. They had read countless pages of computer transcripts and nothing revealed anything they could use. On the latest report, he read through a church sermon DeGeorge attended and to-date that was the biggest thing they had learned about the man. At least on the outside he was a kind, caring godly man. Mitch tossed the report on the desk separating him from Kreed.

"Your gut's wrong this time," Mitch said.

"No, it's not. It just proves what we've always known. They're smart and know how to work the system." Kreed looked over at him and picked up the file.

"So what now? We follow him to the soup kitchen and church?" Mitch ran a hand through his hair and leaned back in his chair. He was pissed they were getting nowhere and fast.

"We're gonna have to," Kreed countered back. Mitch reached over to his office phone and dialed Connors.

"Can you come in here?"

"Sure, hang on," Connors said on the other end of the line. Mitch hung up the phone and looked back over at Kreed.

"He's not gonna go for it." Mitch stretched his legs out in front of him and brought his fingers together, interlocking them, and rested his chin on his knuckles.

"Why not?" Kreed questioned, a confused look crossed his face.

"Budgets." Mitch shrugged and rapped his knuckles sharply against the desk.

"Mitch, I'm telling you, if you want the answers, you need to get them from DeGeorge." Mitch contemplated what Kreed had just said as Connors came inside the room and looked between them.

"What about undercover? Could we place someone on the inside?" Mitch asked.

"We got nothing to help us justify spending the money or the manpower on something like that," Connors said, leaning against the door frame.

"We'd have to get approval. What do we say? We need more to go on than just a gut feeling." Connors looked over at Kreed and then back to Mitch. "Look, I'm not supposed to say anything, but the director's thinking this needs a change. He thinks the case needs fresh eyes."

"You haven't told me that," Mitch spoke up.

"Did you not just hear me say I'm not supposed to? Your director's fighting hard to keep you on the case, but you know how I feel. We're missing the mark, Knox."

"Bullshit," Kreed spoke up. "I fucking told you the answers are with the coffee shop owner. Infiltrate him and something will break."

"And the Marshals are halving this budget," Mitch added. "I can get Director Skinner more involved. Make him approve undercover."

"Look, rumor has it that we have an undercover agent freeing up. She'll be reassigned soon. She's good. She'll become whatever she needs to become. Let me see if she's available. They won't give her to us for long, but she's good enough to see things quickly." Connors didn't wait for their approval, he was just out the door.

Connors came back about an hour later with a grin on his face. Kreed was on his surveillance shift and Brown was pacing. Both Mitch and Brown stopped what they were doing and narrowed their brows, concentrating on Connors.

"We get her, starting Monday," Connors announced and held out his hand for a high-five. He got a round of enthusiastic hand slaps in return.

"Yes! Awesome! How did you get her?" he asked.

"I just laid it out there. Even Kreed's gut feeling, which held weight because he closes most of his cases…" Connors said.

"You mean all of them. I'll bet a hundred dollars Kreed's right on this one too." Mitch shot back before Connors could finish his sentence.

"I'll take you up on your bet, but they agreed with everything. They offered a less seasoned agent, at least less seasoned to me, but I said we would wait. It's only five days. She'll work her way in, and we'll know if we're barking up the wrong tree pretty quickly," Connors assured him.

"When can I meet her?" Mitch asked.

"Maybe Friday. She's expected to close her case Thursday."

"Excellent news!" Mitch was excited about the new development.

"I'm calling Kreed." Mitch dialed Kreed's number immediately and got voice mail. He left a message, inwardly praying Kreed's gut was right.

Chapter 37

Cody finally nodded at some children who stood across the street. They had been staring at him for at least the last five minutes. He could tell they were on a field trip and every so often he could hear them talking about him as they waited patiently in line to take the tour through the capitol building. Cody had come to learn over the last couple of days he'd been in the field, small kids were fascinated by an officer on a horse.

He got it. Most little boys stared at him whenever he was in uniform. Many would eventually muster up the nerve to come over and talk to him whenever they had the chance. And all children loved horses, but put the two together and children were drawn to him and Ranger like moths to a flame. And to top it all off, his horse loved the attention.

Sometimes on occasion, parents let their children get close enough to actually speak to him and touch Ranger. He was mindful of his actions, careful how he handled his mount. Over the past few days, he'd met so many interesting people. He enjoyed his job, and he hoped it showed, giving a lot of nods to the tourists he encountered, and he always returned a smile.

For Cody, being in law enforcement meant he needed to uphold a certain standard. He had to always remain the constant professional.

Cody held on to the reins and backed his horse Ranger into the shade. They were due a break, but he was just so pumped about the job he didn't want to leave. He also didn't want to push Ranger too hard. They were just getting to know one another.

His phone vibrated in his pocket. The faint whistle sounded, and this time, he had to really fight the smile. Thank god no one heard that ringtone. He'd thought he had completely silenced his phone. Man, the hell he'd get if any of his team heard that.

He shouldn't have, but since Mitch had been on his mind twenty-four seven, he palmed his phone, keeping an eye on the crowd as he read the message.

"Can you talk?" Mitch had asked. Instead of sending back a text and wasting the precious few minutes he had, Cody decided to call.

"Shut the door on the way out!" That's how Mitch answered the phone. "Hey."

"Is it a bad time? I figured you could talk," Cody replied.

"Nah, it's fine. I'm waiting for Kreed to call back. What are you doing?"

"Working, Ranger and I are taking a break. So I can't talk long." Ranger shifted his weight under Cody.

"Are you outside? I hear…a lot of noise. Wind maybe?" Mitch asked.

"Yes, I'm on Ranger and the capitol's full of tourists today," Cody answered.

"You're on your horse right now?" Mitch asked.

"Yeah, I probably shouldn't have called."

"No, you should have, that's hot. Damn, the visuals that produces, cowboy."

Cody was silent to that.

"Take a selfie," Mitch urged.

"I'm not taking a picture of myself on this horse," Cody said.

"Please take a picture. I wanna see you mounted and in your uniform," Mitch insisted.

"Mitch…" he started, but the guy cut him off.

"I'm hanging up now so you can take the picture and text me," he said, then hung up on Cody. A text came immediately in.

"Hurry. Don't overthink it. Just do it." And Cody did. He opened the camera button on his phone, stuck his arm out, and clicked the picture. He'd never done anything like that while on the job. He didn't let himself even consider the inappropriateness of his actions. The shot was awkward but showed him and part of the saddle and a bit of Ranger's neck and dark mane. He swiped the photo and sent it to Mitch, before dropping the phone back in his shirt pocket.

"I didn't think you could be anymore sexy than when you were lying underneath me. You proved me wrong. Wear that when I see you next time." Mitch's text came back quickly.

Cody felt the blush rising up on his cheeks at the same time his cock hardened. He tugged his trooper cowboy hat down farther on his head and adjusted himself in the saddle, neither helped. He nudged Ranger forward and forced his mind back on the job. Mitch Knox was exactly the distraction his sister had always warned him about, yet somehow he couldn't find it in him to care. He welcomed the distraction if it meant keeping Mitch around.

~~~

If Mitch sat there staring at that picture of Cody, he'd be left with a full-fledged hard-on and no way to relieve it while sitting in the middle of the FBI building, so he closed the picture and redirected his thoughts as he dialed Kreed again.

"We finally got the break we needed. Your gut better be right on this one. I put down a hundred bucks in your favor. We have someone going in undercover starting Monday!" Mitch said before Kreed could even speak.

"I gotta go home," Kreed spoke quietly into the phone. Kreed was like a brother to him, and that tone he heard had him worried.

"Hey, man, you can't just open the van door like that." Mitch heard someone say, then he heard the door slam shut.

"What's wrong?" Mitch asked. Whatever this was, it had to be bad.

"My little brother was killed." Mitch could hear the pain in Kreed's voice as he tried to register those words.

"What? I thought he was in San Antonio. Did he get deployed? What happened? I'm sorry, man." Mitch sat straight up in his chair.

His heart broke as the momentary shock wore off, and the reality settled in.

"Thanks. No, my dad said it was a training exercise accident, some shit like that. He'd just moved back home with my parents. They said he decided to not re-enlist. He declined orders and was just waiting to get out. I didn't even know that."

"Kreed, man. I'm so sorry."

"I gotta go home. They got the body released last night. I missed their call. Man, my mom's a wreck." Kreed's voice broke as he spoke. Mitch could hear the sadness in his words. Maybe tears had started, but there would be no way Kreed would ever let him know.

"I'm on my way. I'll get you to the airport." Mitch jumped up, searching for his keys.

"No, I'm flagging a taxi now. I'm sorry I'm leaving the case like this," Kreed apologized.

"Don't worry about that. Do they have any funeral details?" Mitch leaned against the desk, not sure exactly what to do. He hated the helplessness.

"I don't know. I'll text you when I know more," Kreed said, and Mitch heard Kreed's signature loud whistle. The one that would stop any moving taxi within a mile radius.

"I'll be there," Mitch promised.

"You don't have to come. I need to get to Dulles International," Kreed said, then Mitch could hear the taxi driver saying something.

"I'll get Ellen to get you a seat," Mitch offered.

"I just hung up with her. I gotta go, Mitch." Kreed's voice choked up. The best Mitch remembered, Kreed had only one sibling who was years younger than him. His parents were older. Mitch had met them one time for just a minute when they drove through Texas to Mexico.

His heart broke a little more right then. He vowed to himself to be better to his family. What if this had been him? He hadn't even *met* three nieces and nephews. He dropped his head in his hand before he rose. He needed to cover Kreed's shifts and find someone to cover them both for the funeral. He'd be there for Kreed. He had to be.

Chapter 38

Cody ran uncharacteristically late and that stressed him out more than the man he rushed to pick up. The last few days had been hard. Cody knew Mitch was grieving at the same time he had been busting his ass, covering both his and Kreed's workloads. Cody was hell-bent on being there for Mitch when he needed him this weekend. In honor of that thought, the least he could have done was arrive to the Austin-Bergstrom International Airport on time. But downtown Austin traffic had other ideas. The roads had been a snarled mess, something he didn't factor into his time when he left this evening.

Cody took a chance and pulled into the loading zone for arrivals. He was at least twenty minutes late, probably enough time to get out of baggage claim, if Mitch had even checked any luggage. Cody drove slowly through the lot, watching as he passed by the people standing outside. Mitch stood out like a beacon to him. He was somewhat alone, looking impressive and intimidating all at the same time. There were people on the sidewalk with him, but they all stayed back, which probably had something to do with the scowl he wore on his face.

Damn, he hoped he hadn't made things worse.

Cody pulled his truck right up alongside the curb and shoved the gearshift into park. He opened his door right about the time Mitch opened the passenger door.

"I'm sorry I'm late." Cody was stuck between getting out of the truck and Mitch getting inside.

"Don't be. Thanks for picking me up. I could've grabbed a taxi," Mitch said, holding the passenger door open. He had a backpack as well as a garment bag with him. Mitch reached back to hang his suit bag on the hook in the backseat when Cody got fully inside and shut the door. Once Mitch got everything settled, he slid into his seat and looked over at him. Cody reached across and lifted Mitch's sunglasses from his eyes.

"You look exhausted."

"I am. This one, for some reason, is really hard on me," Mitch said, putting the sunglasses back in place before linking his hand with Cody's. They still faced one another, neither willing to be the first to look away.

"It's been all over the local news. I'm sorry for your loss. I played little league with him," he squeezed Mitch's hand.

"I wondered about that. He's your age, thought you might have gone to school together or something. Just a kid." Mitch sighed as he sat back in his seat.

"He wasn't a kid. I'm not a kid. At least I don't see us like that. Something's not right with this whole thing." Cody didn't put the truck in gear. Instead, he continued gauging Mitch's mindset.

"That's the military for you. They aren't giving any details. Kreed's family's a wreck." Mitch pointed toward the drive. "We should get going. The cop's circled a couple of times now. He's eyeing you."

"I'm not gonna get a ticket," Cody chuckled. He knew ninety percent of the Austin Police Department. Mitch had to know that. Cody reluctantly let go of Mitch's hand and moved the gearshift back into drive.

"I imagined you driving a big truck like this, wearing that baseball cap you wore the first night I met you. I thought about that on the plane ride. I'm glad you're wearing it now." Mitch took Cody's hand back in his once they'd merged into traffic.

"Where am I taking you? Are you going to Kreed's family's house?" Cody asked after giving Mitch a smile for remembering those details about him.

"I planned on staying with you, cowboy. If it's okay." Mitch winked at him.

"I'd hoped you'd would, but do you need to go by the family's house first?" Cody asked.

"I guess I probably should. You mind going?" Mitch asked.

"Not at all. I planned on going to the funeral tomorrow. I figured I should. I didn't know him well, but you know." Cody gave a shrug as he navigated the small turns of the airport with the massive vehicle he drove one-handed, unwilling to release his hold on Mitch.

"Good. I wanted you to go. I just didn't want to ask," Mitch said. That surprised Cody. He figured he'd be on his own tomorrow. That Mitch would be tied up with the family.

"San Antonio PD's got some news that Eastfield might show up, but it's just a memorial. I didn't think they came to things like that," Cody said, picking his route from the airport.

"I hate those fuckers. Damn, they piss me off. Is anything forming a counter-protest?" Mitch asked, looking his way, very concerned.

"I don't know. It was gossip some of the guys were talking about," Cody answered, cutting his eyes back and forth between the road and Mitch.

"Do they know Kreed's gay?" Mitch asked, fully facing him now.

"Kreed's gay?" That got Cody's attention, because he hadn't known.

"If you didn't know, that's probably a good sign," Mitch replied, pulling his phone from his jacket pocket.

"Kreed's gay?" Cody asked again. He felt a pang of jealousy squeeze his heart even as he said the name.

"Yeah. It's why we teamed up together. We've been doing this a long time. It's just now that people are so accepting. When I first started in all this, I wouldn't have made it without him. He's always had my back. I've had his," Mitch responded, working his phone.

"Do you fuck him?" Cody asked bluntly. He was shocked by his own crude use of words and the possessiveness coursing through him. But damn, how was this the first time he'd heard about this? And absolutely this was not the time to be having this conversation.

Oh shit. I'm an idiot. He'd been saying he would hold Mitch's spot, but Mitch had never given him that guarantee back.

"No. Of course not." Mitch's gaze jerked to his as he waited for the call to connect. Just as he was getting ready to say more, his attention diverted to the phone a second before he whispered, "Hang on," and held up a finger to give him a minute. "Hi, Mrs. Sinacola, this is Mitch Knox. How are you doing?" Cody drove, not listening to Mitch. Having no idea where he was going, he headed toward San Antonio, taking Mitch to see the family, but with each passing mile, the pit in his stomach grew. He gripped his steering wheel a little tighter than normal. Why hadn't he thought of this before? He'd never questioned Kreed sharing a room with him that first night he was in town. He also got the feeling Kreed wasn't into this relationship between them. Just the little things Mitch had said, and now he completely got why. *Fuck!*

"Hey, cowboy? Earth to Cody." Mitch's voice pulled him from his thoughts. Cody glanced over at Mitch who now had his sunglasses pushed up on his head, and the devious grin was back, showing off those gorgeous dimples. Maybe it was more of a smirk, but the dimples were there, drawing him in, and damn, if dread didn't fill him. Mitch meant something to him, and he didn't like that Kreed Sinacola was gay.

"Where am I taking you?" Cody asked, not sharing his thoughts out loud.

"What were you thinking so hard about?" Mitch countered.

Cody didn't answer. He couldn't. The timing was wrong, and he needed space. Maybe distance was more the word.

"Are you jealous?" Mitch turned in his seat, facing him.

"Of course not." At least that was what he wanted Mitch to think.

There was silence between them.

"I don't have sex with Kreed Sinacola. We decided against that a long time ago. We needed to have each other's backs, look out for the other one. He's a couple of years older than me. He came from a military background. He knew the deal way before I did."

Cody glanced over at Mitch, gauged his face. He looked like he was being honest and straight-forward. He couldn't stare at Mitch long because he had to split his time between the road and the man. Cody finally just picked the road to concentrate on. "You never had sex with him?"

"I didn't say that. I have, we did in the beginning a few times. But that stopped a long time ago. We made that decision. It's done. I have no desire to ever go back there again. He's my work partner, we're fluid in the field together. Nothing else. I promise," Mitch assured him.

Cody let out the sigh he was holding, keeping his eyes on the road. "I assumed you'd be holding my spot since you were asking me to hold yours."

Mitch took Cody's hand back in his, made a show of linking their fingers together again. "It's a safe assumption. Look, I'm not gonna hide the fact I'm kind of looking for more with you than someone to fuck. Watching Colt Michaels and Jace Montgomery and knowing their story made me realize that if it could happen for them, then it could happen to anyone. I was open to the idea, but I honestly didn't think I'd find anyone. Then there you were, sitting quietly in a corner, almost unseen. My world's been pretty rocked since then. Meeting you knocked me flat on my ass, Cody. I'm not gonna lie about that to you."

Cody gripped Mitch's hand tighter.

"So it's a safe assumption?" Cody asked, not looking over at Mitch.

"Oh yeah," Mitch answered and raised their joined hands for a kiss.

"I'm driving in the general direction of San Antonio. I'm not real sure of your plans. This is the way I should be going, right?" Cody asked, changing the subject.

"Yeah, let me pull up their address on my phone."

Cody's stomach wasn't roiling like it had before, he might even be back to the happy medium he'd been at when this conversation started, but he still needed to be careful. He hadn't figured Mitch for the settling down type. No way would he have ever gone there. Besides, their distance was enough to make this whole thing between them too hard. This was good for now, but he needed to keep his head straight. This was going to end. The complications were stacked against them. No matter how much he wished it weren't true, six months from now, Mitch Knox would be a memory.

~~~

Mitch watched as Cody navigated the big truck down the older neighborhood street, dodging the parked cars and children playing outside. He'd officially spent almost the whole entire month of October in DC. Riding down this street reminded him it was close to Halloween. He had to look down at his phone to see it was actually October thirtieth.

This part of the country was warm and inviting outside. The carved jack-o'-lanterns were being put out. Decorations were being hung. When had Halloween rivaled Christmas for home décor?

"Right here," Mitch said, pointing to the house that had cars filling the driveway and all out front along the road.

"That's Kreed." Mitch gestured to the guy atop a ladder, doing some sort of home repair. An older man stood at the foot of the ladder, pointing, giving directions. It had been years since he'd met Kreed's family, but he thought that might be Kreed's dad at the base.

Cody parked the truck in the first available spot a few houses down. He turned off the engine. Mitch didn't move, he stayed by Cody's side.

"You've been quiet. I know that's not a good sign."

"I'm just trying to be accommodating." Cody gave him a smile.

"You know I feel better just being with you, but you haven't kissed me yet," Mitch said, scooting closer to Cody.

"It's probably not the best place," Cody started to say as Mitch lifted his arm, moved in, and pulled Cody toward him. Their lips met for a soft brushing. Mitch opened, deepening the kiss. He agreed this wasn't the time for much more, but he'd missed Cody and merely being in his presence soothed him. Besides, they'd just had a pivotal moment in their relationship. Cody had been jealous of Kreed. Very jealous, and that meant he cared. Mitch wanted him to care.

"I'm gonna need you to make love to me tonight. Maybe something tender, meaningful." Slowly he opened his lids to see Cody staring at him.

"You have no problem just saying what's on your mind." Cody leaned in and kissed his lips again.

"Actually, I don't think you'll believe me, but I do. I keep a lot inside." Mitch watched as Cody's brow narrowed. "Come on. Kreed's probably going to need some help with whatever job his dad has him doing." Mitch let go of Cody, got out of the truck, and waited for him at the tailgate.

"Mrs. Sinacola said there was a lot of food. We could stay for dinner." Mitch tucked his hands inside his jacket pockets when Cody slid his in his jeans.

"It's Halloween this weekend."

"Am I keeping you from anything? You don't have to stay if you have plans," Mitch said.

"No, I took off tomorrow, and Sunday I was scheduled off," Cody said as they walked side by side toward the house.

"Knox, it's about fuc...time." Kreed yelled from the top of the ladder.

"It's about time you did some actual work for a change," he called out, cutting across the yard. He reached for Kreed's father's hand. "Mr. Sinacola, I'm sorry for your loss."

"Thank you, Son," the older man replied. His eyes were red-rimmed, and he looked tired. Kreed was coming down as he introduced Cody.

"Mr. Sinacola, this is Cody Turner," Mitch introduced them. Cody was perfect. He extended a hand to Mr. Sinacola's in greeting.

"Sir, I played little league with Derek. I was so sorry to hear what happened." Before Mr. Sinacola could respond, Kreed was in Cody's face.

"It's about damn time I met you. Mitch freaked me out with all the positive energy and smiling he's been doing," Kreed teased, sticking out his hand. Mitch took this as the diversion Kreed needed. He looked as exhausted as his father.

"It's crazy in there. You might wanna grab a ladder and help me clean out the gutters," Kreed offered.

"I'm supervising," Kreed's father declared. "The womenfolk are three feet deep in food in there."

"Your mom said there was food." Mitch watched as Kreed handed Cody the ladder and grabbed a smaller one lying against the side of the house.

"Not worth going in there," Kreed hollered back.

"Cody, don't let him put you to work. Come inside, eat something." Mitch was already several steps away.

"I don't mind helping," Cody said, and Mitch laughed at the gleam on Mr. Sinacola's face. Mitch could see him mentally ticking things off his to-fix-around-the-house list. Cody was in good hands, besides, his cowboy had to see for himself that Kreed was harmless. Those two needed to build a friendship if he and Cody had any chance of making something substantial together.

"Can you use a hammer?" Mr. Sinacola asked, and Kreed just laughed.

"Yes, sir," Cody nodded seriously.

"Well, that's going to come in very handy. Come with me, young man," Mr. Sinacola said.

Chapter 39

Twilight had passed about an hour ago, and Cody worked on hammering several broken shingles back in place. The job had been more than he originally thought. Part of the siding from the house had come loose. Once he got up there, he found a big mess, and he just didn't have it in him to do a half-ass job.

Kreed's father had regularly thanked him for the last couple of hours. He finally sent the man inside when the evening chill came on. Kreed had his own task going on in the shed outside. Apparently with both their boys gone and Mr. Sinacola's age, a lot of things around the house hadn't been taken care of.

What got Cody solidly in the heart was when Mr. Sinacola had said Derek had planned to make these repairs once he left the military and was looking for work. That broke his heart. He and his family worked together all the time. And here this family was all broken apart.

"Homemade Southern fried chicken. It's about the best thing ever," Mitch taunted. Cody looked down and saw Mitch standing in the shadows of the house, holding up what looked like a chicken leg.

"I'm a home-grown Southern boy. That chicken's a staple of my everyday life. It doesn't hold a lot of interest to me. Now pecan pie on the other hand…" Cody called back, jokingly.

"Well, that's a good thing since I ate your share of chicken. Now I'm gonna go find that pie." Mitch grinned, and Cody just chuckled at him.

"I'm almost done. Hang on." Cody finished the last couple of bangs with the hammer, made sure everything was nailed properly and made his way down. Mitch sat on the porch steps. The light from the front door cast a glow on him. He gnawed on that bone, not leaving a scrap behind. Cody had to laugh; Mitch must really like fried chicken. He'd be at home with his mom on a Sunday lunch.

Kreed came from the other side of the house, the tall dark-headed guy wiping his hands on a rag as he came toward Cody. "I'll take that," Kreed said, motioning for the ladder Cody already had tucked under his arm.

"I got it, just tell me where to go," Cody said, already walking toward the garage.

"Dad's got several against the side of the house over there," Kreed responded.

"Go inside or take a seat. I got this." Cody put everything away, turned off the lights, and closed up the garage. He had no idea of the time. He looked up at the moon, trying to judge, until he saw Kreed sitting next to Mitch on the front porch. They sat side by side with the same stance, feet spread apart, elbows on their knees, heads bent toward the other, and they were talking quietly. Both men were about the same size, definitely the same build. They looked good together. No matter what Mitch said, he could see Kreed was his best friend. It showed in their mannerisms. That stomach pit thing happened again, and he slowed his pace, not sure if he should interfere.

It was Kreed who saw him and looked up. "Thanks for helping him tonight. It took his mind off things because he got to boss you around."

"It's not a problem. He's a good man," Cody said, coming to stand in front of them. He felt liked he'd interrupted them and wasn't exactly sure what to do about that.

"Come sit down," Mitch urged, looking up at him as he stood watching them. Mitch moved the chicken bone sitting on the edge of the porch in order for him to take a seat. It would be a tight fit if he sat between Mitch and the post on the front porch. When he didn't move right away, Mitch reached out and took his hand, drawing him down.

"Manual labor's over for tonight," he said, winking at Cody when he sat down. He'd been right about the tight fit. Mitch leaned back and draped an arm around his back, pulling Cody up next to him. Again, there were no inhibitions in Mitch's behavior. He clearly felt comfortable with PDAs, and Cody cast a glance in Kreed's direction, gauging his response.

Kreed stayed silent, watching them. His face softened a bit and Cody glanced back at Mitch who was looking slyly at Kreed.

"He's hot, isn't he?" Mitch asked Kreed and nodded in his direction.

"Yep," Kreed responded after a minute. "Damn, Knox, didn't think you had it in you."

"I told you he was fucking hot. You didn't think I could get a guy this good-looking?" Mitch watched Cody intently and had a big shit-eatin' grin plastered across his face. Cody's cheeks warmed under his gaze and the compliment in Mitch's words.

"How old are you?" Kreed asked him.

"Twenty-six," Cody answered, linking his fingers, matching Kreed's sitting position.

"What's a good lookin' guy like you doing with an old man like him?" Kreed asked and nodded his head toward Mitch.

"I did not fly halfway around the world to hear you casting doubt to my guy about me," Mitch retorted and drew Cody in closer to him. "Besides, I'm not that old."

Kreed gave a bark of laughter. "Said the old man."

"You're older than me," Mitch scoffed.

"I'm not trying to date him. Cody, when you're thirty, he'll be sixty-two." That had Cody smiling, looking back at Mitch who then shoved Kreed.

"Fuck you. I'm like seven years older than him," Mitch snapped.

"You're not counting the dog years. Did he tell you what a dawg he was back when he was your age?" Kreed asked, trying for serious as he looked around Mitch to Cody.

"Okay, that's enough. No more of this," Mitch said, standing, drawing Cody up with him.

"Yeah, you need to know something, you call me. I'll fill you all in about Mitch Knox," Kreed goaded, rising slowly to his feet.

"Don't listen to him. He's got nothing to say that has any value or importance to anything. They have you a plate of food in there." Mitch started moving Cody inside as Kreed laughed out loud at him.

"I need to wash my hands," Cody added as Mitch opened the door and pushed him through.

"There's a bathroom down the hall. Come on, I'll show you," Mitch said.

"I can show him." Kreed offered still from the front porch.

"You just stay outside," Mitch called back. Cody laughed again, looking over his shoulder. Kreed was smiling. He looked younger right then, not so burdened. The moment eased Cody too.

~~~

Somewhere around eleven o'clock, Cody navigated the highway to drive them the hour or so back to his place. His belly was full and he yawned right alongside Mitch who had a couple of whiskey shots with Kreed. Mitch yawned louder again and Cody looked over at him. His eyes were closed, his head was back, and his body naturally shifted with the movement. He was close to sleeping, lulled by the sway of the truck.

After they had gone inside, Cody ate more food than he ever remembered eating. What he saw as he worked outside was a steady stream of well-wishers coming to the house. They never stopped all night long. There was also a large group of women inside, just wanting to help out any way they could. Those women were responsible for the three plates he'd consumed, because they never let his plate get empty. A spoonful of something was always being added.

"Thank you for tonight," Mitch said. Cody looked over and smiled.

"I thought you were sleeping."

"Dozing, I think. Seriously, thank you for tonight. I didn't know when we went over there they were gonna put you to work," Mitch said.

"I don't mind helping. I do things like that for my dad all the time," Cody replied. "I was thinking about grabbing some of the guys at work that knew Derek and taking them over there in the next few weeks. They've got overgrown trees in the back. Their fence is coming down. I think some of them paint. The house needs some work."

Mitch stared at him.

"What?" He felt the weight of Mitch's gaze on him as he watched the road.

"I like you more and more every time I'm around you," Mitch said quietly, and that made him smile. He grinned, staring out into the night, keeping an eye on the road. "How much longer until we're home?"

"About twenty minutes, give or take."

"Do you mind if I sleep?" Mitch asked.

"No, go ahead. The headrest bends in." He motioned behind his head to show Mitch.

"Fancy," he said, lying back, resting his head on the headrest. Mitch appeared to have passed out within seconds of reclining. Cody found he drove a little slower and a bit more carefully, letting Mitch sleep longer. He pulled his truck through the gates of the community parking garage in the back of the complex and parked. Mitch never woke up.

Cody contemplated his next move. He slid his hand across Mitch's thigh, unprepared for Mitch's hand to reach out and grab his. Mitch kept his eyes shut, his breathing even, looking very much asleep, but slid their entwined hands up his thigh, covering his dick, using his hand to help Cody massage him right there.

"I've been dreaming about you," Mitch whispered. "See? You're even in my dreams."

"I dream about you too," Cody confessed, stroking Mitch on his own now. Mitch sat forward, barely opening his eyes, and moved until he reached Cody's lips. He kissed him good and long, almost climbing over the console to get to him. No matter how awkward the position was, Mitch kept Cody's hand on him, massaging his rock hard erection.

Cody thought he heard the words, *I need you.* He wasn't sure, but Mitch's brute force had him now pulled across the seat, on top of the console, almost in Mitch's lap. The kiss turned frenzied in a matter of seconds. Mitch's tongue made love to his mouth at the same time his hands roamed across his body.

"Inside," Cody managed to croak out. "Let's take this inside."

"I'll suck you here, if you let me. No one will know." Mitch somehow managed to slide his fingers in the waistband of his jeans.

"Inside." Cody broke free of Mitch's hold, only getting a foot or so away before Mitch was on him again.

"I hate when you deny me. You do it far too often," Mitch grumbled.

"I don't think I do it enough," Cody teased, and Mitch went for his lips again. Cody dodged the move. "Come on. Inside."

Cody awkwardly got out of the truck, making sure to untuck his shirt before going any farther. He prayed he didn't see anyone going up the elevator. There was no way to hide the hard-on filling his jeans.

"Stay over there," he commanded as Mitch rounded the truck. Mitch didn't listen and came for him, pushing him against the side of the truck and kissing him like he'd never been kissed before. Mitch consumed him in that swirl of tongue, lips, and teeth. When Mitch came up for air, Cody wasn't certain he was holding himself up, and without question, the roll of his hips, matching Mitch's, was completely involuntary.

"Now, we know what's what. Take me upstairs and make love to me," Mitch said, lifting Cody's chin until he stared into Mitch eyes. The raw passion he saw reflected in their depths filled him with need. He leaned in and swiped his tongue across Mitch's lips.

"God, you're killing me," Mitch groaned. "Come on."

~~~

Mitch had no idea where he was going. The passion they'd just experienced had Cody tucked in next to him as they followed people inside the building. Mitch caught the door before it closed while Cody pointed in the general direction the others had walked. The elevator dinged and Mitch moved them toward the noise.

"Hey, man." Mitch heard a masculine voice say. He saw the elevator doors being held, and he pushed Cody forward, getting them inside as the buzzer sounded.

"Thanks," Cody said, reaching for the ninth-floor button, but the guy got to it first. So he knew Cody. Mitch eyed him as he leaned back against the elevator wall and Cody stood next to the guy.

"Eastfield's in town," the guy told Cody. Instead of concentrating on whether the guy was in law enforcement or whether he was straight or gay, Mitch's interest perked upon hearing the name of that organization. This was the first confirmation he'd heard they were here.

"For sure?" Cody asked. Good boy, Mitch thought. Suddenly he wanted Cody questioning the guy until they had all the answers.

"Yeah. They're causing problems downtown tonight. I had to go in. I'm surprised you didn't get called."

"I'm off through Sunday. So they're here for the Derek Sinacola's funeral?" Cody asked, crossing his arms over his chest. Mitch decided the guy worked in law enforcement too.

"Yeah, talking shit all downtown. They love to get people riled up," the guy said.

"I'm attending the funeral tomorrow," Cody replied, somewhat quietly.

"I volunteered to work it tomorrow. Be careful, man." They gave a quick fist bump before he got off on the third floor.

"It's wrong what they do," Mitch said, the lust of a moment ago fading quickly. In its place, a sick hollow feeling twisted in his gut. He believed in freedom of speech, he absolutely did, until it crossed the line to hate. The ding signaled their arrival on Cody's floor a moment before the doors opened. Cody extended an arm, pulling Mitch forward, drawing him out.

"We aren't worrying about that church tonight. We're finishing what you started downstairs. Then you're gonna get a full night's sleep, and we'll get up early and head over to the Sinacola's first thing in the morning. Besides, for every one Eastfielder, there will be four people there supporting the Sinacola family. Law enforcement will cover that by themselves," Cody stated, fishing the keys from his pocket.

"I hope you're right."

"I know I am. I'd be there too, if I wasn't going with you," Cody said and opened the door to his apartment. Mitch walked inside, a little impressed. The clean, small loft-style condo perfectly represented

Cody with a mix of Western, modern, and classic. Mitch smiled as Cody's arms came around his waist and his hard cock pressed against his ass.

"I like your place," Mitch said, reaching both his arms back, pulling Cody's head forward for a kiss over his shoulder. Cody's hands slid down the front of his jeans, and that was all it took for the lust to return. He was hard and ready. Mitch tried to turn in Cody's arms, but he couldn't move with the freaking arms of steel pinning him there, and fuck if that didn't turn him on more.

"Walk to the right," Cody whispered against his cheek before his warm tongue plunged into Mitch's ear. Cody unbuckled Mitch's belt and slid a hand inside his jeans. His cock jerked at the rubbing it got. Mitch popped the button and lowered the zipper on his jeans, freeing himself as Cody finished lavishing his ear with kisses and moved to his neck. "Move, Knox. I'm making love to you in the bed. But I'm gonna suck this first."

Cody tightened the hold on his cock, and every nerve ending in his body went nuts. His senses overloaded, and he actually heard himself whimper.

"Move," Cody growled, pushing Mitch forward as he stroked and nuzzled Mitch from behind. Thank god the space was small—maybe fifteen steps and they were at Cody's bed.

Cody ran his palms up Mitch's chest, over his nipples, and then his arms were above his head, the shirt coming off. Cody never paused in his actions. His hands ran back down along Mitch's sides, sliding over his hips to grip the globes of his ass. Cody pushed his jeans down, flipped Mitch around, leaving the jeans pooled at his ankles with his boots on. Cody shoved him back on the bed, tugging his boots off and ridding him of his jeans in one smooth motion.

The domination thing Cody had going made his dick twitch. He fucking liked that shit, especially with the hot blond cowboy at the reins. Mitch lifted himself on his elbows and watched in fascination as Cody undressed and dropped to his knees. He pushed Mitch's thighs open, crawled between them, and swallowed his leaking cock down to the root.

"Fuck, cowboy," he hissed, dropping his head back to the bed when that mind-blowing heat consumed him.

He arched his hips and eased his cock in and out of Cody's warm, wet mouth, trailing his fingers through Cody's hair. Cody's blond head bobbed up and down on his cock. The delicious rhythmic suction of Cody's talented mouth had his balls tightening against his body in no time.

"Cody, I need you to make love to me, please."

Cody pulled off his dick, and he swore the temperature rose twenty degrees in that small room as those blue eyes slid slowly up his body to meet his gaze. Cody gave him a grin and kissed the tip of his cock, before righting himself. He leaned to the side, grabbing a condom and some lube, tossing it on the bed within reach. Mitch scooted backward toward the middle of the bed, and Cody followed after him. That sexy look focused intently on him. *Fuck!* Mitch spread his legs and Cody crawled between them, their hard cocks brushing together as he slid his body firmly on top of him.

Their lips met when he lifted his head to take Cody's mouth with his. He could taste himself on Cody. The feel of Cody's weight on top of him comforted him. He thrust his hips up, grinding his erection into his cowboy.

"Fuck, Turner," he hissed into Cody's mouth as he continued to rut against him. Cody sucked and licked at his lips, never stopping the sensual assault.

"I missed you, missed this," he said between frantic kisses.

"Me too." Cody scraped his teeth over Mitch's throat.

"Oh, god, I need you in me, cowboy." He took hold of his legs, pulling them back, until his thighs were almost touching his chest, opening himself fully for Cody.

"Please."

Cody sat back, and rolled the condom on. He made quick work of popping the top of the lube and pouring some into his palm. He stroked his dick a few times, his gaze holding Mitch's the entire time. Mitch needed Cody Turner buried deep inside him, moving in him, making him forget the uncertainty of the outside world.

The press of strong fingers against his rim made his muscle flutter. Cody eased a finger past the contracting ring and slid in and out a few times before adding a second. He watched the intense look on Cody's face as he moved those fingers inside his body.

"Now, please."

"Let me stretch you," Cody whispered.

"Just fuck me, Cody," he begged.

Cody withdrew his fingers then dragged his erection along the crack of his ass, up and down his crevice, then teased the tip barely inside.

"Oh, shit," Cody gasped as he pushed inch by inch into Mitch, stretching him torturously slow. Mitch's ass was on fire, the burn and sting quickly fading to a delicious heat and welcomed fullness as Cody started to move.

"More." He wanted more, needed more.

Cody pulled out almost all the way, until only the tip remained at his entrance. He slammed forward, doing that same move over and over. Shivers raced through him. He no longer had a coherent thought in his head. His hands fisted into the cool sheets as Cody used his knees for leverage and pounded wildly into him. Somehow he managed to wrap his legs around Cody, drawing him even deeper.

"Harder, cowboy. Fuck me harder," he demanded as his body strained for release.

Cody had angled his hips, the mushroomed head of his lover's cock brushed that magical spot with every in and out thrust of his hips. Cody fell forward and buried his face in Mitch's neck. Mitch moaned at the prickle of Cody's stubble scraping along his jaw. His warm breath ghosted across his skin. Cody's hand continued moving between their bodies, tugging and stroking him with deliberate, rough pulls.

"Yes." Cody rocked into him as loud pants filled his ear.

Mitch was close, so fucking close. The heat of his orgasm took root, growing in his spine, wrapping around to settle in his balls. A sob escaped from his lips.

"I'm gonna come."

"Don't want this to end." Cody's frantic thrusts slowed. Eager lips nibbled his neck, latching on to his skin and sucking. Mitch was absolutely sure that would leave a mark. Seconds passed as Cody lifted to his elbow, bright blue eyes locked on his, and Cody's grip tightened at the base of his cock, denying his release.

"Kiss me," Cody whispered. Mitch pulled Cody's head down to him and captured his mouth with his. Cody's body surged in and out of him as he pushed his tongue between Cody's open lips. Their tongues convened, twisting and curling around the other. Cody's intoxicating taste burst across his palate. Mitch stared into Cody's eyes, holding his face between his palms, urging him even closer. And the slow roll of Cody's hips had him arching his body for more.

Cody made love to him, slowly, purposefully. Deliberate, long thrusts, stroking him in time with the sway of his hips. The kiss eased, turned tender and loving, a soft brushing of lips. He was so lost to this man. Nothing mattered, nothing existed in this moment, except the two of them. He kissed Cody with all he had, making love tenderly to his mouth with his own. He tried to convey the feelings surging through his soul. The kiss ended with a soft brush of lips.

His orgasm churned heavily in his balls. Cody's cock collided against his prostate, and he groaned as his lover increased the strokes on his dick. He hung on by a thread, needing to come, yet not wanting the pleasure to end.

Cody kissed his way to his ear and whispered, "Come with me. Mitch baby, come with me."

"Yes! Cody…yes!" He erupted on those words, his ass clenching uncontrollably around Cody, rippling and contracting as creamy ribbons of his seed splattered against their chests.

"Mitch," Cody moaned low as his body stiffened and his cock pulsed deep in Mitch's ass. Mitch glanced up at Cody, their eyes locked, and the impassioned look reflected in Cody's beautiful blue eyes wrenched a last soul-shattering spurt from him.

~~~

Cody rolled off Mitch who already snored softly underneath him. He slid the condom down his flaccid dick, tossing it in the trash can next to the bed. He lay back against the pillows, watching the ceiling fan as it turned in circles, and dropped an arm over his forehead and sighed. God, they had good sex. Actually, all the time they spent together was good. He and Mitch clicked, fell easily in sync with one another, and Cody felt the pieces of himself aligning when Mitch was with him.

That can't be good.

Cody forced himself up from the bed. Mitch lay in the exact position he'd been in when Cody had finally let them both come. That was a trick he'd learned from Mitch himself. Apparently he'd been an excellent student.

Cody headed to the bathroom, turned on the warm water faucet at the sink, and grabbed a washcloth while he let the water run until it heated. He looked at his reflection in the mirror. He was different. He might not look different on the outside, but inside, he was a whole new person. Each time he'd been with Mitch, he came back a different man, a changed man, a better man.

The warm water splashed across his fingertips, and he used the wet cloth to clean himself. He thought about the kiss they shared as he'd moved so perfectly in and out of Mitch's body. He smiled and closed his eyes, remembering the way Mitch gasped his name. God, he loved to hear that deep sexy voice utter his name.

Cody reached over and grabbed another washcloth, wetting that one, hoping he hadn't taken too long. Mitch would make a mess if he turned over. He wrung out the cloth and went back out into the bedroom. Mitch hadn't moved. He was passed out and snoring solidly now. That made him smile.

The cloth was still warm when he wiped across Mitch's stomach. Mitch jerked forward, almost colliding with Cody's head. He jumped backward as quickly as he could to avoid the collision. "It's okay. I'm just cleaning you."

Mitch looked around the room before focusing back on him. "I fell asleep."

"I know. I was there." He smiled and lifted Mitch's arm to wipe his chest. When he'd finished cleaning Mitch, he turned back to the bathroom, but Mitch's arms hooked around him.

"Leave it. Let me hold you," Mitch said, his voice still thick with sleep.

Cody discarded the rag, carefully laying it on his nightstand. He reached over and clicked off the lamp, making the room dark. Mitch pulled Cody down as he reached for the duvet, tugging the cover up over them. "It took me a solid week to sleep right again after you left DC."

Cody nuzzled the crook of Mitch's neck. Mitch lay back, bringing Cody in an awkward sprawl across his chest. Finally, after a few minutes, Mitch settled. Apparently this was the way Mitch wanted to sleep. He lifted his arms and ran his fingers through Mitch's hair. Mitch turned and kissed him.

"You're perfect," Mitch mumbled. Cody froze.

Perfect?

Mitch's hold loosened and the snores were back in full force now. Cody slid to the side and Mitch went with him. That seemed to help with the snoring. Cody laid in the dark, listening to Mitch breathe until sleep finally took him too.

Chapter 40

The Eastfield Pentecostal congregation had already arrived. They were set up across the street from the First United Methodist Church scheduled to hold Derek Sinacola's memorial service. Bullhorns blared. Large colorful hate signs waved high in the air to make sure everyone attending could see them even though the church was surrounded three deep with supporters. The Sinacola supporters sang the Marine hymn as loud as they possibly could.

Cody and Mitch drove in the family's processional, as did most of the family's friends, trying to keep the grieving family from seeing the hate spewing across the street, but it was impossible. The Eastfield congregation knew what they were doing and were there to be seen. As each vehicle turned into the parking lot of the church, louder voices yelled scripture verses as signs were lifted higher in the air. Mitch tried to read out loud the signs as he caught glimpses of them: "Soldiers-Die-God-Laughs, God-Hates-Fags, Thank-God-For-Dead-Soldiers. What the hell is wrong with these people?"

After a while, he turned to look at Cody. Mitch realized, his man was the smart one. He kept his eyes focused forward, seeming to not hear or see a thing.

"I hate this," Mitch said, completely disgusted.

"It doesn't matter," Cody replied.

"It *does* matter. They can hate me; that's fine. But why the hell do they take it out on our soldiers?" He really wanted to know that answer. It didn't make any sense to him. Hell, none of this did. Why did these people spew so much hate? Why were they so vicious in their attacks? But what got to him the most was seeing the little boys and girls that couldn't have been more than four or five marching beside their parents carrying hate signs. That really bothered him.

"It doesn't matter," Cody repeated as he pulled the truck into an open space.

"That's all you keep saying. I don't get it." He turned to Cody and stared at him, refusing to leave the truck till he had his answer.

"It's the truth. They don't matter, Mitch. We're here for the Sinacola family. Nothing they are doing over there changes anything. They suck, and Kreed's brother died protecting their right to suck," Cody said, putting the truck in park. "We can't let them get to us." Cody turned to him and smiled. "You look handsome in your suit."

"I don't know. I'm not really a suit wearer." Mitch looked down at his clothes and straightened his tie. "How the fuck do you do that? No one else can do that to me. You make me forget my worries and think about you." He smoothed his hands down his slacks. Stupid protesters forgotten.

Cody chuckled and lowered the rearview mirror, pushing the few pieces of his short blond hair back off his forehead and checking his teeth. "You do look hot."

"You're the one who looks fucking hot. You were made to wear clothes like those." Mitch opened the passenger side door, getting out of the car. Cody was slower to leave as he grabbed some items from his console. Mitch went and stood at the front of the truck. He had a perfect angle to see the haters, and lord, did they hate him. He did something he rarely did anymore—he reached up to check his weapon in his side holster. The familiar feel comforting him in the semi-hostile environment.

Mitch dropped his hands in his pockets and stared at the protestors. He wanted to shoot them the bird, but held himself back out of respect for Kreed and his family. Cody came forward, never looking behind him as though he truly couldn't care less. Mitch wished he could get there.

"Ready," Cody said, sticking a hand out, ushering Mitch toward the church. Out of defiance, Mitch grabbed Cody's hand purposefully and strolled slowly into the house of worship. They walked hand in hand through the mega church filled to capacity, making their way to stand beside the Sinacola family.

"Thank you for being here." Kreed greeted both of them. Mitch hugged his friend tightly.

"I wouldn't let you go through this alone. Anything you need, man, I'm here. Now, don't thank me again. And, Kreed, stop worrying about us." Mitch released Kreed from the tight embrace. "Concentrate on your family."

"I know it was hard dealing with those people out there," Kreed said and stuck a hand out for Cody.

"I don't pay attention to their ignorance. I'm just sorry your family has to deal with people like that." Cody replied, shaking Kreed's hand.

"I would love to shove a few of those signs up their asses," Mitch mumbled under his breath and dropped his sunglasses in his inner suit pocket.

"Son," Mrs. Sinacola called out. Kreed took his mother's hand, and the family started down the long aisle.

"If we were to ever get married, I'd walk you down an aisle like this," Mitch whispered into Cody's ear. Cody turned his head toward Mitch and stumbled a little. "Finally! That calm, cool, collected thing you were doing was wearing on my nerves." Mitch gave a small smile.

"I'm trying to be supportive," Cody whispered back.

"Well, you've accomplished that. Thank you," Mitch said quietly and stopped to the side of the pew and waited for Cody to be seated first.

Chapter 41

"Drink this," Cody instructed as the bartender put a Crown & Coke in front of Mitch and cleared away their dinner dishes. They were hours from sitting in a packed church, listening to the community talk about the Sinacola family and the loss they'd endured. Mitch had teared up several times during the service.

It was a good thing they sat on the edge of the pew, close to a box of tissues. Cody had pulled several from the box during the hour long memorial, handing them over to Mitch, then disposing of them when he began to worry the tissue into shreds.

Mitch hadn't handled much of the service well, and seeing his lover so affected was incredibly emotional to watch. The worst part for everyone concerned was exiting with all that chaos still going on outside. All the hate from the insane church group and love from friends and supporters, but to have it all going on at the same moment, during a time of grieving was really just way too much to handle.

Cody had known going into this weekend that he needed to just be supportive, but he had no idea how much this day would impact him. It would take some time to process all this emotion. He'd never let anyone know how badly that grandstanding from the church had bothered him.

"I like where you live," Mitch said, reaching for Cody's hand and pulling him in for a kiss. "Thank you for today."

"You've said that two or three times. I didn't do anything." He swiveled on his barstool toward Mitch. They were in the space below his loft, tucked away at the end of the bar, out of the way of everyone.

"Yes, you did. And thank you," Mitch said again, lifting his glass to salute Cody. "Let's talk about something else."

"Okay, like what?" Cody asked.

"Like how hot you look in this suit," Mitch said, turning on his stool, leaning one arm on the back of the chair and the other on the side of the bar, effectively caging Cody in.

"That's not a subject I'm comfortable with. Talk about something else." Cody lifted his glass, letting the few ice cubes at the bottom fill his mouth. Mitch took a drink from his glass and resumed the position.

"How about...I want you to come to DC the next time you get two days off in a row—if I'm still there."

"We need to plan it. It'll be too expensive otherwise," Cody started, but Mitch leaned in and kissed his lips to silence him.

"I'll pay. You just worry about coming..." Mitch laughed at his words and took another drink, emptying the glass.

"You're drunk. Let's see if you still feel this way next week." Cody smiled at the very tipsy Mitch; he liked him like this. Mitch had long ago abandoned the tie and suit jacket. His sleeves were rolled up, his shirt unbuttoned to almost mid-point on his chest, and he was all smiles. Mitch was definitely a happy drunk.

"I'm gonna feel this way next week. Are you fuckin' doubting me?" Mitch looked hurt, all except for the half pout, half smile he still wore. "I like you in this suit." Mitch reached over and flipped the tie he'd made Cody wear through dinner.

Cody looked down at his clothes. "It's just a black suit..."

Mitch stopped him by leaning in close and whispering, "Take me up stairs, fuck me hard. You know, like you mean it..." Mitch sucked Cody's earlobe between his lips and ran a hand over his bicep. "I think you got it in you to take control, and I'm drunk enough to let you."

Mitch moved forward, much closer to his face, so close, in fact, he could feel Mitch's breath against his lips. "Say yes. And when you're done, I'll do you."

Cody chuckled. "Are you done?" he asked, reaching for his wallet in his back pocket.

"I'm paying," Mitch said, fumbling to reach for his suit jacket on the back of his stool.

"No, we agreed, you're here, and I'm paying."

"No, you've put yourself out to help me this weekend," Mitch insisted, turning to the bartender across the bar. "I'm paying!"

"No, John, I'm paying," Cody spoke up using his trooper voice, and that had Mitch looking straight at him.

"That's exactly how I want you to handle me tonight," Mitch growled as John came up and took the credit card out of Mitch's hand.

"Let somebody pay for you for once," the bartender said as he swiped the card in the credit card machine located close to them.

"Yeah." Mitch grinned at Cody. "I win!"

Cody rolled his eyes and slid off the barstool, grabbing their jackets and Mitch's tie. He loosened his and reached to undo the first button of his dress shirt as he thought about how best to handle the next few hours. He needed a game plan fast.

~~~

Mitch leaned back against the bar, watching Cody as he spoke to several guys who had just arrived. By their looks, he would probably guess they were law enforcement. Maybe military, who knew for sure, but they seemed to know Cody pretty well. Apparently, they had known him for a few years because there was easy camaraderie between them all.

Another glaring fact, Cody hadn't introduced him to any of them.

Mitch watched them closely. Cody said he didn't hide, but he also didn't flaunt his homosexuality. Today at the church, there had to be police and state troopers there who knew who he was, but he'd walked in and out of the church with his head held high and his hand in Mitch's.

So why hadn't he introduced him to his friends?

Mitch tried to push that thought out of his head. That was the great thing about liquor, it helped cloud his mind so he didn't hold on to anything too long—at least helped him forget until the next day. That was okay too. Cody stood with his back to Mitch. He had a really good view of his cowboy's ass. He knew that perfect bubble butt intimately and everything else that lay underneath those slacks. He also knew how powerful Cody's thighs were when they were wrapped around his waist.

"Fuck…" His eyes were glued to Cody's ass, and he would have missed the questioning blue eyes staring back at him if he hadn't noticed Cody's upper body shift slightly. *Shit*! He must have said the word out loud. He just shook his head and waved them off.

"Don't mind me. I've got a throat thing going on." He coughed for good measure as if to prove his point. Cody kept watching him as he spoke to the crew.

"I gotta go. I'll see you guys later." He heard Cody say as he shook everyone's hand before taking the few steps back to Mitch's side. He didn't reach out for Cody like he wanted to, like he seemed drawn to do every time that hot trooper moved within reach. Instead, he stayed against the bar, forcing his hands inside his slacks pocket to keep them from misbehaving.

"Everything okay?" Cody questioned.

"Absolutely. Buddies of yours?" He smiled, trying not to seem jealous. Damn, being drunk hadn't taken those thoughts away, and he apparently didn't like being excluded. *Huh.*

"I guess. I only remembered one of them from the police academy when I was like nineteen, and I couldn't remember his name."

"Ahhh," Mitch said, extending a hand toward the back of the restaurant where the door was to the elevators.

"What's that mean?" Cody asked, shooting him a look over his shoulder.

"Nothing. Just, I see," Mitch answered, staring down at Cody's ass. "I had a good view from the bar."

"Are you sure you're okay?" Cody asked, stopping at the door, turning back to him.

"Introduce me next time," he said, stepping closer to Cody. Cody stood his ground and didn't back away from Mitch. Cody could have opened the door, pushed them through, but he stood right there, chest to chest with Mitch.

"I didn't remember their names. You saw me looking back at you. I was trying to get you to come introduce yourself so they would say their names," Cody said. And with that, the tension forming in his chest eased, and he smiled, pushing the door behind Cody open.

"So let me get this straight. Looking over your shoulder means come introduce yourself?" He bumped Cody's chest until the cowboy stepped backward.

"Yeah. Everyone knows that," Cody reasoned, taking steps back.

"I didn't know that," he replied.

"Of course you know. I was even giving you the help-me look," Cody stated matter-of-factly.

"What's the look?" Mitch asked, reaching for the elevator button. Cody's whole focus was on him. Mitch kept his eyes on Cody's and laughed out loud when Cody attempted to show him the supposed look. He couldn't help the outburst when all Cody did was widen his eyes and look constipated.

"That's the look," Cody advised, and Mitch backed him against the small wall separating the two elevators.

"Is that so? I'll just have to remember that next time," he chuckled and leaned his head in to kiss Cody's lips. "I just thought you didn't want them to know."

Cody took hold of his waist and pushed him back a step. It was all he was willing to give.

"I told you I didn't hide," Cody's eyes met his.

"I didn't know."

"Everyone knows the look," Cody repeated.

"I didn't." The elevator doors slid open, revealing an empty space. When Cody didn't automatically enter, Mitch reached out and pushed him inside. He was either an incredible actor or sincere. Mitch guessed that straight-forward, good guy Cody had never taken a theater arts class in his life. "But next time, I will," he promised.

"I wasn't hiding you," Cody insisted. Mitch had completely accepted his answer but apparently hadn't made that clear to Cody. Mitch reached back to push the button to his floor.

"I got it. My bad, cowboy. Kiss me," he said, moving in closer to Cody as the doors shut. Cody put a hand on his chest, keeping him a step away.

"I wasn't hiding you. I just didn't remember them. I was trying to cover that," Cody explained again, staring him straight in the eyes.

"Good. I don't wanna be hidden. I wanna be right there beside you." He moved forward against Cody's outstretched hand and reached out, turning Cody's head to the perfect angle. Not taking no for an answer this time, he nipped and licked at Cody's lips until he opened for him. That whole conversation must have sounded crazy. Mitch also got that he'd been a little diva, but Cody had sealed himself inside Mitch's heart today. Now all he wanted to do was to protect what was his, and this man in his arms belonged to him.

~~~

Mitch was on him as soon as the elevator doors closed, their mouths fused together in a frenzied kiss. Cody heard the doors open and reached out, grabbing the sides of the elevator seconds before they shut again. He used the leverage of his body to push Mitch backward. It was like moving a concrete wall. Mitch was powerful, glued to him just the way Cody would normally want him, but he needed them in the privacy of his apartment first. Mitch held on as he walked them off the elevator, out into the foyer. Seconds passed before he finally broke free from the kiss.

"Let's get in my apartment," Cody breathed into Mitch's ear. Mitch fought him a little bit to take back possession of his mouth.

"Right here's fine," Mitch murmured, latching on to his neck, pushing Cody backward several steps. The strong arms holding his waist tightened; their hips now in perfect alignment so their cocks brushed together. An involuntary moan slipped from his mouth, and he ground himself harder into Mitch.

Get a hold of yourself, he mentally chastised himself.

"God, you smell sexy." Mitch ran his nose along his neck, up to his ear.

"I've got something planned. Let me go, so we can get inside." He was surprised he got the sentence out. Mitch had him so hard he couldn't think. His arms tightened around Mitch, but he lost his grip on their jackets and they fell to the floor. He had to get Mitch to his apartment *now*! Cody roughly shoved him away, causing him to stumble several steps back.

Mitch looked up at him. The glint in his eyes said it all. That move had turned Mitch on, and a devious grin spread across his handsome face.

"That's it, cowboy. You know what I want," Mitch growled, pointing his finger at him.

"Get into the apartment, and I'll give it to you," he promised, keeping his distance, because fuck, if he didn't, he'd have Mitch on this foyer floor, banging into him for the whole world to see. He had no doubt Mitch would have loved that idea. Mitch pivoted on his feet as Cody reached down and picked up their jackets taking a wide curve around Mitch as he headed to his place. "Follow me, Deputy Marshal."

Chapter 42

Mitch trailed behind him, keeping his distance. Cody was able to get inside his apartment, discard their jackets, and toe off his shoes before Mitch leisurely strolled inside. Mitch didn't shut the door. Instead, he walked straight into the living room, turned toward him, and cocked his brow.

Mitch's invitation was very clear—give it your best shot. Oh, he would, but he was nervous. He tried to ignore the fact he'd never done anything like this ever before.

"You sure you know what you're asking me to do?" Cody absently reached back and shut the front door. On a thought, he pivoted and made a show of turning the lock. "Take off your clothes. They're too nice to ruin," he stated, trying to be what Mitch needed. He looked at the support beam in his living room as he walked to the bedroom, leaving Mitch where he stood.

He loosened his tie, but let the silk hang as he untucked his shirt. He freed himself of his belt before working the buttons at his wrist. He assessed his bedroom. The support beam in this room might be better. It sat to the side of the room, but he could get Mitch from the beam to the bed if needed.

He lifted the tie from his collar and unbuttoned his shirt. He slid off the dress shirt, and tugged the white undershirt over his head, then he reached for the lube and condoms in the nightstand. He grabbed those as he worked his slacks and underwear down, tossing them on the end of the bed where he placed his shirts. His socks came off as he stood with one hand on the dresser.

"You're sexy as hell," Mitch said from the bedroom door.

"How hard do you want it?" Cody asked, trying to keep his nerve. Mitch was shirtless. That expansive tattooed chest always did funny things to his stomach, and he looked away to help keep his goals in sight. He wanted Mitch Knox in his life like he had never wanted anything before.

"How hard you got, cowboy?" Mitch smirked, walking forward. He was much slower at undressing, and his actions became Cody's very own strip tease. He knew Mitch wiggled his ass and gripped his rigid cock, stroking himself, just for show. It worked and Cody had to force his eyes away from the sight in front of him. He turned on the small lamp on the nightstand and turned off the bright overhead light.

He then took his time to walk across the room and shut the bedroom door to block out the light from the living room. The last thing he did was push back the curtains over the large windows, exposing the view of the Austin skyline. He prayed they were high enough up and dark enough inside the room to keep from being seen by any roving eyes.

"It's a great view," Mitch said, looking out the window before moving his attention back to Cody. Mitch's gaze ran up and down his body, taking him all in. The way he looked at Cody made him grow even harder. "I can't imagine ever getting tired of looking at that."

Cody didn't respond any more than the involuntary twitch his cock gave at Mitch's lust-filled stare. He kept it cool as he opened the condom box and the bottle of lube for easy access. Maybe he could catch Mitch off guard with the way they were standing. Mitch had his back to him for the moment.

Mitch had been trained for the sudden attack, so he slowly slid in behind him, kissed his shoulder, and then his neck. He placed his hands on Mitch's waist. He had to be careful—the steel beam could work for what he had planned if he didn't damage anything on Mitch's body in the execution.

"Trust me?" Cody asked quietly.

"Oh yeah," Mitch cooed and laid his head back on Cody's shoulder, turning in for a full kiss. The exact move he needed. He smiled as he leaned in, lightly kissing Mitch's lips. He took the silk tie from around his neck and slid his palms down Mitch's arms. In that moment, everything changed. Mitch opened to kiss him, and Cody drove their bodies forward, wrenching Mitch's wrists above his head, taking care as they slammed into the support beam. The grunt Mitch gave made it very clear Cody had taken him by surprise and now had the upper hand, if only for a moment.

He ground his hips violently into Mitch's ass as he gripped both wrists in his one hand, and wrestled them up above his head. He tied Mitch's wrists together with the silk necktie and bound him to the steel beam. He was strong and he knew Mitch was just as strong, but in this moment, Mitch gave in to him. "Can you feel me, Deputy Marshal?" He pressed his body against Mitch and held him there, securing the knot as his cock slipped up and down the crevice of Mitch's ass.

"Fuck yeah," Mitch moaned. He pulled and then wrenched at his wrists, struggling to free his hands. Mitch tried in vain to get free. Watching him struggle made Cody hard as hell.

He stayed on Mitch, pressed against his back, as he ran the palm of his hands up and down Mitch's brawny arms. He leaned forward and whispered in Mitch's ear, "Don't fight me, it just makes me harder."

"I want it." Mitch arched his back, grinding his ass farther into Cody. The move fueled Cody's lust, and he involuntarily met Mitch's ass with a solid roll of his hips. He ran his nose up the back of Mitch's neck and inhaled the scent of his skin.

"Mmm...you smell so fuckable," he hissed against the shell of Mitch's ear. He ran his hands to the front of Mitch's chest, pressed his body head to toe against him, and shifted his hips. One hand moved to Mitch's neck and the other hand slid lower, his fingers traveling down Mitch's flat stomach and farther into the closely trimmed hair at the base of his cock.

"Kiss me," Cody hissed into Mitch's ear. At that point, it wasn't a request. The urge to taste Mitch's kiss on his lips overwhelmed him. He tightened his grip on the side of Mitch's neck and jaw and turned his head at an awkward angle, holding Mitch where he wanted him. Effortlessly, he slid his tongue inside Mitch's mouth.

Mitch pulled away and whispered, "I want this...need you," before leaning back as far as he could and allowing Cody complete and total access to his mouth. The little sex noises Mitch made kept him working harder. He gripped Mitch's cock and roughly stroked him. Mitch bucked up into his fist. But the grinding backward Mitch had done had come to an abrupt halt. Now he was arching forward, shoving himself into Cody's hand. Mitch had abandoned the kiss, arching forward, and Cody reached low with his other hand, gripping his balls.

"If you don't want this, you better say something now. It's the last chance you're gettin'," Cody growled into Mitch's ear. He wasn't sure where his words came from, because they certainly were the only rational thought running through his head. He rolled Mitch's balls in the palm of his hand and Mitch widened his stance. The heady smell of their arousal filled the room, shooting straight to his balls.

"Do your best or worst, cowboy. I need this." Mitch rested his head against Cody's shoulder. The movement of his lover's hips urged him to pick up the pace with his hand. Instead of giving Mitch what he wanted, he squeezed his hand, tightening his fist on the base of Mitch's cock to slow things down. Cody bent his head and sank his teeth into the thick flesh of Mitch's shoulder.

~~~

Trapped against a thick steel beam and held in place by a necktie and Cody's hard body, Mitch couldn't move, not that he really wanted to. He was fucking hot as hell from all the teasing his cowboy was doing. Now he was completely at Cody's mercy and damn sure couldn't think of a better place to be. Mitch needed this; he didn't want to think about anything, he just wanted to feel.

Mitch tugged on his wrists again. He wasn't getting loose anytime soon. Cody had tied him up tight, probably been a fucking Boy Scout as a kid. The knots Cody used were a bitch to untangle from. No matter how hard he tried, he couldn't get free, and he was absolutely certain Cody's roving hands and hard dick were the reason for his complete lack of concentration.

"Did you just fucking bite me?" Mitch asked. His muscles tensed and flexed under the strain Cody inflicted on him and the unexpected moment of pain. He drove himself harder into Cody's tight fist. Clearly this would be a two or three orgasm night, and he needed the first one right about now.

Cody's fist tightened on his cock. He held him like a vise, and the buildup rolling through his spine, churning through his balls faded as Cody denied him again.

"Yes," Cody said, releasing his cock, sliding his palms back up his chest to his nipples. Cody mouthed his way across his shoulder, nipping and licking down his spine. Only the sound of their heavy pants filled the room as Cody went to his knees behind him. Mitch rested his forehead against the beam and began to pray.

"You're killing me," Mitch said through gritted teeth as Cody's warm tongue licked across the base of his spine. When Cody's hand caressed the globe of his ass, he held his breath. Cody had done this to him in Washington. And it was one of the most tender, sweetest memories of his life.

"Please," he begged as Cody spread his butt cheeks and circled his rim with his fingers. Mitch's knees went weak, his eyes threatened to roll back in his head as Cody's hot wet tongue slowly slid across his hole. Cody lapped at him, sucking and licking, but when that warm, sweet tongue poked its way inside…Mitch lost it. Cody was a master at rimming and teasing with his tongue. A loud groan escaped his lips. He bucked his hips, pushing back against the tongue inside him. He wanted more. His orgasm built slowly till his legs shook. He was just about to come, and fucking Cody pulled away, denying him again.

"Shhh, you can't come yet. I don't want you to, Deputy Marshal." Cody's lips pressed against his most intimate place. He could feel puffs of breath dance across his wet rim as Cody spoke. Mitch's legs gave way under Cody's assault. Thank goodness the tie held his weight.

"I can't take it," he panted. Cody grabbed his ass cheeks, spreading them farther open, and slipped his tongue deeper inside. "Fuck. Cody…" Mitch's words turned to whimpers.

~~~

Cody held on to Mitch's cock, palming his balls and easing him back to his mouth and hungry tongue. He released Mitch's sac and sucked a finger into his mouth before pressing the digit against Mitch's rim. The desperate whimpers and strangled breaths urged him on, letting him know he must be doing everything right. He slid his finger into Mitch's heat, pushing deeper inside until he felt the spot. He curled his finger, pressing against Mitch's prostate, and then he reared back to watch his finger slide in and out of Mitch's ass.

"Does that feel good?" Cody asked, looking up the long line of Mitch's body. He was perfection. Every cord and muscle flexed and worked together, straining against the tie that bound him.

"Answer me, Mitch," Cody said again, reaching for the lube. He withdrew his digit, coating his fingers with lube before sliding two back in.

"Don't stretch me too much. Just fuck me," Mitch whispered. It took a second to understand what Mitch said. Cody rose to his feet, adding a third finger. Binding Mitch was one thing, hurting him intentionally was another, and Cody resisted the idea of not opening Mitch.

Mitch bucked his hips. He was back to fully supporting himself with his legs now. "Fuck me, Cody."

Within seconds, he'd rolled the condom on and lubed himself up. Mitch tried to look back at him, he moved his head back and forth, attempting to get a better angle, but he couldn't. Cody gripped his cock and aligned himself against Mitch. He was so aroused, so turned on at the sight of Mitch struggling he wasn't sure how long he would even last.

Cody held on to Mitch's hip, positioned his tip at Mitch's entrance and drove himself forward. In one swift plunge, he was buried deep inside Mitch's tight heat.

"Ah, fuck!" Mitch yelled.

Cody growled as unbelievable pleasure tore through him. Mitch was tight, almost too tight. Mitch shoved backward, the force of his body pushing Cody almost completely out. Both hands now gripped Mitch's hips. He used his knees and pushed forward again with such force he drove Mitch up and off his feet, hard into the pole.

"Aghh! That's it...need you," Mitch panted.

Cody pistoned his hips, thrusting forward and pulling almost completely out, only to plunge forward again. Every single time, Cody took Mitch up and off his feet, pounding him harder. The words coming out of Mitch were almost unintelligible, but any time Cody slowed, Mitch used his body to urge him on, tilting his ass up for Cody to take. And he did. Cody drove his hips forward, slamming himself over and over in Mitch's tight, warm channel.

~~~

"Ahhh…Fuck…Cody," Mitch moaned. His knees threatened to give as the line between pleasure and pain blurred for a moment. His body craved what Cody was giving him, his need for this man so strong it went beyond anything he'd ever allowed himself to feel before.

He winced as Cody took his fill, withdrawing only to drive deeper back inside his body. The 'oh, gods' rambled past his lips the minute he had been lifted off his feet, making him sound like a complete idiot, but he didn't care. This was what he craved. Mitch panted as his body headed into overdrive. He began to thrust back against Cody's thick cock, trying to drive him deeper and harder as he began to answer each thrust with one of his own.

If he could only get his hands on his own dick, he'd come with just a touch.

Cody's breath hitched. If Cody felt half of what Mitch experienced, they were a match made in heaven. Mitch had wanted to be possessed by Cody. He'd needed him. Hell, he'd waited for him to come into his life. God, had it been a long wait.

"Just like this. I like it, like this." Mitch hoped the words were clear. "So…good." Each hard thrust of Cody's hips drove Mitch's breath from his body. Closing his eyes, he could do nothing but press closer to Cody and hold on tight as his cowboy took his fill.

"Me too," came a grunted response several minutes later. Mitch got it, he was right where Cody was, so close to coming.

Mitch had worked his bindings till his hands were loose, his knuckles were white from the grip he had on the steel beam, and he kept his fingers locked in position while Cody pounded into him.

He relaxed his upper body against Cody, leaning his head back to rest on his cowboy's shoulder. At that moment, so many raw emotions coursed through Mitch's body, the intensity almost too much to process. Time stood still for him, and with every thrust of Cody's hips, his emotions spiraled deeper, threatening to ignite into one incendiary moment. Without a doubt, Cody Turner was meant for him.

Mitch let go of every barrier and completely surrendered to Cody, allowing himself to be consumed by the raging inferno of this man and the deep love blooming inside his heart. He was falling over the edge. He groaned and fought back his need to come. The small puffs of Cody's warm breath dancing across his sensitive skin didn't help. Every nerve ending was alive and in overdrive.

His hands gave way and the restraint unwound around his wrists. It was a metaphoric as well as a physical decision when Mitch decided to let go of the bonds that had held him. He arched his body against Cody and let his arms drop, reaching back behind him to cup Cody's head in his hands. His fingers ran through his lover's damp hair, and his body melted against Cody's big muscular frame. He couldn't remember anyone being able to hold him so completely before.

He had deliberately waited as long as he could to beg from deep inside his heart. "Finish us."

~~~

Cody felt Mitch's hands come around his neck. He paused slightly and glanced up at the pole. Mitch rested back against him, his body soaked in sweat and trembling. Cody wrapped Mitch tightly in his arms, supporting all of his weight. He ran his hand up the curve of Mitch's neck and then along his jaw as he turned his face toward him. Pleasure had Mitch's eyes hooded. They were slightly opened, but dazed, and he panted through parted lips. Mitch was the most beautiful man Cody had ever laid eyes on, and it occurred to him for the first time since arriving yesterday, Mitch would be leaving him tomorrow. The desolate thought slowed Cody's thrusts, ebbing the release he'd been holding back.

"Hold on, Deputy Marshal."

Cody managed to move them from the beam to the bed a few steps away. He gently placed Mitch down on his bed and thrust deeply into his lover. He gripped Mitch's ass, pulling his hips up while pressing Mitch's shoulder blades and head deep into the pillows. It was the perfect angle; the position was exactly right. "Oh, fucking shit, that feels..." Mitch started.

With each thrust of his hips, the pillows gave way underneath Mitch, one after another fell to the floor beside the bed. He smoothed his hand over the beautifully detailed skull and rose tattoo in the center of Mitch's back and bent in to kiss the ink. Sitting up taller on his knees, he punched himself harder and faster into Mitch.

"I love being inside you," he whispered and gripped Mitch's cock. His thumb circled Mitch's sensitive head, then delved into the slit, spreading the beads of moisture across Mitch's swollen tip. Cody stroked him harder, matching every stroke of his hips. Only gasps and pleasure-filled moans filtered through the bedroom. Damn, Cody was addicted to the sound and the feel of the man who fit so perfectly with him.

Mitch was absolutely made for him.

His lover gasped for air and his body clenched around him. Mitch was about to go over. He never slowed the movement of his hips; he welcomed the pressure building in his spine. It was something he couldn't continue to hold off. He was close, so close. Mitch's tight heat gripped him, threatening to make him lose his control. He ground his teeth together and forced himself to wait.

"Come for me," he managed through gritted teeth, stroking his lover faster. Mitch moaned and pushed his hips back, driving his ass against him.

"Cody, fuck," Mitch gasped as his chute contracted hard and the heat of his orgasm ran over in Cody's hand.

"Yes...Mitch..." Cody lost it at that moment. The power of his release took his breath. His body vibrated uncontrollably; his muscles stiffened and his toes curled as he emptied himself into the condom in Mitch's ass. The world darkened as he fell forward, completely spent.

Chapter 43

Cody stayed glued to Mitch for a good ten minutes after they had both came. Mitch rolled over and removed the spent condom from Cody. For a while after that incredible sexcapade, Mitch was certain he'd died and gone to heaven. Once he centered back into himself and realized heaven was a six foot four inch blond-headed angel, he woke enough to find he was wrapped around a very silent, barely breathing Cody. Mustering the energy, he trailed a hand up Cody's back and that had a startling effect. Cody jerked and suddenly sat up, looking down at Mitch, completely out of sorts.

"I must've fallen asleep," Cody said, his voice rough from sleep and his breathing shallow.

"I know, cowboy," Mitch laughed, and Cody settled back down on top of him. He looked too exhausted to do much more than rest. Mitch liked him right on his chest. He liked to feel his heart beat against his cowboy's.

"I don't remember anything after you came," Cody breathed into his ear.

"It was kind of mind-blowing," Mitch said with a chuckle. "I didn't know you had that in you."

"I didn't either," Cody replied.

"Ahhhh." Mitch smiled and held on to Cody a little tighter. He liked the idea of this being something only he and Cody shared.

"You don't tie every guy to that pole, do you?" Mitch asked, feeling a little lame that he needed the obvious reinforcement.

"No, I'd hurt 'em." Cody answered and pushed himself up and off Mitch. If he had more energy, he would have rolled with him, but he didn't. His body still attempted to recover from the confusing sensations vibrating off his skin. "The guys I've dated are smaller. I'll clean us. I just have to get my body working with my mind."

"I'm having that problem myself," Mitch said. He closed his eyes, taking a mental note of his body parts. He wiggled his toes and felt relief when they worked. He hadn't known for sure if they would. After such a life-alerting event as the sex he'd just had, he was certain parts of his body had gone permanently as numb as his brain.

The bed moved, and Mitch opened one eye, seeing Cody stumble as he sat on the side of the bed. On a big breath, he rose and stood there a minute. Mitch got it. He should try to get up too, but his body resisted that thought on such a major level that he gave in and closed his eyes again.

He must have fallen asleep because the next thing he knew was Cody back beside the bed, wiping a warm cloth on his body. Again the sensations were odd and still hard to register. The rag was warm, but left his skin cold, and he shivered.

"Did I hurt you?" Cody asked immediately, sounding concerned. Panic flashed in his cowboy's eyes as their gazes met. "You said you wanted it rough. Was I too rough?"

Mitch reached out, taking a hand and wrapping his fingers around Cody's thigh, giving him gentle caresses with his thumb.

"You were perfect. Might be the best sex of my life. Kiss me."

Cody studied his face before leaning in to kiss his lips. "Are you sure?"

"Nah, I changed my mind it's definitely the best sex of my life." Mitch kissed the top of Cody's head. "I just need a small nap," Mitch said. Cody moved from under his hold and came back with a blanket, covering him. It was a sweet gesture, one Mitch would absolutely thank him for after he woke up from his nap.

~~~

"What time is it?" Mitch asked from the bedroom door. Cody stepped through the patio door to grab the steaks he'd cooked on the grill. He'd put some athletic shorts on, but Mitch hadn't bothered and wore nothing but his birthday suit.

"Can I come out?" Mitch asked, looking around. The question was odd, until he realized all the living room and kitchen lights were on and the curtains were opened wide.

"Hang on," he said and turned off the grill, lifting the lid, before coming back inside. He quickly walked from light switch to light switch, turning off the overhead lights. The television was on, volume turned down low.

"You can wear some of my shorts," Cody said, scooting past Mitch who stopped him as he passed by.

"Where are you going?" Mitch asked, sticking a hand out to draw Cody closer. Mitch turned them both, embracing Cody in his arms. "My legs work. You didn't comment on that."

"Did I hurt you?" Cody questioned again. He'd been worried about that since he'd gotten out of bed. It was the main reason he hadn't crawled back in beside Mitch and slept the rest of the night.

"Not at all, and stop asking me that," Mitch chided, kissing his lips. "Is that food I smell?"

"I made you a steak, just in case." The sound of laughter came from outside the front door.

"Is that kids?" Mitch appeared distracted by the sounds.

"It's Halloween. We open up the building for trick-or-treaters," Cody explained.

"Do they knock on the door?" Mitch asked. He seemed to like that idea.

"I put the bowl of candy outside so they wouldn't wake you."

"What? You know what I would do when people did that? I'd dump all the candy in my bag," Mitch said. Cody pulled away, entering the only bathroom in the apartment.

"But you were bad; hopefully they aren't," Cody teased. "I put a note on the bowl, telling them to get one piece."

"Oh, that should do it," Mitch laughed.

Cody went to the closet in the bathroom and pulled out a pair of shorts. "These should fit." He dangled the shorts in front of Mitch.

"You're skinnier than me," Mitch said, taking the shorts and eyeing them.

"Is that a bruise?" Cody asked.

"Where?" Mitch said, looking down. Cody turned Mitch, giving him a full inspection.

"Shit, man, I'm so sorry." Cody ran his fingers over the bruises at Mitch's hip and looked back up at Mitch a little panicked.

~~~

Mitch saw something flash in Cody's eyes. He wasn't sure exactly what put that look there, but he didn't like seeing it on this man. Since Cody wasn't being forthcoming in what bothered him, Mitch turned to the mirror and moved his body around. As he looked at himself, he realized how funny it was to know you were forever changed on the inside, but the outside looked completely the same. He started to say those words, but his eyes met with Cody's in the mirror. They clearly weren't on the same page right this minute.

"I have no idea what you're talking about," Mitch finally said.

"Here." Cody pointed out four or five little marks marring the skin around his hips. They were so faint Mitch hadn't seen them during his cursory inspection. They looked like they could have come from Cody's fingertips. As far as Mitch was concerned, they were love marks, made during unbelievably good sex, but based on the uncertainty rolling off Cody, he didn't see things that way. Not only did he not see it like that, he'd brushed past Mitch and left the room.

Mitch ran his fingers over the marks and smiled. He loved being marked up by his handsome cowboy. There was no pain, just discoloration. His ass on the other hand was going to ache sweetly for a week. Both were exactly what he wanted to take back to DC with him. If he couldn't have Cody there with him, he'd have Cody's mark across his heart and on his skin. Mitch grabbed the shorts and pulled them on as he went in search of Cody.

The lights were still off. Cody stood in his kitchen with his back to him, pouring something into a pot. He tapped the can on the side, trying to get everything out. Mitch came in behind him, wrapping both arms around his chest.

"Stop being so concerned. I loved every minute of what we did tonight. I wanted everything you gave me. I asked you to make it rough," Mitch said quietly behind him, resting his chin on Cody's shoulder.

"I think I did a little harder than rough," Cody said. He didn't move out from beneath Mitch, but he also didn't turn around. His concentration stayed on the contents of the pot heating on his stove.

"Well, whatever you did, do it just like that every time I ask. I haven't slept that good in a long time. Although it would have been better sleeping if you would have stayed in bed beside me," Mitch added quietly.

Cody didn't say a word. They stood like that for several minutes as the beans began to boil. "Oh shit, are those Ranch Style Beans?"

That eased the tension and made Cody laugh.

"I love those things. You can't get 'em in New York, did you know that?" Mitch stepped back a little to turn Cody around. "Stop being down. There's no reason. I have less than twelve hours before I have to board the plane. Who knows when I'll be back? I want to eat this food, maybe drink a beer or two, and then make love to you before I close my eyes again. Fair?"

Cody nodded.

"And I might need a pillow to sit on if we're eating at that table." Mitch chuckled.

"We can eat on the couch," Cody offered, grinning at Mitch as he spoke the words.

"Okay, but I might need a pillow there too. We'll see where this goes." Mitch moved away from Cody. "Where're the plates?"

Cody reached over and opened the cabinet closest to Mitch's head before taking a couple of beers from the refrigerator.

"This looks delicious," Mitch said as he began to load his plate with the dinner Cody had cooked him. Yeah, he was totally in love. Cody sucked him, rimmed him, and fucked him until his ass throbbed, and then cooked the perfect meal for him…steak and beans. They were a match made in heaven.

Chapter 44

"My turn," Mitch said, rising from the sofa with a yawn. The clock on Cody's microwave showed one in the morning. He could sleep on the plane tomorrow, but he was missing time snuggling with Cody. They didn't seem like they were at a point where they could relax easily together and cuddle on the sofa since Cody sat in the only chair right beside the couch.

They'd eaten and watched a Thunder versus Mavericks basketball game. They talked easily about the game, about the teams and players. Cody followed sports more than Mitch, but he could hold his own enough to communicate on the topic.

The chair had been close enough to Mitch's side of the sofa that he could hold Cody's hand. It was more finger play than official handholding, but Cody participated, so that did count in the closeness Mitch needed. He wasn't a hundred percent certain, but Cody's distance may have been from earlier, still put off by the tiny, and thrilling, bruising he'd caused. Mitch hated that Cody felt that way and had to set things straight. He actually had to set them both straight, and there was only a few hours left to do it all in.

For the first time ever, he resented how much traveling his job required. He could have used more time here. Time was what they needed and what they didn't have. He held his hand out to Cody.

"Come on, big boy. It's my turn," Mitch said, and Cody glanced up with a questioning look on his face. "I'm done with the foreplay; now I want your ass."

"I'm not sure watching basketball's considered foreplay," Cody said, giving him that smile he adored as he reached for the remote.

"And I'm certain it is." He was in Cody's way, and he refused to move as Cody stood.

"How's your ass?" Cody asked carefully.

"It's perfect. Kiss me," Mitch said, lifting his hands to Cody's face. He took his lips in a soft slow kiss. In this, Cody participated. They devoured each other's mouths.

"I wanna make love to you, Cody."

Cody turned off the television, plunging the apartment into complete darkness. Exactly what he needed for what he had in mind.

"Come in here," Mitch growled, stopping Cody from dropping his shorts where he stood. He led them to the long bank of windows in Cody's bedroom. Mitch hadn't really noticed the brilliance of the room until the curtains were opened and he looked out into the night. He doubted anyone could see them this high up and there was a perfect view of downtown Austin spread out in front of them. "Here. Don't move."

Mitch grabbed the lube and a condom from the dresser and dropped his shorts as he stepped back to Cody who looked completely confused. Mitch placed the items in his hands on the ledge of the window as he lowered Cody's shorts and kicked them with his foot in the general direction of a side chair. "Stop looking so confused and be here with me. Be in this moment."

~~~

Cody wasn't sure what he was supposed to do. He stayed by the window when Mitch went to his dresser, but he just wasn't picking up what Mitch was trying to do. Maybe that was the plan. Mitch was back, standing in front of him, completely nude. His cock was hard, rigid, and jutted out in front of Mitch as if asking for his touch. When Cody reached down, Mitch swatted his hand away.

"It's my turn, let me seduce you," Mitch said, placing both hands on his shoulders. "Now, turn around."

Cody did. He'd seen this view every day for the last two years he'd lived here, but tonight it was different somehow. The complex he lived in was upscale, very high-end, and his two rooms weren't more than eight hundred square feet. It had been all he could afford, but he loved his home. Loved being here, and he loved Mitch being here too.

"Stop overthinking it, cowboy," Mitch purred against his ear.

Cody forced himself to go with the flow as Mitch moved in closer behind him. All those emotions from earlier came barreling forward as Mitch tugged him against his chest and ran his nose up the back of Cody's neck. The move caused his swollen dick to plump even further and brush against the cold window he was pressed to.

Closing his eyes, he rested his forehead on the glass and concentrated on breathing. He'd need his wits about him to get through the next hour if this sensual torture was what Mitch had in mind.

~~~

Buildings lit up the Austin skyline with thousands and thousands of lights as far as he could see. The main highway in town ran in the distance, flashes of lights racing through his mind. His heart kept steady time, thumping wildly in his chest. He absolutely didn't want to leave tomorrow. He wanted to stay here, holed up in this apartment with the man he loved. Insecurity hit with that thought, but so did the thought of pleasing Cody. He licked along the path his nose had just taken.

Cody shivered in his arms and Mitch's smile widened. He loved that his touch had triggered the reaction.

He pressed his naked body along the length of Cody's back, so they were skin on skin and kissed and nipped at his neck. "It's beautiful, isn't it?"

He waited for Cody to show some sign he'd heard him, and eventually he nodded, but didn't say a word. He ran a hand up Cody's chest and covered his heart with his palm. The beat matched his own.

A frantic rhythm of something magical binding them together. At least he hoped Cody felt the same.

"I need you in my life," Mitch whispered against his cowboy's skin. Cody shivered again, and Mitch pulled him closer, caressing his arms, softly brushing his lips across his shoulder. "I need us, Cody."

Cody turned his head to look at him, and something flashed in his eyes as he leaned back for a kiss. When Cody tried to spin completely around in his arms, Mitch denied the move and held him tight against the window.

God, how he needed this man. He'd never wanted anyone as much as he wanted Cody. Mitch took advantage of the moment and leaned in, capturing Cody's mouth in a heated kiss. The kiss lingered as he slid his hands down, stroking Cody's leaking cock. He loved how his kiss could so easily undo this man.

Mitch eased his hand between Cody's ass cheeks and found his entrance. He slid a finger into Cody, working him open as he reached for the lube on the ledge. He dribbled a few drops on his fingers and pressed two into his tight opening.

"You're so fucking hot, baby," he growled and added a third, enjoying the view of his fingers moving in and out of Cody's perfect ass. He curled his finger against Cody's gland and smiled at his reaction.

"Agh, yes!" Cody hissed. "Make love to me."

He reached for the condom, taking time to roll it in place, then spread Cody's cheeks. Gripping himself, he pushed the tip of his cock against Cody's tight ring of muscle. Mitch shuddered as he slipped inside his lover, slow and steady, inch by inch. Cody's palms slammed against the window, then slid down the glass as he grabbed for anything to hold on to. He could see Cody's reflection in the window, and he couldn't tear his eyes away from the image. Cody Turner in the throes of passion was an incredible sight to behold.

Mitch bent his knees and built a rhythm with his hips, something he could hang on to. He pulled Cody's back against his chest and held him tightly, nuzzling into his neck. He drove in and out of his heat, giving Cody everything he had. Cody's brawny arms reached back behind him, and his hands tangled in Mitch's hair, holding him there. The move was hot, sexy, and possessive.

"I love you," Mitch whispered next to Cody's ear.

~~~

Cody allowed the sensual assault, but dear god, did he have his limits. Mitch didn't play fair. His touch, the caress, the care he took resonated deep inside Cody's soul, reaching past any of the barriers or warning signs he'd ever been able to construct. He was opening to dangerous territory and completely unable to stop himself.

As much as he promised himself he'd give this one to Mitch, let him have his time, Cody couldn't help but reach back and cling desperately to the man holding him with such care. It took several long seconds for the words to penetrate. When they did, he tensed. The words scared him. As much as he wanted to stay right here in this moment, he also had to know if Mitch spoke from the heart or from his cock. Cody turned at the waist. Mitch never stopped moving in and out of him, but their eyes met, and he locked on that deep gaze.

"I do. I love you, Cody Turner." Mitch's lust-filled voice proclaimed the words again, and he saw truth reflected in those caramel orbs. Mitch meant what he said. Cody devoured Mitch in a life-altering dance of dominance. Tongue, teeth, and lips collided in the heated kiss. He held Mitch's head in place and kissed the man like he'd never kissed another before him. Hungry, probing, searching and exploring every crevice. Mitch's tongue brushed against his, and he moaned as he took in the sweet taste of his lover's mouth. Mitch's words blanketed his heart and embraced his soul; the moment was beautifully devastating, and Cody knew right then he'd never be the same man he was when he walked into this room tonight.

~~~

He'd said what he'd intended, and if kisses were words, Cody had definitely returned the sentiment. Mitch gripped Cody's hips, tore from the kiss, and took a step backward. He pulled Cody's hips away from the window and pushed his upper body down so he could get a better angle. He watched Cody's hands splayed out across the glass, holding his body in place. Perfect.

He drove deeper and harder into Cody's welcoming body. With every thrust, he searched out Cody's prostate. And considering all the sexy sounds coming from Cody, he figured he was doing it exactly right. He moved his hand down, taking Cody's rigid cock and stroked hard and fast. "You're so…fucking…tight."

The window rattled loudly as Cody's head and body slammed against it with every thrust he gave. The musky smell of their sex and the sounds of flesh slapping against flesh filled the room. His hand slid up from Cody's hip to the base of his neck. He tangled his fingers in Cody's hair. Cody whimpered, begging him to finish, as his body gave several shudders before he tensed in Mitch's arms and his ass contracted tightly around him, drawing him deeper. That was all it took.

His hard thrusts never slowed, and holding back his release became impossible. He groaned against Cody's neck, unable to control his release any longer. Mitch's driving rhythm finally faltered as his body tensed hard and pleasure crashed over him in mind-numbing waves of ecstasy. He rode wave after wave, and with a shout, he spilled himself deep inside Cody's body.

As he finished, he realized he wasn't going to be able to continue to stand on his own two feet much longer. Before the darkness claimed him, Mitch took two or three steps backward, dragging Cody with him. He held Cody against him as he tumbled them onto the bed.

"I meant what I said," he whispered against Cody's shoulder, rolling them to their side. Cody belonged with him. After tonight, there was no doubt in his mind. The smile spread across his face, and he closed his eyes, gathering Cody in his arms. He let the sated feeling lull him into sleep.

Chapter 45

"Wake up," Cody said, running a finger across a sleeping Mitch's perfectly shaped lips. Cody looked up at the clock on the nightstand. It was already eleven in the morning. Mitch had to leave for the airport by eleven thirty. They had gone to bed early this morning, but Cody had gotten up, fixed coffee, breakfast, showered and dressed, and Mitch had never stirred.

"Can you get a later flight?" he asked softly. When Mitch still hadn't moved a muscle, he sat on the side of the bed and watched for his chest to rise and fall just to make sure he was breathing.

"Mitch Knox, open your damn eyes," Cody said, and the long eyelashes that had fascinated him for hours two nights ago finally fluttered open.

"You make an annoying alarm clock," Mitch mumbled and snaked an arm out from under the cover, draping it across Cody's waist. He tugged and then tugged again. "Shit, you're too big to force to lie down and cuddle with me."

"It's a little after eleven. We have to leave in twenty minutes to get you there on time," Cody explained. Mitch returned to lying on his back, his hand brushing Cody's thigh. "Can you get a later flight?"

"Kiss me good morning," Mitch said, and Cody eyed him. They hadn't showered last night when they were done. If he leaned in there, he'd probably get stuck in bed, and there would be no chance Mitch would get to the airport on time.

"Can you get a later flight?"

"Are you playing hardball?" Mitch asked. When Cody just stared at him, he chuckled. "No, Kreed's meeting me at the airport. I planned to fly back with him."

"Then up! I have coffee, bacon, and biscuits waiting," Cody said and stood, taking two or three steps toward the door. "I packed your bag. It's in the bathroom. Now get up. Kreed needs you."

Cody left the room and shut the door behind him, but he stayed there, listening until he heard his mattress squeak and muttering coming from the room.

"All I wanted was a kiss," Mitch yelled his way before the bathroom door shut a little too hard.

Cody just rolled his eyes. Did Mitch seriously not know what he looked like? It was never just a kiss with him.

~~~

Ten minutes later, Mitch was showered and dressed when he opened the bedroom door in a huff. His booted feet thudded across the hardwood floor as he entered the room. He dropped his bag on the small kitchen table and ate up the distance between himself and the sink where Cody stood washing dishes.

"That was fast," Cody said, looking at him over his shoulder, splashing the suds from his hands.

"New rule. Kisses in the morning, then shower. You in the shower would have been better," Mitch said, wrapping both arms around Cody and hugging him tight. That bulge in his jeans grew more solid as he rubbed against Cody's blue jean covered ass.

"How's your ass? Sore this morning?" Cody asked.

"I meant what I said last night," Mitch said, ignoring the question. While he was in the shower, he realized he didn't have the time to wine and dine a response out of Cody. He wished he'd had a solid week here with Cody to get things settled between them, because there was absolutely no telling when he'd be back.

"Are you sure?" Cody questioned. He'd gone completely still and turned in Mitch's arms. His own instinct had him tightening his hold.

"More so than I've ever been in my life," Mitch said. Cody had an array of emotions crossing his handsome face until he pulled away. He couldn't go far in the small kitchen, but he did put as much distance between them as he could.

Mitch turned with him, taking Cody's place against the counter, and eyed him the whole time. Had he judged this situation incorrectly? He'd thought they were on pretty safe ground when he'd said those words last night. But in all honesty, he had no measure to go by. This was uncharted territory, emotions he'd never experienced before. His heart sank, and he forced himself to stay quiet. He wouldn't rush Cody or push him, no matter how bad his heart began to ache.

Shit. So this is what rejection feels like.

"I made you a couple of biscuits with bacon. And a travel mug of coffee," Cody said. His back was still to Mitch as he fumbled with the food.

Fuck the food. Mitch ran a hand over his face. Fuckin' shit. Now he was going to have to leave like this.

"I love you, too," Cody whispered very quietly, still facing away from him.

Mitch shifted his eyes to the back of Cody's head. Had he heard that right?

"What did you say?" Mitch needed those words reinforced.

"You heard me," Cody responded, and Mitch was across the kitchen, again at Cody's back, wrapping him in his arms, tugging that hard body against his.

"Say it again," Mitch said. It took a full minute for Cody to respond.

"I love you," Cody said, and he worried his bottom lip as Mitch turned him around.

"Does that pain you?" Mitch asked. The words were exactly what he wanted, but the tone was off.

"I didn't expect this so suddenly. And I can't really see how this is gonna work. We've been lucky or I guess unlucky if you count the reason for this visit, but you got to come here. It could've been months before I saw you again."

"It's only this case that's got me tied up right now, and I can't see how they can justify this team much longer if we continue to come up with shit. My home base can be anywhere; I just have to be on call and go when they need me. I can be here," Mitch explained.

"Like move in here?" Cody asked, and the shock showed on his face.

"Well, I guess not…" Mitch said, and that little needling in his heart pricked at him again.

"No, you could. It just feels so fast, and surreal," Cody said in a reassuring tone.

"I know. I could get a place around here until you're ready for more. I don't want to push you."

"You could stay here," Cody said again. Then added, "It's just moving really fast."

"That's how I am. I don't pause very often, especially if I know it's right," Mitch said. Cody's front pocket on his shirt beeped, drawing Mitch's eyes down. "What's that?"

"My phone. It's time to go," he said, but neither moved. They both just stared at the other.

"Kiss me," Mitch demanded, leaning in and covering Cody's mouth. Responsible Cody kept the kiss short and pulled away.

"Grab your mug. I'll get your bags." Cody was gone from the kitchen. Mitch didn't want to leave right then. It was only obligation and consideration to Kreed that had him moving. Otherwise, he'd have flown out first thing in the morning, or hell, what would he have to do to get removed from this case? For the first time in a while, he thought again that fresh eyes needed to take things over.

On those thoughts, Mitch picked up the coffee mug and took a long drink, amazed at how instantly coffee perked him up. He could go back with Kreed, give the guy a week or two to get back in the swing of things, and then officially pull himself from the case. He could offer to consult with the new team investigating the crimes. Surprised at how good that felt, Mitch reached for the biscuits that were all wrapped up. Cody had cooked for him. Why did he love that so much? He unwrapped one and took a bite.

"Are these homemade?" Mitch asked as Cody came back, opening the front door.

"Yeah, did you get your wallet?" Cody asked.

"You make homemade biscuits? I might have just died and gone to heaven," he stepped past Cody out into the hall.

"It's just that Bisquick stuff, not the real from scratch kind," Cody stated matter-of-factly.

"And he knows the difference. If I already didn't love you, I would right now," Mitch added.

"Did you get your phone and wallet?" Cody repeated again, pushing the down button on the elevator.

"I did. Thank you for taking such good care of me." Mitch gave Cody a smile and walked over to kiss his lips.

"Am I mothering?" Cody asked with a wince.

"In a good way," Mitch confirmed and kissed him again.

The elevator dinged, ending the moment.

Chapter 46

Sunday morning traffic wasn't terrible. Cody put it off to the big Halloween festivities from the night before, but whatever kept people at home was a great thing. He'd driven to the airport and back in less than an hour.

He parked his truck back in the designated spot, got out, and walked into his building. He should have been on his way to his parents for Sunday dinner, but Cody talked to Sheila about twenty minutes ago to let them know he wouldn't be there today.

It was lame. He never missed their weekly dinner, because he knew how much his mom loved her whole family being there, but he missed Mitch. Missed him bad, and the highs and lows of this relationship were settling in.

Cody rubbed his eyes as he rode the elevator back up to his place. The emotions churning through him wanted him to drive back to the airport and just wait out front until the plane took off. Who did things like that? Girls mainly, he supposed.

He unlocked the front door and walked inside. His apartment felt empty. How was that even possible? He'd been alone in here since the day he bought the place, but now the loft reminded him of Mitch, and since Mitch was gone, it was lonely.

Damn, I've got it bad.

Cody's phone vibrated in his front pocket. He fished it out, seeing Mitch's picture light up the screen. That was new too. Mitch had that way of tinkering with his stuff, yet making the phone better in the end. Funny how Mitch was the only person in the world he'd be okay with digging through his stuff. He answered the phone on the third ring.

"What are you doing?" Mitch's sexy deep voice asked. Cody saw Mitch's suit jacket on the back of his chair.

"I just got home. I forgot to pack your suit jacket," Cody admitted, lifting the coat in his hand and drawing the fabric to his nose. He breathed Mitch's cologne into his lungs. Ah, he missed him so much.

"I can get it next time," Mitch said quietly. "I don't wanna go."

"I was just thinking that same thing," Cody anchored the phone on his shoulder as he slid Mitch's jacket on one arm, then the other. He shrugged the coat onto his shoulders, surprised at how well the cut fit. He'd thought Mitch was bigger than him.

"Hang on, that's Kreed," Mitch said and clicked over. Cody kept the phone to his ear and went to the bathroom mirror, looking at himself with Mitch's jacket on.

"Hey, wanna come pick me up? Kreed's staying another few days."

"Can you stay that long?" Cody asked, shocked at how his whole attitude just perked up.

"No, I gotta go back in the morning. If you'd rather me fly out today, I can," Mitch offered, the excitement of a few seconds ago faded.

"I'll come get you and take you back in the morning." Cody's doorbell rang. "Hang on, somebody's here."

Cody dropped his phone inside his front shirt pocket. He went for the door, looking out the peephole. A guy in a suit stood outside his door. Okay, not something he saw every day. Cody opened the door and had a badge shoved in his face.

"Agent Peter Langley with the Central Intelligence Agency. Are you Officer Cody Turner?" a tall, thin middle-aged man asked.

"I am," Cody responded, looking over the badge. It was genuine, but what in the hell? If this was work-related, he'd have been called to the office.

"I need you to come with me, sir," Agent Langley advised.

"What's going on?" Cody asked, not budging.

"Sir, we'll explain that to you when we get downtown," Agent Langley said.

"I need some information before I just go off with you, Agent Langley," Cody felt around in his pockets. His keys were there. His cell was in his shirt pocket.

"It's regarding your recent time spent with Deputy Marshal Mitch Knox." Mitch's name caught Cody's attention. His heart jerked in his chest, and he stepped out the door, locking the deadbolt as he followed the agent downstairs.

"Has he done something?" Cody finally asked as he got on the elevator. Agent Langley remained stone-faced. The man never said another word.

~~~~

Mitch ducked his head, moving quickly through the crowd of people, trying to find a quiet place. He shoved a finger in his ear and concentrated. He could hear all of Cody's conversation and that voice talking to him was familiar.

Frustrated beyond belief, Mitch ducked into an airport gift shop and found the back door. He went through, even at the protest of the clerk, and listened closer to the conversation. When he realized what he was hearing, his heart slammed in his chest. He'd heard that fucking voice before.

Thinking quickly, he activated the recorder on his phone and ever so carefully dialed a three-way call to include Aaron, praying the man picked up. If he didn't, at least the voice would be recorded.

Karma was on his side. Aaron picked up on the third ring. Mitch started talking before he said hello.

"I'm recording this call. Can you detect the voice?" Mitch asked quickly and efficiently.

"Give me a second," Aaron said.

He palmed his wallet and waited as he listened. The clerk or security would be through that door any minute. He needed them to remain quiet and step away, so he held open his wallet, showing his badge, ready for when they walked in.

"I'm hooked up. Can you narrow the voice down? Have you heard it before?" Aaron asked.

"Its recent, and he said he was CIA." Mitch specified, trying to listen and talk at the same time.

"Did he use a name?" Aaron asked.

"I didn't catch it. He hasn't said it again. They've gone silent," Mitch whispered. He concentrated hard on keeping his cool as the panic began to set in. He could think of no reason the CIA would need to talk to Cody about him. Fuck if the panic didn't accelerate.

"All right, I need the recording from your phone. I didn't get enough," Aaron said.

"He'll speak again. Can you trace the call?" Mitch asked.

"Sure," Aaron answered. Mitch could hear typing as well as Cody walking. He was leaving the apartment. Everything in his heart didn't want Cody leaving that building with the guy.

"He's in downtown Austin. It looks like an apartment building," Aaron said.

"It's his place." As Mitch had expected, security entered the small room. He kept his arm held out with the badge for them all to see. There were three or four of them, but Mitch kept his head down, listening to anything said, but still watching the guards. After a second, he lifted his finger to his lips and shooed them from the room.

~~~

Cody stepped out of his building and the brightness of the sun blinded him. He shaded his eyes and looked around the parking lot. Only then did he realize he still wore Mitch's suit jacket. He felt a little bit like a fool as he followed the agent to a car backed into the farthest parking space in the lot. The car had federal-issued written all of it. He assumed the vehicle was probably an old Buick, something along those lines.

"You'll need to ride in the back," the agent instructed.

"What's this about, now?" Cody asked again, because he couldn't get past the fact that something about this whole scene didn't feel right.

"You know the drill. We'll talk downtown," he said, opening the back door.

The agent extended a hand, stepping back after opening the door. Cody stood there, staring at him and finally followed directions only because if he'd been on this assignment, he'd hate getting shit from the guy he had to bring in.

Cody ducked his head and angled his big body into the cramped backseat. After both legs were inside, the agent shut the door after him.

"Good, faggot," Agent Langley hissed loud enough for him to hear through the closed door. Cody's nagging doubt turned to full-fledged panic as he tried to bolt. His reactions were quick, but the door couldn't be opened from the inside. He slammed against the door and searched outside for the guy, trying to keep his eyes on the agent. Glass separated the front and the back seats virtually making a quick escape impossible. He couldn't give up, he needed to find a way out of this car.

Cody angled his body to ram his elbow into the window. Only then did he see the flash of metal as the sun caught the gun barrel being aimed his way. *Shit!* Cody went for the dive, but he was too late. The first bullet struck him somewhere in the chest, knocking the breath from his lungs as glass shattered around him. He was forcibly shoved backward, slamming into the back of the seat. The second bullet ripped through his shoulder, and the searing pain rendered him powerless.

Cody fell to the side. He couldn't get enough air in his lungs, and the pressure in his chest was excruciating. His body wouldn't cooperate. He tumbled forward, and picked up a faint clicking noise from underneath the vehicle. The darkness began, filling in from the sides. Shit, his vision blurred. Mitch and his family filled his thoughts. The lack of oxygen proved too much. The darkness took him.

~~~

"Fuckin' shit!" Mitch bolted up, yelling at Aaron. "Where is he? Where the fuck is he?"

"He was still in the parking lot when the phone went dead," Aaron said. Mitch heard the intensity in his tone, and Aaron was slamming the keys to his keyboard as he typed. "Hang on, Mitch. I'm patching you through to 9-1-1."

"What's your emergency?" Mitch heard a dispatch officer say. On the need to get to Cody, he was up and out the door. Airport security had stayed close by, no doubt trying to keep an eye on him. Whatever the reason, he was thankful to see them. He needed immediate help.

"I'm Deputy US Marshal Mitch Knox. I've been on a telephone call where a local state trooper in Austin, Texas, is being kidnapped. I believe there were shots fired," he told the dispatcher a little desperately before turning to the airport security. "I need a ride."

"My truck's outside," the security guard said.

"Do you know the address of the incident?" she asked. Aaron, who was still on the call, spouted out the information he'd gotten before Cody's phone went dead.

"They made it outside his apartment complex. Cody was loaded into a vehicle when I heard a possible shot and the phone went dead," Mitch added. He could feel the panic taking over, making him helpless. Shit, he was so fucking worried about Cody. He forced himself to remain calm. He had to use his head, think rationally, when all he really wanted to do was scream.

"We have officers on their way. Can you identify the trooper involved?" the dispatcher asked.

"His name's Cody Turner," Mitch answered and stumbled as he said Cody's name. Fuck, what had happened? And his next most immediate thought was how he'd just found Cody. No way could he lose him now. That sent a crashing blow to his heart.

"Oh no," the woman finally said. For the first time in this conversation, she left the standard communication dialog she was required to give to each caller. He could hear her advising the officers en route to the scene. "Sir, my boss is taking over the call."

Thank god the security guard ran. Mitch followed, ducking around to the arrivals entrance. The airport security's white truck sat right out front. Mitch entered on the passenger side and then thought better. He scooted all the way over, taking the driver's side before the guy made it to his side of the truck.

"I'm driving, get in. I need your phone."

Mitch activated the speaker and dropped his phone on the dash as he waited for dispatch to continue the call. He started the truck and took the phone being offered by the security guard. He dialed Cody's number and pushed send.

"You keep pushing this number until someone answers," Mitch said, giving the guy a hard, no-nonsense look. Seconds later, he peeled out of the parking space, taking corners faster than he should.

"Deputy Marshal Knox, I'm Officer Carmichael," a new voice began, and he immediately interrupted him.

"I'm at the airport. I need an escort to the scene. I'm heading south leaving terminal…" Mitch looked around. "Where the fuck are we?" Mitch bellowed. The fucking guy should have seen he had no idea where he was. What the fuck!

"Terminal C," the guard said. "Still no answer."

"Terminal C. I'm heading south," Mitch advised.

"Just a moment," he heard the new dispatcher say. "All right, we have an officer en route to you. What are you driving?"

"A white F150. It's airport security," the passenger answered loudly for Mitch, totally redeeming himself. In a softer tone, he said again, "Still not answering."

"Fuck!" Mitch yelled, the anxiety of the uncertainty was getting to him. He couldn't lose Cody. Not now. Had he just listened to Cody's last few minutes alive? His mind spun out of control. Had he heard Cody being killed? There was no way he knew that for sure. Colt survived the attack, so had the Greyson kid, Mitch reasoned, trying to calm himself. He refused to consider that neither of those men had been shot at point blank range. Mitch said a silent prayer, begging for Cody's life.

"Deputy Marshal, there should be a patrol car on you at any minute," the new dispatcher informed. An Austin PD patrol car pulled up beside Mitch and pointed forward through the window. Mitch nodded. The officer turned on the sirens and punched the vehicle forward. Mitch did the same as they flew through the streets of Austin toward Cody's complex.

~~~

Mitch pulled into the entrance of Cody's apartment complex where the gates were now draped with yellow crime scene tape, marking the area off. The officer that stood at the entrance, keeping everyone out of the parking lot watched him, yelling as he motioned him to move on.

Mitch threw the truck in park and got out, still gripping his phone, and he worked his wallet out of his jeans. The officer was on him, but he held his badge in the guy's face, ignoring him completely. He forced himself to concentrate, to focus on Cody, not the havoc that now stole his coherent thought.

Mitch passed the indignant tenants littered along the sidewalk who stood outside the iron rod fencing. Officers from every single area of law enforcement agency were on hand. For Mitch, they were a clusterfuck of people, but when one of their own was hit, things turned out like this.

The dread that consumed him had his brain going numb. He could feel himself going into survival mode. His body's way of protecting him from the news it was about to hear.

"Deputy Marshal Knox, I'm Sergeant Johnson. I was first to arrive." The officer met him a few feet inside the gate and walked him toward a car. Mitch assumed this was where they'd found Cody. From this vantage point, he didn't see anyone inside the car. Generally that was a good sign, right? It had only taken him twelve minutes to get here from the airport. Officer Johnson slowed, but Mitch was having none of that. All the vehicle doors were open, but everyone stayed several feet away.

"What'd you find?" Mitch finally asked the question he'd been dreading. He went for the car, bracing himself just in case Cody's body was still inside. The officer stopped him, and Mitch reared back to punch the guy.

"There's a clicking noise. We think there's a bomb attached to the undercarriage. The bomb squad's on their way."

"There isn't a bomb. He just used that method on his last victim. He wouldn't do it again so soon," Mitch said distractedly, pulling out of the hold the officer had on his arm. He centered into himself as he glanced inside the front seat and then to the back. The car was empty except a massive blood stain on the rear seat and floorboard.

"Where is he?" Mitch finally asked, so relieved he hadn't walked up on Cody's dead body.

"They took him to University Medical," the officer said. He'd stayed several feet away, clearly not convinced of Mitch's explanation.

"What are his injuries?" Mitch questioned, surveying the blood stain. He'd seen far worse, but never from someone he loved. He steeled his heart for the answer and closed his eyes.

"No one's told you?" the officer asked, clearly surprised. Mitch didn't answer; he just waited as he gripped the frame of the car for support.

"Turner's cell phone saved his life. He was shot at almost point blank range. The cell was in his front shirt pocket and took the hit." Mitch stopped listening and dropped his head in his hands. He bent over, trying to fight back the overwhelming relief flooding his body and to keep from hyperventilating.

The tears he'd been holding back broke free. He bent his knees and dropped down, crying in earnest now. Cody had lived. How was that even possible? After a minute, he felt something at his shoulder and glanced to the side to see a handkerchief being handed to him. Sergeant Johnson had braved the supposed bomb to help him out. Several moments passed as Mitch gathered his composure and pulled himself together.

"Why do you think there's a bomb in here?" Mitch finally asked after he dropped his sunglasses in place to help hide his red-rimmed eyes.

"The clicking sound was going off when we arrived. It was only because it was Turner that we went near the car," the officer said, standing at a distance again.

"You better be fuckin' glad you went after him," Mitch mumbled.

"Say it again, I couldn't hear you," the officer yelled back.

"Nothing." Finally Mitch turned his attention back to the car. "The supposed bomb misfired is your guess?"

"What else could it be?" he shot back, a little defensive. Mitch lowered to his knees, looking under the car. There was nothing there. Then he went to the front of the car, pulled the lever to pop the trunk and headed to the back of the vehicle. Against the officer's advice, he lifted the trunk. *Fuck.*

"You got another body in here," he yelled out. He ignored the foul smell of death and looked around without touching anything. "No bomb, but he's been in here a while. The ticking's coming from him. I need to know the specifics when you ID this guy."

"Shit," the officer declared, immediately tapping his chest as he began talking to headquarters.

Mitch forced himself to consider the case. Cody was alive, and this had officially become ground zero. What had made the killer come here? The obvious answer seemed to be the only one that came to mind—this was a message to him. But even more importantly, why now had he done such a sloppy job?

Blinding rage at your sexual orientation, echoed through his mind.

Mitch looked around the parking lot, then at the building. "How much surveillance do you think's pointed this way?"

"The city's covered. That's one thing we've done right," the officer said as the bomb squad approached the car.

"You need to stay behind the line until we're done surveying the vehicle." Mitch ignored them completely as he looked out toward the road, trying to identify the cameras. Sergeant Johnson followed behind him, keeping one eye on Mitch and another on the car.

"You didn't ask, but Officer Turner was also shot in the shoulder," the officer said quietly. "We aren't supposed to give that information out. They're keeping this on the DL. I guess because of you guys."

"Was he conscious?" Mitch asked, palming his phone to call Aaron.

"He wasn't when he left here," the officer said, stepping back behind the imaginary line the other officers maintained. All eyes were on the team at the car.

"Who's heading up this investigation?" Mitch probed.

"I'm not sure yet. I was first to arrive. It's mine right now, but my direct supervisor's en route," he said.

"All right, give him my card. I need to talk to him. I'm working with the FBI on a special assignment. I need that car kept together."

The officer kept his eyes forward, watching the bomb squad work as he tucked Mitch's card in his pocket. "I need a ride to the hospital."

"Parks, take him to University," the officer called out, still staring at the vehicle. It was only then that Mitch remembered he'd called Aaron.

Damn, he needed to pull his shit together. Cody needed him on his A game right now.

"Are you there?" Mitch asked into the phone, following Officer Parks to his squad car.

"Yeah, I've got Connors on the phone. I identified the voice and didn't know who else to call when you didn't answer. Hold on, let me connect us," Aaron said.

"Connors, Knox, you both there?" Aaron asked.

"Yeah," they said, pretty much in unison.

"Did you tell him?" Connors immediately asked.

"Not yet. Mitch the voice ID is coming back a match for Special Agent Peter Langley. He's not Central Intelligence. He's Secret Service, and he was also the one on the Greyson detail," Aaron said.

"We interviewed him. He's flagged, but his alibis held up," Connors said.

"Fuck, do we have any idea where he's at?" Mitch asked, getting in the passenger side of the patrol car.

"I've got a team forming now to head to his house, but my gut says that he's there in town with you," Connors stated.

"Who all knows this? I don't want him to go into hiding before we get him," Mitch responded, buckling in.

"We have to act. He's attacking you personally now," Connors said.

Mitch went silent. This was completely personal, a message straight to him. Langley had to have been watching him, and Mitch never noticed. *Think!*

"Okay, we think he works alone and leaves town after each strike. We've gotten nowhere in the cases, and he knows that. At some point, he'd get cocky and arrogant—we know that. Now is that time, he's gotten careless."

"True, but does he know he didn't complete the job?" Connors asked.

"How do you know he didn't complete the job?" Mitch questioned him, worried.

"I checked. It was me," Aaron replied. "Connors is the only one I've told. I know to keep that on the DL."

"So he wouldn't stick around," Mitch said, but he needed to get by Cody's side, keep him safe, just in case they were wrong. He turned to the officer driving. "Step on it for me."

The lights went on, the siren was left off so he could hear, and the car accelerated. "He'd think it was a direct hit to the heart. That would eliminate a survivor," Connors added. "There's no way he knows that we ID'd the voice."

"I've got the street surveillance cameras that surround the building. If you give me a little more time, I'll get into the security cameras of the building," Aaron added.

"I don't even want to know how you do that so fast," Connors said.

"Remember, Connors, that's within his jurisdiction. He's national security. You know he has access to everything," Mitch tossed out in Aaron's defense.

"Still, Knox, he's amazing. No wonder everyone's freaked out about him. Besides, we've got a positive ID on his voice. All done the legal way. We don't need to jeopardize the case by doing under the table procedures," Connors said. Mitch hardened. They had a small window to work within. Soon the news stations would pick this up, and the guy could hide if they didn't have him in custody first.

"Keep working, Stuart. Connors, see if you can find out if he's boarded a plane. Good chance we can catch him when he walks off if he's headed back there. Stuart, I'm authorizing you to access the Marshals' intelligence system to help get a visual on the suspect."

"Already there," Aaron started and then stopped himself. "I mean, sure thing, I'll get on that for you. I can find out if he's boarding a plane, too."

"I got that," Connors said. "Stay in touch, Knox. I'll message you if he is, and we'll take him at the airport." Connors disconnected from the call, leaving Mitch still on the phone with Aaron.

"Stuart, is there any chance he's still in town?" Mitch asked.

"There's always a chance. He's crazy, man. He's broken his patterns. He's not thinking clearly. It makes him more unstable. It's why I called Connors; otherwise I never would have," Stuart said absently, a little distracted.

"Faster!" Mitch turned to the officer behind the wheel and demanded. The sirens went on, drowning Aaron out.

Minutes later, Mitch stared helplessly at the swinging doors of the OR. Being high level federal law enforcement gave him special privileges—one was that he was able to get this far into the hospital without being family, but no matter how he tried, he couldn't get any farther. Cody was being operated on, and until he got to see his cowboy face to face, the nagging ache wouldn't fade.

The lingering doubt that perhaps the killer was still somewhere close by wouldn't let him go. Per a text message on a choppy signal, Connors arranged FBI security here in the hospital. Apparently, that decision hadn't been popular with the Austin PD. The hospital was being flooded by the local police, as well as State Troopers, who packed the downstairs waiting room. The unity touched Mitch's heart, but not enough to join the local police department in their fight to continue to provide security for Cody.

He absolutely did not believe they could handle this crime by themselves. There was no way they knew the severity of these offenses, and as for the suspect, currently Cody Turner was the only person on the planet able to give a positive ID.

It made sense that the killer would come back and finish the job. Mitch hardened his heart at the thought. The panic and desperation that hovered just below the surface fled as anger began to take hold. As the helplessness ebbed, he started to think a little more clearly—a first since he'd heard that gunshot through the phone.

No question, Agent Langley had come after him personally. Mitch would be staying right here in Austin to protect what was his until the FBI was in place.

In his moment of clarity, Mitch walked across the hall to a bank of windows and glanced down at his phone. His signal increased by one bar. That had to be enough. He dialed quickly, calling the two people he knew would help. First, his director in Louisiana.

"Director Skinner, sir, he's hit me personally," Mitch said, staring out the window, completely unaware of the world outside the glass.

"What's happened?" Skinner asked.

"Sir, he got to my boyfriend this morning. But he's made a mistake. He'll be back once he realizes that," Mitch relayed the information, steeling his heart.

"Do we know who this is?"

"Yes, sir. He's being tracked down, but if we let him slip through the cracks, he'll be back to finish this job. Once he finds out Cody's not dead, he'll have to return to cover his tracks," Mitch reaffirmed.

"What do you need from me?"

"I need backup. I want our guys on this. I want him arrested the minute we find him," Mitch answered.

"Of course, I'll arrange it now. What else?" Director Skinner asked.

"I want my dad to oversee Cody's care. We need security to transport him here. And I need security detail on my family. Once Cody's stable, I want him up there with my dad. I don't care about the investigation. He's safer away from here." Mitch ran his palm along his jaw. All he could think was that he needed Cody away from this place as soon as possible.

"I'll arrange that. Tell your father to contact me. Does Connors have your whereabouts?" the director inquired.

"Yes, sir. Thank you, sir," Mitch let out a sigh of relief.

"Keep me updated, Knox. Watch yourself. I can't say I didn't see this coming. It worried me, Son. Because of who you are, I should have put someone else on the case. You and Kreed watch yourself." The director ended the call. Mitch was wound up so tightly, the moments of relief hit him hard. Mitch stood there, shaking off all this unwanted emotion keeping him from thinking reasonably. Instead, he searched his contacts until he found his father's phone number.

"Hello, Son, your mom told me you called her." His dad sounded happy, and with all the background noise, he thought he might be in the middle of something.

"I need you, Pop," Mitch spoke quietly. All that emotion he'd been fighting came out in those four words. It was always hard talking to his parents. Just their voices brought out the inner love and compassion that no one else on the planet had seemed to ever have.

"Where are you, Son?" his dad asked, and Mitch heard the immediate change in his tone from Dad to Dr. Knox. There was movement on his dad's end of the line. The background noise slowly fading away as he sought out somewhere he could hear the conversation more clearly.

"I'm in Austin, Texas. They got him, Dad. Just like with Colt; they got him." Mitch lowered his head to the big windows. He bumped his forehead against the cool glass, having to remind himself Cody was alive. God, what would have happened if the killer had succeeded?

There was silence on his father's end of the line for several long seconds until he finally said, "Your guy?"

"Yes, sir," Mitch responded immediately, his voice broke on the words.

"What's his condition?" his father asked, the professional tone masking the concern. He knew his father did that for him, to help him stay strong.

"All I know is that the cell phone saved his life. It took the bullet to his chest. He's got another in his shoulder, and he hit his head somehow. He's in surgery."

"All right, I'm on my way." There was never any question his father would do this very thing. The weights were slowly lifting off his shoulders. Getting Cody the care he needed while protecting him from another attack were his two main focuses. The people in Mitch's life were taking over, taking care of him and Cody.

God, the fucking tears were starting again.

Mitch dug his thumb and forefinger into his eyes, pushing them away. He'd cry for hours, just not right now. Later. Much, much later, when he was all alone and no one could see.

"Dad, I need you to call Director Skinner. He's arranging your flight and security for you and the family until this bastard's caught. If we don't get our hands on this guy soon, Cody's gonna be a big target. I want him to go back home with you and mom when he's stable. I want him far away from here until we get this resolved," Mitch said firmly.

"All right, Son, whatever you want. Can you text me the director's number now? I'm at a game and need to get your mom home before I leave," Dr. Knox replied.

"Thanks for doing this, Dad. I'll send the text now." Mitch ended the call and immediately sent his father a text with Skinner's phone number. He waited until he got the return text from his father confirming receipt. As he turned away from the window, a tall, blond-haired man entered the secured area. There was an older woman flanking him. Mitch looked at the two. They had tears in their eyes, a panicked look that Mitch totally got, and they eyed him as closely as he watched them.

They had to be Cody's mom and dad. Damn.

Chapter 47

Mitch steeled his spine and walked straight to the distraught couple. He absolutely didn't want to meet them this way. Certainly, he'd never wanted to apologize for allowing their son to be put in harm's way, but he manned up and stuck out his hand.

"Mr. and Mrs. Turner?" They both nodded. "I'm so sorry," Mitch started, clasping Mr. Turner's hand first.

"You're Mitch." A woman entered the room, catching Mitch off guard. There was no denying the family connection. She was tall, blonde, and pretty, dressed in a business suit and high heels. She was no-nonsense and there in front of him, sticking her hand out to him.

"I'm Sheila, Cody's sister. He's Cody's new boyfriend," she said to her parents. "Have you seen him yet?" she asked him. Mitch looked from her to her parents. She was most definitely taking the lead, something it looked like his mom and dad were accustomed to.

"Sheila, let's meet him," Mr. Turner started, but she stared at Mitch, ignoring her parents, waiting for him to answer her question.

"I haven't. I've only been here about fifteen minutes. He was already in surgery when I arrived." Mitch looked between the three of them.

"They came down and got us. He's supposed to be in recovery now. We can see him soon," Mrs. Turner said.

"I don't even know that much. I only got this far in because of the deputy marshal badge," Mitch admitted. That seemed to frustrate Cody's sister. She looked at him hard, then did an abrupt turn, focusing on her parents.

"Mom, you need to come sit down," she said, ushering her mom to the chairs in the middle of the room.

"How did I not even know Cody had a boyfriend?" Mrs. Turner asked her daughter.

"I talked to him about noon today. He told me. He said he was going to come tell you and Dad this week sometime," Sheila answered, her voice fading. As much as he wanted to hear whatever else she had to say, Mr. Turner was still standing in front of him, waiting for the women to get out of hearing range.

"What are they saying? I've heard 'a random act of violence' on the radio coming in, but I can't get through to anyone who knows anything. Damn Sunday, nobody's fuckin' working, and I'm not buying it," Mr. Turner spoke up. The years in law enforcement left the older man shrewd, and you could see the wheels turning as he worked through the situation.

"Sir, as much as I hate to say this, I'm not at liberty to say," Mitch responded honestly.

"So there is more to this?" he asked. Mitch sighed and just gave as much as he could at this moment.

"Yes, sir. It's much bigger." Mr. Turner's face turned hard. This wouldn't be the end of their conversation, and thank god, the doctor chose then to enter the room. Otherwise Mitch may have caved under the intensity in Mr. Turner's eyes.

"Are you Cody Turner's family?" the doctor asked.

"Yes, sir." That same attitude Mr. Turner just gave him was there all over Sheila's face. She was the first one to the doctor.

"How is he?" she asked.

"He's holding his own and currently in recovery. It'll be a while before he wakes," the surgeon informed quickly and efficiently. "Are you Deputy Marshal Knox?" he turned, looking directly at Mitch.

"Yes, sir," he answered.

"Officer Turner regained consciousness in the ambulance. He gave me very strict instructions to talk to you and no one else. I had to promise him and then repeat the words back to him before he would allow surgery. He said, a special agent, CIA, badge authentic. The suspect was tall, lean, muscular, graying hair, brown eyes, a scar along his left cheekbone, and one under his right eye. Hate-related," the doctor repeated Cody's words and looked visibly relieved he got them all out. "He also felt sure you would be here."

Mitch pulled his phone out, typing into the notes section as the doctor spoke. He repeated the words back to him. "Is there anything else?"

"Yes, but it was only if he didn't make it through. Since he did, I'm not to say," the doctor added.

Mitch was having none of that. He tossed out his own hard stare, trying to match that of Cody's sister. "Tell me what he said."

It took a full minute of silence before the doctor responded. "He said he meant what he said this weekend."

Those words were said in a completely different tone than the first. They had meaning and stole Mitch's breath away. He nodded, looking down at the phone, pretending to type. He felt an arm at his back, patting him, and he looked down at Cody's little mother trying to give him comfort while her son lay in recovery just a few feet away.

"What are his injuries?" his father asked, breaking the silence.

"Someone was watching out for him. His chest wound was nothing really, just deep bruising. Shards from the protective case on the phone had been embedded into his skin, but other than that, the bullet didn't penetrate. The one in his shoulder didn't cause irreparable damage. He was very lucky."

"Were there any other injuries?" Sheila questioned.

"At first we thought he may have a closed head injury, but he's been downgraded to a nasty contusion. It'll heal. He was unconscious when he got here. Probably the pain and shock took him under," the doctor said.

"Can we see him?" his father asked.

"Yes. They'll be back to get you in a few minutes." The doctor nodded and gave a small smile.

"Thank you, doctor," Mr. Turner said as the swinging doors opened. Two suits stepped in, silently taking their places. Mitch suspected every entrance into this part of the hospital would have the same security detail in place by this point.

His phone rang, and Mitch went back to the far side windows, trying to get as much signal as he could. He saw Aaron on the caller ID and answered immediately.

"It's him. I got proof, well, sort of positive ID. You can't see his face super-well, but it's his height, build, profile, and the rental he's driving's registered to him. He'd been in Austin for a few days. He got there Friday, per the rental."

"Is he on a flight?" Mitch's heart rate sped up.

"You haven't heard back from Connors?" Aaron asked.

"No."

"Hang on, I'll get it. You guys are too slow."

"We don't all have the skills you do, Stuart." Mitch prayed they got that son-of-a-bitch.

"Hot damn, man! You got your break! He's on a non-stop to DC, flight three eight seven. His boarding pass was scanned about thirty minutes ago. Want me to call Connors?"

"No, I got it. Thanks, man. I owe you," Mitch said, disconnecting the call. He dialed Connors's cell phone.

"He's on flight three eight seven out of Austin; we know where he's going, Knox." Connors supplied immediately.

"Good. You going after him?"

"We'll get him the minute he steps off the flight," Connors assured.

"Don't lose him. It'll be a crowded flight. Don't take chances."

"Do I ever? We're notifying the airlines now. We'll get him, I promise," Connors responded. "How's Officer Turner?"

"The surgeon just told me he can identify him. Aaron's got us a good visual from the street view and proof he'd been in town this weekend."

"You know we can't use his video work." Connors and his stupid rules.

"He'll tell us where to get the best shots. Look, man, take it as a gift and be thankful we have it," Mitch said. It wasn't until he felt all eyes on him that he realized he'd probably said those words a little too loudly, perhaps a little too roughly. "I'm heading to the local office as soon as I'm done here. I'll get the footage myself."

"It's gonna blow things up around here to arrest a Secret Service agent. We need to have our argument ready," Connors stated.

"Don't fucking say a word to any other department until we have him. When I get done here, I'm heading back there. I want to talk to him myself." He made his way to the bank of seats facing the waiting room door.

"Mitch, I'm not sure that's wise."

"You'll be there. You'll stop me if I take it too far, but we gotta get him to say something to tie him to those other cases." He sat in the chair away from everyone. He didn't want anyone listening in on the phone calls he needed to make.

"Then get back here today. Sunday's our only excuse for not advising everyone," Connors said. "I gotta go. I've got to pull this arrest together."

"Get him, Connors," Mitch said.

"Got it."

~~~

By the time he got through the phone calls, Mitch found himself alone in the waiting room. Not completely alone, the two FBI guards stationed by the door were the only other people left in the room. Completely confused, he took a second look around the room again.

"They went through that door. They tried to get your attention," one of the guards said. Mitch didn't hesitate. He gave a nod and hurried through the swinging doors that had earlier kept him separated from Cody.

The freedom of shoving the doors was fleeting when he came face to face with a wall. He could go right or left, with no direction as to what was down either long hall. Mitch stood there a minute before sticking his head back through the swinging door.

"Did you see if they went right or left?" Mitch asked.

"Left," the guard said, fighting back a grin.

Mitch was off, going left. Several missed doors and wrong turns later, he found a back entrance into the recovery area. He walked in on what had to be ten people lined against a wall. There was a security guard stationed by this door, a nurse's station in the distance, and rows of curtains to his right. Mitch nodded at the guard by the door and looked the people over who stood to his left. They all stared at him. After a quick assessment, he guessed some of these were the Turner siblings. Every other one was blond. Mitch could pick out some of Cody's features in everyone with blond hair.

Sheila stepped out from around the curtain and caught sight of him. "Mitch, come in. He's here," she said, ushering him around the curtain as the rest watched. Cody lay in bed, his eyes closed, with his mother and father on either side of him. Cody's mom was crying, and Mitch had no idea what that meant. She held on to Cody's hand.

"Has he woken yet?" Mitch asked quietly, staring at Cody. His hair was a mess, his skin very pale, and he was bandaged around the shoulder and chest. He breathed evenly, and his eyes were closed, but moving. Mitch thought he was beautiful.

The overwhelming relief was staggering, and he wondered how many more times his heart could go through the high and lows of today and still continue to beat. He walked to the end of the bed, rested a hand on Cody's foot, and squeezed.

I love you, he mentally told Cody.

"They haven't said anything else. The nurse is going to let him sleep a little while longer, then wake him up," Mrs. Turner said.

"I'm gonna have to head back to DC," Mitch started.

"Did they find the person who did this?" Mrs. Turner looked up at him, her eyes full of hope.

Right when Mitch was going to have to say he couldn't discuss the case, her husband stepped in.

"Connie, it's an open investigation. He can't tell us anything," Mr. Turner advised his wife.

"I'm sorry," Mitch added, not entirely certain why he apologized, but he did with the crestfallen look she gave him.

"Mom, Dad, can we give Mitch a minute alone with Cody?" Sheila asked. "I think Cody would want that." Mitch looked up, surprised, and cut his eyes between the three of them, until his mother finally nodded. She kissed Cody on the forehead and squeezed his hand before leaving the small room. Cody's dad followed along after them.

"Take your time, but we can hear everything you say. The curtains don't provide much buffer," Sheila warned him before she left. Mitch turned back to Cody, and his heart seized a bit in his chest. He hated seeing him in this condition. And then the guilt that had been lingering on the outer surface of his frantic thoughts finally came crashing down on him.

Cody wouldn't have been here had it not been for Mitch.

"We know who it is. He's not gonna hurt you again," Mitch whispered as he reached out the palm of his hand, stroking Cody's cheek, and he leaned farther down to Cody's ear. "I'm sorry I let this happen. I haven't been able to see well enough on this case. I should have anticipated this."

Mitch kissed Cody's cheek, and then kissed his lips. He let the tears he'd been holding back, fall freely. "I love you. You do everything the doctors say to do. Don't be stubborn. I'll be back as soon as I can. You're protected, Cody, you don't have to worry about another attack."

Cody's eyes fluttered before they slowly slid open. Mitch kept caressing Cody's face with his palm. He sniffled and wiped at his nose as Cody's eyes focused in on him.

"You're crying," Cody barely whispered. The sound of his voice must have alarmed him because he closed his eyes and blinked. Cody tried to move, but the bed just jerked a little.

"Be still. You just came out of surgery; they removed a bullet from your shoulder," Mitch said, staying as close to Cody as he possibly could, assessing everything he knew to look at. Cody's eyes were focusing, and the color to his skin was coming back. His voice was weak.

"Why are you crying?"

"I'm relieved, that's all." Emotion crossed over Cody's face and then something changed.

"He's CIA. The badge was real. He's tall, lean…"

"The surgeon told me. I'm going after him now. I was just telling you goodbye."

"He's part of a hate crime group," Cody replied.

"I know. I was on the phone still. I heard him, I heard everything." Mitch slid his hand in Cody's.

"The phone saved me." Cody smiled.

"I know. I'll be thanking Apple soon enough. Your whole family's out there," Mitch nodded toward the door and squeezed Cody's hand.

"When are you coming back?"

"As soon as I can. My dad's coming here. He's on his way. He's a doctor, but he knows his shit and everybody to call. He's gonna watch out for you while I'm gone. You don't have to make this decision now, but I'm gonna want you to go back home with him. Get you outta here."

Cody stayed quiet, just staring up at him then closed his eyes again. Mitch could tell he tried to fight to stay awake, but lost the battle and kept his eyes closed.

"You need to sleep. I love you," Mitch whispered quietly and kissed Cody's hand and then his lips before he rose. He took some paper towels from a drawer dispenser and rubbed them across his eyes and nose before discarding them in the trash. He stepped out from behind the curtain. Cody's family was all right there, but so was Kreed.

"He woke up, but he's back asleep." Mitch smiled at Cody's parents as he walked to Kreed and stuck out his hand. "Thank you for coming."

"I'm heading back with you," Kreed informed him, very no-nonsense.

"I got this—" Mitch started, but Kreed stopped him.

"He attacked you. Enough said." All of a sudden he felt like such a girl. He had to fight to keep the emotion of his partner's words at bay.

"I need to get security in there with him. Hang on." Mitch went to the FBI agent guarding the door and brought him inside Cody's room.

"Stay here. You go where he goes. Got it?" Mitch waited for the yes sir from the kid before he continued on. "And get someone else on the door. Your replacement stays with him too, twenty-four seven. Got it?" he asked the suit that he'd placed in the corner of Cody's little room.

"Got it," the guy said. This time, Cody's mom was back in place beside the bed. Probably a sister was in the room. Cody was awake, his eyes following Mitch, actually all eyes were on Mitch but Cody's were the only ones that mattered.

"I'll call you tonight." Mitch struggled right then, but fought it and leaned in to kiss Cody's lips again. "Promise me to do everything they asked of you."

Cody nodded and whispered softly to him, "Be safe."

"You worry about getting your strength back. Nothing else." Mitch squeezed his hand, then forced himself from the bed. He didn't acknowledge anyone but Cody's father and motioned for him to follow him out.

"Mr. Turner, I've arranged federal security for Cody and your family. You need to call my director. Here's his number." Mitch stood to the side of the elevator, scribbling Skinner's number on his business card. "My father's a world-renowned surgeon, and he's on his way. Not to take over anything, but to be a second set of eyes. He'll be looking for you to go over things and give his thoughts. He'll give a good opinion on things for you."

"Thank you," Mr. Turner said.

"I'm very sorry this happened. I should've been more prepared."

"Come on, man. The elevator's here," Kreed said, holding the door.

"I'll be back in touch tonight." Mitch was on the elevator, his eyes on Mr. Turner as the doors closed.

"It's not hard to see what Cody's gonna look like when he gets older," Kreed smiled.

"Yeah, he looks just like his dad," Mitch agreed.

"Did the cell phone really stop the bullet?" Kreed asked, sounding amazed.

"Yeah, that's what they're saying. I haven't seen it for myself yet," Mitch answered.

"Holy fuck, he sure must have an angel watching over him."

"Fucking A," Mitch mumbled and gave a halfhearted fist bump to Kreed's raised hand. Things were just too close to home on this one. If everything went okay from Connors's end, he had approximately six hours until he was face to face with the fucker who shot Cody. Just the thought had him chomping at the bit. He had to get some sort of confession out of the guy. Something to tie him to the others before morning. Before the politics of DC took over.

Chapter 48

Cody rested with his eyes closed, wishing everyone inside his room would leave. His entire family packed into the hospital room, making the large area seem much smaller. He slowly and carefully breathed in and out through his nose, ignoring the throbbing in his shoulder as well as the discomfort from his chest. His cell phone had done a bang up job at stopping the bullet by lodging bits of the protective case and phone cover into his skin. The impact had his chest so sore, he could barely breathe without wincing. He should be thankful for the pain, it meant he was alive, but right now his mood was deteriorating by the second.

Another couple of minutes passed before the general sounds in the room began to quiet. Cody hoped they'd gotten the hint that he needed peace. Right when he truly thought the whispered voices were preparing to leave, the door to his room opened. Things got too quiet too quickly for his loud family to have left the room so fast. Surely his sisters would be over here kissing his cheeks like they had done about a million times since he'd been assigned a room.

Cody cracked an eye open and then turned his head as a well-dressed, older man walked into the room. He wasn't well-dressed as much as he just looked like he had money. Lots of money. He wore a New York Panthers collared shirt, pressed blue jeans—the kind that showed they'd probably never seen a day of manual labor in their existence.

For some reason, he knew he should know this man, but he couldn't place him in his fumbled brain.

"Hello, I'm Dr. Knox," he said, coming to stop in the middle of the room among all of his family. Cody looked closer at the doctor, associating the name, but nothing about the man resembled Mitch.

"I'm Johnny Turner, thank you for coming all this way." Cody watched his dad shake the doctor's hand.

"It's not a problem at all. Is this our patient?" Dr. Knox asked. Cody's heart stirred as the doctor looked his way. Mitch had his eyes. Dr. Knox then gave him a small smile and there were those dimples.

Cody tried to adjust himself in the bed. He lifted his good arm to check his hair, but exhaustion had him dropping it in mid-motion.

"This is Cody. He's our youngest. This is my wife, Connie, and the rest of our crew." Dr. Knox extended a hand to his mom and looked at the rest of his family, but walked toward the bed, that special smile still in place.

"It's very nice to meet you," Dr. Knox reached out to take his hand. Cody tried to give a formal shake, but the medicine made him weak. Dr. Knox changed the hold as he gripped Cody and held on as he stood over him. "I wish this were under better circumstances."

"You live in New York," Cody responded. Dr. Knox's smile broadened.

"I do. Mitch asked me to come and look at the care you're getting. I wanted to stop in and make sure you're comfortable with his idea before I introduce myself to your doctors."

"Yes, sir, but I don't wanna put you out. I don't think it's as bad as it could've been," Cody stated.

"You got lucky. No question there," Dr. Knox agreed. "Since you're good with me being here, I'll head down to the nurse's station, get in touch with your doctors, and give any opinions I think necessary. Is there anything you need before I go?"

"Just sleep." Cody glanced over at his family. Dr. Knox followed his gaze to see his entire family watching them.

"We have a crew like this back home. Drives Mitch a little crazy. I'll see what I can do," he laughed. He didn't lower his voice, speaking loud enough for everyone to hear. "You get some rest. Mitch has this place locked down as if the president himself was in this hospital. If you need me, I'll leave my phone number at the nurse's station. Buzz them and they can get a hold of me." Dr. Knox released Cody's hand to straighten his blankets.

"Thank you for coming." Cody was touched by Mitch's father's actions. "I'm sorry you came all this way. I think I'm fine." Cody's eyes drooped, the medication making him drowsy.

"Mitch never asks anything of anyone. He's worried. I'll be his eyes here to evaluate that worry for him," Dr. Knox said, and Cody had no idea how to respond so he didn't. Dr. Knox patted his legs and turned to his family. "Can I talk with you outside?"

It was crazy how much Cody appreciated that gesture. When his family left the room, a security guard came inside and stationed himself at the door, but never made eye contact with him. He didn't even care and fell asleep within minutes of having an empty room.

~~~

Patience never came easy for Mitch, but this plane ride from Austin to DC had just about killed him. Sitting for hours, after so much drama, had Mitch fighting off moments of serious panic. First and foremost, he worried about Cody. Leaving that man had been about the hardest thing he'd ever done, and he wasn't certain he would have left if Kreed hadn't shown up.

Kreed was the voice of reason. Something he never considered about the guy before. Kreed also had a clue as to what Mitch was feeling for Cody which was just weird to him. He'd known Kreed ten plus years and never had the guy given any clue that he'd had someone important in his life.

Neither Kreed nor Mitch had their laptops. Mitch had left his in the airport security truck. Who knew where it was now. Kreed had left DC without his. About halfway through the flight, Kreed got internet on his phone, but text and signal were still impossible. The lack of communication hadn't helped Mitch's mental state at all.

When they landed, both their phones went nuts. They were ushered off the plane first. Actually he and Kreed stood by the door, phones in hand, before the flight attendants were even unbuckled. Mitch ignored the looks as Kreed glanced over his shoulder.

"Are you calling Connors or the hospital?" Kreed asked.

"My dad sent me a text. I need to call him," Mitch answered, wondering why in the hell he was putting the call to his father before finding out if Agent Langley had actually been apprehended.

"Cool, I'll call Connors." The doors opened, and they ate up the distance to the gate. By the time they hit the terminal, Kreed gave him a thumb's up and slapped him a high-five. Mitch participated, but listened only to his father talk about Cody's condition.

"He's good, Son. I can't find anything I'd change or recommend that they aren't doing. I've heard some rumbling that the Austin PD wants to be more involved. They don't like being pushed out, but that's the only conflict. Only family members are allowed in his area."

"They aren't supposed to release any information on his condition until we get this done on our end," Mitch informed his dad, following Kreed through the airport with a finger stuck inside his other ear.

"Pieces are getting out. Lots of speculation, but his medical team here is very solid."

"When can he leave?" Mitch asked.

"Probably in the next day or two," his father answered.

"Can he travel?" He had to dodge two women who were huffing and puffing, slowly pulling their oversized suitcases behind them.

"With some pain, yes, but you'll have to talk to him about that. I think there may be some resistance to that idea," his father answered.

"From him?"

"No, just everyone here wants to take care of him." Mitch let that settle in. He was glad Cody had a community wanting him well, but he wanted Cody out of there, hidden. Tucked away from anyone that could hurt him.

"What's he doing now?"

"When I left his room, he was sleeping."

"All right. When you see him again, tell him I'm thinking about him. I'll call him tonight when I get a chance. If you can get him alone, tell him we got the guy, but only if he's alone."

"Good work, Son." His dad seemed proud.

"Thanks, but we should have had him before now." Mitch could see the exit just a few feet away. God, he wanted to talk to that son-of-a-bitch that shot Cody.

"Don't do that to yourself, Son. No one's more dedicated to this case than you," his dad said. Mitch was silent as he followed Kreed to an unmarked car parked in the front of the airport, a driver waiting inside.

"Dad, tell him I'll call him tonight. Thank you for being there."

"I will. I won't leave the hospital until we talk again," his father promised.

"Thank you." Mitch disconnected the call as they headed to the detainment center.

"He was arrested without incident. Skinner had the place swarming with our guys. He walked off the flight, picked up what was happening, and surrendered to them. They're holding him on-site until we get done with him. He'll be booked and taken to Petersburg in the morning. That gives us about twelve hours to get what we can," Kreed informed.

"Have they talked to him at all?" Mitch asked.

"Minimal. They're waiting. Connors is holding everyone off. He's kind of being a little badass. Barking orders 'cause he's got the highest clearance on-site right now."

"Thank god it's Sunday." Mitch sat back in his seat and prayed the drive would go quickly.

"Yeah, thank god or we wouldn't get this chance with him. So, you got a plan?" Kreed asked, and Mitch turned and looked his way.

"I just need a confession. However that happens is my plan."

"Okay, buddy, sounds good to me, we'll get something." Kreed assured him with those final words, and Mitch knew this rested squarely on his shoulders.

~~~

With herculean effort, Mitch pushed Cody from his mind and stood there staring through the double-paned glass window at Agent Langley. He sat at a table in a small room, his hands linked together, staring back at the darkened window, completely alone. He looked like he didn't have a care in the world.

Connors had the Austin surveillance camera footage printed as well as the voice audio extracted and burned to his computer, all in an effort to convince Agent Langley to talk. In Mitch's mind, of course they had their guy. The video feed was perfect. The voice recording an exact match. Crazier things had happened to free fugitives, but they had done the best they could in pulling this case together very quickly.

Mitch could feel the tick in his jaw working the longer he stood there. This was going to be an hours-long process. The guy was trained to keep his mouth shut. He also knew the law. All he needed was time.

"Let me go in." Mitch didn't take his eyes off the man sitting in the small room.

"There are better trained interrogators. I've called in favors—" Connors started.

"I have a way of getting under people's skin faster than anyone. It's the only way he'll talk," Mitch cut Connors off.

"Knox, you have to be careful."

"Just let me in there. I've got a plan. It'll take a few times, but I'll get him talking." Mitch opened the door to the room, not waiting for permission. He checked his sidearm with the security guard at the door. He didn't trust himself not to shoot the guy where he sat, which would be incredibly satisfying in the short term, but not so much if he sat in prison for the rest of his life.

He entered the interrogation room. Agent Langley's eyes connected with his, and he held the stare until the agent turned away. There was no look of remorse in the guy's gaze. Nothing that indicated he knew how much trouble he was actually in. Mitch glared at him, coming to stand directly in front of him. He crossed his arms over his chest, letting the bulk of his muscles be as imposing as intended.

"You were looking for me?" Mitch cocked his head to the side, studying the guy. "I'm here. I'm not sure I heard your message clearly. Care to repeat it?"

"I have a right to an attorney. I'm exercising that right."

"We both know this is bigger than that. You can't target a senator's kid and keep all your rights. I'll make a deal with you... You talk, confess what you've done, why you did it, and who else you're working with, and you might get a nice plea deal." The guy smirked at Mitch.

"I'm exercising my right to an attorney."

"Ain't gonna happen. You're a big enough man to target unsuspecting men, but not big enough to have that conversation with me now? I fuck men, but you know that, don't you? We have positive ID of you at the scene of the crime in Austin." Mitch grinned as Langley gave the slightest narrowing of the eyes before forcing the passive features back in place. "Got anything to say now?"

"I want my attorney."

"Ain't gonna happen, we've got you now." Mitch placed both hands on the table, leaning in. "What'd you do, follow me?"

"Attorney," the agent said.

"Was this all a big show to gain my attention? Did I turn you down at one point? You aren't my normal type. I tend to like my men younger and prettier than you." Mitch leaned completely in, getting in the guy's personal space.

Agent Langley didn't like that at all. After a moment of chicken, the calm façade wore off, and the agent leaned back in the seat, creating distance. Hate and disgust were clear on his face, and he stayed silent. That spoke volumes. Mitch had his strategy.

He said nothing more, but turned to leave the room. As he shut the door behind him, he re-holstered his weapon, then grabbed his phone and set the alarm for one hour. He'd be back in there talking about the homosexual lifestyle, accuse the guy of being closeted, and let him tick like a time bomb. Langley would give. He'd talk before morning, for sure.

"Let me handle him, Connors. Don't let anyone in there, and don't fucking argue with me right now. I'll be back in an hour." Mitch headed to his office to call Cody.

Chapter 49

"Mr. Turner," Cody heard in his haze of sleep. He tried to turn away from the voice. Anyone using words like mister wasn't anyone he needed to talk to right now.

"Mr. Turner, I need to give you your medication." Cody cracked an eyelid, saw the nurse, and gave in as he opened both eyes. The place was wrong, so was the nurse, and he tried to rise. A long string of curse words flew from his lips as he registered the pain in his body and carefully laid himself back.

"Settle down, sir. You're okay. This will help with the pain," she said swiftly and efficiently. Clearly this was not her first time with disorientated patients. Cody let her drop the tablets in his mouth and took a sip of the water she held. They did that three more times until everything on the tray was taken. She turned away and entered information into a portable rolling computer before she looked back to him.

"You slept through dinner, can I get you another tray?" He looked in the direction she pointed to see covered dishes sitting on the hospital bedside cart. The pain in his arm was a little too much to consider eating anything and he shook his head.

"His parents are bringing him some warm soup from the dining room," someone said from the corner of the room.

"All right, Mr. Turner. Here's the call button. Call the nurse's station if you need anything. It's almost time for your vitals. The aide will be around soon." The nurse packed up her portable cart and left. Cody's eyes landed on the man attached to the voice, but recognition took a second more to sink in.

"Dr. Knox?" Cody asked, still a little uncertain if he had dreamed the earlier exchange or if this was Mitch's father in the room.

"Yes, you remember. Pretty impressive after everything you've gone through today," Dr. Knox said, rising, walking toward him.

"Why are you here? Wait. Not that I'm not thankful…" Cody started, but stopped as a hand reached out to him.

"Mitch couldn't be here. He needed someone watching over you. I volunteered." Dr. Knox stood beside the bed, patting his leg. "Make sure you let them know when you're in pain, especially these next twenty-four hours. No need to live with it right now."

"Yes, sir," Cody nodded, staring at the older man. He had a memory of thinking Mitch looked absolutely nothing like his father. Dr. Knox was a shorter man, balding, very excellent bedside manner. Then he remembered the smile and the dimples he'd caught glimpses of earlier.

"I'm sorry you came all this way."

"I wouldn't be anywhere else. Son, Mitch wants you to know they have the suspect in custody now. They still have security tight around you, but he's working hard to alleviate the threats."

"He blames himself, doesn't he?" Cody asked.

"He has always taken on other's burdens, but I've always figured that's what makes him so good at his job," Dr. Knox answered.

"What are they saying about my arm?"

"You've had good care. If you do what they say and promise to do your physical therapy, you'll be good as new. But they'll keep you in here another day or two, for good measure. Your phone took the hit. I suspect Apple's going to have a field day with that one," Dr. Knox said, smiling warmly down at him.

"Mitch found the suspect pretty quick," Cody said, relieved the agent had already been taken off the streets.

"Yes, he did, and I promised him I'd call once you woke. Are you up to talking to him now?" Dr. Knox asked, pulling his phone from his pocket.

"Yes, thank you, sir. I hate that Mitch called you away from your job and family because of me," Cody replied, watching as Mitch's father dialed the number.

"He's never asked anything of his family since the minute he pushed himself out of the nest. I'm very happy to be here for him and you, Cody. It's not an imposition," Dr. Knox responded and lifted a finger to Cody, silencing him.

"Son, do you have a minute? Cody's awake," he heard Dr. Knox ask. "Here, Cody."

"Hello," Cody said, watching as Dr. Knox turned from the bed and walked toward the door. He ushered the guard out of the room before he stepped out too.

"How you feeling?" Mitch asked, his voice turning soft as he spoke.

"Okay, sore, tired," Cody replied honestly. "What's going on? Your dad said you have him in custody."

"Yeah, we have him. We're just trying to get him to talk."

"Was he really CIA?" He tried to push himself up in bed and winced, but kept quiet. He didn't want Mitch to know he was in any pain.

"No, he's Secret Service, but he left too many clues this time," Mitch trailed off.

"You still there?" Cody asked when Mitch became silent.

"Yeah, babe, I gotta go. I just thought of something. Can I call you back?" Mitch asked, distracted.

"Yeah, sure." Cody hoped Mitch couldn't hear the disappointment in his voice.

"I just thought of a new angle to get his confession. If it works, I can get back there with you a little faster. I love you, Cody. I'm not sure I could have handled losing you. I knew you were important to me, but you freaked my shit out. I don't ever want a repeat." Cody felt the exact same way. The emotion of that statement ran strong inside him. Too strong.

"They told me you got help to me fast," Cody said, instead of what he really wanted to say. "Call me later. Go do what you need to do."

"Say it back to me. I won't ever put you in that position again, I promise." Mitch had a way of pulling Cody out of his shell, making him face his feelings and uncertainties.

"You didn't do this, Mitch. He's a sick fuck; just like those guys that beat up Mr. Spencer. You can't take this on, but you can find justice. Go get him. Not just for me, but for all those men," Cody replied.

"Say it back to me, so I know you mean that."

"I love you," Cody said, and there was silence again.

"I can't imagine ever getting sick of you saying those words to me," Mitch said. "I gotta go. I'll call you later. I love you."

The phone went dead. Cody stared at the ceiling, and a smile formed on his face. Those new love feelings made him momentarily forget all the obstacles that lay between them.

~~~

"It hasn't been an hour," Connors informed him when he came busting through the side office. He ignored the window, ignored everyone, including Connors as he checked his weapon and went back into the interrogation room. He barely schooled his features and started in on the agent the minute he entered.

"You left too many open ends on this murder attempt. Where did you see me with him?" Mitch demanded as he stalked across the room, coming to a stop right in front of the table separating the two of them. He was met with silence. A bored expression crossed the agent's face.

"Attorney," Langley said in the same uninterested tone as his facial expressions.

"Did you follow me to Austin?" That was a question that burned his ass—how did this guy even know about Cody?

"Attorney," the Secret Service agent repeated.

"Or were you there already?" He placed his hands on the table and stared at the suspect.

"Attorney." Agent Langley pretended to yawn.

"In what capacity were you there?" Mitch asked.

That got him silence.

"Yeah, I'm getting it now. When did you see me? It could have been here. He's been here, but I'm not thinking that was it. You freaked on this one. Blew your identity. Something made you crazier than you already are... Did you see us here or in Austin?"

"Fuck you, I want my attorney."

"It made you so crazy to see me, you fucked yourself over. You didn't see the plan through, you reacted from the gut. Well, you know what? He lived, and he's gonna keep on living. I'll make damn sure of that," Mitch spat, getting closer to the guy as he watched his eyes burn with hatred. He had hit his mark.

"You aren't a card-carrying member of that church. I've checked that. So what is it? Are you in the closet? Or are you mad at the government?" Mitch asked, watching him closely. All he could see was sheer disgust on Langley's face.

Mitch moved in for the kill.

"That's fucking it, isn't it? You're gay and mad at the government. You spent time in the military, hiding yourself. Did you fall in love in there? Was it unrequited? Have you twisted it in that fucked up brain of yours to make it the government's fault how you turned out?"

Mitch rounded the table, standing close enough to bend in, getting all in Langley's personal space, and whispered the worst insult of all to a homophobe. "If you're so lonely, I'd of let you suck my dick. All you had to do was ask."

The agent leaped out of his chair, swinging both handcuffed hands toward Mitch's face. "He should have died. I should have come after you," the enraged agent bellowed. Mitch was standing too close. The fist came out of nowhere and caught his jaw, whipping his head back, sending him stumbling backward. He lifted a hand to the window, stopping the guards from rushing in. They didn't have enough information yet, and he needed a confession that would come from the unguarded words of a fanatic's rant.

Langley tackled him and Mitch let it happen. He'd hoped the motherfucker had a short fuse. One after another, double-fisted punches pummeled down on his face.

"You lying faggot! I killed him, and you're next. I'm coming after you next, you filthy cocksucker." Mitch felt the belligerent agent being wrestled off him. The force and impact of the agent's blows zoned him out, but he didn't need to hear any more. Connors and the video feed would pick up the rest.

Mitch sat up, and after the stars faded, he saw it took three guys to subdue the enraged agent. The man was a badass and very well-trained; he could have overpowered the Greyson kid all on his own.

Mitch got to his feet with some of the most vile accusations about his sexual orientation still being flung his direction. He made his way out of the room, rubbing his sore jaw. Langley's outburst was sure to leave a mark.

"You okay?" Kreed asked, handing him a wet paper towel and ice pack as he entered the office.

"Yeah. You get all that?" Mitch asked Connors.

"Yeah, he's still raging. You made him crazy. He just implicated himself to the Greyson case and the justice's bombing. We got enough." Connors looked satisfied, still staring into the room.

"So let's book him and go after the owner of the coffee shop." Mitch wiped the blood from his nose, not peering back through the window. Langley was everything wrong with this world. Mitch didn't need to look his way again.

"Kreed's already brought him in." Connors grinned at him.

"Really?" Mitch asked Kreed, giving him a fist bump.

"Yeah, he's in holding room two. He's doing that same bullshit Langley did, saying attorney over and over. But he's scared. He'll break soon enough," Kreed offered.

"So they worked together to get Elliott Greyson out of the coffee shop." Mitch said the obvious out loud. "Just like you thought."

"We have enough to book Agent Langley. It'll take some creative talking, but I'll book the shop owner too. We'll get it out of him," Connors stated, sitting back in his chair. "Brown just sent a message. They have Langley's computers. They've just started the sweep of his house. Based on what they're saying, we have our men."

 Chapter 50

Cody sat on the side of the bed, wincing as his older sister, Sheila, tugged a T-shirt down over his head and pulled the material over his arm. "Stop being such a baby."

"I was fucking shot yesterday. Can't you be a little gentler?" he winced.

"It's your own fucking fault. You're too damn big. Who needs all this muscle? No one. It's a stupid double extra-large shirt," she chided, not paying him any mind.

"Mitch likes it," Cody tossed out, then immediately began to blush.

"I bet he does. You didn't tell me things got so far along. He was a wreck waiting to hear from the doctor. He cried in the waiting room. It was kind of sweet."

"It sort of all just came together this weekend." Cody smiled, sliding his feet into the flip-flops she'd placed for him on the floor.

"He sure is a good-looking thing. I can see why you'd be so into him. So what happens now? Are y'all going to keep living so far apart?" she asked, going to the other side of the bed.

"I don't really know. He said he could move here." Cody blushed, eyeing her as she slipped a hand between the mattress and the rail. "What are you doing?"

"Dad left this for you. I didn't think you'd remember. You're really good at looking people in the eye and coming off like you listen." She pulled a pistol out.

"Hey! Be careful with that." Cody took the gun, checked the safety, and kept the Glock pointed away from both of them. With the gun still in Cody's hand, Dr. Knox entered the room, then his mom and dad. Mitch trailed behind them. Everything faded away as their eyes connected. Mitch looked exhausted, and bruised yet when he smiled at Cody, his body stirred, even under the influence of all the pain medicine.

"You shouldn't be leaving today," Mitch said, bypassing everyone as he came closer to Cody.

"What happened?" Cody gasped when he saw Mitch's busted lip and the bruises on his handsome face.

"Let's just say I pissed off the bad guy." A sheepish grin spread across Mitch's face before he winked at him. He still had a hold of the gun as Mitch stalked closer, not stopping until he lifted Cody's chin with his thumb and kissed his lips.

"I haven't brushed my teeth yet," he warned, knowing the warmth in his cheeks had to be a bright red blush.

"I don't care. Do you need help into the bathroom?" Mitch asked.

"I already went. Does your face hurt?" Cody gazed into Mitch's eyes.

"No, and you need to stop worrying about me. This is a small price to pay to get the confession we needed. Besides, you're the one who got shot and is now trying to sneak out of the hospital early."

"You really got him to confess?" Cody asked, ignoring the part about his being shot.

"Yep, I did." Mitch nodded.

"Good job!" Cody lifted his face, and Mitch bent in and kissed him.

"Ahem…" Cody's dad was beside them, ruining the moment until he realized he was relieving him of the pistol he held.

"I'm glad you remembered this." His dad checked the safety on the weapon, before tucking the gun inside the waistband of his jeans.

"You were too out of it, but I saw that look in your eyes," his father said proudly, whacking him on the back. Cody winced as his shoulder shook under the pressure.

"Dad! That's his bad shoulder."

"Oh, Son, I'm sorry. I didn't think," his dad started.

"It's okay, Dad. Is the wheelchair here?" he asked.

"What's up with you trying to leave?" Mitch questioned. "I think you need to stay and rest another day."

"He's hardheaded, Mitch. That's something you need to know about him before this gets too far. He hardly listens to anyone," Sheila said at the end of the bed, and all Cody could do was stare at her.

"Is he hardheaded? That's something I haven't seen yet." Mitch laughed.

"Oh my god, Cody. He doesn't know that when you get something in your head, it's impossible to remove?" Sheila feigned a look of horror.

"Shut up, Sheila," Cody shot back, giving her a very clear *I can't believe you right now* look. "I'm going home."

"Back to our house," his mom confirmed, gathering the few belongings his family had brought to him.

"Not if she doesn't shut up," Cody said, and that had everyone but Cody laughing. He struggled to get out of bed, to stand on his own two feet, but Mitch was right there to hold him in place. Cody was determined though—he'd walk out of the place if he had too. He wasn't staying another second. Between his family and the constant hospital staff interruptions, he needed to go home and get some sleep.

"What about all these flowers?" his mom asked, looking through the drawers, making sure she got everything.

"Give them to the nurses or other patients. I don't care." Cody started taking small steps toward the door.

"I'm gonna get you situated at your parents." Mitch supported his weight by holding his good arm and waist as he walked. "You know, they're bringing you a wheelchair."

"I'm fine. Just get the car." Cody tried breathing deeply through his nose, hoping to manage the pain in his shoulder.

"They have a back way for you to leave. There are a lot of media people out front," his mom said from behind him.

"Why's the media here?" Cody stopped, completely confused with why reporters would be interested in him.

"Because you're a local hero," Sheila explained.

"You stay away from them. Don't talk to them at all," Cody warned his sister. She'd make this into a production and opportunity to push every single product and belief system she had.

"Too bad for you, the family voted me a spokesperson for you. I talked to them last night." She smiled brightly.

"I think I've changed my mind. We might need to go to your house." Cody looked over at Mitch and his father who stood right beside him ready to catch him if he fell.

"You have an open invitation," Dr. Knox said from behind Cody. The wheelchair was pushed through the door, and Mitch helped him over to the seat. The team of security was there by the door and that confused Cody. What had he missed over the last twenty-four hours?

"I thought you made an arrest," Cody asked as he sat down.

"We did, I'm just covering my bases," Mitch said, helping to adjust him until he sat comfortably. "I'm not taking any more chances where you're concerned."

"Ah…" He heard a collective sigh from his sister and mom behind him.

"I like Mitch," his mom said in a soft voice.

"Me too," Sheila actually agreed, which was just very weird all in itself. When he turned in Mitch's direction, Mitch's eyes were on his family. He was smiling broadly, making his dimples stand out more than usual.

God, he was in trouble.

~~~

Three black Tahoes sat in an underground garage. Mitch understood this was overkill and a waste of taxpayers' dollars, but he didn't care. Cody was too important a package to not arrive in one piece. As far as Mitch was concerned, he'd have Cody under lock and key for eternity to make sure this never happened to him again.

Once Cody realized this was his transportation, he jerked a panicked gaze up to Mitch. As a matter of fact, every eye looked at him as though wondering what he had planned, but he ignored them all and moved forward, giving everyone their riding assignment.

"Your dad and I are hoping for a bait and switch. Mr. and Mrs. Turner, Sheila, and my father are in the front SUV. The driver's a deputy marshal friend of mine based out of Dallas. Y'all are going to take the long way home. The two SUVs behind you are blacked out for show. If the media takes the bait, they'll follow your parents," Mitch explained.

"We're going home by way of Round Rock before we cut back and take Dr. Knox to the airport," his father added. Round Rock had to be at least an hour north of where the Turner's lived.

"I thought you said you got the guy," Cody questioned again, concern entering his voice.

Mitch leaned in. "We did. Shhh, you're giving me a complex."

"Oh, that'll throw them off, for sure. How are you two getting home?" Sheila questioned.

"Once I know they followed, we'll go to the farm in my rental," Mitch detailed. "If it all works out right, we'll be at your parent's house about the time you hit Round Rock. I'll call you, Mr. Turner," Mitch continued, pushing Cody with him to the truck to open the door and help the others inside. His good friend Brody Masters was the driver of this truck, and he hopped out, helping everyone inside.

"Dr. Knox, I've known your son a long time, sir. He's had my back more times than I can count." Brody extended a hand to his father who'd gotten in on Mitch's side. Mitch had called in all those favors Brody owed and got him down here to make this run.

"He's a good son," Dr. Knox said, taking Brody's hand. His father smiled brightly at the compliment. That had Mitch narrowing his brow and listening closer. Something wasn't right, but he'd slept about a minute the last few days, and it didn't connect right away.

"I bet he is. sir, I've got a son that I adore..." Brody started, giving Mitch the eye and everything connected then. Colt's autograph.

"You're such a douche." Mitch chuckled and immediately glanced around at every one. "I'm sorry for the language. Don't bother my pop about that, Masters. I'll get the autograph next week."

"What did I miss?" his dad asked, humor in his eyes.

"Mitch's is my son's god-uncle," Brody started with laughter in his voice.

"I'm not, Dad. Don't listen to anything he has to say. I've seen his son once, and that was years ago. Get your ass in the car and shut up, Masters." Mitch shut the door on his side and motioned for his dad to roll down the window. "Call me when you get to the airport."

Dr. Knox nodded and patted his arm. "Cody, it was a pleasure, Son. I want you two to come to New York as soon as you can travel."

"Thank you, sir," Cody's voice sounded off, and Mitch turned back to look at him. Mitch smiled, when he discovered his tired cowboy had been in the middle of a yawn.

"Get going. I've got to get him home. Call me to confirm they followed you guys, Mr. Turner," Mitch said, going back to Cody, not waiting for an answer.

Mitch loaded Cody into his SUV. He got him settled, adjusted the seat back some, and Cody closed his eyes. He waited as he listened to the reports coming his way. When Mr. Turner finally called, his heart was relieved. Most of the media followed along behind the decoy caravan.

Mitch put the rental in drive and slowly pulled out of the parking garage. He took the back way that Mr. Turner had told him about, and as they hit the highway, he felt home-free. He could get Cody home without drama. Mitch looked over, and Cody was awake, staring at him.

"Are you really feeling all right?"

Cody nodded. "It's more my chest where the phone embedded in my skin. I'm just sore and bruised. I wanna know everything that went down."

"I'll tell you everything tonight. I promise. Your parents invited me to spend the night." Mitch smiled.

"If you're gonna be there, I could just go home," Cody tried again.

"No, everyone knows where you live now. You need to be away from everything. We should really go to my family's house," Mitch tried again to get Cody to agree.

"I don't want this to be the first way I meet them," Cody said, lifting his bandaged arm. "Your dad came all this way."

"You're a hardheaded man, Cody Turner. Good thing I'm so head over heels or I might have to question this." His teasing worked, and

Cody gave him a smile. Mitch reached over and patted Cody's thigh. "Sleep. The medicine makes you tired. We can talk later."

"Are you staying in town for a while?" Cody asked.

"Yeah. I'll have to give my final reports and probably fly back to DC at least once, but I'm taking vacation after that. I already told Skinner. I have about a million hours, so I can stick around and help get you solidly back on your feet."

"Thank you." Cody let out another yawn.

"You don't have to thank me. I want to. You're my cowboy. I love you," Mitch whispered. Cody was sleeping before he ended the sentence.

~~~

Later that evening, Mitch sat on the front porch swing of the Turner's home, enjoying the cool country breeze. Cody rested on the lounger next to the swing and one of his little nieces—there were too many, and Mitch couldn't remember her name—sat close by. Out of all of them, this little girl loved her Uncle Cody the most. She couldn't have been older than five, but she sat on the floor of the front porch and held Cody's hand, working the iPad in her lap.

She never said a word as she let Cody rest. She just wanted to be with him. Quiet nieces and nephews were something completely foreign to Mitch. Even though he didn't get to see his own nieces and nephews as much as he should, he always heard them in the background whenever one of his siblings called.

He played a game on his cell phone, keeping a constant swing going back and forth when Connors interrupted with a phone call. He answered on the first ring, even though he was pretty certain that allowed the zombies time to eat his character. He hated that shit. Zombies were ruthless killers in the video game world.

"Knox," he answered.

"I've got a pretty big update. We got a full confession and statement that Langley worked completely alone. He met with his attorney and the guy came back with Langley's written and signed account of each death and accident. He gave enough information to undoubtedly tie him to the scene of each crime. He admitted he planned to go after your friend Montgomery, not Michaels. He also admitted he changed the video feed in the back of the coffee shop," Connors said, clearly very relieved, maybe even happy they had finally solved this case. "The only discrepancy is that DeGeorge admitted giving Langley access to the security system."

As Mitch listened, he got up off the swing and took the steps down so he could hear better and have a little more privacy. Something felt off. "Why the abrupt change?"

"I guess he figured he was busted after going off on you," Connors replied, and that earned him a solid, *Huh*, from Mitch.

"What's gonna happen to DeGeorge?"

"Kreed had already caused him to slip up. The guy knew the video feed had been changed. He's being charged as an accomplice to the crime right now. Hey, hold on. Brown just walked in," Connors said. He could hear someone in the background talking. An intense conversation going on.

"Shit, Knox, I'm putting you on speaker," Connors said. Seconds later, he heard Paul Brown talking.

"They found Langley dead in his cell," Brown said loud enough for Mitch to hear.

"Who confirmed that?" Connors asked.

"Anne just called me when she couldn't get you to pick up the phone. Young just got the news," Brown informed them.

"I thought they had him on suicide watch?" Mitch asked.

"They did. He asphyxiated himself with his pant leg," Brown explained.

"You're kidding me?" Connors replied. "So we got the confession and he killed himself? That's convenient."

Connors tone was off and Mitch got it. He stood there thinking things over as he kicked at the grass with his boot. "Where's Kreed?"

"He's on his way to verify all this himself. You know how he is. He doesn't take any information blindly, but he was there with me when Anne called," Brown said.

"Okay, I'll call him later. Connors keep me posted on what they need from me," Mitch said.

"How's Cody?" Brown asked. Mitch looked up and Cody was watching him. The minute their eyes connected, Cody leaned in and whispered something to his niece. She jumped up and scurried off.

"He's doing good, I think. He needs me. I gotta go." Mitch was already taking the steps back up to Cody as he disconnected the call.

"Need some help?" Mitch asked and took over for Cody to help raise the lounger. He'd had trouble getting the lever to hold.

"I heard a little bit. What happened?" Cody questioned, his eyes on Mitch.

"He confessed to every case then killed himself." Mitch sat back down in his same spot on the porch swing because it was the closest to Cody. He just stared at his cowboy, letting the news of Langley's suicide sink in.

"So you're done. You solved the case?" Cody asked and Mitch leaned in to kiss him.

"I think you solved the case, but we'll see what happens. You never know when you're dealing with all this political shit." There was silence for several long moments between them.

"You're gonna go stir crazy if you hang out here every day with me. You know that, right? You're used to traveling free," Cody said randomly as he glanced apprehensively at Mitch. Cody could change a subject in a heartbeat and usually did when he decided to talk, which wasn't all that often.

"No, I'm not, Cody. I keep telling you, this is where I want to be. I'm a changed man. You changed me." Mitch held Cody's gaze as he leaned in, lifted his hand, and ran his palm down Cody's cheek. "Almost losing you scared the shit out of me. I'm here for as long as you want me."

Cody raised a hand to hold Mitch's against his cheek. Cody visibly swallowed, another sign Mitch was learning that the words about to be said were impactful, so he listened closely. "I don't think I'll ever want you to leave. You're the part of me that's been missing. I'm off when you're not around."

"Those are the words I wanted to hear." Mitch leaned in and kissed Cody. When Cody opened for him, he deepened the kiss, letting all the love he felt remove the lingering doubt he had about this case for the moment.

"I love you," Mitch whispered. He couldn't seem to say the words enough.

"I love you, too. Forever." And that earned Cody another kiss.

Epilogue

"As sexy as you look in my childhood bed, you need to get up. The crew's gonna be here in about an hour," Mitch whispered, sliding his palm up and down Cody's back. He heard the words and agreed he needed to move, so he turned over, but instead of getting up, he snuggled deeper inside the warm bed.

"Is it still snowing?" Cody drew the covers up and over his head. Mitch tempted him, but not as much as the comfort of the down mattress.

"Yes, just special for you." Mitch tugged the blankets down, exposing Cody's face. He snaked a hand out from under the covers and ran his palm across Mitch's thigh. "Come lay down with me and keep me warm."

"You're a tease. You won't sleep with me because my family and the Montgomery-Michaels duo are right down the hall, which sucks for me, so get your ass out of bed." Mitch yanked the covers back down and the blanket ripped completely off his body. When the cool air hit his warm skin, Cody's eyes popped opened. *Shit!* Mitch wasn't going to give up, so he might as well get moving.

"It's Christmas Eve. You could be nicer," Cody complained, sitting on the side of the bed, rolling the stiffness from his shoulder. He felt more than heard the quick kiss Mitch placed on the top of his head.

"I love you. Shower and come downstairs. Mom's got breakfast cooked." Cody looked up, yawned again, and that earned him a kiss on the lips even with his morning breath.

"I'll be down in fifteen," Cody mumbled, rising and doing a full body stretch, his sweatpants dipping low. He laughed when he heard Mitch's grumble as he slammed the door behind him.

~~~

Mitch sat at the end of the sofa, his arm stretched across the back, hugging Cody's shoulders. He kept him right there pressed against him. A raging snowstorm churned outside the windows. The curtains were pushed wide, giving them a front row view of the winter wonderland surrounding them. His mother made sure all the drapes in the house were open, so Cody could get his first taste of what a white Christmas truly meant. This year Mother Nature really put on a show.

All of his older brothers and sisters, with their children, were there visiting. Everyone had grown so much. His oldest brother, Matt, had become an old man since he'd seen him last, but he supposed that was what happened when you were nearing fifty. Matt's oldest child was close to graduating high school. Mitch had actually kept her at about twelve years old for the last five years, and he was shocked to find out how much she'd actually grown. She looked very much like a young woman. That was just too weird for him.

Currently the family sat gathered around the brightly lit Christmas tree in the living room, passing out presents to all the grandkids that wouldn't be able to stay for Christmas day.

"I told you they were loud," he leaned his head, whispering into Cody's ear.

"You've experienced more than enough of the Turner hospitality. You know this ain't got nothing on them." Cody looked over at Mitch, grinning from ear to ear. "How's the tattoo?"

"Hurts like hell. Why'd you let me do that?" he asked, smiling back at Cody who bumped him in the shoulder.

"Ah, young love." Mitch cut his eyes up as Colt came to stand behind them.

"Leave them alone," Jace said as he took a seat on the floor in front of Mitch and Cody.

"No, he can keep going this time. I am young," Mitch teased, nodding firmly. "It's why I love coming home. I'm the baby."

"You have a niece almost your boyfriend's age," Colt snickered, and that earned a frown from Jace. Mitch laughed and pointed down to Jace.

"You're in trouble for messing with me so much. You better sit down before he makes you leave the room."

"Hey, Dr. Knox, did you know that Mitch got a new tattoo a couple of days ago?" Colt hollered.

"He did?" That earned a solid scowl from his father when he glanced over at him. Mitch cocked his head back to Colt.

"Really? This is how you wanna play?"

"I wanna see!" Pretty much every one of his nieces' and nephews' voices rang in complete unison. His family was a straight-laced crew. He was the only one with body art. Mitch untangled himself from Cody who just grinned at him, and he leaned down to kiss those perfect lips as he rose.

He tugged his shirt up, letting the crew admire the artwork on his chest.

"I think that cross is cool," his sister Lori said, the only adult to really come and examine him. "Is this one new? *For those I love I will sacrifice*. That's so cool. Did it hurt?"

"Like a bitc...crazy." He caught himself before he said the bad word out loud. That would be two strikes according to the look on his dad's face.

"Have you seen enough?" He glanced down at the littlest nephew who must have been around three and half years old. The little guy's big brown eyes bore a striking resemblance to his own, and when he smiled, he had the biggest dimples. This was the one everyone said reminded them of Mitch.

"I want that," he said, pointing to Mitch's chest. He bent at the knee and lowered to the floor to let the little one examine his chest all he wanted.

"Cody, how you feeling, Son?" Dr. Knox asked, changing the subject.

"I'm good, sir," Cody answered.

"Such good manners," Mitch's mom cooed, making Mitch smile at her comment.

"Mini-Mitch, come sit by Pop-Pop before Mitch gets in trouble for showing you all that," Matt called out. That was the one part of him that his dad didn't like. His father wasn't a tattoo guy. He never really said anything to Mitch about the tattoos. He just gave a look that let Mitch know he didn't agree.

"Hey, Dad, did you get enough sausage this morning? I saw Colt in there hoarding some in his pockets," Mitch remarked, standing after his nephew got bored with looking at the ink on his chest.

"What?" Jace gasped as he looked back at Colt.

"Yeah, Mom made some for you, Jace, and Colt ate your sausage, too," Mitch quipped, stepping over the wrapping paper littering the path back to Cody.

"Man! That's getting old. Jace, I did not eat any more than my share that was cooked for me. He's messing with you. He's still peeved because our wedding photo replaced his baby picture in the hall. Don't listen to his lies," Colt exclaimed, coming around the couch and taking a seat next to Jace. Mitch looked around and all eyes were on the couple now sitting on the floor.

"I'm not lying. I'm quite certain he ate your sausage this morning," Mitch chuckled and dropped down in his spot on the couch.

"Really? You're gonna do that here?" Colt huffed, his face turning red as he looked back at Mitch. His brothers actually laughed hard at that. His sisters and sisters-in-law clearly didn't get the joke by the looks on their face. He knew better than to look over at his dad.

"We've got the Skype call, Mitch. Do I just answer it?" his mom asked from her place on the couch across the room.

"Yes, ma'am." This time the freshly inked skin resisted the movement and prickled as he stood.

"Where're you going?" Cody asked.

"Hang on, babe." Mitch went to his laptop and connected the few steps that Aaron had arranged for him until he was able to use the remote control to click on the big screen TV. Cody's entire family popped up on the screen. They had a huge family between the two of them.

Mitch watched as Kylie sat up front on her grandfather's lap, her eyes scanning for Cody. He knew the moment she saw him because she lifted her new Princess Barbie, the one they had given her, with a giant smile on her face. Mitch found he wanted that same kind of relationship with the little mini-me nephew he'd bonded with since he'd been home.

"Knox family meet the Turner family." Mitch waved his hands around. His dad knew them and stepped in to make introductions as he went for Cody who looked completely confused. Of course, Cody still wouldn't get what was going on, which was for the best. He liked shock and awe. He extended a hand and pulled Cody up, purposefully stepping on Colt in the process. "Oops...my bad."

He tugged Cody across the room, knocking wrapping paper out of the way as he went. Once he got to the center, the chatter came to an end as he turned and smiled. Cody's red face said it all, and god, he loved that blush on his lover's cheeks. His guy wasn't comfortable being the center of attention ever and certainly not in Mitch's family's home. He stared at Cody, lost in his eyes. Suddenly his mouth was dry and his heart hammered in his chest. This was it, he'd been so excited and sure of himself, but now, the thought of forever with Cody humbled him. He wanted to make Cody the happiest man on earth.

"I've brought us all together today to share in this moment. I already asked your dad, he gave his half-assed approval," Mitch teased as Cody's dad started to chuckle. Neither would ever say how worried Mr. Turner was by what Mitch was doing. Mitch understood Cody's father's concern was well-founded simply because all of the ignorance surrounding gay marriage, especially in the South. But Mitch loved Cody, and this was the man he wanted to spend his forever with.

"Cody, this may seem a little rushed. I just didn't know when everyone would be together again, and my feelings aren't going to change no matter how much time passes. Since I first laid eyes on you, I knew I had to have you. That feeling has only grown stronger as I've gotten to know you. I love you and I know without a doubt you're the only man for me."

Mitch fished around in his pocket until he found what he was looking for.

"You're supposed to have that ready," Matt called out from across the room and was immediately shushed by all the females. He lowered to one knee and looked up at Cody who stared down at him with the most intense look he'd ever seen. Mitch got it, his heart pounded wildly in his chest, pumping the blood through his veins so loudly he swore he heard the roaring in his ears. He opened the box and lifted the ring, holding Cody's gaze with his.

"Cody Turner, will you do me the honor of marrying me? Please. Make an honest man out of me." Cody stood silently. He'd spent the better part of the last few months with the man. Cody was proud and strong, but he worried over their lifestyle like his father, even if he never said it out loud. He waited on baited breath for Cody's answer. Cody's brilliant blue eyes never strayed from his. His cowboy loved him, no question there; he saw the love reflected in their depths.

Silence filled the room, but Mitch wouldn't have heard anything anyway. His heart, mind, and soul were connected only to this man who always took his time to respond to life-changing events. So he continued giving Cody enough room to grasp the importance of the moment.

Mitch always pushed, Cody took things slower. They balanced each other.

After what felt like fifteen minutes, Cody finally nodded. That was all anyone needed. Cheers erupted from both living rooms. Mitch stood and pulled Cody to him, no resistance to this PDA in front of their families.

"Thank you! I love you," Mitch proclaimed loudly.

"I love you," Cody said, burying his face in the crook of Mitch's shoulder. Mitch could feel Cody's heart hammering in his chest. Cody lifted his face to kiss Mitch's neck before he whispered in his ear, "You completely surprised me."

"I wanted to," Mitch whispered quietly. He closed his eyes and pulled Cody against him even tighter if that were possible. "I love you so much, Cody Turner."

~~~

Four hours later

Aaron Stuart sat at one of his computer screens in his downtown studio apartment. He'd dodged the Christmas Eve festivities with the fam, feigning illness, since he really couldn't stand his new sister-in-law. Crazy gold-digger was only after his brother's money, and she'd scored big this time around. She was on her fourth marriage and this time got pregnant to secure her spot on his brother's bank account. Interesting the things he could find out about people online.

His idiot brother was too in love to believe his findings, so he deserved what he got in the end.

Tyler Connors earlier email had bothered him all day long. Elliot Greyson had had a breakthrough moment in counseling yesterday. A wave of memory was back, but he didn't identify Agent Langley as his abductor. Actually, he been more than adamant that he was one hundred percent convinced they didn't have their man where his case was concerned.

Connors decided to wait and clue Mitch in after the Christmas holidays. The Marshals and the FBI had arranged for him to take some time off. He'd become too high profile after Cody's attack. His face was recognizable so they kept him on the down-low. He'd probably get assigned to a desk on his return, bury him in piles of paperwork.

After that email, Aaron had sifted through the miles of files he had on the case. So they hadn't gotten all their men. That meant the information was somewhere inside the data, hidden, just waiting to be found. He pulled up all the video coverage he had on Agent Langley. Aaron watched the in-custody interview between Agent Langley and his attorney. There was no audio, but he suspected they'd exchanged some valuable intel, whether directly or using code. He pushed that file out to his desktop. He'd investigate the attorney soon.

Next he re-watched the coverage of Cody's accident, leading back to the coverage of Kreed's brother's funeral. He bounced his leg as he watched the hate spew from those supposed Christians' mouths. As a gay man, it was hard to stomach. The leg twitch helped him concentrate and kept his anxious feelings manageable. He didn't know how Mitch had kept so calm amidst all the hate. How had he not taken out his gun and shot them all? He would never understand how people who called themselves Christians could be so cruel. Aaron slowed the feed and concentrated on the picture in front of him, looking for anything that might help. That was when he saw him. Aaron almost missed the lawyer.

He rewound, slowed the video feed, and stilled the screen on the familiar face. Langley's lawyer was part of the hate group picketing the Sinacola funeral. Why in hell hadn't anyone caught this before now? Better question, how had he missed this? *Damn.*

Pulling up his phone, he went to call Mitch and stopped. He didn't want to be the one to tell him there were now holes in the case. Instead, he tried Connors on his cell. The agent didn't pick up, but he was traveling for the holidays. He then called Kreed. He hated bothering the guy during this particular Christmas. Mitch had told him he'd gone home for the first time in years. Maybe he would answer.

"Kreed Sinacola," a deep voice barked over the Christmas music playing in the background. "Hang on, I can't hear you. I'm going outside." Seconds passed and the background noise quieted. "That's better."

"Kreed, it's Aaron Stuart. I hate to bother you, but are you busy? This is important."

"Hey, Aaron, nah, it's fine. What's up?"

"I was going over the footage on the Langley case, and I think I might have found something," Aaron replied, his eyes back on the attorney as he captured a print screen and sent the photo to Kreed's phone.

"Well, of course you have. Tomorrow's Christmas, you know that right? This couldn't wait twenty-four hours?" Kreed sarcastically replied.

"Probably not."

A Nice Guys Novel 3
Coming 2015

About this Author

Best Selling Author Kindle Alexander is an innovative writer, and a genre-crosser who writes classic fantasy, romance, suspense, and erotica.

Send a quick email and let me know what you thought of *Full Disclosure* to kindle@kindlealexander.com. For more information on future works and links, check out my website at www.kindlealexander.com. Come friend me on all the major social networking sites.

Books by Kindle Alexander

**If you loved *Full Disclosure* then you won't want to miss
Kindle Alexander's bestselling novels:**

Always
Double Full, A Nice Guys Novel 1
The Current Between Us
Texas Pride
Up in Arms

* * *

True love will stand the test of time, *Always*!

"Be prepared to cry and cry while reading this pure love story of Avery and Kane's journey of self discovery, love, lust, heart wrenching scenes and hot and I mean hot male-male sex." —*Paul Berry, Gay Media Reviews*

"But be assured Kindle Alexander fans will love this book, they have delivered what I would call a true romance that even those readers like me, that can be a bit skeptical at times will love... be assured there is nothing cheesy or too saccharine about *Always*, it's just the perfect love story!"
—*Monique, Sinfully Sexy Reviews*

"If I could rate it higher than 5 Pennies, I would. I don't think there are enough words to convey how much this book touched my soul."
—*Penny Pam, Penny For My Thoughts Book Blog*

"Always by Kindle Alexander takes on a life completely of its own and it is unlike anything she has published before. Always is an epic love story of two men that transcends time."
—*Tania, Scandalicious Book Reviews*

"Regardless of whether you're a seasoned m/m reader or if you're stumbling into this genre for the very first time, I urge you to give this extraordinary book a chance. I have no doubt whatsoever that it will leave you speechless."
—*Natasha is a Book Junkie*

The word is out on *Double Full*

"Kindle Alexander knows the rules of romance and she applies them good."
— *Elisa My Reviews and Rambling*

"You can't help but love Jace and Colt and suffer their heartbreak right along with them." —Tanis, *Scandalicious Book Reviews*

"I was drawn into this book from the first paragraph!"
—*Dirty Hoe's Book Blog*

"These two hunky men had me in tears, their love for one another is magically." — Jennifer Robbins, *Twinsie Talk Book Review*

"It's a really steamy story, and I put this on my GRL TBR list and was everything I hoped." —Jessie Potts, *USA Today*

"*Double Full* is a compelling and fabulous read!"
— Monique, *Sinfully Sexy Book Reviews*

"Double Full will be in my heart for some time to come."
—Paul Berry, *Gay Media Reviews*

Everyone's talking about
The Current Between Us

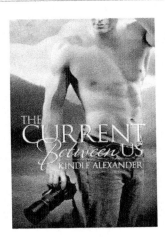

"Ms. Alexander has become one of my favorite M/M authors; check that one of my favorite authors. Her characters are mature, well rounded and seem to find a place in my heart." —Denise, *Shh Mom's Reading*

"I will recommend this to those that love family stories, hot men coming together and discovering love, a twist that will raise eyebrows and a very happy ending." —Pixie, *Mmgoodbookreviews*

"I loved this book! Everything about it was just perfection...great characters, suprises, and the story...seriously, it was so sweet and romantic and just really good reading." —Christi Snow, *Author*

"Kindle Alexander has given us another great book. The characters Trent and Gage   grabbed my heart and haven't let go. This isn't just a love story, it has a mystery going on that keeps you hooked." —Teri, *The Bitches of Eastwick Book Reviews*

"Loved this book!!! This is the second book I've read by Kindle Alexander. The first one was *Texas Pride*. I was hooked right from the beginning. It's an amazing love story." —Brenda Wright, *Twinsie Talk Book Review*

"This book is an excellent love story, where even the most hardened heart and disillusioned soul can find the romantic streak hidden deep within and see it blossom into something neither thought possible. I fell in love with the author, her writing and the characters... just go read it!!!"
—Monique, *Sinfully Sexy Book Reviews*

"This is my first book by Kindle Alexander and I have to say that I loved it! I am a fan of the m/m genre especially when there is a beautiful and touching story behind it." —*Three Chicks and their Books*

"If you enjoyed Texas Pride you will love *The Current Between Us!*"
—*Swoon Worthy Book Reviews*

Rave Reviews for
Texas Pride

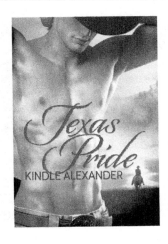

"I would DEFINITELY like this to be a series...hint hint to Kindle Alexander!!!" —Brenda, *Twinsie Talk Book Review*

"I have a severe case of book hangover. Seriously readers – you need to read this book. Ten stars for me!" — **Foxylutely* Blog*

"The end of this book was so well done!" —*Shh Mom's Reading*

"Definitely a great read...I didn't want this sweet story to end." —Christi Snow, *Author*

"Recommend this to those who love cowboys and movie stars ...and a very happy ending." —*Mmgoodbookreviews*

"I highly recommend it." —Samantha, *Passionate Books*

What readers are saying about *Up in Arms*

"*Up in Arms* is a compelling, fascinating drama that honestly explores the conflict of love in the military without taking away from an enchanting romance." —*Joyfully Reviewed*

"This story not only follows these men's love affair, which is sweet and sexy, but we also see the aftermath of how they deal with tragedy. I love these boys, how they interact, how they overcome, how one of them blushes *sigh*."
—*The Bitches of Eastwick*

"This is a tender love story…. She taps all the sensory elements that binds a romance reader to the narrative, characters, conflicts and resolutions."
—*Blackraven Reviews*

CPSIA information can be obtained at www.ICGtesting.com
Printed in the USA
BVOW07s1009270615

406455BV00010B/239/P